FEMME FATALES DON'T
PLAY BY THE RULES

I couldn't believe it. I literally *could not* believe my eyes. The woman in the slinky dress and the big man by the door had taken out all nine of the bodyguards, and as I watched, she killed a sixth man from the crowd around the table.

But it wasn't random, a corner of my brain realized. She passed up easy kills, bypassed the people between her victims. She wasn't a homicidal maniac out to kill everyone in sight. She was taking *targeted* kills, exactly the ones—and *only* the ones—she wanted.

And then I saw something else. Something she didn't see.

The plainclothes floor cop came out of his chair to one side of the lavatory arch and his pulser was in his hand. I saw it rising, lining up on the woman in the black dress, and I knew it was none of my business. I knew exactly what I needed to do, and that was what she'd *told* me to do: head for the nightclub's lavatory, lock the door, and not open it for anyone until the uniformed cops got there.

I *knew* that . . . and I didn't do it.

I didn't recognize the sound I made. It was deep, guttural, primal. It came from the pit of my belly, from a heart filled with hatred for the system that had taken my parents, was killing my brother by centimeters. It came from deep down in the soul of me, and the *other* modification I'd inherited from my great-great-grandmother popped out of the tips of my fingers . . .

—from "Recruiting Exercise" by David Weber

NOIR FATALE

Edited by
LARRY CORREIA &
KACEY EZELL

A Baen Books Original

Baen Publishing Enterprises
P.O. Box 1403
Riverdale, NY 10471
www.baen.com

ISBN: 978-1-9821-2473-1

Cover art by Dominic Harman

First printing, May 2019
First mass market printing, July 2020

Distributed by Simon & Schuster
1230 Avenue of the Americas
New York, NY 10020

Library of Congress Control Number: 2019000752

Printed in the United States of America

10 9 8 7 6 5 4 3 2 1

To all the femmes fatales who are about the noir life.

And to all the men who love them.

Acknowledgements

First, thanks to Toni Weisskopf, Jim Minz, and all of the phenomenal staff at Baen Books for allowing us to pursue this labor of love. Thanks also to our contributing authors for making this process so easy, and for giving us such fantastic stories. Additionally, thanks to Sharon Rice-Weber and Shawn Holsapple for their assistance in coordination, to Glennis LeBlanc of The Missing Volume for her timely suggestions, and to Rich Groller, director of programming at LibertyCon, for giving Kacey the chance to sweet-talk Larry into this project. Finally, thanks always to our families, for all the things.

Contents

xi Editor's Introduction: Kacey Ezell

xv Editor's Introduction: Larry Correia

1 AIN'T NO SUNSHINE: Christopher L. Smith and Michael J. Ferguson

35 RECRUITING EXERCISE: David Weber

65 SPOILS OF WAR: Kacey Ezell

91 THE PRIVILEGES OF VIOLENCE: Steve Diamond

127 A GODDESS IN RED: Griffin Barber

151 KURO: Hinkley Correia

179 SWEET SEDUCTION: Laurell K. Hamilton

219 A STRING OF PEARLS: Alistair Kimble

251 HONEY FALL: Sarah A. Hoyt

281 THREE KATES: Mike Massa

325 WORTH THE SCARS OF DYING: Patrick M. Tracy

363 THE FROST QUEEN: Robert Buettner

395 BOMBSHELL: Larry Correia

437 About the Authors

Kacey's Introduction

I blame this whole thing on Raymond Chandler and Chris Smith.

Back in 2015 or so, I was living in Albuquerque, NM, and just really starting to dedicate myself to writing professionally. I started the practice of writing at least a set minimum number of words a day and found my creativity flowing as a result. During this time, Chris Smith (aka my Wonder Twin and/or my Aggressive Muse) and I started talking about detective novels and the noir subgenre. I'd loved *The Maltese Falcon* as a kid and said that I was interested in learning more. He suggested that I check out *Farewell, My Lovely* by the late, great Raymond Chandler.

At the time, my youngest was a toddler who had recently transitioned to a twin bed, and so it became our bedtime routine that I would lie down with her, sing her some songs, say a prayer (we're religious) and then cuddle quietly together until she fell asleep. In order to keep from falling asleep myself, I started reading via the Kindle app on my phone and took Chris's advice to check out Chandler.

Wow.

Color me instantly hooked. Not only did Chandler craft some of the most beautiful phrases in the English language, but he absolutely pulled me into the seamy, smoky underworld of the genre. I became a fiend for noir. I devoured the movies *Mullholland Falls* and *Chinatown*. I burned through several other Chandler novels. My dreams echoed with the taps of high heels on darkened pavement and I couldn't get rid of the image of a lone streetlight beaming down through a black-and-white misty scene. I imagined myself as a femme fatale, working every angle to further my own ends...

A story started to take shape in my head. I think I wrote it in about two evenings. When I was done, I sat back and read it and thought: "Wow. I really need to publish this." Buzz was starting to heat up about the *Black Tide Rising* anthology from Baen, and so I started to scheme how, exactly, I could get Baen to produce a noir-themed anthology.

Enter Larry Correia.

I'd read the Monster Hunter International series about a year prior, and had liked it enough to comment online. A friend of mine saw the Facebook post and said that in his opinion, the Grimnoir Chronicles series was even better. With Chandler hot on my brain, I bought *Spellbound* for my Kindle and started reading. Once again, I was hooked. Here again was that gritty, seamy feel, but with a delicious fantasy twist and some really compelling femme fatale characters. I devoured the entire series and wondered if I would ever have a chance to pitch my anthology idea to the man himself.

A year or so later, I got my shot.

I was slated to attend LibertyCon as an "also attending" guest for the second time. Larry himself was scheduled to attend as well. With the wheels turning in my head, I reached out to Rich Groller, the amazing director of programming at LibertyCon and pitched a panel called "Panel Noir: a look at the intersection of noir and genre fiction." I suggested that Larry's fans might be interested in hearing him and some of the other guests at Liberty (of which there are hundreds. I'm not kidding. LibertyCon has the highest guest to attendee ratio of any con in the United States) discuss how science fiction and fantasy writers use noir tropes and devices to enhance their stories. I volunteered to moderate and even dressed for the occasion as a femme fatale in a pencil skirt and backseam stockings. It was a blast. The panel was well attended, and the audience really got into the discussion. I was thrilled.

Through sheer serendipity, the schedule that year was such that the annual Baen writers' dinner followed immediately after Panel Noir. So I traipsed over to the Hot Chocolatier in Chattanooga, TN, in my femme fatale costume and waited for just the right moment to walk up to Larry and say:

"Hey, Larry, thanks so much for doing that panel. Did you enjoy it? What would you say if I said I had an idea for a similar anthology where I'd do all the work, you put your name on it, and we both make lots of money?"

Or words to that effect. As you can imagine, an avowed capitalist such as Larry Correia was intrigued by my presentation and listened to my full pitch.

"I'm really busy this year," he said. "But it's a good idea. I'm in. Let's approach Toni about it next year."

And that's what we did. Toni Weisskopf really liked the idea of an anthology focused around the theme of the femme fatale archetype in fantasy and sci-fi fiction. Larry and I got the go-ahead and reached out to some of the best in the business to see what they'd give us.

And boy, did they give us their best.

The anthology you hold in your hands contains thirteen completely different, totally original stories. Some of the characters will be familiar faces, some will be new loves. Every story contains at least a modicum of the gritty darkness that underlies polite society. And every story contains a unique take on the archetype of a woman with her own agenda, ready to reach her goals by any means necessary.

I hope you enjoy this love letter to the femme fatale. We have definitely enjoyed bringing it to you. And I hope that when you've finished reading the stories, you're able to remember that sometimes the hero doesn't get the girl, but he does the right thing anyway.

That, my friends, is my definition of noir.

—Kacey Ezell

Larry's Introduction

When Kacey came to me with a pitch for an anthology of noir themed sci-fi and fantasy stories, it was an easy sell. I love noir. As a kid I read a lot of Louis L'Amour. He was known for his westerns, but he also wrote hardboiled detective pulp stories. Reading a collection of those had caused me to check books by Raymond Chandler and Dashiell Hammett out of my local library.

It was fantastic stuff. Tough guys, seductive women, scheming crooks, weary cops, fast talkers, all competing, not to see who wins, but to be the one who doesn't lose the most.

I've been a fan ever since.

When I started plotting the novel *Hard Magic*, it actually started out with a typical epic fantasy setting, except then my friend and author Mike Kupari said something to the effect that everything was cooler back when men wore hats, and it kind of stuck. So I took all those fantasy elements and stuck them into 1932 Great Depression Detroit. My weary knight became a detective. I kept the wizards. Strangely enough, it worked really well.

Personally, I had a lot of fun mixing noir with fantastic elements. So when I was presented with the idea of getting together a bunch of other writers to see what they could do with femme fatales in fantasy or sci-fi settings, it was a no-brainer for me. I was hooked from the get-go. Kacey is clever like that.

When putting together a collection of stories, noir is one of those things that can be hard to define. I'm not the kind of writer who gets hung up on arbitrary genre rules. Depending on the creator, noir can be a vibe, a look, a lifestyle, or an attitude. The characters can be morally ambiguous or heroic, jaded or naïve. It can take place in seedy back alleys, or glittering nightclubs...or in this case, nightclubs on spaceships.

We've assembled some of my favorite authors in this anthology, and they all had different, creative takes on the subject. There are some stories from well-known authors writing in their popular franchises, and some from newer writers in settings you've never seen before. Either way, if you like what they've done here, I'd encourage you to check out their other work.

I truly hope you enjoy reading these as much as I have.

—Larry Correia

Ain't No Sunshine

Christopher L. Smith and Michael J. Ferguson

Flavor burst onto his palate like a mouthful of fireworks. Yes! That inevitable and delightful burn of heavenly nectar from an earthbound distillery. The haunting sound of the Miles Davis horn and the heady smoke-ladened liquor paired so well it made him feel like the gods themselves had designed this moment.

I can get used to this, thought Slade, taking a second sip. Would that he could afford this Earthside hooch more often. *Maybe this PI thing will work out after all.*

It wasn't his intention to go into the private investigation business, but with the success of his first case, the possibilities became more plausible. The transition from "search and destroy" to "search and rescue" had been easier than he'd thought, and brought with it a fulfillment he hadn't expected. The money didn't hurt, either. While not "buy an island and retire" good, it was "I could get used to this" good, at least for his initial case. Enough for him to seriously consider making it a career. Hang out the shingle—Isaac Slade, Private Eye. Had a nice ring to it.

He looked about his single cube dwelling, small even by station standards. Clean and organized in military fashion, if a little dingy around the edges. Despite his best efforts, some of the grime refused to budge. He'd made his peace with it, accepting it as something that wouldn't change. Granted, his cube wasn't in the best sector of the station. One of these days, though . . . It would be nice to move up to a place in a location he could bring a woman without the associated embarrassment.

Perhaps if he had applied himself a bit more while in the Marines he'd be pulling down a captain's or even a major's pension. Once he traded his nugget for a silver bar, he felt he had arrived at the perfect comfort level. As first lieutenant he never had to make the big decisions and only took orders from his captain. Most of the time anyway.

"Money talks and BS walks," his gunny had said the day he handed Slade his old antique knife. "It may be the root of all evil, but you can't do fuck all without it!"

With the near empty glass in one hand, he grabbed the bottle with the other as he got up from the "kitchen" table to move over to the chair in front of the display. Two long strides and he flopped into the autoform chair. It moved immediately to his preferred alignment, lifting his legs and adjusting to a perfect spinal position. These days, it was well beyond his paycheck to find old-fashioned furniture that could fit a person over six foot four, so he'd had to make a minor compromise to his preferred aesthetic.

The chair was the only thing he had that could be considered "modern." Artificial intelligence had made some major leaps in the last hundred years, but Slade just couldn't bring himself to trust it. Only one more thing to break, or make a mess of things, as far as he was concerned. The less complicated and intrusive, the better. Even his vid unit was an old 3D version with no voice command.

He'd stopped using his military implant the second he was discharged, declining the offer to upgrade to the civilian spec version for free. He'd gone so far as to have it removed with his last check, effectively segregating himself from the majority of the world's tech. "Off the grid" was difficult these days—practically impossible—but in his mind, every little bit helped.

Slade knew his atavistic nature made him an odd-ball in this day and age, but he also knew just how much humanity was stripped away by modern tech. As "connected" as everyone was, they seemed more and more distant. Modern interactions seemed to have no soul to them. Not his style at all.

He put down the bottle, finished what was left in the glass, set it next to the bottle and picked up the remote from the table by the chair and turned on the display.

Maybe it's time for a little R and R. Catch the shuttle over to a geosync and take the elevator down Earthside and get some real gravity under my feet. See a beach, walk on some sand, talk to women in bikinis.

A few seconds into his fantasy, he realized his display was still blank.

"What the hell?"

He stared at it, trying to figure out what was

happening. Signal but no feed. He switched to another channel, then another. Nothing.

"Great. Another glitch," he said, mentally adding another bullet point to his list of things he didn't like about technology.

Finally, he got something—a local feed. Station news mostly, but at least it was coming in.

". . . behind the continuing glitches," the announcer said. "The unprecedented interruptions of operations is puzzling engineers and techs stationwide. We've not been able to get a direct answer from Lagrange Analytic on the cause."

"The glitches are blamed in at least one death. Lagrange Analytic's Senior Vice President and Chief Operations Officer Salome Deveraux, died earlier today. Head of security, Damian Rains, told Station One News the preliminary exam suggests the death was caused by a catastrophic failure of her access node implant at ten a.m. station time, when the glitches began . . ."

Slade leapt out of the chair, still holding the remote.

"Salome?" he whispered.

He needed to go to the office. He grabbed his fedora from the hook by the door and rushed out.

Slade lifted the brim of his hat slightly as Dennis Collier walked into the office. His friend, carefully juggling his lunch and a small package, kicked the door closed behind him. Shifting slightly, he tossed the parcel on the desk they shared.

"Where you been?" Slade said, looking up from the slate. He'd been going through what little there was about Salome while he'd waited.

"A man's gotta eat. Came for you today," Collier

said, sitting down and nodding at the package. The smells from the lunch bag suggested something laced heavily with saffron. Again. "You're in my seat."

At just under six feet tall, and especially with his leaner frame, Collier didn't have the same issues as Slade when it came to furniture. Slade felt no remorse over taking his partner's chair.

Slade didn't answer as he opened the package, carefully sliding his knife along the top edge. Turning it upside down, he eased the contents into his palm. A smile flickered unbidden, but unashamedly, across his lips. He'd get back to Salome momentarily, right now he just wanted to enjoy the moment.

"I don't get it, man," Collier said, tucking into the couscous mixture, "We have vids, slates, etc., available. What is it about books?"

Slade ignored him, breathing in the scent of the yellowed paper.

"It's just..." he said, placing the book on his desk after a moment, "it's just that it feels more real, you know? The pages have weight, smell, texture. Like you're a part of the story, not just reading it."

"Whatever, man," Collier said, pointing at Slade's hat. "You don't see me wearing a fez, do you? Seems too much like you're living in the past."

"Ah, but the past was *cool*," Slade said, smiling. "The style, the panache, the way things were done."

"We live on a station that we flew to in a space-ship, bud. How can you possibly say that's not *cool*?"

"Don't get me wrong, ain't nothin' wrong with progress, and I got no hassle with where I am," Slade said. "But c'mon—you have to admit, the sense of adventure, the thrill, it's missin'."

"That's another thing—listen to yourself. And don't give me that 'poor black sharecropper ancestor' crap. 'Ain't nothing.' 'Got no hassle.' You are a college-educated man, not some hayseed hick from East Texas. Why try to sound like that?"

Slade's grin grew, causing his partner to roll his eyes.

"Like I said, man. Panache." He picked up the book, turning it so Collier could see the cover. Slate tapped the picture. "Easy Rawlins was a smooth talkin', tough walkin' sonofabitch. I like his style."

"Whatever you say, Slade. I'm not gonna argue with you." Collier pushed back from his meal. "So what was so urgent that you actually came into the office? I figured you'd be taking some R and I by now."

"Rest and Intoxication? Yeah, that was put on hold," Slade said, getting his mind back on task. "Remember me talking about a woman named Salome when we were in the service?

"We were friends back in the day," he said, not waiting for an answer. He carefully placed the book on the desk. "Came up together before I enlisted. Went to the same college and all. Well . . . she's dead. Died this morning. They're saying it's part of these weird glitches we've been having."

"I think I heard something about that on the local feeds. Nothing coming in from outside. Salome Deveraux, right?" He wiped his mouth with the back of his hand. "What of it? Sounds like a tragic accident to me."

"I can smell something is wrong, and it's not just your damned curry. I feel it deep down—just can't shake it. The same way I felt when something was hinky on patrol. This whole thing's not on the up and up."

"So what do you want to do about it?" Collier said, giving him his "you gotta be kidding me" look.

"I think we need to go see Rains."

"Great! I'm sure he'll be thrilled."

"Gentlemen, to what do I owe the pleasure?" Rains said. He stood and walked around the large desk to greet them before they could walk further into the office. "I don't believe we have an appointment."

"As if you're booked solid," Slade said as he pushed past the smaller man to flop into one of the four chairs. "Mind if I sit?"

"Look, Damien," Collier said. Rains raised an eyebrow slightly before Collier continued, mollified. "Inspector, my partner here thinks all these glitches and interruptions the station is going through might not be wholly responsible for the demise of Ms. Deveraux."

"Oh?" Rains said, eyebrow shooting higher. The expression, coupled with Rains' small, dark eyes, somehow made the man look even more ratlike to Slade, if that were possible.

No, rat is wrong. he thought. *Weasel.*

"I know what you think." Slade leaned forward. "Just give me something to go sniff around and I'll be out of your hair so you can get back to...inspecting."

"Well, I suppose I can let you see the prelim autopsy report." Rains went back to his desk and lifted the clear rectangle of his tablet. "Would you like me to send a temporary link to your implants?"

Slade gave a sharp wave of his hand.

"Ain't got one. Just hand me the tablet, will you?"

Rains glanced at Collier before tapping instructions on the tablet and handing it to Slade.

Slade felt the frown take over his face as he studied the words and images on the tablet, brow furrowing involuntarily. Since it was clear, Collier would be able to see the same thing, only in reverse. Slade shifted to let him have a better view.

"Well?" Collier said, gesturing.

"I'm no expert, but it seems the damage is very localized," Slade said, handing the tablet to his partner. "Not like frying from a glitch—I'd think that should have taken out more of the neuroelectronics. This looks like a controlled overload, like blowing a fuse."

"You're right about one thing, Slade." Rains looked disgusted, snatching the tablet from Collier before huffing back to his chair. "You're not an expert. Not to mention this report is preliminary. Come back when you have a doctorate in medical tech."

Rains looked back and forth at the two men, finally throwing his hands up in a helpless gesture.

"I don't believe anything untoward caused Ms. Deveraux's death," he said. "This is an old station—the oldest in the system. The retrofits are not going as planned. Typically overbudget and delayed. Something about scarce rare metals."

He paused, looking between them again. Slade kept his expression neutral. Rains sighed dramatically before continuing.

"Fine. If you feel you must duplicate effort, then you should probably seek out Ms. Deveraux's heir apparent at Lagrange Analytic. A Ms."—his eyes became distant for a moment as he checked his implant—"ah yes, a Ms. Lydia Vadinov."

That got Slade's attention, setting off a myriad of emotions. Some good but most not so much. Lydia,

Salome, and Slade's complicated past made this case more compelling and personal.

"Yes. Judging by your reaction, I take it you know her," Rains said. "She was in charge of the day-to-day for the retrofit. Though, I suppose, now she'll be in charge of the entire project."

Slade nodded at Collier, then jerked his head toward the door.

"Thank you, Inspector," Slade said as they turned to leave. "We'll keep you in the loop if we find anything new."

"While you're at it," Rains' voice came from behind them. "You might want to speak with Samantha Deveraux, the victim's sister. She handled the procurement."

As they left Rains' office, Collier pulled Slade off to the side of the corridor out of the way of the foot traffic. There was more than the usual amount of people in the corridor, likely due to issues with the transit pods.

"Look, Slade, we should split up to save time," Collier said. "You take this Vadinov woman and I'll go see Deveraux."

He held up a hand before Slade could speak.

"I know you know them both, but Samantha just lost her sister. I'm thinking a stranger might be easier to deal with than a friend"—he gave a knowing look—"especially one that had history with the deceased."

Collier was right. Slade felt his emotions ebb, argument dying on his lips. He nodded.

"Yeah, I feel ya. I'll give her a heads-up you're coming by. Let her know you're okay, dig?" Slade gave a slight grin as he said the last, enjoying the pained expression on his friend's face. "I tried to reach her on the way to the office but I couldn't get hold of her. I still want to see how's she doing. Give my condolences, you know?"

"Understood. We'll meet up afterwards to compare notes."

As Collier walked off, Slade went to the nearest com corridor to give her the heads-up about the visit.

Little Sunny Deveraux, all grown up and putting all her nerdiness into the station retrofit. Slade had to admit he hadn't been a very good friend to her since he returned from the "policing action" on Callisto. For that matter, he hadn't seen much of Samantha or Salome. He'd have to make an effort to visit more, now that Salome was gone.

He placed his thumb on the com's "call" button, a picture of an old-fashioned rotary telephone, activating the screen. One of the original pieces of tech from the station's early days, he found it comforting in its relative obscurity.

Name and number? the screen read.

"Samantha Deveraux, 92647." He appreciated the little hourglass icon as well. An atavistic hanger-on from an earlier time. How many people would even know what that is these days?

"Hello?" said a female voice he recognized. Audio only, no video. Either the gremlins were still running rampant, or Samantha was being cautious.

"Sunny, it's me—Slade." The screen came to life. Not gremlins then. Deveraux's upper torso filled the screen, a deep blue satin robe drawn tightly around her shoulders. He took a second to examine her face.

She had been crying, it seemed, and had hastily

prepared herself for a video call. Her hair spilled out of a top bun, stray dark brown locks cascading down her neck. Her nose and eyes were rimmed in red, and both were running.

"What do you want?" she said, sniffling.

"Sunny, I just wanted to say how sorry I am for your loss. I wouldn't be bothering you right now if it wasn't important."

"Save your sorrow for someone you care about, Slade. Haven't seen hide nor hair of you in months." She shook her head slightly, dislodging more hair from the bun. "The only time I see you is when you're sniffing around Salome. If she wasn't dead, you'd still be a stranger."

"I know I haven't been a very good friend of late," he said. She wiped her nose with a tissue and tossed it to the side. He imagined the floor piled with snotty, tear-soaked tissues, and repressed a shiver. "I get busy with stuff and forget to do the real things I should pay attention to. It'll be different, you'll see. I'm here to support you, Sunny, I swear."

"It's Samantha. Only people close to me get to call me 'Sunny.'" If she saw Slade wince, she ignored it. "What's so important? I'm sure you didn't call just to explain what a lousy asshole you are."

"Right." He gave up on trying to convince her of his sincerity for the moment. "Look, my partner is on his way to talk with you about Salome. His name is Dennis Collier. We don't think it was an accident. We're working a couple of leads and could use anything you've got. He'll be there shortly."

"Not an accident? You think she was killed?" Her voice dropped. "Murdered?"

"I think it's possible. You should get yourself cleaned up enough to have company." Snotty, tear-soaked...

"I have a right to wallow as much as I want," she said, eyes becoming hard under the tears. "If he can't understand why I look this way, then tell him to piss off and leave me alone!"

"Fine. I'm sorry I said anything." He shut his eyes and took a deep breath. Staying calm was key.

"I didn't ask for this, Zac. I'm not paying a private investigator to look into 'It's possible.' Rains told me it was a closed case."

"No. This is on me. I'm the one that's kicking up all this mess, and I owe her—you—this much," he said, fighting to keep his voice level. "Just, please, talk to Denny when he gets there. Tell him anything you can think of that might have been out of the ordinary or caught your attention as odd. In the meantime, I'm on my way to see Lydia Vadinov."

"That prime bitch!" she snarled, features twisting. "If it is murder, I'd put her at the top of my list. She hated Salome for parachuting into that position over her."

"Sam, let's not jump to any conclusions..."

She ignored him. "Lydia thought she was next in line. She never had a chance and the chip on her shoulder was so big it made her walk funny." The anger fell away as she teared up again. "Well, I guess she finally beat Salome."

"I'll suss out what's really going on, Sam. I have a nose for such things. There will be justice for you and Salome." His eyes narrowed. "I promise."

❖   ❖   ❖

Lydia Vadinov. She had been one corner of a sexually tense triangle back in college, with he and Salome as the other two. Both women were fiercely competitive in nature, and it permeated into all aspects of their lives. Each was always ready to throw down, in order to outdo the other, no matter the subject. Grades, fashion, bedroom games, it didn't matter. Kept him on his toes—not to mention exhausted and happy.

He and Lydia had parted on strained but civil terms way back then. Since he'd been on station, they'd met up a few times, but it didn't feel right. Since then, he'd done his best to avoid her. Not difficult to do, considering the social and literally physical rings they moved through. She and Salome, being rich, socialite businesswomen, wouldn't have had that luxury.

He snorted at the irony.

Could it be that she was jealous enough to take things a step too far? It didn't feel right, but yet, the stakes were much higher than before. He'd reveled in it at the time—two smart, white-collar women fighting over his blue-collar ass—but it hadn't been healthy for any of them. Perhaps Lydia took the competition a little too seriously?

With the pods all jacked up, he figured he would take a maintenance belt ladder upspoke to the .75g area where Lagrange Analytic had offices.

He had been a station rat back before the Marines. Fresh out of college and looking for adventure, he came to L5 because it was the most affordable space habitat. He quickly discovered why.

It was old, very old. The first large space station ever built, it was state-of-the-art at the time. Now, it was mostly a tenement. A lofty version of its inner-city ancestors, locked into geosynchronous orbit.

Of course, that made it very affordable and desirable to Earth's lower-class citizens, especially in those countries that had issues with overcrowding. Many of the residents were "encouraged" to relocate here by their "benevolent" governments, often at the business end of a rifle.

He knew every corner. Gentrification only went so far, a fresh coat of paint over the mildew and rusted corruption underneath. Those areas—the unseen and unmentioned places the well-to-do tried to ignore— that's where he and his cohorts made their home.

He slipped into a back corridor unnoticed, the smells of curry and cabbage fading behind him. Flickering lights, their affliction more obvious due to their fewer numbers, did more to bolster the darkness than vanquish it. In the farthest corner, beyond the limit of the last stuttering circle of illumination, he found a maintenance hatch. Pulling Gunny's knife from his back pocket, he used the blade to ease the panel off the lock screen and hit the override. Just like back in his rat days.

The hatch gave way to a narrow corridor, connecting all the "back of house" necessities for station life. Plumbing, fiber optics, electrical, waste retrieval, etc., it was all here, hidden from the upper crust.

Slade covered the hundred meters to the belt ladder with brisk, long strides. He stepped onto it, activating the mechanism.

This brings back memories, Slade thought.

He felt lighter as he ascended, the gravity easing as he moved closer to the center of the station.

Each ladder shift became something of a dance as he adjusted to the sensation. His younger self dared him to jump for the next ladder; his wiser current self slapped that down, hard. Missing the landing would put an end to his new career in short notice.

Just as that younger voice decided to speak up again, it was time to get off. He landed lightly on his feet in a semilit corridor similar to the one he started in. Only the floating, glowing, alphanumeric level designation differed.

Slade walked slowly for a few moments to adjust to the weight he'd lost, getting his "grav-legs" under him. With a grin, he let his younger self come out, sprinting down the corridor to the maintenance hatch. The lock was designed to keep people from getting in, not out. He hit the large exit button and slowly opened the hatch, peeked out to make sure the coast was clear, then slipped effortlessly into the foot traffic with no one the wiser as to how he got there.

So much for the easy part, Slade thought. *Now what do I say to an old friend that just might be guilty of murder?*

"Isaac?" Lydia looked up from a glass and chrome desk as Slade walked into her office. "So this is what it takes for you to show up around here. Death and the station falling apart around us?"

She stood up and walked around the desk, the rustic curls of her long black hair slightly buoyant in the reduced gravity. Her smooth skin, tanned and healthy as though she just walked off a beach, looked as though she hadn't spent months living as a space mole. Her tight skirt, along with the brightly colored scarf adorning her neck, gave the impression of a model playing at big business.

To his eyes she looked even better than before.

"You look...great!" Slade said, his brain deciding to shut down. Lydia walked up to him and, rising slightly on her toes, kissed him on the cheek.

"At a loss for words. I'll take that as a compliment," Lydia said, smiling. She indicated two chairs and a couch near a coffee table to the left of her desk.

"This office is bigger than my apartment," he said, taking in the room. Data banks sat to the right of the desk, dwarfed by the massive monitors behind it. He turned and saw two on either side of the door, similar in size. All were showing different angles of the same scene, giving the illusion of windows overlooking a beach. "Very impressive."

She sat on the couch, carefully smoothing her skirt and crossing her legs. He took a chair.

"You should see Salome's. The boss has it even better." Lydia looked down, a sudden catch in her voice. "Had."

"Lydia," Slade said softly. She raised her head at her name, allowing him to look her squarely in the eyes, "I have to ask—how enticing is her office to you? I mean, how badly did you want that office to be yours?"

"I am quite sure I don't like your insinuation," she said, eyes growing hard. Genuine indignation, or just good acting? "Are you suggesting that I might have something to do with her death?"

"You have to admit, the competition between you two didn't always stay on the rails."

Lydia sat back, crossing her arms.

"I've seen you, what, twice since you returned?" It had been four times, but two of them were all fun. She didn't give him a chance to correct her. "I had to hear you were back through the grapevine and it was me that came to you. Now you waltz in here and accuse me of murdering a childhood friend?"

Her face twisted, like she smelled something awful. "The nerve of you. You have no idea the relationship I have ... had ... with Salome. What makes you think I'm capable of committing such a horrific act?"

Slade paused. He wanted to answer carefully, with a little forethought. After all, he was accusing a friend and former lover of murder. A friend he hadn't seen much of, granted, but one he still cared for deeply. That realization hit him like a finely aimed left hook. He didn't want to lose her, too.

"Lydia, you have to admit, it all lines up." He ticked points off on his fingers. "The competitive nature of your relationship with Salome is well documented. It's no secret—you were pissed that she got the job, the job you figured was by all rights yours. You told me that yourself."

"I did no such thing!"

"Honey, you talk in your sleep," he said gently. He raised another finger as he continued, "You have the know-how, and access, to create a feedback loop in the implant. Take a step back, calm down, and be reasonable."

"Calm down?" Her voice rose an octave between the first and last word.

He looked at her, trying to keep his face expressionless. She met his gaze with ferocity and a side of anger before standing abruptly and walking to her desk. He recognized the action as her way of getting under control. Ever conscious of outward appearance, Lydia hated losing composure in public.

"You need to leave. Now." She held up a hand as he opened his mouth, cutting off any reply. "I mean it, Isaac. You have no authority here, and as far as I'm concerned you're trespassing."

"Lydia, I'm trying to get to the bottom of this. Salome's death wasn't an accident."

"No, I get it, Slade," she said, shaking her head. "You're convinced I had something to do with it. I'm your prime suspect, our history be damned. Get out of here before I call Rains."

"Fine. You know where to reach me if you want to talk." He turned and walked towards the door. There was no reasoning with her when she got defensive.

She said nothing further as he left, the door closing with a whisper over the icy silence behind him.

Slade went back to the office mollified after meeting with Lydia. Collier was already there, sitting in "his" seat.

"How'd it go with Ms. Vadinov?"

"Let's just say I had to leave before I became the next victim," Slade said, shrugging. He sat in the other chair. "She'll come around and want to talk again later, she always does. She just needs time to think it all through. So what did Sammy have to say? Anything useful?"

"As a matter of fact, yes." Collier leaned forward, clasping his hands as he leaned his elbows on the desk. "But I don't think you're going to like what she had to say. There's no love lost between Samantha

and Lydia. She thinks that if it is murder, then Lydia
had something to do with it."

"I gathered that from the conversation I had with
her. I have to admit that Lydia looks like the prime
suspect but I can't help feeling like I'm missing
something."

Collier said nothing but made a "go on" motion
with his hand. Slade sighed and continued.

"They may have been competitive, but they were
good friends as well. Like sisters from another mother."
He shook his head, "It's hard to explain."

"Tell me, Slade, if it is murder, who else had something to gain?" Collier leaned back, combing his hair
back with his fingers.

Slade thought a bit. Collier had a point. Only one
person came front and center, no matter which way
he looked at it. Still, there was a nagging feeling in
the back of his mind that it wasn't that easy.

"There's always more than one angle," Slade said.
"Maybe Salome saw something she shouldn't have, or
one of the contractors had a beef. Maybe she had a
relationship sour. Could be anything."

"You're grasping at straws," Collier leaned forward
again, a smug look on his face. "You're inventing
boogeymen. Look, it's all about Occam's razor. The
simplest solution is usually the right one."

"It wasn't when we looked at Salome's body."

Collier waved him off. "Bah—you don't want it to
be her, is all. I get it; I really do. She's a looker, and
you two have history."

Was that all it was? Slade thought. *Am I thinking
with the wrong body part?*

"Hey! I found something you'll appreciate," Collier

said, changing the subject. He reached into one of the side drawers and pulled out something wrapped in an oiled cloth. Placing it on the desk, he pushed it toward Slade. "Check it out."

Slade reached over, pulling the object closer. He knew what it was before he unwrapped it fully.

"You've got to be kidding!" Slade's grin threatened to split his face in two. "A Ruger Standard? With the red eagle medallion...this is from what? 1949? 50? Where the hell did you get this?"

Slade picked up the pistol carefully from its position between the two loaded magazines. It was in excellent condition and freshly cleaned. He checked the chamber before loading it, seating the mag with a slap. He felt like a real PI, the hard-as-nails sleuth with the classic heater, ready to crack the case. He raised the .22, aiming at the wall away from Collier and sighting along the barrel.

"Sweet Jesus's Mama! This had to cost you a fortune!"

"Nah, won it in a poker game. The guy had a major tell," Collier said, chuckling. "Poor sucker definitely didn't know what he was betting. I figured you'd get a kick out of an antique like this, Mr. Hardboiled Gumshoe."

"You betcha." Slade dropped the mag, checked the chamber again, and placed both on the cloth. After carefully wrapping everything up, he slid it back over to Collier. Still smiling, he said, "Great gun to have on a station by the way. Low caliber. Won't pierce the walls. Well, that was a moment of delight on this otherwise shitty day."

"I thought it might make you feel better," Collier

said, returning the gun to the drawer. "Go home. Get some rest. We'll talk more later, maybe over dinner and a drink. It'll do you some good to step back for a bit."

"You ain't lyin' 'bout that."

Slade entered his cube, thoughts buzzing through his brain like electronic gnats. Bright flashes of ideas that would zip away as soon as he tried to pin them down, taunting him with how close he could get. If he could only slow them down enough...

The bottle of high-quality hooch sat where he left it. He went over, plopped into the autoform and poured himself a snort.

Then, with a frustrated sigh, added more.

Lots of ways to think about this case, but only one way that covered all the bases, Slade thought, taking a sip. *If not Lydia, then who? Lydia knew Salome was qualified for the job. Could simple jealousy and pride be reason enough to kill a long-time colleague and friend?*

It didn't jibe with Lydia's style. Competitive, yes—she was ruthless when it came to winning—but she was honorable. Salome had been the same way, preferring to "win" against Lydia by using what she had, not sabotaging the other woman. It's how they were able to remain friends.

The display com announced an incoming call, causing his thoughts to scatter like cockroaches scurrying from the light.

"Lydia Vadinov. Will you accept?"

"Hell yeah!" He said, before getting himself under control. Not knowing her mood, he tried for "passive polite." "Lydia, how nice of you to get back to me."

"Save it," Lydia said curtly. "How soon can you get back to my office? I have something to show you."

"Not long," he said. She cut the connection without another word. Slade downed his drink, hopped up, and made for the door, grabbing his hat on the way out.

Slade calmed himself before allowing the AI to announce his arrival. The doors pushed aside and he walked in, not knowing what to expect.

"You got here fast," Lydia said, looking up from her desk.

"I know a shortcut," he said. He'd only stopped long enough to shoot a quick message to Collier about where he was going.

No kiss this time, he thought. To her, he said, "Hello again, Lydia. Feeling better?"

"I'm *fine*, Isaac," she said flatly. He recognized the look on her face. Not angry, just...disappointed. "It doesn't mean I don't hate your guts right now."

Okay, so more than disappointment. Slade walked over to the desk.

"Just following the evidence, baby girl."

"Then you should have followed it more closely." Standing suddenly, she walked around the desk, stopping about two feet away. For a long moment, she said nothing, looking him in the eyes. Her impossibly high heels brought her almost to his height.

If I didn't know better, I'd say she was about to...

Her right hand came up so fast that he didn't have time to flinch before it made contact. The sound was deafening in the silent office.

"That's for not giving me the benefit of doubt!"

Slade rubbed his left cheek. If he had lighter skin,

there would be a full handprint there. Even so, he wouldn't be surprised if it was at least partially visible.

"I deserved that. You feeling better?"

"Much," she said, smiling slightly.

"Well..."

She stopped him, putting an index finger to his lips while pursing hers. "You're like a dog with a bone, Slade. You get an idea in your head and, right or wrong, you build up a story to support it. But you got me thinking." She walked back to her desk, the computer coming to life as she tapped something into it. "I was worried about the glitching and what effect it might have on autonomic systems throughout the station. I mean, we all have access nodes."

She stopped, giving him a look.

"Well, most of us, at least. So, if this was indeed an accident, why haven't more people been affected? There should be more cases of failure, up to and including death." She tucked a buoyant curl behind an ear. "So, I did some digging."

Slade moved around behind her, watching the screen as she clicked through.

"When I checked the logs, they showed this computer as the source," she said, bringing up the appropriate file.

"You're not making a case for yourself, Lydia. It's all right there, in black and white."

"You see what I mean, Slade? You won't give up what you assume you already know. If I were guilty, would I have called you up here?" She looked over her shoulder at him, her expression showing exasperation and disappointment. "That's what I don't understand, Zac. You know me. I'm not some random suspect you've never met before. I thought we...I thought you and I..."

"It doesn't matter what I think, or feel, or desperately want to believe, Lydia." The words didn't ring true in his head, but dammit, those gnats were still eluding his grasp. He moved away from her again, heading back towards the door. "What matters is that everything still points to you. You had the motive, the means, and the ruthless streak to do it. What I don't get is why you called me up here. Are you trying to convince me to cover for you?"

"No! No, you don't understand—I couldn't have done this!"

"Oh? The woman that clawed her way to the top of this ladder, who told me in as many words that she'd do anything to make it to the top? She couldn't have cut down anyone in her way?" He spun, frustration coming to the surface. "I'm not going to risk going to jail because you and I had a good time."

"I'm going to ignore that for now, because I need you to quit being so damned stubborn and listen: I'm not only saying I wouldn't have done it—I'm saying I *couldn't* have. I've been hacked. I don't have the codes any longer; my login was changed."

Lydia turned her screen to face him. Like he'd said, it was all there in black and white. The internal log showed Error code 505. "Password and login unrecognized." Dated the day Salome died. Service ticket request for new password created and received at 0800. He thought back to the autopsy—Salome's time of death had been closer to 0930.

"It's very subtle," she said, pulling up the page source. "Just a few lines of code here and there. It allowed me to access the other systems but locked me out of that section until the scheduled update at 0915."

"Why didn't you say something earlier?"

"You mean when you were accusing me of murder?" She stared at him, unflinchingly meeting his eyes with hers. "Honestly, it didn't occur to me that it was more than just another glitch until you came up here."

Either this was a very elaborate lie or . . . she didn't do it, and someone wanted to make it look like she did, should anyone dig deeper.

Like me.

Those gnats started slowing down, still eluding his mental grasp, but letting him see them better.

"Lydia, has anyone else used your office recently?"

"No," she said, shaking her head, "I haven't even allowed the cleaning crew in here recently. I've been practically living out of this office since the project began."

That made sense when he thought about it. That competitive streak again. Lydia wouldn't want any detail to be missed, just to prove that she was the better woman.

"What about Salome? Was she as diligent?"

"I'm not sure," she said, frowning. "I mean, I didn't keep tabs on her, but she also had a workstation in her apartment."

He caught a gnat, then another. Just as things started to fall into place, Lydia's eyes widened.

The muffled cough behind him caught his attention, turning his gaze away from Lydia. Collier stood there, smoke drifting lazily from the suppressor screwed into his .22. Slade blinked slowly, realization of what had happened coming shortly after.

He looked down—expecting to see a bloody rose growing across his chest. It took him a second to realize he wasn't hit.

"Slade..." Lydia said weakly. "I..."

He spun, lunging for her as she toppled forward, catching her before she hit the desk. He lowered her slowly to the floor, carefully working his way around to her side. For now, her pulse and breathing were thready, shallow, and rapid, but *there*, as her system went into shock. She was alive, at least for now. He pulled off his shirt and pressed it to her wound, placing her hands on it.

"Hold this here as tight as you can," he said. "Just hang on for me, baby."

Slade looked up at Collier, eyes pleading for an explanation even as the pieces fell together in his mind. As he stood, he felt his features harden.

Collier smirked at him, keeping the pistol leveled. The nine remaining rounds would last him until the end of Slade's life.

"Let me guess," Slade said, taking a step toward his former partner. The gun came up just a little, aiming squarely at center mass. "Salome found something fishy with the retrofit project. She's only working a hunch and doesn't want to go to Rains until she's sure. Wouldn't want to give any appearance of mismanagement, especially with Lydia watching. Goes looking for someone on the outside, and up pops your name."

Collier kept smirking, giving him a slight shrug. Slade took another careful step forward, keeping his hands at his side but in view. The Ruger stayed steady, but Collier's gloved finger tensed ever so slightly. Slade continued.

"Long story short, she hires you to suss things out. Which you did, with your not-too-shabby investigative skills. Only when you discovered what was really going on, you threw in with the perp for a big payday." He rubbed the stubble on his chin and cheeks with his right hand as if to aid his thought process. "You wanted to split up earlier, so you could take Samantha out of the picture for a clean getaway after you finished tying up the loose ends here. Am I close?"

He squared his shoulders and placed his hands in the back pockets of his jeans. He inched a booted right foot closer to Lydia.

"Not bad," Collier said, nodding, "Not too shabby yourself. But you are wrong on some essential facts. Yeah, Salome hired me to track down the culprit. She had a lot of it figured out, so it wasn't that difficult. What I didn't expect was who it led me to."

He almost looked...was it happy? His eyes sparkled.

"It led me to the smartest, most incredibly stunning woman I have ever met. The first time I saw her, she stopped me dead in my tracks. It led me to..."

"Samantha Devereaux," Slade said, finishing the sentence. He tried not to look shocked, although by Collier's expression, something had flashed across his face.

"I know, right?" Collier's grin spread as he spoke. He gestured as he continued. "Your problem is you still consider her a child. Little Sunny in glasses and braces who used to cramp your style with Salome. Take it from me, pal, she's definitely not a little girl anymore. She also knew you might be the wild card."

"What, she flash some skin, and you were all in?"

"Don't be crass, Slade. Do you know what cobalt is?"

"Sure. It's used for all sorts of things, like blue glass

or high-strength durable magnetic alloys. Weapons, too." Collier's jaw dropped a bit. Slade couldn't help but grin. "What? I know stuff!"

"Okay, so you're familiar with it," Collier said. "Anyway, it's very expensive and hard to come by, unless there's a huge project with deep pockets."

"Like fixing up a historic space station, home to a major corporation."

"Exactly."

"And this has to do with Sunny...how?" Slade knew the answer, but he needed to keep Collier talking, giving him time to get his boot a bit closer.

"Let's just say the high strength durable magnetic alloys aren't very durable currently. Samantha siphoned off about half of what was intended for the station." He shook his head, as though overwhelmed with his fantasy. "Zac, you have no idea what that kind of money can buy! It's close to half a billion Elons, enough to buy two spaces on the Martian Colonies. Good spaces. Orbital now, dome when it's done, and a quarter billion left to play with."

"How do you plan on getting away with shooting Lydia and your partner in cold blood? It's not like I have a working implant to fry my brain with."

"Here's the thing, pal; I don't want to shoot you. If I did, I would've already. So, I'm giving you a choice." It was Collier's turn to look pleading, his features softening slightly. "Leave her, we all jump ship, and live fat, rich and happy. All the R and I we can stand."

"And the other option? How do you plan on explaining that?"

"That's the easy part. You suspected Lydia and came

here all in a huff, dead set to punish the murderer of
your college sweetheart. Only she was armed and shot
you before you wrestled away the gun and shot her."
He put on a look of sorrowful resignation. "Unfortunately, you both bled out before I could get here.
How did you get here so quickly anyway?"

"Trade secret. Do you really think that story'll fly?"

"Believe me, the good Inspector Rains will be only
too happy to take the path of least resistance. Especially with a reasonable fee to cover any paperwork.
He's looked the other way for years. I'll make it fly."

"Neat little gift-wrapped bundle for the news feeds."
Slade let out a humorless chuckle, covering the sound
of his boot against the floor. "Thought of everything,
did you?"

"I can't take all the credit," Collier said. "It was
Samantha's plan. I'm just doing what I was told, like
a good Marine."

Slade nudged Lydia hard in the side. Her scream
filled his soul with guilt, but he quashed the feeling,
hard. There'd be time to feel bad later. Maybe.

Collier, surprised by the sound, looked away for
only a second. Just enough time for Slade to push
off hard, lunging to his left, away from Lydia's prone
body. As he dove, he pulled the knife from his back
pocket, pressing the button as it came forward. In the
same fluid motion, he snapped it toward his former
partner. There was another coughing sound, and fire
lanced across Slade's shoulder. He ignored it, rolling
to his feet and throwing himself at the other man as
the gun went off again.

He hit him at the knees, his mass causing Collier
to topple even in the fractional gravity. Slade used his

size to his advantage, pinning the other man as he locked a hand around the pistol. Another shot hit the wall as Slade drove his free hand into Collier's nose.

His former squad mate was only fazed for a second, lashing out with his own free hand in a haymaker that caught Slade on the temple. Fireworks exploded in front of his eyes, blinding him briefly. He rolled to his right, pinning Collier's arm before he could land another. Out of the corner of his eye, he saw his knife, just within reach.

Collier met Slade's eyes at that moment, determination written on his face. He'd seen it too.

Slade forced the gun hand backward and down, keeping the muzzle of the pistol pointed at Collier's body. His fingers, inches away from the knife's hilt, scrabbled against the floor, straining to make contact. Collier fought back, trying to get enough leverage to bring the gun around.

Slade snapped his neck forward, slamming his forehead into the other man's bloody nose with as much force as he could muster, then again for good measure. Collier went limp briefly, giving Slade the moment he needed to grab the knife, rolling as he did so. He put the blade against Collier's ribs and finished the roll, letting his weight come down on the hilt.

Collier's gasp turned into a gurgle as his body went limp. Slade moved off of his friend, kneeling next to him.

Collier looked at the knife sticking out of his chest, crimson petals blossoming around it. He chuckled weakly, blood flowing from between his lips. "You and that stupid feeling of yours. Couldn't let it go this time. You just had to scratch that itch, didn't you?"

His laugh faded into a wet cough, scarlet foam spraying the air. "A switchblade! A fucking switchblade!"

"I assumed y'all'd appreciate the gesture," Slade said. "An old-fashioned solution for an old-fashioned guy. Like I said, the past is cool."

The gun fell to the floor, followed by Youcef Collier's head, his dead eyes staring at nothing in particular.

Slade stood, taking a moment to check his shoulder. It stung like all get-out, but was only a flesh wound, the blood flow only a trickle. A soft groan brought his attention back to Lydia. He crossed the office, knelt down beside her, and brushed a stray curl from her face.

"Sorry I had to kick you, baby girl, but hard times call for hard methods." He reached across her, pulling her arm closer. The bracelet on her left wrist looked like just another piece of high quality jewelry, but she'd told him what it really was. He tapped the synthetic sapphire in the middle, alerting security to her position.

"Help will be here soon, honey. Just hang on a little longer." He pulled the scarf from around her neck, tying it across his blood-soaked shirt on her chest.

The large video panel behind him came to life, the beach scene replaced with a face he barely recognized. He pushed himself to his feet, and after a moment of stunned inaction, walked over to the monitor. Smooth coffee and double cream skin occupied most of the screen.

"Hello, Zac."

"Sunny? Is that you?" *My god what a transformation.*

"I told you before, it's Samantha, and even that is only temporary." She gave him a brilliant smile that made the siren's call even more alluring. "Not the little girl in horn rims and braces any longer, am I?"

"I'd say not." He forced his mind back to the matter at hand. "Why? What happened with Salome that drove you to hatch this plan?"

"To tell you the truth, I've been planning a move on sister dear for my entire life." Her lovely face took on a sinister cast. He had to admit, it was terrifying and arousing at the same time. "I hated that bitch! Forever in her shadow, never living up to her status. Working for her was the final insult."

Damn, Slade thought, as she arched an eyebrow, the gesture coming across as an invitation. He could almost smell the pheromones through the screen. *She's getting to me too. Glad we're not in the same room.*

"Salome got everything she wanted—always," Samantha said. "I got nothing, no matter how hard I worked. I was constantly compared to her, and never measured up. Do you know what that feels like, Zac? Don't answer—I know you don't. You met some criteria of hers."

"I feel we're missing the sad violin music," Slade said. "It's over, Sunny. I'm coming for you. Even Rains can't deny your guilt or Youcef's culpability."

"I wish you luck with that endeavor, you're going to need it." The camera zoomed out, revealing her surroundings as it pulled back. No wonder Collier fell for her so hard. "Drink it in, Zac, this is the last you'll see of little Sunny. There's no extradition from the Martian Colonies to Earth space, not that it matters. They won't know who I am once I get there."

"Where are you?" Slade said, focusing on the background. It didn't look like anywhere on the station.

"Dear Zac, I'm on the cruise ship *Asimov*, on an intercept course with the Martian orbital. Did I forget to mention that when last we talked?"

"You weren't in your quarters then, I take it."

She shook her head. "Things were getting a bit dicey, what with all the systems issues. I thought it a good idea to get a head start on my new life." She hit him with that smile again. "I'm in your debt though. You saved me the trouble of having to tidy up around there. Poor Youcef. He didn't understand that he wasn't invited, and I didn't have the heart to tell him otherwise."

She pulled a long braid over one shoulder in a move so sensual it made Slade shudder.

"Of course, had things gone as planned," she continued, "Mr. Collier would have experienced another unfortunate access node failure."

"Yeah, there's a lot of that going around lately." He snorted. "You had his nose so open he didn't have a chance. You played him like a stacked deck, but you weren't planning on me getting involved."

"Yes, you were the only wild card, one I underestimated. You've just got big, black and stupid written all over you. Living in the past like some historical vid drama, with your bizarre colloquialisms. You play the part well—it's something of a pleasant surprise to see the truth."

"Spare me, Sunny. You just can't murder three people, steal a half billion Elons and get off scot free. I'll find a way to get to you."

"Dear, dear Zac, that is exactly what I am doing. Soon we will go dark and only the AI will be awake to ignore your pleas," she said, dazzling smile growing more radiant with her gloating. "This section of the ship is considered Martian soil, already through customs, sanitation and clearances."

"This isn't over," he said, not quite able to convince himself of their sincerity. "System Central will come knocking, and I'll be right there with them."

"Earth and Mars aren't getting along these days. I suspect the rich and infamous are tired of paying Earth to be rich and infamous." She smiled that deadly, alluring smile. "You can try, Slade, but I suspect you'll die broke and bitter before it happens."

The camera filled with her face again as she moved closer.

"Goodbye, Isaac Slade. If you're lucky, I'll see you in Hell."

The screen went as blank as his mind felt.

Coming out of his daze, he made a promise.

"I will find you, Sunshine, if it's the last thing I do," he said, meeting his gaze in the reflection of the dark monitor. "Mama didn't raise no quitters."

Recruiting Exercise

David Weber

Confidential
Official Internal Security and
   Mental Hygiene Police Use Only
Access Authorization Level Gamma Seven

RE: Homicide Investigation MT3-137-56-A732
Excerpt, Surveillance System MT3-42-1693-04;
   7/14/73
Positive ID Hilaire Becquerel, NP-342-8879-1736
Positive ID Samuel Rochefort, NP-491-3275-4291

Excerpt begins:
ROCHEFORT: Cheez, Boss! I thought they'd
   never cut you loose! Are you all right?
BECQUEREL: Do I *look* all right? Pour me
   another one, damn it.
ROCHEFORT: How hard they gonna hammer
   us on this one?

BECQUEREL: How the hell am *I* supposed to know? Wasn't my idea for the idiots to come here. And not my *fault*, either! You know that.

ROCHEFORT: But who *was* she? I mean, the big bastard was bad enough, but *her*—!

BECQUEREL: How do I know? Paschal checked her license at the door, right?

ROCHEFORT: 'Course he did! Never would've let her into the place if her docs hadn't showed green. You know that.

BECQUEREL: Yeah, I do. I do. Hit me again.

ROCHEFORT: Boss, I think you'd better cut back on the booze. You need to go home, get some rest. Cops'll be back tomorrow, and you're gonna need a clear head.

BECQUEREL: I know. I know! Damn it, Sam—of all the stim joints in all the towers of all Nouveau Paris, why'd she have to walk into *mine?*

Excerpt ends.

None of it worked out the way I'd expected.

Not after the moment I got through the door, anyway. Up to that point, yeah. It was just as depressing as I'd known it would be, but what do you do when you don't have family anymore; the databases list you as "recidivist," which means you're untouchable for any legal employer; the government's keeping two thirds of your BLS; you've sold everything you own; and the only person in the entire world you still have to love needs a doc bad and the local clinic won't jump him to the head of the queue without a bribe? I'll tell you what you do. You sell the last thing you have—yourself.

Which is why I went through that door. Didn't tell the doorman why I was there, of course, because I wasn't licensed. You can't get one of those in Morocco Tower without knowing the right people or black-market cash in hand. And, unfortunately, the "right people" knew all about me. No way in hell they would've licensed me even if I'd had the cash. That's what happens when both your parents get picked up by the Mental Hygiene Police and never seen again. I was seventeen when that happened. Tomorrow would be my twenty-second birthday.

Hell of a birthday present.

The guy at the door let me in. From the look he gave me, I was pretty sure he knew the real reason I was there, all gussied up. I'd spent almost all my dwindling pile of credits on that outfit, and I'm not proud to admit it, but I'd stolen the cosmetics. Then again, old Bonneville was a suck-up to Marteau, the Hundred-Ten Floor manager, so I didn't feel too bad about it. Marteau was the one who'd stood and watched Mom and Dad being disappeared for "deviant behavior" and then made sure his goons were first into the apartment to steal the best stuff—not that it was all that good—before anyone else got to it. Besides, if Bonneville didn't want people stealing stuff, he should get better cyber security. That server of his leaks like a sieve if you know where to look. And the greedy old bastard had stiffed me on the off-the-books IT work I'd done for him. There'd been no way to make him pay me for work I was legally barred from doing in the first place, and he knew it. Just like *I* knew he wanted into my pants. He'd made that clear enough when he didn't hand over the credits, so in a way, I'd just collected what he owed me through different channels.

Probably should have closed the back door when I left instead of posting it on the darknet, I guess. But he'd really, really pissed me off.

Anyway, they let me in, and as the sights and sounds surrounded me, I tried to look like I had at least a clue about what I was doing. It wasn't what I'd expected. Or, rather, it was exactly *what* I'd expected, just not *who* I'd expected. Lunete had told me there'd be some big spenders at the Lisbon, but I'd thought she was talking about roof-tier Dolists. About the ones who run the protection rackets or jack the prices for basic maintenance on the contracts their Dolist manager buddies throw their way. But these weren't "my" class of people after all. Not all of them, anyway.

An actual, honest-to-God piano sat at one end of the single huge room, the ripple of its notes coming clearly through the background mutter of conversation as the very dark-skinned pianist stroked the keyboard. I stood there listening, looking around, under the haze of smoke—most of it old-fashioned tobacco, but salted with euphor and dream weed—that was too heavy for the ducts to dissipate properly. Or maybe the Lisbon's owner just liked the atmosphere and he'd dialed down the fans. The lighting was awful, but it was the kind of awful somebody takes pains to arrange. The kind that leaves lots of darkness for those who want to be discreet. Not that too many people in the Lisbon seemed all that concerned about discretion, judging by the live sex show on the stage and the well-dressed people calling encouragement and tossing credit slips.

"Welcome to the Lisbon, cutie," someone said

and I looked away from the stage and its...improbably energetic occupants. The waiter was older than me—seems like all the world's older than me—and as Mom had said, back in the days when she still laughed sometimes, he looked like he'd been ridden hard and put up wet. But at least he was smiling.

"Thanks," I said.

"First time here?"

"Yeah," I acknowledged.

"Well, you're gonna have to buy at least one drink or tab, and Paschal—he's the guy on the door—expects ten percent off the top." I blushed at the devastating accuracy with which he'd assessed my reason for being there, and he shook his head. "Way it works, cutie," he said almost gently. "And at least it's only ten percent. Down-corridor at Jamie's, the house takes twenty percent."

"Yeah, I'd heard that," I lied. "Reason I thought I'd try my luck here tonight."

"Well, good hunting," he said. "Was I you, though, I'd stay away from table ten. People there'd really like someone your age. Too much."

He gave me a long, steady look, and I managed not to swallow nervously before I nodded. Then he nodded back and disappeared into the crowd, and I headed for the long, polished, old-fashioned bar. It looked like it was made out of real wood. I wasn't sure it actually was, but it did have a real live barkeep behind it.

I would've preferred an AI dispenser, for a lot of reasons.

"What'll it be?" he asked over the piano, his eyes resting knowingly on my breasts, as I slipped onto one of the barstools. That was one of the reasons

I'd have preferred an AI. Then again, I've *always* preferred computers to people. Probably because no matter how "brilliant" the system may be, I know it's not really self-aware. Not really judging me.

Not really looking for what it can squeeze out of me before it throws me away.

"Something sweet," I replied. "What do you suggest?"

And that was another of the reasons I'd have preferred an AI. It wouldn't have cared about the fact that I didn't have a clue what went into most mixed drinks.

"How much kick you want?"

"Not too much." I gave him my best attempt at a knowing smile. "Want to keep my head clear for later."

"Oh, I think that's a really good idea, chickie." His smile was a leer. "But, in that case, I'd recommend the piña colada."

"Sounds good," I said, and he got busy with his bottles and mixers and things. It didn't take him long.

"That'll be a cred and a half," he told me, sliding it across the bar, and I bit my lip in dismay. That was a lot of money for a single not-that-big glass with some kind of paper or plastic umbrella sticking out of the top. It was for me, anyway.

"Sure," I said and swiped my uni-link over his terminal. I didn't tip him. I hoped that wouldn't piss him off, because I couldn't afford any trouble. But I couldn't afford the tip, either. Not yet. Maybe I could toss him a little something when I left, assuming I had anything to toss anyone.

To my surprise, he didn't even seem to notice, and I picked up the drink. I removed the stupid umbrella, took a sip, and got another surprise; it was actually good. Maybe a little *too* sweet, but it reminded me some of the coconut cake Dad used to bake. A mixed blessing. The memory might warm me, but I didn't need to be thinking about him or Mom or what they'd think about my plans. Not tonight.

I turned on the stool, sipping the drink—very small sips; I wasn't much of a drinker so I didn't know how much "kick" it really had and I needed it to last as long as I could manage before I had to cough up for another one—and surveyed the big, crowded room again. There were a lot of singles, men and women, and not a few of them were looking in my direction. The lighting might be bad, but there was enough of it to show off my long purple hair. Wasn't a dye job, that hair. Great-Grandmother—or maybe it was Great-Great-Grandmother—Faustine had been designed in a lab somewhere, and her genotype had kicked up hard in my case. The hair wasn't the only thing they'd modified when they built her, either.

It was the most visible, though, because it was long and sleek and the same deep, vibrant shade of purple as my eyes. It fell in a thick, silky cascade from the white ribbon I'd used to confine it, and I'd programmed my skimpy little dress to flow back and forth between pristine white and canary yellow by way of antique ivory to contrast with it. Nothing flashy; just enough to draw the eye.

The rest of me's not as striking as the hair and eyes, but it's good enough to get by with. If it hadn't been, I wouldn't have been here tonight.

"Hi there, honey," a man said, sliding onto the stool beside mine. "You look lonely."

He was probably at least twice my age—hard to tell with prolong, of course—and one of the people

I hadn't expected to see here tonight, judging by the cut of his expensive tunic and the elegance of his grooming. He dressed like a Legislaturalist, not a Dolist—not even a really well-heeled Dolist—although I couldn't imagine what Legislaturalists were doing at the Lisbon.

"Maybe that's because I *am* lonely," I replied, trying very hard to hide my nervousness and sound like I'd done this before.

"Well," he leaned towards me slightly, laying one hand on my thigh just below the dress's hemline, "maybe we could do a little something about that later tonight. Wouldn't do for a sweet thing like you to go home lonely, now would it?"

"No, I think that would be a terrible idea," I told him.

"I'm working right now," he said, and my heart sank a bit as he twitched his head in the direction of one of the tables.

It sat like an occupied island in a small sea of empty tables and the number "10" floated in the air above it. The dozen-plus people sitting around it were as expensively dressed as he was—maybe even more so; I wasn't all that good at estimating costs for the sorts of things the "better sort" enjoyed in Nouveau Paris—and most of them seemed intently focused on the activities on the stage. Two of them didn't, though. A pair of men with their heads close together, obviously deep in some sort of discussion.

"Friends of yours?" I asked lightly.

"I wish!" He shook his head. "No, employers. Gotta make sure nothing . . . unpleasant happens."

He twitched his tunic open for just an instant with the hand that wasn't busy sliding steadily higher as it stroked the inside of my thigh. Just open enough for me to see the butt of the pulser holstered under his left arm. I wondered if he'd done that to impress me with how important and dangerous he was or because he thought it might turn me on.

"Probably be another couple of hours," he said. "Then I'm off duty for the rest of the night." He smiled knowingly, and his fingers slipped still higher. "You wait and come home with me, and you won't be sorry."

"Really?" I tilted my head and I gave him my best sultry smile.

I'd practiced it in front of the mirror before I gave Cesar his meds—what there were of them—and tucked him into bed and slipped out of our miserable little closet of an "apartment." One whole room and an attached bathroom, and—as Manager Marteau had pointedly told me—lucky to have that after our BLS was garnished every month to pay off Mom and Dad's fines.

At the rate we were going, we'd be done by the time I was fifty.

"Really." He winked and leaned closer and I felt his lips on mine. At least he didn't have bad breath, although that was about the only good thing I could say about it. Then he drew back and gave my thigh another squeeze.

"Break's over. Gotta get back to work," he told me. "Call me Hercule. And don't you go away! I'll be back."

"And I'll be here," I promised him with another of those smiles.

He chuckled, then snapped his fingers arrogantly, and the barkeep looked up instantly.

"Anything else my friend here wants, put it on my tab," he said.

"Whatever you say," the barkeep promised, and my new "friend" climbed off the stool, gave me another of those kisses, and headed back across the floor. An equally well-dressed woman standing to one side of the door watched him come, then nodded brusquely to him as he took her place by the door and she headed for the arch that led to the lavatories.

Now that I'd followed "Call-Me-Hercule"'s progress across the room, I realized he and the woman weren't alone. There were at least three more people—obviously bodyguards—scattered strategically around the bar, and there were four more standing none too discreetly two or three meters back from table ten itself, surrounding it in a hollow square. Despite the fact that I'd just made my first commitment as a prostitute—or perhaps because I wanted to think about anything besides the fact that I had—I felt my eyebrows rise as the level of security sank in.

It wasn't a surprise that any Legislaturalist would have some security. Given how universally beloved the Legislaturalists in general were, bodyguards made an awful lot of sense. But nine of them was pushing the upper limits. Usually, you wouldn't see more than three or four, at most, outside the ranks of the senatorial families. And what in the world would someone like *that* be doing at the Lisbon?

I sipped my piña colada, grateful that at least I wouldn't have to pay for any more pricey drinks, and gazed at table ten, wondering if Call-Me-Hercule was one of the people my friendly waiter had tried to warn me about. With my luck he was. But maybe he wasn't.

The waiter hadn't sounded like he was talking about the hired help. And there was something about—

My nostrils flared as the two men who'd been leaning into their discussion straightened and I saw them in profile at last. Carmouche. That was *Senator Carmouche* on the right. He'd been all over the HD and public boards for the last couple of months, ever since he'd stepped down as Secretary of Security to become Secretary of War instead. What was *he*—?

"Child, what are you doing here?" a voice asked beside me, and I twitched in surprise, then looked at the speaker.

It was a woman with a very pale complexion. Her hair was almost as long as mine, but it was blacker than a near-raven's wing, and her eyes were dark in the lighting. There was a large mole on her right cheek, big enough I wondered why she'd never had it removed, but she had what was probably the most beautiful bone structure I'd ever seen. She was also petite, at least five or six centimeters shorter than me despite her high-heeled shoes, with the graceful, slender carriage to match that bone structure.

Just looking at her made me feel too tall, gawky, and plain.

Not to mention young, unsophisticated, and out of my depth.

"Excuse me?" I replied brilliantly to her question.

"I asked what you're doing here." She shook her head. "This isn't the sort of place you ought to be."

There was no condemnation in her tone, only compassion, but I felt a sudden surge of anger. Who was she to judge whether or not this was where I "ought" to be? And I didn't need her compassion. I didn't need *anybody's* compassion. I'd made it on my own for five miserable years in the teeth of everything the fucking system could throw at me, and if she didn't think I could go on doing that, then the hell with her!

"I'm working," I said shortly, taking in her black, elegantly cut, revealing gown. It was vented hip-high on either side, with a high, round neck but a plunging keyhole bodice that showed a lot of cleavage. Its fabric was programmed with a moving pinprick pattern that gleamed against its black background, flowing like a constellation of stars, and it must have cost at least a hundred times what my dress had.

"Like you," I added in a pointed tone.

"Oh, no," she said, shaking her head with an odd little smile. "You're not working at *all* like I am, child. And you shouldn't be 'working' here at all. It's not where someone like you should be."

"And how do you know what 'someone like me' should or shouldn't be doing?" I demanded.

"Sheath the claws," she told me, and I suppressed a sudden, totally inappropriate giggle at just how apropos that was. "I'm not criticizing. But you remind me of someone. Someone I lost a long time ago."

"And who might that be?"

"Just someone who was...important to me." The woman's expression changed, and for just an instant, the kind of sorrow that wrenches the heart right out of someone looked out of her eyes at me. Her hand rose to touch the only item of jewelry she wore—a silver unicorn on a beautiful chain around her neck—and she shook her head. "Just someone I cared about."

"I'm sorry," I said, and I meant it. That sudden

spike of anger had died under the weight of her unspoken grief.

"It happens." She shrugged. "It happens way too often, in fact. But that doesn't change the fact that you shouldn't be here. You've never done this before, have you?"

She ran the hand which had caressed the unicorn down the fabric of her gown as she spoke, and I knew exactly what she meant.

"Why do you say that?" I challenged.

"Oh, quite a few reasons." She smiled again, crookedly this time. "Like the fact that you didn't show the doorman your license, which means you're not legal. And you're young—God, what? You all the way up to twenty by now?" She shook her head. "And then there's you and Hercule. I'll admit he's probably the best of a bad lot, but that's not saying a lot in this case. You're likely to get hurt, going home with someone like him."

"He didn't seem too bad," I argued, wondering whether I was trying to convince her of that or myself. "A little...touchy-feely, but after all—"

I shrugged uncomfortably, and she nodded.

"You're in public right now," she pointed out, "and his boss is trying to keep a low profile. But, from what I've heard, his tastes are...esoteric, shall we say?" I realized she was watching me more closely than it seemed as she dropped "esoteric" on me, as if testing my own vocabulary. "And he likes his bedmates young and inexperienced. I think it's their 'innocence' that attracts him, and not in a good way, if you know what I mean."

"You seem to know an awful lot about him for

someone so much older than me," I said just a bit snippily.

"Oh, I do know quite a bit about him." There was very little amusement in her smile. "Goes with the job."

"I see." I cocked my head at her. "Why are you telling me all this?"

"I don't really know," she admitted. "Oh, you do remind me of someone. That would probably have been enough. But you're young, and you're in trouble." My eyes widened, and she snorted softly. "Child, you have no *idea* how many people I've seen in trouble! It's in the way you move. That's probably part of what attracted Hercule, too, now that I think about it." Her gaze went unfocused as she contemplated something only she could see, then she nodded. "Yes, he'd like that. Like stalking the wounded fawn. Like knowing you're only doing this because you're desperate. That'd give him even more control, wouldn't it?"

My blood turned to ice. If she really did know anything about Hercule, and if what she knew was as accurate as what she'd just effortlessly deduced about me, then . . .

That distant gaze refocused on me, and she gave herself a little shake.

"Let's just say I don't like seeing people in trouble, and that I like watching someone else take advantage of their trouble even less. So take my advice, child. Get off that stool and walk out of here." She reached into the stylish little purse hanging from her right wrist and extracted a small data chip. "Take this. It's the contact information for the CRP outreach office down on Seventy-Five. Whatever your trouble is, they can help."

I took the chip with fingers that trembled slightly.

The CRP—the Citizens' Rights Party—was tolerated (barely) by Internal Security and the rest of Nouveau Paris's police forces. Everyone knew it was really the political mouthpiece of the Citizens' Rights *Union*, and the CRU was the next best thing to a terrorist organization. In fact, if the People's Republic had been the sort of place which could possibly have produced terrorists, that's what it would have been called by the newsies. As it was, its members were merely "thugs" or "hooligans," which the Citizens' Rights *Party* dutifully denounced at regular intervals. Despite which, anyone associated with the CRP automatically went into InSec's files. As the daughter of a pair of known recidivists, they'd love to have *my* name on their list!

"I know what you're thinking," she said. "But InSec doesn't worry much about the CRP's outreach." She snorted again. "They'd have to put a quarter of the people in Morocco Tower on their lists if they did that! Your manager's worse than most, I'm afraid," she added, twitching her head unobtrusively in the direction of table ten.

I followed the gesture, and my jaw tightened as I realized the man Carmouche had been talking to was none other than Charles-Henri DeRosier, the Dolist manager responsible for Morocco. And she was right about him. He set the tone—and the example—for the scale of graft which wouldn't hand over the basic medical services my baby brother needed to stay alive without extra payment. They were there. They were available and they came free of charge . . . officially. Even the Legislaturalists insisted on that. But no one actually got them in Morocco Tower without paying off the right people. And they—and he—got away with it because he was one of the heavy hitters among the managers. Morocco wasn't the only tower whose votes he controlled. He'd never be a Legislaturalist, but in his own way, he had more power than anyone outside the very highest reaches of the Legislaturalist dynasties. Enough that it actually made sense for someone to find him allied with someone like Carmouche. God alone knew what the two of them might be cooking up over there.

Whatever it was, there'd be credits in it. *Lots* of credits.

The familiar rage burned inside me as I recognized him, but I choked it down. You learned early to live with your anger in Morocco Tower, assuming you wanted to live at all.

"Go," the woman said again, and this time there was an additional edge in her voice. An urgency that could almost have been anxiety... but wasn't quite. "Get out of here. Go home, climb out of that dress, and go talk to outreach. I know somebody who can put in a good word for you before you get there."

"But—" I began.

"No buts, girl! Just turn around and walk—"

She broke off suddenly, her lips tightening, and I looked a question at her.

"Too late," she said very softly, reaching into that purse again. She wasn't looking at me; she was looking at the electronic mirror behind the bar. The one that showed the enormously tall, broad-shouldered man who'd just walked through the corridor door. He was as well-dressed as she was but at least thirty centimeters taller than her, and he carried a fashionable shoulder bag.

"Get off the stool," the woman told me in that same soft voice, never looking at me, never looking away from the mirror. "Go into the lavatory. Close the door. Don't come back out."

"But—"

"Be as smart as you look, child! Now *go!*"

I looked at her for an instant longer, then slid off the stool, turned, and walked away as nonchalantly as someone whose nerves had just been turned into tuning forks could manage. Unfortunately, she'd waited a moment too long to give me my marching orders.

I'd almost reached the arch between the bar and the lavatories when it happened.

The doorman said something to the big guy. I couldn't hear what it was, but it was obviously the wrong thing, because an enormous left hand reached out, twisted itself into the front of his tunic, and hauled him up onto his tiptoes.

"What the hell did you just say to me?" the big man demanded, and *everyone* heard him. The doorman started to say something, and got shaken like a toy before he could.

"Of course I'm sure it's the right place, idiot!" the big man snarled. "What? You want to see my invitation?"

His right hand delved into his shoulder bag while he continued to shake the hapless doorman with his left, and I realized I'd stopped moving. The confrontation had drawn my attention, and I paused, staring at it like every other set of eyes in the place.

And because we were all staring at *him*, no one noticed *her* when she toed off those high-heeled shoes, slid from her stool, and started casually towards table ten.

"All right, *here's* my invitation!" the big man announced, and his right hand came out of the bag.

With a pulser.

A very *big* pulser, with a long barrel. Much too long—and probably too powerful—to carry concealed like Call-Me-Hercule's.

I froze. I admit it. I flat out *froze*, staring at him in disbelief. If every eye had been attracted to him before, they were *riveted* to him now, and I saw Call-Me-Hercule twisting around towards him, his hand darting into his tunic.

It was an unfortunate decision on his part.

The pulser seemed like part of the big man's hand. He didn't even look at Hercule, not really. He only swung the weapon to the side, pointing it as naturally as he might have pointed his finger. And then it whined shrilly and the back of Hercule's head exploded in a gory fountain of red, gray, and white bone splinters.

The screams began then. You could tell which patrons' brains were faster than others. The really quick ones had started out of their chairs when the killer first raised his voice. Now they dived for the floor, and the next quickest launched themselves to join the early starters. The rest of the patrons simply stood or sat, as frozen as me, while the other bodyguards scattered around the room went for their weapons.

Pulsers shrilled, and the doorman's scream died in a cloud of aspirated blood as at least a half-dozen darts sliced into and then out of him. Blood and bits of tissue sprayed across the big guy, and the solid darts were hitting him, too. But unlike the unfortunate doorman, they seemed to have no effect on *him*. He went to one knee, his face and the entire front of his head disappearing behind some sort of opaque-looking shield, and laid his pulser across his forearm like someone on a pistol range. It snarled, and I realized he was firing single shots, not the full automatic spray coming back at him.

And as I realized that, I also finally realized the woman from the bar was moving. In fact, she was racing towards table ten on her bare feet.

The bodyguards around the table had whirled to face the threat out of pure spinal reflex. The closer of the two came together, planting themselves between the big man and their charges as they brought their own pulsers into play. One of the men they were protecting saw her coming, though, and pointed at her with a shout of alarm.

"Get *down*, you idiots!" she shouted back at the people seated around the table. "*Get down!*"

The man who'd seen her stiffened, then started out of his chair in obedience to the authority in her shout as she came within two or three meters.

And that was when they discovered what she had in her left hand.

I'd seen vibro blades before. The floor police don't much like them, but they tend to wink at them, even in Morocco Tower. Not because they approve of armed Dolists, but because self-defense is a practical necessity, especially on the rougher floors, and they'd rather see us armed with weapons with a maximum range of thirty centimeters, the legal limit on any civilian vibro blade, rather than with pulsers like the one in the big man's hands.

But this vibro blade was different. The woman

was still a good two meters from the table, passing between the two nearer bodyguards, when the first security man's head suddenly flew from his shoulders in a spray of blood.

The man who'd seen her coming stepped back in shocked disbelief as her hand came slashing around and the second bodyguard went down as instantaneously as the first, and then *she* was flying through the air. She landed in the center of the table, barefooted and incredibly graceful in her high-vented gown, and another severed head bounced across the tabletop and onto the floor.

She twirled like a dancer as Senator Carmouche exploded from his chair. He started to leap away from her, but he'd made the mistake of coming to his feet rather than simply dropping to the floor. That brought him into reach of that impossibly long, illegally silent vibro blade, and he went down without even a scream as the blade sliced diagonally downward, completely through his skull and out the other side.

The Lisbon was a madhouse. Screams and shouts were everywhere. The gun battle at the door continued, although the big man had already dropped three more of the dispersed bodyguards. He ignored the last one for a moment, and picked off one of the two remaining close-in bodyguards, the ones on the far side of table ten, with a perfectly placed headshot from at least twenty meters. The last bodyguard, unfortunately for her, was still distracted by the gunfight. Her attention was obviously split between that and the carnage closer at hand, and she hesitated—ever so briefly—trying to decide which threat was greater.

The woman from the bar settled the question for

her. She continued across the table, almost as if it were a trampoline, and landed in a crouch—right leg bent sharply under her, left leg fully extended—and spun. The vibro blade hit the bodyguard at knee level, and she shrieked as her legs were sliced out from under her. She went down screaming, twisting in pain and trying vainly to reach the damage, and the woman finished her with a single, economical thrust, then bounced back to her feet and towards the table.

DeRosier had gotten his chair shoved back from the table, but he was tangled up with it. Or maybe it was just panic that made him so clumsy. Whatever his problem might be, though, it was like watching a *guépard* take down an Old Earth sheep. She moved with deadly, flowing grace, and he bleated in terror, just like a sheep.

Until the vibro blade slashed across his torso at an upward angle and spilled his vital organs across the floor.

He went down, and she continued her trajectory back across the table. Another of the men flew backward. His head was still attached, but only by the spine, and blood spurted everywhere as his heart continued to pump frantically.

She spun, cutting down a fourth man, then a fifth.

I couldn't believe it. I literally *could not* believe my eyes. She and the big man by the door had taken out all nine of the bodyguards, and as I watched, she killed a sixth man from the crowd around the table.

But it wasn't random, a corner of my brain realized. She passed up easy kills, bypassed the people between her victims. She wasn't a homicidal maniac out to kill everyone in sight to make a statement. She was taking *targeted* kills, exactly the ones—and *only* the ones—she wanted.

And then I saw something else. Something she didn't see.

The plainclothes floor cop came out of his chair to one side of the lavatory arch and his pulser was in his hand. I saw it rising, lining up on the woman in the black dress, and I knew it was none of my business. I knew exactly what I needed to do, and that was what she'd *told* me to do: head for the lavatory, lock the door, and not open it for anyone until the uniformed cops got there.

I *knew* that . . . and I didn't do it.

I didn't recognize the sound I made. It was deep, guttural, primal. It came from the pit of my belly, from a heart filled with hatred for the system that had taken my parents, was killing my brother by centimeters. It came from deep down in the soul of me, and the *other* modification I'd inherited from my great-great-grandmother popped out of the tips of my fingers.

I hit his back, keening like a fifty-five-kilo banshee, and my hands reached around his neck. But I didn't grab it. No, the curved two-centimeter claws sank into the front of his throat, pulled in opposite directions with a horrible soft, *dragging* feel, and something hot and slick—and far thicker than I'd ever thought blood was—exploded across my hands.

The floor cop went down with a gurgling scream, and I found myself kneeling on his spine, looking up through a tangle of purple hair, as the woman from the bar spun towards us. Her eyes narrowed, but then she shook herself, scooped up the cop's fallen pulser, and turned back to the bloodsoaked survivors cowering around the table.

"On the floor, all of you," she said in a cold, flat voice, beckoning with the barrel of the pulser, and they fell over themselves obeying her, going to their knees and—without instructions—clasping their hands behind their heads.

"This is your lucky day," she told them then in that same icy voice. "None of you have made it onto the list...yet. I'd recommend trying really hard to keep it that way. If you see me again, 'lucky' is the one thing you *won't* be."

She held them for two or three heartbeats, more paralyzed by her merciless eyes than by the pulser's muzzle. Then she took two steps back and looked at me, still crouched on the body of the man I'd killed, trying to comprehend what had just happened.

"We're going now, girl," she said. "I think you'd better come with us."

I stared at her, my brain mostly blank. But it worked well enough to tell me the one thing I *couldn't* do was stay here. I scrambled to my feet, trying not to think about the stickiness dripping from my hands, of the blood spreading across the floor, and stumbled towards her.

"Good girl!" she said encouragingly, tossing the pulser away and tucking one amazingly strong arm around me. "This way!"

I don't really remember crossing the room. I do remember that she had the presence of mind to scoop up her discarded shoes. And I remember she paused in the vestibule long enough to grab a fashionable evening cloak from its hanger, and I remember the big man reaching into his bag again, pressing a small device of some kind against the outside of the power door between the vestibule and the club itself.

"Got it," he grunted, and punched a button.

"Security systems?" She'd already slipped back into her shoes. Now she swept the cloak around her, concealing the blood which had splashed across her gown, and another small unit came out of her evening bag. She tapped a control, and I gaped as a cloud of dust seemed to envelop her ever so briefly. It cleared, drifting away like smoke, and the black hair was platinum, the complexion darker even than mine in spectacular contrast, and the eyes . . . the eyes were the most brilliant topaz I'd ever seen.

"Don't gawk," she told me with a chuckle, and I noted that the mole had disappeared, as well. "Nanotech. And getting rid of it takes the bloodstains with it."

She looked back at the tall man, whose handsome and regular features had vanished. Now he looked like someone had used his face for a punching bag—more than once. But it was a very, very tough-looking, competent face, and he was even bigger than I'd thought he was.

"Security systems, Kev?" she repeated, a bit louder.

"Down and done," he reassured her. "The worm took out everything they've recorded for the last three days. Don't know what they might've downloaded to InSec or the floor cops before Carmouche got there, but they haven't got crap from the moment you walked in the door. Locked down their net connection, too. They are *off* the web and out of coms until we say different or they get a really good cyber tech in there."

"Good. Door?"

"Not opening it without cutting gear for at least a couple of hours. And"—he tapped the unobtrusive earbud in his right ear—"the other teams locked down the other doors. We've got at least half an hour before anybody in there figures out how to get the word out."

He'd been stripping off his expensive—and blood-soaked, courtesy of the unlucky Paschal—tunic as he spoke. Now he reversed it, pressed something, and it reconfigured into a totally different cut and color. He unfastened something from around his neck and dropped it into his shoulder bag, then grimaced as he touched his side gingerly.

"Remind me to tell them they need better kinetic damping," he said. "Wouldn't be surprised if I've got a couple of busted ribs."

"That's what quick-heal's for," she told him. "And it seems to've kept the darts out of your hide just fine."

"Only because they aren't allowed to load explosive darts inside the tower."

"Bitch, bitch, bitch." She shook her head. "I swear, Kev, you'd complain if they hanged you with a golden rope!"

"Nah. Gold's about right for me . . . assuming they couldn't get platinum. Maybe a few diamonds set here and there." He frowned thoughtfully. "Rubies, you think?"

"Oh, shut up!" She chuckled and shook her head again.

"Gotta say, this pop-up face shield's really neat," he continued, patting the shoulder bag. "Wish we could get our hands on more of 'em."

"Be grateful for what we've got. I don't know who our 'mysterious benefactor' is, but he's got a Beowulf accent. There's a limit to how openly Beowulf can risk antagonizing the People's Republic."

He nodded. Then both of them turned to me, and

I realized they'd been chattering with each other at least in part to give me time to stop hyperventilating.

"Hold out your hands," the man said. I extended them shrinkingly, and he sprayed them with an aerosol from his bag. It felt cold, like an alcohol spray, and then it tingled. When I looked down again, the sticky, drying blood had disappeared.

"Useful little solvent," he said, putting the aerosol away again. "Won't fool a good forensic sniffer—too many traces left—but the trick is to look so innocent nobody runs a sniffer over you." He cocked his head, examining me critically. "Can you program that dress to a darker color?"

"S-sure," I said.

"Then do it. The darker the better."

I keyed up the app on my uni-link and tapped icons. The dress turned a darker purple even than my hair, and I looked back up at him.

"Good!" He nodded approval. "Solvent's good for getting blood off skin, and you managed to keep most of it off your dress. But not all of it. That's dark enough nobody's likely to notice before we get you off-corridor again."

"Off—off-corridor?" I repeated. "Where?"

"Well, I guess that sort of depends on you," the woman said. "Kev says the worm killed the security systems, and I'm sure he's right about that. But it can't do anything about human memories, and a lot of people saw you in there, honey. And, pardon me for saying so, but your coloring's even more . . . memorable than mine. Odds are InSec can get a pretty decent working description of you, and I'll bet you're from right around here, aren't you?"

I nodded numbly as I realized how right she was about how easy I'd be to find. God. What was going to happen to me and Cesar *now*?

"So, you've got to disappear. Drop completely off the grid." My eyes widened, and she shook her head quickly. "Don't worry. We can do that. Have to move you to another tower, but we can do that, too."

"And my brother?" I heard the anxiety in my own voice. "My brother—Cesar—he's sick. Real sick. And the floor doc wants extra cash to move him up the queue. I don't think he's going to make it if I can't get it, and that's why—"

I broke off, realizing I'd been babbling, and she glanced up at her companion. He looked back down with a shrug, clearly making it her decision, and she turned back to me.

"Any other family?"

"No." I shook my head. "We're all that's left since they took Mom and Dad."

Her mouth tightened, and those magnificent topaz eyes turned bleak and hard.

"Then of course we'll get Cesar out, too. And I'm pretty sure we can get him the medical help he needs. But where and how we do that's going to depend on you."

"What do you mean?"

"I mean you've got potential, child. You . . ." She paused and shook her head. "I can't just go on calling you 'child' or 'girl.' What's your name?"

"Ninon," I said. "My name's Ninon."

"Ninon, then. You're quick, you don't freeze, and from the sound of things, you don't have any reason to love Legislaturalists."

She watched my expression, then snorted.

"No, you don't. Well, neither do I. Or Kev here. Or our friends. So, we can just hide you away somewhere, or we can recruit you instead."

"*Recruit* me?" I stared at her in disbelief.

"You've got the talent." She shrugged. "The only real question is whether or not you've got the motivation. This was a little more . . . spectacular and hands-on than usual, but this is what we *do*, Ninon."

"I still think you should've let me just use a bomb," Kev grumbled. "Been a lot quicker and simpler, and we can't afford to lose you doing shit like this, Ellie."

"Bombs aren't very precise weapons," she pointed out. "And I might add that if I'd let you play with your toys this time, our friend Ninon would probably be among the statistics about now."

"Point," he conceded.

"You're CRU?" I asked, looking back and forth between them. If even a quarter—hell, a *tenth*—of the news reports about it were accurate, the Citizens' Rights Union was about as bloody as "thugs" and "hooligans" came. Like Kev's bomb, the CRU wasn't a precision weapon.

"Kinda, sorta, in a way," Kev replied. "Me, I was part of the CRU from the beginning. Hardcore, too. But my friend here, she's more idealistic than me. And I'll be damned if she didn't convince me to see it her way. Who would've thought it?" He shrugged. "Anyway, we're *technically* CRU. But what we really are? We're Aprilists."

I inhaled sharply. Aprilists? They were *Aprilists*?

"'S right," he said with a lopsided grin. "Reason she wouldn't let me use a bomb. I tend to revert to CRU default settings sometimes."

I nodded slowly, almost mechanically. From everything I'd ever heard, the Aprilists scared the Legislaturalists worse than the CRU ever had. Everyone knew there weren't many of them, compared to the CRU, but they were smart, their operations were carried out with meticulous precision, and in their own way, they were even more merciless than the CRU. But their target selection was very different. Even PubIn, which wasn't about to give any batch of "thugs and hooligans" good coverage, had to admit the Aprilists took out only those they held directly responsible for the regime's actions, and they were scrupulous about avoiding collateral damage . . . like dead schoolkids in their parents' air car.

"The decision's yours," the woman said. "Don't hurry to make it, though. We've got to get moving anyway. So think about it on the way to the safe house."

"Think about it?" I threw back my head and laughed. There was a little hysteria in the sound, but no hesitation. "What's to *think* about? These bastards took my parents and they're killing my baby brother centimeter by centimeter. Of *course* I want in!"

"Crap!" Kev said with a deeper, rolling laugh of his own. "Little girl reminds me of someone else!"

He looked down at the woman, and she shrugged.

"The bastards are still our best recruiters, damn them," she said. Then she looked back at me. "All right. You want in, you're in."

"Just like that? You get to make the decision for everybody else?"

"Hell, yes, she does!" Kev snorted. "This here's Brigade Commander Delta, honey."

I gasped. The gray net knew that name, that title, but no one knew a thing beyond that. No one knew whether "Brigade Commander Delta" was old or young, male or female. But at last I had a face to put with it, and it was nothing like the towering giant I'd always imagined. I'd expected someone more like Kev, I supposed, but he was clearly following *her* lead.

"It's just a title," she said, shaking her head. "And I started from pretty much where you are right this minute." She touched the silver unicorn, still visible at the neck of her gown. "We all start from pretty much where you are right this minute. And I can't promise you we're going to win in the end, or even survive. But I can promise you that if we don't, it'll be because we died trying. That good enough for you, Ninon?"

"That's *more* than good enough for me," I replied, holding out my hand. She looked at it for a moment, then gripped it firmly.

"Then welcome to the Revolution, Ninon," she said. "Buckle up tight."

"Why do I think Admiral Harrington and President Pritchart are well suited to negotiating an actual peace agreement between us and the Star Empire? I'll tell you why. It's because for all the differences between them, I cannot *imagine* two women who are more alike under the skin!"

> —Senator Ninon Bourchier,
> Senate Foreign Affairs Committee,
> Republic of Haven,
> Speaking to reporters,
> 01/05/1922 PD

Spoils of War

Kacey Ezell

On a muggy afternoon in August, steam rose from the broken asphalt arteries of the nation's capital city. My heels tapped wetly on the pavement as I walked. Breathing felt like trying to suck air through a wet sponge, but I moved at a brisk pace. What remained of Washington DC was a cesspool of a town, but at least in this part, moving with a purpose meant I was less likely to be disturbed.

The lettering on the door said "Ra"..."tel." The faded, peeling letters looked as if they'd been painted on, rather than programmed into the glass of the door like a modern sign. The center part of the name had been completely obliterated. I pushed the door open, expecting to hear an automated assistant. Instead, I walked in out of the muggy air to the sound of tinkling bells.

The office inside was small, square, and dingy. I blinked in the sudden dimness. A window hung with crooked, ancient-looking blinds threw bars of shadow over the floor, the single, sagging chair, and a rickety end table.

"Can I help you?"

He was tall, with a chiseled jaw just imperfect enough to be natural and dark hair that fell forward into his eyes. He wore his shirt open at the neck, with no tie, and his cuffed trousers looked well made, if creased from sitting.

I conjured up a tired smile.

"Well," I said, "you obviously didn't let peacetime turn you soft."

"Never saw the sense in it," he answered. His voice was dark and handsome as he was. He'd stood up when I entered the office. Now he stepped around the antique metal desk and held out a hand as big as my face. "Ray Martel. And you are?"

"Dying for a drink," I said, tilting my head to the side. I watched his eyes search my face. I could almost hear his thoughts assessing me, wondering about me. Who was I? Why was I here? What kind of trouble was I in, and would I bring it to his door?

"Have a seat," he said, instead of any of those questions, and gestured to the chair by the window. I gave him another version of my tired smile and put just a hint of sway in my walk as I moved to take the seat. Ray Martel watched me for a second longer than necessary, then turned to the cabinet behind his desk. He pulled out a bottle and two highball glasses.

"Interesting aesthetic you have going on," I said as he poured me a drink, then one for himself. "Very mid-twentieth century."

"Developer before the war was doing a whole noir gentrification thing," he said as he carried two glasses over and handed me one. "Liked the idea of having a PI who fit the décor. When I came back, all I had was my license, the lease on this place, and the clothes in the closet. Don't know what happened to the developer, but I'm still here. People do like their nostalgia."

"Poetic," I said, "considering that film noir was largely a response to the world wars of the early 1900s."

"If you say so," he said, lifting his glass to his lips. "It pays the bills."

"Mmmhmm," I replied, taking a drink of my own. I savored the whiskey burn before meeting his waiting eyes.

"Mr. Martel," I said, the whiskey giving my voice a bit of a rasp, "My name is Nina LaFleur. I believe you knew my brother, Edward, during the war."

Some of the suspicion cleared from Martel's eyes, and he walked back to sit in the creaking swivel chair behind his desk.

"Eddie. Sure, I knew him. Good kid. Talked about a sister some. That you?"

"Yes."

Martel's face creased with the ghost of a grin.

"Eddie LaFleur. Haven't thought about him in forever. Best shot I ever saw with a laser rifle. Not a bad hacker, either. How's he doing? I haven't seen him since I took an IED blast and got sent home."

I rolled the glass between my hands, then set it down on the end table. I reached into my purse for my vape case and snapped it open. My fingers trembled just a bit as I pulled out the thin cylinder and put it to my lips, my eyes flicking up to Martel's for permission. He nodded, and I inhaled, focusing on the brief jolt of nicotine into my system. The sweet taste of caramel mingled with the whiskey remaining on my tongue.

"My brother said that you were one of the best men he'd ever known," I said softly, watching him through the milky tendrils of my exhale as it drifted upward in the still, stale office air. "He said that if I were ever in trouble, I should find you."

I took another hit, delaying the inevitable, as if not saying the words robbed them of some truth.

"My brother is dead, Mr. Martel."

Martel closed his eyes briefly. I'd seen them do that before, the ones who came home from the war. They wouldn't show any other sign of grief. Eddie once told me that with all he hated about the war, he came to love the men he fought beside. I didn't speak. I'd had my time to mourn Eddie. Let this stranger have his.

He opened his eyes, and the suspicion was back.

"I'm sorry for your loss, Ms. LaFleur, but why come to me? If Eddie was murdered, the police will find his killer."

I just looked at him.

He shifted slightly in his chair, making it creak again. But he didn't speak. Stubborn, like Eddie said.

I took another hit and exhaled, letting the cloud screen my face.

"Mr. Martel," I said softly, "neither of us is a child. The police have ruled Eddie's death a suicide."

"And you think it wasn't?"

"I know it wasn't. You said it yourself. Eddie was

a crack shot with a laser rifle. If he was going to kill himself, that's how he would have done it. He wouldn't have jumped from the Key Bridge with a weight tied to his ankles."

Martel blinked.

"Eddie hated heights." His voice was low and thoughtful.

I took another drink. Outside, a delivery drone rumbled by. The floor vibrated under my shoe.

"All right. Who would have wanted to kill your brother, Ms. LaFleur? Eddie wasn't the type to make enemies, from what I could tell. He was always making everyone laugh."

Sadness curved my lips in a smile that I knew looked like Eddie's had done, once.

"He was still like that after the war. Some men came home without their laughter. Not Eddie. If anything, he laughed more, lived more. Everything was going so well for him. He had a great job working for Kolorotech. Do you know them, Mr. Martel?"

"Kolorotech? Sure. Cybernetic enhancements, right? Medical tech company, made their name doing upgrades on wounded soldiers back from the war. Eddie was working for them? I remember him as more of an artistic type. One of the only times I ever saw him really angry was when that story came out about how the enemy had looted the Louvre and destroyed some of the ancient European works of art."

"Eddie worked in Kolorotech R&D to help develop their cybernetic eye suite," I said, allowing my smile to deepen as grief threatened to choke me. "Specifically, he was working on the ability to allow human beings to see in spectra other than just visible light."

"You mean like near-IR? We already do that."

"Yes, but it takes additional machinery, which is still crude, even a century after its invention. Imagine if you could simply blink twice, Mr. Martel, and suddenly you had perfect color night vision. Or if you could watch a sunset in the UV spectrum. Imagine the art you could create then. Eddie certainly did."

"So why kill him? Seems innocuous enough."

I took another calming drag before speaking again.

"When were you injured, Mr. Martel?"

"April of '75," he said. "During the last attack on the enemy stronghold."

I nodded. Eddie had told me this story many times.

"During that offensive, in the Alps, right? You were a squad leader, were you not?"

"Seems you know I was," he leaned forward, his eyes sharper than they had been. "Eddie's squad."

"My brother spoke highly of your leadership," I said, before taking another pull from the vape and inclining my head through the smoke. "He said you saved his life more than once."

"Well, he saved mine, so we're even." Martel's voice was tight as we got closer to the subject of his wounding.

"Yes," I said softly, letting the word out on a curl of vapor. "When you were hit. Your squad surprised a platoon of enemies who weren't where they should have been. The blast knocked you off your feet, embedded shrapnel in your shoulder. But you were also shot. You took rounds in the neck and upper thigh. Actual bullets, the ancient kind. The rest of your squad was killed. Eddie dragged you out and got you to the medic."

"Look, lady," Martel said, looking at me with hot, unfriendly eyes. "Your brother was a damn good man, and I'm sorry he's dead. And if you want to hire me, I'll do my damnedest to help you find who did it. But I don't need to hear a play-by-play of the end of the war. Not from you. Not from anyone."

I took another drag and exhaled, letting the cloud hang in the air.

The rest of our conversation went about like you'd expect.

I suspected that Martel couldn't decide if he loathed me or wanted me, but it didn't much matter. At the end of the day, I had the credits and a case and he was, after all, a businessman.

I left the office just as the setting sun sent its light slanting through the sagging steel skeletons of ruined buildings lining G Street as they ran toward Garfield Park. Occasionally, through the noise of airborne and ground traffic, a few notes of the "Star Spangled Banner" came drifting up from the old Marine Barracks at 8th and I, a block or so to the south. United States Marines hadn't been stationed there since DC's first orbital bombardment during the war, but they still had the bugle calls and such on an automated timer. Some people thought things like that still mattered, I guess.

I turned my face to the setting sun and started to walk west down the steaming sidewalk, through the flat, greasy smell of garbage permeating the air. Just a few blocks toward the ruins of the old Capitol, and the mag rail that would take me back to Alexandria.

❖ ❖ ❖

Some seem to think there's a romance to living in a building that's four hundred years old. If by romance you meant sagging stairs, uneven floors, and drafty windows, you'd have it nailed. The house had once been owned by some business partner of George Washington's or something. Legend had it that revolutionaries had met here for tea before heading off to Gadsby's Tavern down the street. Personally, I thought the legend was a load of bunk. Who drinks tea before heading out for ale and treason?

The current owner was a hard-eyed, fleshy matron in her fifties named Belinda Ellis. Mrs. Ellis claimed to have lost her husband in the war. She had a bad dye job and talked too much, but she minded her business and let me mind mine. We got on swimmingly.

I waved tiredly as I passed her sitting outside with a glass of wine, watching the cleaning bot sweep the front steps of her historic landmark. My feet ached in my pumps as I walked around to the back entrance that led to my rented lower floor. I needed a drink and a hot shower, not necessarily in that order.

Thirty minutes later, with my second drink in hand, I spoke a quick command and eased down into my sofa as the mournful notes of old jazz spilled into the air. I leaned my head back and let my wet hair spread out on the cushion behind me as I drew in a deep breath and refused to think about anything. Anything at all.

The edges of my mind had just started to soften when there was a pounding on my door. I startled up, nearly spilling my drink that I set hastily on the nearby end table. The streetlights switched on and cast sudden, sharp shadows through my windows as

I yanked open the end table drawer to reveal the charged snub-nosed energy pistol I kept there.

"I'm coming," I called out as I slipped the piece into the pocket of my satin bathrobe and fluffed my drying hair. One last tug to ensure that I was at least nominally decent, and I opened the door.

Martel stared at me with a face like a hanging judge's.

"You wanna tell me why you've got two thugs tailing you home?"

"You wanna come in?" I asked, letting out a sigh as I pushed the door wider.

He stared at me long enough without saying anything that I shrugged one shoulder and stepped back. Either he'd follow me in or the door would close. He followed me in.

"Drink?" I asked, walking to the small bar I kept against the wall.

"Bourbon," he replied, his voice clipped.

I poured the drink and turned to hand it to him. His eyes flicked down to the V at the front of my robe, and then back up to my eyes as he took the drink.

"Mr. Martel," I said as he sipped, "I'm an accountant. My primary employer is a company known as McHenry-Key Industries. Do you know them?"

Martel shook his head in the negative.

I smiled a small smile. "I'm not surprised. On the surface, they're an import/export business. Some planetary, but mostly spacegoing commerce with the orbital, Mars, and lunar colonies. In reality, they're a business front for the profiteering operations of a man named Maxwell Rothesky II." I watched his face as I said it. Sure enough, his eyes widened and the glass came down from his lips. Outside, the mag rail whistled as it sped by on its track.

"You work for Junior Rothesky? The Boss of Baltimore?"

"Not officially," I said, "but yes. I started right out of college. I came to Mr. Rothesky's attention when I identified an irregularity in the books that led to proof of a subordinate's embezzling. Mr. Rothesky dislikes disloyalty in his employees." As I spoke, I refreshed my own drink, then walked back to sit on the sofa. I leaned back against the armrest, enjoying the slide of satin on my skin.

"So why is he having his thugs follow you?" Martel asked, moving to sit on the opposite end of the sofa. "Were you disloyal?"

"No," I said softly. "But I think Eddie might have been."

"What did Rothesky have on your brother?"

I pressed my lips together. "Tech," I said lowly after a few minutes.

Martel's eyebrows went up. "Tech?" he asked.

I took a drink and nodded. "How much do you remember about the night you were shot in Bavaria?"

Martel's expression slammed shut like an airlock door. "What?"

I held up a hand. "Please," I said softly. "I'm not trying to hurt you. I just . . . What do you remember?"

"Nothing," he said, forcing the word through gritted teeth. "My entire squad dead but Eddie and me, and I don't remember a goddamn thing."

I reached out my free hand to touch his arm where it lay on the back of my couch. He jerked away, but his eyes thawed just a bit.

"Mr. Martel, that night your squad surprised a detail of enemy soldiers in the middle of the forest. Did you never wonder what they were doing there?"

He just stared at me. It didn't last long. I couldn't draw it out.

"Eddie told me," I said, my voice going quiet, as Eddie's had always done. "He told me about the surprise, how your forward men died in the initial blast. How you were hit, but ordered the squad to return fire. How when it was over, there were only the two of you left. You passed out. He dragged you into a nearby cave, just in case anyone else should happen by... only it wasn't a cave. It was the entrance to an abandoned twentieth-century salt mine. And the enemy had been using it to store stolen tech they'd looted from the industrial centers of Europe."

I took a drink and a moment to beg Eddie's forgiveness for the story I was about to tell, for I'd once sworn on my very soul that I'd keep this secret forever.

"Mr. Martel, you weren't the only thing rescued that night. Eddie brought some of the tech back."

"Some of the tech? What does that mean? What tech?"

"I don't know," I said, shaking my head sadly as the lights from a passing autoflyer slanted through the blinds and flashed across my face. "I don't know what, exactly, he got out. He never told me specifics. But he did tell me it was priceless. Notes, maybe? Diagrams, blueprints? Your guess is as good as mine. It couldn't have been large, given the circumstances."

Martel snorted softly. His mouth twisted upward at one corner.

I let my own smile deepen in acknowledgement of his understanding. "In any case, very near the end of the war, I got a letter from Eddie. It was vague, but I understood it. He was asking me to put him in touch with my boss—with Mr. Rothesky. He had something that he needed to get into the country without a lot of questions. When he came home, he told me the full story . . . or as much of a full story as he would say."

"So Eddie finds this stolen tech, steals some of it, and Junior helps him fence it?" Martel asked, sipping at his drink.

I shook my head. "Not fence. Import. Smuggle, I guess. I don't think Eddie told Mr. Rothesky's people what he was bringing in through the orbital colonies, he just paid the asking price."

"Where'd he get the money for that?"

I gave him a level look.

"Ah," he said, raising his glass to me. "Little sister to the rescue. Junior pays his employees well, does he? The loyal ones, anyway."

"Well enough," I said, in my best "not your business" tone.

He let out a short bark of laughter and took a drink. Irritation flashed through me, then faded, leaving the familiar exhaustion and grief that blanketed everything these days. I closed my eyes and leaned my head back again.

"I don't know how, but Rothesky must have found out what Eddie had. Or he found out *something* anyway. Eddie sent me a message. He said he didn't want to come to me because he didn't want to turn Junior's suspicions my way. Mr. Rothesky has trusted me for a very long time. If he thought I was being disloyal now . . ."

I stopped, opened my eyes and rolled my head to the side so that I could meet Martel's gaze. He looked as raw as I felt. I quit fighting and let my grief, exhaustion, and loneliness tangle up inside me until I felt I could barely breathe.

"I'm so tired," I whispered, apropos of nothing. Another drone drove by. Headlights swept across the line of my body. I watched him watch. His wounded desire pulled at my own. The false promise of comfort hung in the air.

I lifted a hand to the sash of my bathrobe and tugged. The silk slithered open, leaving my skin pale in the dimness. Martel took another drink before putting it down and moving toward me.

His lips tasted like bourbon.

"What did Eddie's message say?"

Martel's voice was partially muffled from passing through the bathroom door. I knotted my bathrobe sash once more before waving a hand over the bio-metric lock and walking back out into my bedroom.

He lay in my bed, his chest bare, the bedsheet bunched around his waist. One muscled arm curled up behind his head, while he smoked an honest-to-goodness cigarette with the other one. I gave him a lazy smile and crawled up onto the foot of the bed. I held out a hand and he handed me the cig. It wasn't as harsh as I thought it would be. The smoke filled my mouth and warmed down into my lungs. I felt light and loose, better than I had in weeks.

"Where did you find these?" I asked, coughing just a little. "They're illegal to sell."

"I roll my own," Martel said. "You can still buy

pipe tobacco and rolling papers from religious specialty shops."

"Aren't you afraid they'll give you cancer?"

"We all gotta die sometime. You said Eddie sent you a message." He reached out and took the cig back as he changed the subject, then leaned forward to catch a strand of my ultrasonically cleaned hair with the fingers of his free hand. "What did it say?"

"He said he was in trouble," I said, exhaling and letting the smoke twist upward between us. "And he was sorry he'd made trouble for me, too. He told me to find you. Said you'd help me."

"Help you do what?"

"Something about seeing the beauty in the world," I shrugged. "Typical Eddie. Part of me thinks he knew, even then, that Mr. Rothesky wasn't going to let him go. If Mr. Rothesky knew about the tech, he'd likely have taken it in exchange for Eddie's life...but you know how Eddie was."

"Wouldn't be bullied," Martel said, snorting softly. "He'd have died first. So what, he stashes it?"

"That's what I'm thinking. He said you'd help me. I think...I think he meant for us to find the tech after he was gone. After it was safe."

"It's never gonna be safe," Martel pointed out. "Not if Junior Rothesky's after you for it."

"Mr. Martel—"

"Really? 'Mr. Martel'?" Amusement threaded through his voice as he dragged on the cigarette once more and handed it to me. "Call me Ray, sweetheart."

"Ray," I said, smiling and accepting the cig. "I can take Rothesky down anytime I want to. I have his books. His real ones."

Martel's eyes widened, and he nearly choked on his smoke.

"You mean—"

"I mean that I can take my books and waltz right in to the FBI's organized crimes division and hand them enough evidence to ensure a power vacuum in the Baltimore criminal underworld for the next decade. Not to mention all of the orbital and colonial shares they'd be able to seize by forfeit. The U.S. Government's been looking for a way to put the space corporations like McHenry-Key in their place ever since the war. They just haven't had the excuse they needed. I can give them that excuse. I haven't done so before now because...what's in it for me? Rothesky pays well, as you've pointed out, and I'm a loyal employee. But loyalty goes both ways. Rothesky killed my only brother." And I could have saved him, if only I'd known in time. I took another drag and tried not to drown in my own bitterness.

Martel leaned back against the headboard again, and sat rubbing his fingertips together as he mulled this over.

"So you want to go, find this tech, then do your dance for the FBI? Then what? You're crazy if you think Rothesky can't reach out and touch you, even if he's in custody."

I smiled again, and this time it was sad.

"I think that's why Eddie sent me to you. You can help me disappear. I've got plenty of money. Hell, we can disappear together." My smile grew and I put the cig between my lips and crawled over the bed toward him.

"Think of it," I said. "We could run away together

to some little podunk colonial town in the middle of nowhere on Mars. Change our names, start over. We could leave it all behind, Ray. Rothesky, the war, everything. We could just be Joe and Betty Grumble, or something like that."

I laid my head on his bare chest. A chuckle rumbled under my cheek, and he stroked my hair as I curled into him and lifted the cig over his body to put it on the bedside table. When my hand came back, I rested it over the scar tissue on his shoulder. He stiffened slightly. I needed him to relax.

"Well," I murmured. "Why not? Why couldn't we?" I pressed my lips to his neck, his chest, and heard his answering sigh of pleasure.

"Joe and Betty Grumble, huh?"

"Yeah, I always liked the name Betty. Very retro small-town America." I lifted up a smile at him, but my smile faded at the intensity in his eyes. One big hand came up to cup the side of my face.

"You want to be Betty Grumble?" he asked softly.

It had been a very long time since I believed in love. Other than between Eddie and me, love had always been something that existed for other people. But right there, something flashed in Martel's gaze. Something deep and dangerous. Something that knifed through me and set my nerves tingling.

"Sure thing, Joe," I whispered, before he hauled me in for a rough, almost desperate kiss.

"There's something I want to show you," Martel said later. Much later, in fact. He was sitting at my tiny kitchen table while I poured him a cup of coffee. Real, honest-to-goodness coffee was a luxury since the war, but I had the money, so I indulged. He sniffed deeply and grinned at me in appreciation.

The tension of the night before had evaporated into a dreamy kind of giddy delight. We were Joe and Betty at the breakfast table: pouring coffee, eating eggs. Plotting the takedown of a major crime boss. Typical Saturday morning.

"What's that?" I asked as I slid into the chair next to him, my own coffee mug cradled between my hands.

"I've been thinking about what you said Eddie told you. He said I'd help you, but he didn't say how, right?"

I nodded, blew the steam off the top and took a sip.

"Eddie sent me something a little while ago. I know I said I hadn't thought of him in years, but that was a lie. About a month ago, I get this package from him, with a little note. The note says, 'Thanks for saving my ass all those times. Here's a little something to help you find the beauty you need in your life.'"

I went very still.

"Is that exactly what it said?" I asked, putting my coffee down before my trembling hands could spill it.

"Yeah, why?"

"Because Eddie's message to me also referenced 'the beauty I need in my life.' That's what he said you'd help me find. I think that phrase means something. I think it's his code for the tech. What was in the package?"

"A painting. Looked like a local scene, but all abstract and stuff, with crazy colors. Eddie signed it at the bottom. It was nice."

I reached out and took hold of his hand, gripping his fingers.

"Ray. A local scene? I think...we gotta see that painting!"

"You got it, Betty," Martel squeezed my hand back and gave me a smile.

We left my apartment about an hour later to the sounds of birds singing. The air was young and cool, and the sunlight filtered through the leafy green of the trees that still lined King Street. The Alexandria Farmer's Market was in full swing, and I smiled at a mother looking through the produce with a baby on her hip.

We hopped a hover cab to take us up to the mag rail station so we could catch the express into DC. The hover cab stopped at the corner of King and St. Asaph, and I turned to say something bright to Martel.

I never got the chance. He grabbed my hand and pulled me after him as he stepped out of the hover cab and started walking quickly up St. Asaph.

"Ray? *Ray?*" I asked, struggling to keep up with his long-legged stride.

"Hush," he said, his voice flat and clipped. He ducked into the doorway, pushing me ahead of him into the heavy sweetness of a boutique candy shop.

"Welcome to Sweet Life!" an automated greeter sang out. Neither Martel nor I paid any attention.

"Ray! What—?"

"We're being followed," he said, moving so as to block me from view through the store's big picture windows. "Rothesky's boys I spotted tailing you home yesterday. They're not keeping as much distance today."

"He must be getting suspicious." For just a moment, I allowed fear to register on my face as I looked up at Martel.

He smiled briefly and touched my cheek. "It'll be okay. We'll lose them. They're expecting us to take the express into DC. We'll walk down to the river and take a watertaxi instead."

I took a deep breath, steeled my nerve, and forced a smile and a nod.

"Keep your head down and follow close behind me. I doubt they know what I look like. I know neither of them made me coming to your place yesterday, and I'm pretty sure I spotted them before they got a look at my face today."

"Loitering is not permitted in the Sweet Life," the automated greeter said. "You must select a product or vacate the premises."

"We were just leaving," Martel said and pulled me after him into the street. My hand felt hot in his massive grip.

We got about twenty steps down the sidewalk before a blast sizzled by over our heads. Muffled screams echoed off the bricks around us as we ducked and began to run. Martel pulled an energy pistol from his coat pocket and ran into an alley. He pushed me down and joined me behind a pair of ancient-looking heavy plastic recycling bins. A stray cat yowled her displeasure as we disturbed her and a pair of orange kittens, but that was the only sound...

...Except for the footsteps echoing louder and louder on the sidewalk nearby. I held my breath, both for the stench of the bins and out of nerves. Martel's body tensed beside me. I reached into my pocket and pulled out my own little energy pistol. Martel glanced at it, then nodded in approval. I gave him a tight smile.

The footsteps rounded the corner and slowed to a stop. Martel looked through the opening between the bins and held up two fingers, then pointed at me and to the left. I nodded to show my understanding: two men. I was to take the one on the left.

"Hey, Miz LaFleur," one of the men called out in a voice like gravel in a metal drum. "We just want to talk to you. No need to be afraid." I heard a deep chuckle, quickly stifled. My eyes cut to Martel. He held up three fingers, then slowly lowered one, another . . .

On the count of three, we both stood up, knocking one of the bins over with the suddenness of our movement. My man on the left startled backwards, then went to raise his gun. He was too late. I squeezed three times, and two bolts seared through his torso high on his chest. The third hit somewhere in the vicinity of his right cheekbone and boiled his eye in its socket. He dropped without another sound.

I hadn't noticed Martel's gun going off with the sizzle of my own weapon ringing in my ears, but as he stepped up to the fallen body of the other thug, I can only assume that he shot, too. He took a moment to rifle through their pockets, removing cash, their jewelry, watches, and phones. Either he was trying to make it look like a robbery, or he was gathering identifying data. Could go either way.

I felt numb, as if the blast from my gun had stripped away any feeling or stimulus from the world around me. I blinked twice as I realized that Martel had me by the arms, shaking me none too gently and calling my name.

"Joe," I asked, my voice sounding high and lost, like that of a little girl.

"Yeah, sweetheart," Martel said gently, taking the

pistol from my nerveless hand and putting it into his pocket. He wrapped his fingers through mine and kissed me on the head. "You did good. Real good. Come on now. We're going to get you out of here."

I don't remember much about the rest of the trip down to the river and back up to the apartment over his office in DC. Inputs from the rest of the world came back slowly, but by the time he pushed open the door to his flat, I could hear the gentle whirr of the ceiling fans.

"Come on in," he said. "It's not as nice a place as yours." He sounded a little self-conscious about it. I almost wanted to smile. Almost.

"Where's my gun?" I asked, my voice still sounding strange to my ears.

"Here," he said, pulling it from his pocket and holding it out to me. I wrapped my fingers around its small, familiar weight, and put it in my own pocket. Then I sighed and made my way to an overstuffed chair.

"I never shot anyone before," I said softly.

"I'm sorry about that," Martel said, and he sounded genuine. I met his eyes again, let him see me gathering myself enough to give him a small smile.

"Better them than us, I suppose."

"That's right," he said. "That's exactly right. You just remember that, sweetheart. And don't worry about the cops. When we go talk to the FBI, we'll tell them about being followed by those thugs. I've got all their data. I'm sure they're listed as Rothesky's known associates. And my PI license includes license to carry, so I'll say the gun was mine. They shouldn't fuss at you about that."

I shrugged. I didn't much care about breaking

Alexandria's gun laws, but I knew he wouldn't like hearing that.

"I just want this to be over," I said instead. Martel came over to my chair and bent to wrap his arms around me. I hugged him back, hard.

"Me too," he said softly. "It will be. Soon."

I nodded again, then took a deep breath and squared my shoulders.

"All right," I said. "Let's see Eddie's painting."

Martel let go and got to his feet. He disappeared back into another room while I pulled my vape out of my pocketbook. I took a deep, calming hit and waited for him to return.

I wasn't waiting long. Martel came back with a small parcel, still half-wrapped in self-sealing plastic. I looked up at him, puzzled. He shrugged and looked a bit uncomfortable.

"I didn't know where to put it," he said, handing it to me. "It's not exactly my style."

I chuckled and blew out a cloud of vapor, then dropped my vape back into my bag.

"Eddie would have a fit anytime I blew clouds anywhere near his art," I said by way of explanation. "He'd accuse me of trying to destroy his canvases with moisture." I let some humor leak into my tone as I took the parcel and began to strip away the layers of protective packing material.

"Ah, Eddie," I sighed as the painting revealed itself to me. It was definitely his. Bold strokes of bright, aggressive color assaulted my eyes, and it took a moment for me to find the coherence, the composition of it. But it was definitely there. As I considered my brother's handiwork, details leapt out at me: a shape like and yet unlike an anchor in the middle. A fence. Ripples of water. I let out a gasp and raised wide, excited eyes to Martel's.

"I know what this is!"

"What, the painting?"

"Yes! You were right, this is a local scene. See the water here? That's the Potomac."

"I figured that much. But what's the rest of it?"

"See this?" I said, pointing to the anchoresque shape in the middle. "I know that shape. Down at the end of King Street, near the water. On . . . Strand, I think? There's an art gallery known as the Torpedo Factory. I think it actually was one during the war. Not this last one, World War Two, almost two centuries ago. Anyway, there's this sculpture outside, with a plaque and things. That's what this looks like! Ray . . . I think Eddie hid whatever he had in the old Torpedo Factory Art Gallery."

Martel nodded slowly.

"Okay," he said, sitting back on his heels. "Okay. So, here's what we're going to do. I'm going to go down to this Torpedo Factory and check it out. Alone."

I looked up quickly.

"What?" I asked.

Martel's chin was set like a brick in mortar. "Sweetheart, Rothesky's people are looking for you. They probably killed Eddie. They definitely tried to kill us. You're not going back to Alexandria today . . . maybe not for a while. They still don't know what I look like. I can get down there, move around, check things out. In the meantime, you stay here, where it's safe."

I opened my mouth like I wanted to protest, but then closed it without saying anything.

"You're rattled," he said, nodding. "I can see that. Stay here, relax. Make yourself at home. I'll be back before you know it."

I swallowed hard, and then gave a tiny nod of assent. He stood up.

"Wait," I called out, and surged to my feet. The canvas and plastic slid to the floor with a clatter. I threw my arms around Martel's neck and took his mouth with my own. He met my kiss with a feverish heat as his arms wrapped around my body like steel bands.

"Be careful," I whispered against his lips.

"You got it, Betty," he whispered back, and let me go.

I stepped slowly away and picked up the painting, then watched him walk out the door.

I listened to Martel's key turn the ancient lock. His footsteps echoed away down the hall toward the cramped stairwell.

One more deep breath, and then I began to move. First things first: the painting. I turned to his credit chip of a kitchenette table and set the painting down. Using only my fingernail, I scratched gently at the thick bead of paint Eddie'd left on the corner of the canvas. Sure enough, it lifted and tore easily down toward the middle.

A dark brown eye and the world's most famous enigmatic smile looked up at me through the rent canvas.

Excitement like lightning sang through me. I carefully and quickly rewrapped the parcel, then pulled out my burner phone. A few minutes later, I had a luxury hover cab en route to take me to Union

Station. From there I'd take the mag rail to Dulles Shuttleport, and then we'd see.

While I waited, I typed out a quick message on my phone for Martel to see when he got back.

I don't expect that you will ever forgive me, and I don't imagine I can blame you. I can only hope that the gift I left for you at the Torpedo Factory will be of some comfort. Those books are, in fact, Rothesky's actual expenditures. All of them, in excruciating detail. As promised, this should be enough evidence to make the FBI sit up and take notice. You'll be safe, and Eddie will be avenged. I'm sorry to have to ask you to do the dance for me though. But something tells me you're a fine dancer and will have no problem at all. Do us both a favor. Don't bother trying to find me. The dream is over now. All that's left is a memory to comfort me on long, lonely nights.

Thank you,
Betty

My phone buzzed to let me know that my hover cab was waiting. I took one last look, remembering the taste of bourbon on his lips. Then I put the phone on the table, gathered my brother's treasure up under my arm, and went out to catch a mag rail train in the steamy mess of a DC afternoon.

The Privileges of Violence

A GRUNT'S EYE VIEW STORY

Steve Diamond

My father was a piece of trash, but never let it be said that he was a quitter. Most of what I learned from him boiled down to ignoring everything he said and did. But never giving up? That was from him. Well, that and a weakness for beautiful women.

I had a small office in the Directorate S building in Cobetsnya. That office—along with new living quarters— was my reward given to me by the Chancellor to the Tsar. If anyone asked—which no one with any measure of intelligence did—I'd cleaned up a small mess caused by one of the Tsar's enemies. In reality, there had never been any mess. I'd simply followed the Chancellor's orders to . . . remove . . . one of the Tsar's up-and-coming political rivals.

Easy. Clean. By summer, no one would even remember that potential rival's name.

No one besides me, that is. But that was my secret.

My knowledge. A man in my profession can never have too much secret information.

My office wasn't much bigger than an average closet. But in the Directorate, that was a blessing in disguise. Less space for spies—from within the Directorate, and from outside—to ply their trade. I had a desk. It even had drawers. My own chair, and another opposite me on the other side of the desk. I had one item on the surface of the desk: a clock. It had been a gift from my mother before my father had beaten her to death.

I'm told he was rotting in a prison in the northern, frigid wastes of the Tsar's Empire. With any luck, he'd frozen to death and had been used as mortar for the prison walls.

The clock was small and elegant, just like I remembered my mother. Midnight approached, and along with it, the limits to my stamina for the day...or perhaps "night" was more accurate. I put the unfinished reports from the "mess" I'd cleaned up in my desk and shut the drawer. The Chancellor didn't want any record of what had actually happened.

My latest promotion put me at the topmost levels of the Directorate. The new apartment was nice, as was the increase in rations, but I couldn't help but feeling like I was still falling short of my potential. "Directorate" was the short name for the Directorate of Surveillance and Observation. Our job was to watch the citizens of Kolakolvia and prevent them from harming the Tsardom or themselves. Standard policing. It was easy work. Boring even.

But there were always rumors. Rumors of hardworking, trustworthy individuals at my level in the Directorate being placed in another organization—one run personally by the Chancellor. More power. Better housing. Extra rations. Real work beyond which I was currently executing. Hunting down the Tsar's true enemies.

I needed to be part of that organization, if it existed. No matter the cost.

With nothing more for me to do for the day, I closed and locked the door to my office before making my way toward the exit. The Directorate S building stood several floors high. The carpet was well worn, and the plaster on the walls peeling. If you knew where to look, you could see the bloodstains from former Directorate officers who hadn't done their jobs well enough.

I walked by the closed door leading to my partner's office. I didn't like having a partner, but that was a requirement of the job. I figured it was to breed paranoia and distrust rather than do any actual good. My partner's name was Vasily Bodlen. A brute of a man, he preferred to solve all issues by breaking bones. I could appreciate that attitude in many situations, but I also found words and threats to be equally effective, and much less strenuous. Threaten to put a man's wife in a prison camp, or murder his son... it all worked rather well.

Bodlen had left early, leaving me all the paperwork. It was odd. As single-minded as he was in doing his job one broken bone at a time, he never went home early. I'd ask him about it tomorrow. He'd been gone a lot lately, saying he was on jobs he couldn't talk about.

I took the stairs down to the ground level and pushed my way through the entryway doors. Neither set of two guards on either side of the door acknowledged my leaving. They never did. Guards at Directorate S knew better than to disobey even the smallest of rules. No one wanted to chance being turned into one of the Cursed as a punishment.

The grounds between the doors and the outer fences were devoid of any brush or stone. The Chancellor insisted the "killing ground" be kept clear.

I pulled my coat closer and walked the distance to the outer gate, then turned left towards my assigned housing. Spring in Cobetsnya—the capital city of Kolakolvia—was essentially winter with slightly less snow. This late in the evening—or perhaps better to say this early in the morning—my coat did little to keep the chill from seeping into my bones.

The paved road of Alexandr Prospekt stretched out before me and behind me, running for miles in both directions. It was the main boulevard that bisected Cobetsnya from west to east. The road was wide enough for carriages to pass each other six across. There was talk of putting a rail system through the middle of it, but I doubted that would ever happen.

Directorate S resided in a void along Alexandr Prospekt. No buildings allowed for a city block surrounding it: Chancellor's orders, and what the Chancellor ordered, the Tsar approved. Government-assigned housing began immediately outside the one-block perimeter.

I wasn't overly jaded, nor was I patriotic enough to be blind to the ugliness of the housing complexes. Large, gray, and identical from one to the next. My rooms were only a few blocks up the road.

The cold was bitter, and my breath exploded from my mouth like cannonfire. I should have worn a hat.

Scuffing to my right.

Muffled cries.

In Cobetsnya, most civilians learn to keep walking when unfamiliar sounds reach their ears. You never know what lurks in shadowed alleys. If you are lucky, it will just be some starved citizen waiting to kill you for your food vouchers.

If you are unlucky...well...it may be something wanting to eat your corpse or steal your children.

I had a hunch the sounds I heard were of the more natural sort. If what hid in the shadows was unnatural, I'd probably already be dead. I walked beyond the mouth of the alley, then stepped quickly to the bordering wall and pressed myself against it. I wished I had a pistol, but the Chancellor didn't let Directorate officers carry them. It's always about control.

I pulled a long knife from its sheath under my coat. Moonlight glinted off the curved blade. A butcher's blade for butcher's work. I wasn't the best with it, but I'd been trained well enough.

My hope was for only one assailant. More than that, and I'd have to be lucky. But that was the job, and I needed to make a name for myself. Recognition comes to the ruthless.

When I entered the alley, I went in crouched, and with my blade ready to paint the walls a more lively color. Six quick steps put me into the shadows, and I saw a man straddling a separate, prone form. The man had a knife in his hand—a small thing, easily concealable—raised to strike down. He turned as my blade took him in the kidney.

He screamed in pain, and turned to slash at my throat. I blocked it with a forearm to his wrist, then ripped my knife free. His body had turned so he completely faced me, so I jabbed him three quick

times in the abdomen. On the last, I pulled the blade
to the right, gutting him.

To the man's credit, he didn't give up, even as his
blood and intestines spilled out. His head lashed forward, caught me on the cheek. If I hadn't turned my
head at the last moment, my nose would have been
flattened. His off hand caught my wrist, but I could
feel him weakening. I kept his own knife from my
throat, and inexorably pushed my gleaming blade to
his face. The point sank into his left eye. I expected
another scream, but it didn't come. I twisted my knife,
he spasmed, and it was over.

The man collapsed to the ground, and for the first
time I got a clear look at the other figure.

She'd pulled herself to the west wall of the alley,
knees pulled to her chest. Long, golden locks of
hair spilled over her eyes, and a purpling bruise was
emerging on her left cheek. She stared at her fallen
assailant, mouth open, eyes wide.

"You . . . you . . ."

"Killed him," I said. "Yes. I did. Are you alright?"

She closed her eyes, took a deep, shuddering breath,
then nodded.

"Hospitals don't open until the morning," I said.
I bent over and wiped my knife on the shoulder of
the dead man's jacket. "I'll give you a moment, then
I'll take you to my place. You can stay there tonight."

As I began searching the man's pockets, I saw her
nod out of the corner of my eye. A quick glance
showed her eyes still closed. Her lower lip trembled
a little, but that was to be expected. She straightened
the skirt over her legs over and over.

"Did he—"

"No," she immediately interrupted. "That's not what this was about... though I suppose he might have gone that way... after..."

She trailed off, and I didn't feel like pursuing it further. The man's pockets were empty. Completely empty. It didn't make any sense. He should have had identification papers. Food vouchers. Maybe actual currency. I didn't even see the sheath for the knife. I pushed up his sleeves checking for tattoos. Nothing.

"Check under his collar," the woman said. At the sound of her voice I looked up and found her staring at the corpse. Her expression was sad and horrified. "I thought I saw something when he was... when he..."

"It's alright," I said. "I understand."

I pulled down his collar and saw the tattoo the woman had mentioned seeing. I didn't recognize the design. Three overlapping circles that formed a sort of triangle. The middle where they all overlapped was filled in.

"Do you know what this is?"

She shook her head.

I stood up, then held out my hand to the woman. "We should leave. We don't want to be around the body too long. Never know what will show up."

"We're just going to leave... it... here?"

"Would you rather we attach strings to it and walk it home like a marionette?"

She flinched. "No. It's just... did you have to kill him? So violently, I mean?"

"I prefer his death to yours or mine." I wiggled the fingers of my extended hand. "Come. I think we both could stand getting cleaned up. I'll make us tea, and you can tell me what you were doing out so late."

She took my hand, and I pulled her up. Standing, she was almost as tall as I. She smiled slightly, then glanced again at the body and winced. I put my arm around her and steered her out of the alley.

"By the way," I said, "my name is Kristoph Vals. I work for Directorate S."

"Helena. Helena Sarchev. Thank you for saving my life."

She was weak-kneed the remaining distance to my home and had to be supported as she walked. I didn't speak, nor did she. When we reached my assigned housing, I helped her up the stairs to the third floor, steered her around the loose board on my doorstep, unlocked my door, and helped her inside.

I quickly lit the lamps in the entry, and then those in the corners of the small sitting room. Light revealed my recently acquired home. I ushered Helena to a chair in the corner, by which stood a diminutive bookshelf that held all twelve of the books I owned. She all but fell into the chair. I pulled off my coat and held it in the light. The front was covered in blood. I sighed. My laundress, Ms. Alsteder, would be furious when she saw it.

I left Helena in the front room and went through my room into the lavatory. I lit another lamp there and looked at myself in the mirror. I had blood on my face and a wicked bruise where the man headbutted me, but I was otherwise no worse for wear. I turned the knob on the sink and waited for the water to arrive. The pipes groaned, but finally water trickled out. I rubbed at my face and neck, then scrubbed my hair as quickly as I could. I pulled a towel from where it hung next to the mirror and dried myself off as I returned to the sitting room.

Helena was still in the chair, eyes wandering around the room, taking in the details. Truth be told, there wasn't much to take in. A small desk with a chair. A threadbare rug in the middle of the floor. An artist's rendition of my mother's portrait on the wall. Of course, the chair she sat in and the nearby bookshelf. That was it.

"You have a nice home, Mr. Vals."

"Please, call me Kristoph. I think after what happened tonight, we are beyond the point of formalities." I smiled in an attempt to make light of her near tragedy. "And thank you. I was recently assigned these quarters. They are bigger than my prior lodgings, and I'm afraid I don't have the furnishings to actually *fill* the space.

"Now, Helena," I said, pulling the desk chair over to sit beside her, "I know you are tired, but I think it's time you told me your story. What were you doing out so late? This isn't the military quarter. Surely you are aware of the civilian curfew?"

"I am aware," she said. "But I didn't have a choice."

"Why is that?"

"People have been following me since I entered the city a few days ago. I returned to my room at the boardinghouse two blocks south of here and found it a wreck."

"It had been searched?"

"Yes," she said. "My mattress and pillows ripped open. The drawers of the dresser pulled out and emptied. There were even holes in the walls."

I leaned forward in my chair. "Helena, what were they looking for?"

She hesitated. "You say you work for the Directorate?"

I nodded.

"I know this is horribly rude of me. After all, you just saved my life. But... but... can I see your identification papers?"

A moment passed without my moving. It wasn't the strangest of requests, but neither was it normal. I had to admit I was curious. I got up and crossed the room to where I'd hung my coat, and pulled my papers from the inside pocket. I handed them over to her and sat back down, waiting for her to be satisfied.

She opened the small packet, and she gave a slight nod when her eyes reached the sigil of Directorate S; a twelve-pointed star with an open eye at its center. She handed the papers back, then reached down the front of her blouse and pulled out a folded document. She hesitated a moment, then handed it to me.

"Do you know what this is?"

I took the paper, unfolded it, and found myself looking at a drawing. Maybe "drawing" wasn't the best word. Scrawled across the paper in precise, neat script were a series of old Prajan runes. Every man in my profession knew what they were, what they symbolized.

This series of runes had caused incredible levels of death.

It was the phrase that brought a golem to life.

"I know what it is," I said, "but why should I care? It's no good to anyone. You can't just draw this in some mud, or scrape it into stone and hope to have a killing machine at your command. It takes a dozen priests who have trained in those magics for decades."

"I'm aware."

"Are you?" I couldn't say why, but I was getting angry. Maybe because it was late, or because I'd had to stab a man in the face less than an hour ago. I held up the paper so the writing faced her. "This phrase is why we've been at war with Almacia for the better part of fifty years. This phrase is why the Tsar and Chancellor want us to invade Praja."

"I know," Helena said quietly. "I'm from Belgracia."

Now that was interesting. Belgracia didn't even exist anymore as an independent country. Kolakolvia and Almacia had traded off occupation of the tiny city-state for hundreds of years. It was now in our control. Belgracia was barely worthy of historical text, except for the time they'd risen up in an attempted revolution. Prajan priests had summoned a dozen golems, which massacred the Almacian occupiers. Fortunately, our own army had been stationed nearby. We stormed in, ravaged the city, and managed to kill off the remaining golems.

It cost us thousands of soldiers.

And it had been worth it. From those dead golems, we'd harvested enough pieces of the summoning phrases to double the size of our armored infantry known simply as "The Wall."

"Do you have any idea how hard it is to kill a golem? Have you ever seen one in action?"

Helena shook her head.

"Imagine a creature of stone, earth, wood, or some combination of the three," I said. "More than twice the height of the tallest man. It can run faster than a horse, and it never tires. It can effortlessly rip a man in half. Guns barely touch it. Heavy artillery is the only way to stop it, and that's no sure thing. They are the most terrifying thing in existence—I imagine even fae things would hesitate to come up against a golem."

"Surely you don't believe in those wives' tales? Fae don't exist. That's just old superstition."

"You keep on thinking that," I said. "You don't need to believe in them. When you see your first corpse-eater, you'll become a believer real fast. But that's not what we are talking about." I pointed at the first rune. "When we manage to kill a golem, the full summoning phrase breaks apart. Usually it crumbles into dust. Sometimes, though, a letter or two will survive. The Chancellor embeds them into the armored suits members of the Wall wear.

"Just one letter turns that armor into a piece of mobile artillery. Imagine, nearly indestructible armor made from the latent magic from one piece of a phrase from a dead golem." I sighed and leaned back in my chair. "Why were you bringing this drawing of the summoning phrase to the Directorate headquarters? We're just the police."

"My father is—was—a farmer." Her voice trembled a little. I was willing to bet her father was recently deceased, and that I was about to find out why. For some reason, a shiver crawled up my spine. "Like I said, we are from Belgracia. Well, what's left of it. A few weeks ago, he was plowing a new field he'd recently cleared of trees. His plow got stuck. He called out to me and my five brothers to help him free the plow, and to dig up whatever it had gotten stuck on. We figured it was some leftover tree roots.

"Took most of the day," Helena continued. She rubbed her hands together and looked down at them. "I can still feel the blisters. Anyway, we ended up pulling up a whole bunch of stone and wood, all twisted together. Ended up having to hook our horses to it to pull it out of the ground."

I leaned forward again. I knew where this was going, but I needed to hear her say the impossible. "What was it?"

"The thing was shaped like a man, but missing a leg and an arm," Helena said. "You asked if I'd ever been witness to a live golem. I haven't. But I've seen a dead one. And on its head was carved that full 'phrase' you hold in your hand. If you look closely, you can see it isn't a drawing. It's a rub that I inked in."

I looked closer at the drawing in my hand. It was true. My mouth had gone dry.

"How was it dead if it had the full phrase?"

"We don't know. But the stone around it flaked away without too much effort. My father chipped away at it for a whole night until he was left with a small piece of stone engraved with the phrase."

"You have a full, intact golem-summoning phrase?"

"No," she said. "That's why I'm here. It was stolen. Men broke into the house, killed my father and brothers, and ran off with it. I followed them here, to Cobetsnya."

I didn't sleep that night. Helena took my bed while I tried sleeping in the chair. My mind turned her story over and over, looking for flaws. It was incredible. A full phrase. If a single rune could power a walking suit of armor, what would the full phrase do?

If I could find the stolen carved phrase and give it to the Chancellor, surely I'd earn my place among the rumored secret police. How could I be denied? A full phrase could be the key to unlocking the magic, the key to magical progress everyone knew the Chancellor was searching for. I would be a national hero.

I would also need to tread cautiously.

If anyone else in Directorate S found out about this, they would do their best to find the phrase themselves. Take the glory. My glory. They wouldn't hesitate to put me in the ground and leave me for the corpse-eaters. I couldn't tell anyone. Not even my partner. *Especially* not my partner. He'd break Helena in half to get the information from her.

The chair was beginning to hurt my back, so I stood and walked to the window. In the moonlight I looked at my pocket watch. Dawn was still a few hours away.

A sound from my bedroom arrested my attention. On quiet feet I moved to the doorway, where I saw Helena tossing and turning. Some sort of nightmare. Doubtless the memories of her experience in the alley invading her sleep.

How much could I trust her? How much could I trust anyone, really? Training for Directorate S officers is brutal, violent, and filled with paranoia. My own kill test—the final portion of my training—had been a suspected traitor to the Tsar. I've killed many since. Just the nature of the job . . . but . . .

. . . but . . .

I wanted to trust Helena. It wasn't her fragility. I didn't think she *was* fragile. To come all this way by herself, after her family had been killed, in search of a stolen phrase. That was strength. She could be lying to me. She was almost certainly not telling me the whole truth. But I didn't care.

A squeak outside my door.

The floorboards had been stable when I'd moved in. Most people would have been overjoyed by that small miracle in Cobetsnya. The entities responsible for construction and maintenance weren't known for their attention to detail, nor exquisite craftsmanship. They were known for cutting corners and working the bare minimum to collect their allotted basic income. Working hard never got any of them anywhere, so why bother? I'd been overjoyed to be selected for the Directorate. Paranoia aside, it was one of the few professions where the Tsar and Chancellor allowed for hard work that led to a certain amount of advancement. Violence had its privileges.

My first night in this new housing block, I'd loosened the floorboard—an old trick I'd learned in training.

The floorboard squeaked again.

I smiled.

There's very little as satisfying as knowing you are about to be ambushed or attacked, and being able to flip it on your attacker.

I didn't have time to wake and warn Helena. There was a risk involved in her not knowing what was coming. I didn't know how she would react when things got messy, especially so close after her prior incident. She could turn to hysteria, or be as calm as a veteran soldier.

How many were outside? I had to assume multiple. I grabbed my coat and wrapped it around my left arm. The folds and layers of thick fabric would help just enough if my soon-to-be assailants were the slashing types with knives. I pulled my long knife free, stood against the wall behind where the door would open.

The light scraping of tools being inserted into the lock reached my ears. Pseudo professionals. My heart began hammering, not in fear but excitement.

The lock clicked, and the door pushed slowly inward.

I hid in the shadow of the opening door, using the door as cover, waiting to see the first person enter. A figure clad in black passed into the open space of my home. Through the crack in the hinged side of the door to my right, I saw another shadow pass by, then nothing. Two of them then.

Around the edge of the open door, I saw the first figure walk toward Helena's sleeping form. The second took ahold of the door and began closing it behind him. Neither bothered to check around the door. They obviously hadn't cleared rooms before. Always have to watch doors and corners. I smiled again and stepped out from concealment.

Too late, the trailing figure thought to look behind him. He turned—and received the edge of my blade across his throat. He made the smallest of noises before blood arced out over me. The lead figure spun around in time to see his companion drop to the floor. He rushed me with a shout, and just beyond him, I saw Helena jerk awake.

The man facing me was far bigger, and his reach, therefore, longer. He held the blade well. No matter how skilled I was, one tiny mistake could determine which of us joined his companion in jerking on the ground, trying to hold his throat closed.

My attacker swung at me, keeping me from getting in too close. His knife hand was quick, and he looked to be strong. I could dart in and hope to block his swing with my arm. Stab him a few times. Or I could—

A pillowcase, as if by magic, enveloped his head from behind.

I didn't waste the opportunity. I rushed in, blocked

a wild slash from his knife with my coat-wrapped arm, and stabbed him through the temple. He dropped like a child's rag doll. I kicked the knife from his hand, and let the life spasm out of him. I looked back behind me and saw the other man still stubbornly clinging to life. I walked over, bent down, and pushed my blade into his chest. He convulsed once, then went still.

Under his blood-soaked hands, I spotted the same tattoo.

When I got back up to go check the other dead man's neck, I found Helena suddenly in my arms. She was sobbing. "I'm sorry," she said into my chest. "I'm so sorry."

"You did fine, Helena," I said, smoothing her hair. "More than fine. You have nothing to be sorry for. You are alive. I'm alive. Had you been anywhere else, those results may have been different for you. Had you not helped me, I may not have lived either."

"They were after *me*."

"Indeed. And the information they think you have. They obviously think you have the summoning phrase. Or they are sure you know where it is."

"But I don't. I'm looking for it too."

"They obviously don't believe that. These aren't the men who killed your family?"

She shook her head.

"Well," I said, "then we only have one option. We need to find the phrase and get it to the Chancellor before either of us gets killed. I'm going to need your help. Can you do that for me?"

She looked up into my eyes and smiled.

That smile was the kind that could keep a man warm in the coldest winter. It wasn't broad, nor was it even. The right side of her mouth looked happy, the left a little shy. I knew I was in serious trouble. *She* was serious trouble.

I couldn't have been happier.

Not everyone in Directorate S goes about the Tsar's business dealing death or acquiring information. Some recruits just aren't cut out for that sort of work. We also employ individuals who have a talent for cleaning up messes. I'm decent at it. Others in the organization must be touched by the fae because they can make bodies and blood disappear like magic.

I left Helena in the room, had her wedge a chair under the door, and went to get my favorite cleaner. Her name was Petra.

As beautiful as Helena was, Petra made the other woman look completely average. Her dark hair and almond-shaped eyes marked her as one with blood from the southern, conquered provinces. The Tsar didn't care. Neither did the Chancellor. If you had talents, you were put to use.

When I first met Petra, she was neatly dismembering a corpse. She'd stood up, held out a bloody hand, and introduced herself. For a moment, I thought I was in love. But behind those eyes, something darker seemed to coil and uncoil. I shook her hand, suddenly worried that I would offend her, and I'd end up disappeared. I never once made a pass at her. We'd become, well, not exactly friends . . . I don't think she understood the meaning of that word. There wasn't really a word for what we were. More than professionals with mutual respect. Could you be lovers without any sex or romance? Could you be close to a person just to make sure you stayed alive? Somewhere in there, Petra and I existed.

She came to the door in a thin robe that hid almost nothing. Her home was north of Alexandr Prospekt, where electricity was available, if rationed. She had earned this home, the type of home I hoped to have—if not better—once I found the summoning phrase.

"Darling Kristoph," she said with a yawn and breathtaking stretch. "Why are you here before dawn? Do you have any idea how tiring it is cleaning up after all of you?"

"Petra," I said. I took her hand and kissed it. Again, this wasn't a gesture of romance, but of self-preservation. "I am in need of your services."

She winked at me. "I bet you are. Give me a moment." She closed the door in my face, and I was left waiting on her.

In spite of everything, I was energized. I felt . . . happy. The men attacking my home—they must have followed us from the alley—had all but confirmed the veracity of Helena's story. She'd been, perhaps, too free with her inquiries. Whoever these men were, they thought Helena had information. Their tattoos weren't familiar, which bothered me. I thought I knew the signs of all the local gangs.

The door opened again and Petra came out, looking like she was on her way to a ball. She carried a large canvas bag. Tools of her trade.

"Would you like me to carry that for you?" I asked.

"Ever the gentleman, my Kristoph. But no. I never let men touch my valuables." After we'd walked for several minutes, she sniffed. "You have a woman. I smell her on you."

"I saved her from a mugging," I said, skirting around the truth. No matter the relationship between Petra and me, sharing the full story with her wasn't a good idea. But the best lies are the ones that don't stray too far from the truths they twist. "Then two more members of the same . . . gang, I suppose . . . followed me home to seek some sort of revenge. I dispatched them as well."

She stared at me for a moment. It wasn't pleasant. "Why do you say they were part of a gang?"

"Some tattoo. One I hadn't seen before, but they all had it. Three overlapping circles making a triangle shape. The center where they overlap was filled in. Sound familiar?"

"No," she said slowly, "and I don't like not knowing."

"That makes the both of us."

"I'll look into it." She stopped in front of my building without my prompting. "Here we are."

"You have the location of my home memorized? I was barely assigned it."

"I know where all the Directorate officers currently reside."

"And do you track our movements as well?" I made it sound like a joke. It wasn't.

Petra looked confused. "I know most things. I am very good at my job." Without waiting, she walked through the door and up the stairs to my home.

Petra stared at the mess, unmoving. Helena was in my room, out of view, not wanting to see what was about to happen.

The cleaner nodded once, then opened her bag. She pulled out a battlefield surgeon's saw and several bottles. Some held amber-colored fluid, the others rust-colored.

"This home is assigned a bathtub, yes?" Petra looked in the direction of my room where the tub was also located.

"Yes," I answered.

"Porcelain?"

"Yes."

She put away the amber liquid. "This won't take long. Where is the body of the other man you say you killed?"

"Left him in an alley."

She nodded. "I imagine the corpse-eaters will find him and drag him down. At worst, the dogs get him. Good enough. Now, don't bother me."

Petra left a half hour later. The liquid—an Almacian alchemical creation I knew she bought off the black market—dissolved the corpses in my tub without leaving a mark. She even had something to take away the bloodstains on my floor.

Helena was asleep again. Poor thing was exhausted. She'd done well, though. Tougher than some of the officers I worked with. I wedged a chair under the door handle, then collapsed back to my chair.

I don't remember falling asleep, but suddenly I was awake again. Sunlight was streaming through my window. I pushed myself out of the chair, stretched my aching back, and went to wake Helena. She was curled under a blanket, wisps of hair lying across her cheekbones and nose. She looked younger in her sleep. More vulnerable, if that were possible. I was about to clear my throat to wake her when someone pounded on my door. Helena's eyes sprang open. She had a look of momentary confusion on her face, then her gaze found mine. I put a finger to my lips and motioned for her to get out of sight.

"Yeah?" I yelled at the door.

"It's Vasily. Let me in, we need to talk."

I pulled the chair away from the door and let my partner in.

"You look like a corpse, Kristoph," he said, brushing by me. He went straight to my desk, opened the top drawer, and pulled out my bottle of alcohol and a glass. He poured himself a measure and downed it in a single swallow. I suppose I should have been grateful he didn't drink straight from the bottle. "What happened?"

"Rough night," I said. I needed him to get to the point, and then get out. "What do you want to talk about?"

"There's a rumor going around about a full summoning phrase on the black market. Some woman claims to be selling it. You heard about it?"

I shrugged. "No. You sure it's the real deal?"

"Doesn't have to be to be worth checking into. If it's real, the bosses want it locked up tight in the vault at the Directorate with all the other phrase pieces we haven't converted into armor for the Wall." He paused to pour another drink. "If you go looking for this thing, I want in."

"Why would I bother?"

Vasily's drink stopped just short of his mouth. His eyes narrowed. "I know you, Kristoph. I know you want advancement. And now I know you *are* looking for the summoning phrase." He set the glass back down, then pointed at me. "You're not freezing me out of this."

My partner wasn't normally this pushy. "I'm sure I don't know what you're talking about."

"You do. I want to know what you know. Did you already find the girl?"

I held up my hands, doing my best to play dumb. Vasily was either smarter than I gave him credit for or...

...or he already knew.

He'd left early the day before. The same day I'd had two lethal encounters with the people looking for Helena. He'd been gone a lot lately over the last few weeks.

Wait.

Helena's family had been murdered just a few weeks ago. Had Vasily been gone around that time? I couldn't remember. Could he have heard about the discovery, then gone down and killed them all, stealing the phrase? Either to sell or turn over to the Chancellor himself. But before he can do either, he hears the rumors of Helena's interest and realizes he needs to clean up a loose end?

It made sense. It wouldn't have been the first time a Directorate officer had been ordered to kill a few farmers—officially, or by some rogue members—to acquire pieces of golems. Then he spins it as an investigation. Asks for his partner's help. No matter what I did, he'd end up following me.

I needed to get him set off on something else to buy some time.

"Alright, alright," I said. "I had a run-in last night after you left early. Caught a guy mugging a girl who was on her way to our offices. I killed the guy."

"The girl? She here?" He turned to walk into my bedroom.

"No," I said, then pointed down at the floor to shift his attention. "She ran off. But two more followed me home, and I killed them right there. Had to call Petra. She just left. Anyway, someone must have thought this mystery girl came home with me."

"How do you know the girl was coming to see us?"

"She said as much before running. Told me where she was staying. A boardinghouse a couple of blocks south of us. I imagine she was referring to the one on Victory Prospekt."

"You sure she said she was at the boardinghouse on Victory?"

"She didn't mention it by name," I said with a frown. Something in Vasily's tone . . . like he already knew she was staying there. Maybe he did. There were so many contradictory details in what he was telling me. They didn't match Helena's story. "But you and I both know there's only one boardinghouse that way."

"Right. Sorry. Must have slipped my mind." He was distracted. Obviously lying. "Did she have the item on her?"

I shrugged. "I was busy staying alive. Why don't you head over there and check it out? I'm going to see about tracking down the guys that attacked me." I pointed at him the same way he'd done to me. "But remember, I brought you in on this. I was going to keep it all to myself. If you screw me, I'll make sure Petra knows it. You know how protective of me she is."

Vasily paled, nodded, and was about to leave when I said, "Oh, she said her name was Helena. Does that verify any of the rumors you heard?"

It was there and gone, but I saw the recognition. He knew her name. Without another word he left and slammed the door behind him.

I put the chair back under the handle—a little paranoia never hurt anyone—and walked into my room. Helena was huddled in the corner to the right, knees to her chest just like in the alley. She had tears running down her cheeks. There aren't many things worse in life than seeing a beautiful woman cry.

I knelt down beside her and took her trembling hand. "Helena, what's wrong?"

"He...he was one of the men who killed my family."

"You are sure?"

She nodded. "I recognized the voice, then risked a look. I'll never forget him. He cut my father's throat, then snapped his neck...I...I think just for fun."

That certainly seemed like an accurate representation of Vasily's tactics.

She pulled my hand to her tear-damp cheek and said, "Don't let him kill me. You know that's what he wants, don't you?"

"I do," I said. Her skin was so soft beneath my hand. She looked up with tear-filled eyes, and I couldn't help myself. I leaned forward and kissed her. Her arms wrapped around me, pulling me closer. I tasted the salt from her tears, and for the first time in years, I felt like I could truly trust someone.

I broke away and stood up, pulling Helena up with me. Her cheeks were flushed, and she ran hands over and through her blond tresses.

"Nothing will happen to you, Helena. I swear it."

"Are you going to lock me in a room? Like one of those relics Vasily says you keep locked away?"

The truth was, I was considering it. I didn't want her anywhere near danger. But that look in her eyes. Like she was feeling betrayed by something I hadn't even done yet. So instead I gave her my most reassuring smile. "Of course not. I need your help."

That crooked smile reappeared on her face, and she stood up on her toes to kiss me again. "What do you need me to do?"

"I'm going to introduce you to an information broker. You're going to tell him you want to sell the real summoning phrase. You're going to tell him you want to sell it to this group with the tattoos on their necks, because the one they stole was a fake. You can prove it with the real one in your possession."

"It's a trap."

"Indeed, my dear Helena."

"So they bring the one they stole. What... what are you going to do with whomever shows up?"

I took her hand and kissed the back of it. "Helena, I'm going to make sure they can never hurt you again."

I waited in the shadow of an alley across from a water dispensary. The line out front was longer than usual. With the weather just beginning to warm, even the slightest increase in temperature meant an increase in water consumption. The sad part was knowing how few of the people in line would actually receive their allocation, ration voucher be damned. The bulk of rations went to the wealthy aristocrats, and the majority of the remainder went to the military in their endless war against Almacia.

There wasn't anything I could do for the poor, and

their station in life was set. But I could improve my own lot in life, unlike them. All it would take was reclaiming the stolen phrase.

The information broker was the guard midway through the line. His uniform was the cleanest of all the guards. Not clean in a normal way, but in the fanatical sense. His name was Donal Gelan. He knew how to get in touch with every black-market dealer, every gang, every prostitute, and every hired killer in Cobetsnya. He ran the business with his brother Abert.

By all rights, we should have shut him down years ago, but in truth Donal was too valuable. Patriotism only went so far, even among the police of the Tsardom. We all needed things—information to illicit goods—from time to time. Donal was the best way. Rather than setting up shop in a specific place, he maintained his position as an enlisted guard. No one knew why.

After an hour of waiting, Helena was nearly there. She held a yellow handkerchief where Donal could see it, one of the many ways to show one needed to speak with him.

Donal approached her and motioned for her to step out of line. He took her out of earshot from the line and acted as if he were questioning her. The waiting masses wisely kept their gazes averted. Garnering the attention of the guards, no matter the situation, was generally more trouble than it was worth.

After a few moments, Helena walked away from the line, head bowed in mock submission. Behind her, Donal was already walking away from his post—normally an offence worthy of a firing squad, but his fellow guards knew better than to report him.

I pulled Helena into the alley. "You set it up?"

She nodded. "I told him I didn't think it would be possible for him to set up a meeting for tonight, just like you said. You were right. He took it as a challenge. Said to meet back here after nightly curfew."

"Good. Now we wait." I gave her a reassuring smile. "This will all be over soon."

The night's air was frigid. Brittle. Harsh.

The perfect night for violence.

We both stood in the same alley as earlier in the day, awaiting the thieves and murderers whom we would rob and kill.

"Now, this looks a lot like you cutting me out of the deal."

We both turned and saw Vasily approaching from the opposite side of the alley. He'd either followed us or, more likely, knew where we would be waiting because he was part of the gang that had killed Helena's family and stolen the summoning phrase.

"Didn't think you'd want to be part of a waiting game," I lied.

"Right. And who are we waiting for?"

"I think you know."

"You'd be right."

I wanted to spit back a curse at him, but words weren't going to accomplish anything. Helena hugged me close, arms inside my coat.

Vasily nodded past me. "Looks like the people we are waiting for have finally showed up. How much is the payout? What did the girl here offer you?"

I frowned at that. His words didn't make sense. He should already know all the details of this exchange. For the first time, a tickle of unease wormed its way down my spine.

All the inconsistencies...

Before I could ask Helena about it, Donal's connections stepped into earshot. There were only two of them. If this was all of them, that would mean there were five total, plus Vasily.

Five...

"You have what we want?" one called out.

"I need to see that you are who you say you are," I replied. "Show us the item."

One of the men—he had bright blond hair that shone in the moonlight—pulled a rectangle-shaped stone from his pocket and held it up. I could barely make out carving on it. It was the summoning phrase.

"We have the real one over here," I lied. "Did you bring the money?"

"Money?" the blond man said, smiling. "I think you misunderstand why you are here."

"I haven't misunderst..." I trailed off, that smile sticking in my brain.

Uneven. The right side happy, the left a little shy...

It all hit me at once.

I looked down at Helena, who still had her arms around me. She had a soft touch. So soft, in fact, that I didn't even feel her pull my knife free. But I felt when she stabbed me. That's a pain I'd never experienced before. Hot pain, cold shock. And the—worse still—the horrible realization that I'd been played.

All the inconsistencies between stories. All her looks. Her shyness. Five brothers and now five total members of some unknown gang. Those looks of horror hadn't been because I'd killed random people. She'd made them because I'd killed her compatriots.

But what did she want? What was Vasily's arrangement?

As I slid to the ground, hand pressed to my side, Vasily stepped forward and said, "We had a deal! You weren't gonna kill him! We—"

Helena moved fast. So unbelievably fast. Vasily was not a man to be trifled with, but she made him look like an amateur. She stepped close to him, her hand a blur as she stabbed him over and over in the chest. Had that been five times? Six? My partner stumbled back, hit the wall of the alley, then slid down. He grabbed at his chest as blood leaked from him.

Helena bent over him and went through his pockets. She pulled out his identification papers and stuffed them into her coat.

The blond brother stood over me, his own knife drawn. He dropped the stone he'd held up earlier, then grabbed my hair and put the point of the blade to my eye. "This is for my brothers," he said, then drew his arm back for a stab.

"No," Helena said. Was her voice soft? Far away? Maybe that was the blood loss and shock doing funny things. "Leave him be."

"But—"

"Touch him and I'll gut you from throat to crotch, brother," she said.

The blond brother snorted in disgust then walked off down the alley. Helena knelt next to me and set my knife down on the ground in the expanding pool of my blood.

"Vasily said you had a weakness for women." That smile again. It was still beautiful. She was still beautiful. "For a member of the police, you are so poor at reading people. So is your friend Vasily. I spent weeks with him—not the smartest man. You should know that he didn't want you dead, it's true. He didn't like you, and he was selling you out, but he didn't want you dead.

"I like you, Kristoph. Don't worry about killing a few of my brothers. They are dumb as bricks, and about as useful." She leaned in and kissed me. It was a spot of warmth in an encroaching cold. "You've done Belgracia a favor today. With your papers and Vasily's, we may just be able to get into Directorate S unchallenged. We'll take whatever your vault has and use it to declare independence. Thank you."

She got up and began walking away. She had only gone a few steps when she stopped and said without turning, "I hope we meet again under more honest circumstances. I think . . . I think we could have been special together."

Then she was gone.

I was losing a lot of blood. One look showed Vasily was at the edge of death. How long did he have? Minutes? His blood and mine together would be enough to draw a corpse-eater. I had no desire to see one of those ghoulish creatures break up from the ground, and I desired even less for it to mistake me for one of the dead and drag me back under with it.

As I moved to crawl away from the alley, my hand touched the summoning phrase Helena's brother had dropped. I grabbed it and held it up. Lead. As fake as her story. I put it in my coat pocket anyway.

I crawled. I crawled all the way north to Alexandr Prospekt. I had no help. I had no voice to call to the darkened houses surrounding me—not that anyone would come to help. I took a handkerchief from my pocket—the bright yellow one Helena had used early in the day—and shoved it against the stab wound. Then I shoved myself to my feet and shambled along the thoroughfare. I don't know how long it took me to reach Directorate S. How many times had I fallen, then gotten back up? I imagine I'd left quite the blood trail.

The guards outside were dead, wounds in their backs.

The front doors were wide open, and I made my way through them and down into the basement where the vault was. I encountered the occasional corpse. I couldn't understand why there were so few people inside, but then remembered Vasily and I were to be inside as well. But we'd been drawn out into the betrayal. The vault's doors were opened too, and inside were three blood-spattered bodies. One of them a Directorate officer, the others the remaining brothers. Their wounds were in the back as well.

Written in the blood next to them was, "For you, Kristoph."

I smeared the message with my boot. She knew I'd follow.

The room hadn't been ransacked. There was only so much one woman could carry, after all. But I knew she'd taken what few pieces of summoning phrases we had stored here.

Strength left my legs, and I collapsed.

❖　　❖　　❖

I woke up in a bed, Petra staring down at me.

"My darling, Kristoph," she said, dead eyes staring down at me. "You live." She leaned down and whispered in my ear, "The Chancellor is here to see you. Get your story straight." She kissed my cheek, then moved away.

Then the Chancellor was at my side. He had long, greasy hair and a hooked nose. His skin had the look of a person with a fever.

"Kristoph Vals," he said, tasting the name. "I need you to explain why I have dead Directorate officers and why I am missing valuables from the vault."

I took a moment to try and sit up. I knew right away it was a bad idea, but I needed a moment. I had a choice: lie or tell the truth. Get caught in a lie, and I'd be executed. Tell the truth, and maybe I'd be shot for incompetence. I opted to try the middle road.

"I suspected Vasily Bodlen was a traitor," I lied through clenched teeth. The pain was a great masking agent for the lies. I moved more to keep the pain fresh and real. "I thought, for weeks, he was working with freedom fighters from the remnants of Belgracia. With a woman named Helena Sarchev—at least I think that's her name; I just found out about her the other night."

Now for the tricky part. Stay close to the truth. Admit just enough error to keep below suspicion, but not enough to seem like I was untrustworthy and stupid. "I was fooled at first, Chancellor," I said. "She staged a mugging, which I thwarted. Then had two more of her people come to my home. I killed them as well. Petra cleaned it."

The Chancellor looked over his shoulder at the woman, who nodded. "Continue," he said.

"I found out where Vasily and Helena were meeting, overheard their plan, and tried stopping them. I killed Vasily, but got hurt in the exchange."

"Why didn't you get help?"

"Didn't know whom I could trust. If Vasily was compromised, then who else could be? It was my job to handle it without bothering you."

The Chancellor nodded again. So far, so good.

I told him where I'd left Vasily's body. "Maybe the corpse-eaters left it. I'm sure I left a blood trail another officer can follow. I got to our headquarters, found I was too late, and they were already in the building. I got down to the vault, found a dead guard and"—I grimaced in pain; had to sell this part—"I surprised Helena and the two men with her—I think they were her brothers—I killed them, but Helena used the distraction to get away. I'm sorry, Chancellor."

The Chancellor's fevered face split into a ghastly smile, and he began clapping.

"Vals, you certainly have a talent for stories and lies. I am impressed." When I began to protest, he held up a hand, cutting me off. "The trouble, Vals, is you aren't quite convincing enough. You don't fully commit. You lie without knowing all the facts. You say you killed your partner?" He waved a hand, and an orderly pulled a curtain open to my left. In a bed next to me was Vasily, very much alive. Unconscious, but alive.

"I assumed . . . I—"

"You assumed," the Chancellor said. "Never assume. If you are going to lie, you have to believe the lie like your life depends on it." He leaned in closer. "Because right now, Vals, it does. Do you understand what I am saying?"

I nodded. The threat was clear.

"Good." He leaned back in his chair, considering me. "Every story needs a villain and a hero, Vals. No exceptions. What I need you to do is choose your role. Let's clarify your story. Vasily, over there, actually was a spy working for Belgracian freedom fighters. You apprehended him while suffering a grievous wound. You then, while bleeding to death, followed the freedom fighters back to our building, where you managed to stop most of them. Does that sound like what actually happened?"

With Vasily's form at the corner of my vision, I nodded.

"Excellent. Isn't that excellent, Petra? I think we have found someone we can trust, don't you?" Petra nodded, a small smile on her lips. "Have no fear, Vals. The traitor, Vasily Bodlen will be severely punished for his crimes, and you will be rewarded as a hero to the Tsar. Belgracia, you said? Perfect. We'll execute every child there until they give up the freedom fighters.

"You have done us a favor, Vals," he said, and stood. He was a terrifying man, so I didn't say a thing. He reached into a pocket and pulled out a small pin— an open eye with two crossed swords behind it. He bent over my bed and affixed it to the lapel of my convalescence robe. "You no longer work for Directorate S. You work for me. Welcome to Section 7. I expect great things from you."

When he'd left and been gone for a few minutes, Petra returned to my side.

"Congratulations on your promotion," she said, and kissed my cheek.

"You work for him too?"

She met my question with a flat gaze. "Obviously. Can you make sure your lie becomes the truth?"

I hesitated. Then I said, "What lie?"

Petra smiled and winked at me. "Say that in the mirror a few times, just in case. You know what this means, don't you?"

"What?"

"Working for the Chancellor directly is different than being an officer for the Directorate. Greater scrutiny. The Chancellor expects nothing but harsh brutality from his agents. Your story of heroism plays to that requirement. It's an expectation now. Can you live up to that reputation of violence?"

I thought of my father, and the violence he'd inflicted on my mother and me when I'd been a boy. Like it or not, I was going to need to have more in common with him than I wanted.

"Without a doubt."

A Goddess in Red

Griffin Barber

Some nights, it is far easier to be an immortal monster than others. I don't complain in order to obtain a measure of sympathy that—if you knew the monstrous things I have done—would, of necessity, be false.

No, I merely state facts as I know them.

I see you misbelieve me. Perhaps I should let you decide then?

Very well...

"Honestly, I don't know what he sees in you," I said to my reflection in the mirror as I carefully managed the warmth, and by extension, rose of my cheeks. I was well-fed in those days, and preserving a healthy appearance was easy for one of my skill and experience.

My faithful servant of seven turns, Mennon, smiled from his position behind my left shoulder. I had a wonderful dressing room then. I remember little of the rest of the house on Sukep Row, but I so enjoyed the dressing room. A high-ceilinged corner chamber, well lit by floor-to-ceiling leaded glass windows that were only just coming into vogue at the time. Mennon was always sure to have some new gown or frock for me to wear, as well as fresh gossip from all walks of life.

I miss Mennon on occasion, and not merely for his ability to flatter. Good help is so hard to find. Especially if one is a necromancer, feared and loathed by so many ignorant souls.

"You are a great, ageless beauty, Select."

"None of that," I said. My practice of the Art of Necromancy had offended the traditions of the Select, and they'd revoked my membership long ago. Not long enough for the memory to lose its sting however.

"What, flattery?" he asked, knowing full well what I meant.

"Mennon, do not make me regret taking your oath." I did not need loose lips revealing my nature to the public at large. Most Select showed special vigor in hunting those expelled from their ranks. In order to preserve their monopoly as the only legitimate organization for training those with Talent, the Select were required to aid the temple witch hunters in hunting down Pathless. Some bastards enjoyed it.

His smile disappeared. "Very well, mistress. No more. But to your question: surely he knows, mistress?"

"Undoubtedly. Yet still he courts me."

Mennon made a flourish, as if to present my beauty before an adoring audience.

I sniffed derision, though I must admit the red gown set off the jet hair and golden eyes I had at the time to good effect, and the gown rewarded the efforts I made to ensure my figure was acceptable to modern tastes.

"Perhaps he has some ulterior motive?"

That gave me pause. I was not used to the unTalented seeking me out because of my practice of the Art. At least, not for its use. Normally, such unTalented persons sought my destruction, and met their own. The life of a necromancer is, of necessity, solitary beyond a certain point. Even those who have the Talent, who don't seek me out simply to destroy me, merely want to become my apprentice. Most hope to gather for themselves some measure of immortality.

Yezzul Flint was not possessed of Talent, though his fingers and nimble mind possessed a magick all their own. He was, in certain very small, very secretive circles, known as the greatest thief of his generation. Those circles also whispered that he was so favored of the god of thieves that he'd become a Shepherd of the Crooked Path. It was those same small circles, and their secrecy, that led to our association and, eventually, that evening's assignation.

"Perhaps he requires your help in some endeavor?" Mennon asked, daubing my favorite scent in the hollow of my neck.

"Perhaps."

Deciding I would learn Yezzul's motives in due course, I twitched the gown, settling it to check the fit. Pleased with the result, I gave Mennon leave to carry my compliments and a small gratuity to the tailor. He would, of course, skim, but then I prefer my servants corrupt. How else does one know which way they will turn in a crisis, oathsworn or no?

❖   ❖   ❖

"So then I said, 'Lady Setep may believe I was here solely to partake of her charms, but that doesn't make it so!' Her man pulled a blade, but I was already out the window and on my way by the time he had it ready."

Yezzul was handsome, his amber-green eyes were lively, and his style of storytelling even better than his stories, so I rewarded his efforts with a smile and an inviting look.

His eyes sparkled playfully in the candlelight. Had I a heart that beat without my iron control, I'm sure it would have skipped a beat.

I gestured at the golden brooch that had occasioned the story and raised my glass. "To stealing hearts as well as beautiful things."

Nodding, he raised his glass. "To beautiful things."

We drank. Wine has no effect upon me, but I find it salubrious to pretend, even among those that may know something of my nature.

At length, when I decided I had enough of wine, banter, and flattery, I looked at him from under lowered lashes and asked, "What do you want of me, Yezzul?"

He leaned in, kissed me lightly on the lips, and said, "If it pleases you to do so, we would share our bodies, and then . . ."

"And then?" I asked, stifling a yawn spawned in my doubt that he would furnish me with a novel response.

"And then . . . I will ask your assistance in a matter of procuring beautiful things without paying their owners."

I had a strong urge to devour him then. I didn't act on it however, simply watched him a moment, considering. He was pretty enough, and his banter creative, but what pleasures he could provide appeared limited by a lack of creativity. After the many turns of my unnatural existence, I grow bored with everyday happenings. And this time, I had even grown bored with the exercise of my Talent, something I hadn't thought possible. Time to continue the exercise and mastery of my Talent being my primary reason for seeking out immortality in the first place.

I must have been silent too long because he said, "You do not seem excited at the prospect."

I placed a hand on his cheek, ready to rend his unlined, youthful face should I decide to end him or should he become even more boring. His sparkling eyes stayed my hand. That, and the desire to learn what he thought should excite me.

"While you are a beautiful man, I have many beautiful things already. I also possess plenty of coin to purchase more, should I want, and making you some minor charm that will help you obtain more of the same scarcely appeases my desire for novelty."

He smiled all the wider, surprising me.

"Why do you smile?" I asked, unable to resist the urge to smile back.

He looked at me with those sparkling eyes and lowered his voice to a conspirator's whisper. "Well, Mistress Sunderhaven, I don't propose you make me some charm to ease my way, I want you along with me on the job itself. Indeed, I think you will find both the item I intend to obtain and the holder of it of . . . particular interest."

I gave a startled laugh when he told me what we would steal. A little while later, I gave him my body. A little after that, he told me who would suffer the loss. I laughed the harder. Before I let him slip into an exhausted slumber, we'd begun laying plans.

For the next season or so, Yezzul Flint sought to teach me the skills of a thief. I cannot say I was particularly gifted at any of the more technical disciplines, though I did apply myself diligently to learning what I could. I have a habit of, once interested, attempting to excel in a field of endeavor, so I came to resent the fact that Yezzul's time frame did not allow me the luxury to train beyond a certain minimal proficiency. I did manage to impress him with my ability to move quietly and, when in the dark, become part of the landscape when still.

The latter I suspect was due more to being a necromancer than any natural, inborn ability. If one does not require breath to sustain life, one does not make even the slightest movement to draw the eye. And since my limbs do not fatigue in the normal fashion, I could hold position for durations that even the most disciplined thief found impossible.

On learning of this ability to remain still for prolonged periods, Yezzul quickly began finalizing the plan with this new knowledge.

The irony was not lost on me: in search of diversion, I would have to submit myself to a period of inactivity so lengthy as to drive most people mad. Of course, I have been called mad before, on more than one occasion. And yet, I am still around to speak of the thin line between genius and madness, between the normal and the monstrous, while my accusers can no longer accuse anyone.

The only true difficulty I had with the training

was Yezzul's odd insistence that no one be hurt, let alone killed, in the doing of it. I mocked the idea at first, but he was firm about this one point, refusing to offer a reason.

One night that summer when there were nights warm enough to make stolen flesh half remember old desires, I took him to my bed again. When we were sated, I again asked why, and refused to accept half answers.

He smiled at me, those sparkling eyes making even my dead heart warm. "Because Istar, the Lord O' Sevens, requires it. Otherwise we on the Crooked Path are just like the noble-born, the gods-sworn, and the common robber who beats a man flat for a few smuts."

"What's that? Powerful?"

He shook his head, made the sign of sevens and said, "Merely violent. Taking what we want by hurting people... it's what they do. If we want his favor, we must hold ourselves to a better, higher standard, and accomplish by wit and nerve what others resort to the blade and fist for."

"But what happens when your wits fail you?"

He laughed and kissed my neck where it met the shoulder. "Why, then we run."

By the fall of that turn, Yezzul pronounced us ready. Within a tenday, final preparations were complete.

I was placed in a barrel bound for the Ducal Palace of White Boar as the Three Sisters rose in the night sky, silver and red slivers of their full selves.

A carter Yezzul had groomed for nearly a year took charge of me, rolling my barrel to his cart and up a wood plank to rest among the legitimate ones. He knew nothing, this carter, save where he was to leave me and what he would be paid for it.

The ride to the ancient palace was long and jarring, so I will not bore you further with details. Eventually, the cart stopped, closely followed by a muffled conversation that filtered through wood and lead as little more than a susurration at the edge of perception. I heard someone thump a barrel. I was not concerned. We'd expected the guards to make such checks.

A bit of shifting, and the cart jerked into motion again.

I confess to heaving a great sigh as we passed out from under the gates without incident. The lead sheathing surrounding me was not merely dead weight, it was intended to prevent the wards placed on the gates detecting Pathless monsters such as me trying to enter the palace.

Not that there are many Pathless like me. Necromancers have always been fewer in number in relation to the Soul-Mongers. The former require Talent and training in the Art, the latter only a thirst for power and an ear for the mutterings of some would-be god sent forth from the Pathless Dark.

As we crossed the new flagstones of the palace's servant court, the cart moved far more smoothly. Within a few moments we stopped again. More muffled talk, a clatter, then the cart shifted under me as the first of the barrels was rolled off. This wait was more nerve-wracking than the previous ones, as any accident that cracked my barrel would make for the type of interrogation that rarely ended well for anyone. The wait ended in another roll, this one far longer and faster than the previous one. Were I still subject to living frailties like dizziness, I would surely have lost whatever I'd last eaten.

The seemingly endless tumbling ended in a series of thumps, followed a while later by the sound of another barrel being placed atop mine. Were I a true devotee of Istar, I would have given a prayer of thanksgiving. As I was not particularly devoted to any god—old or new—save perhaps Hesh and her bloody-handed vengeance, I remained silent. Over the next few measures, I was jostled a few more times as barrels were placed in the cradles Yezzul's intelligence gathering had claimed were used. Then, nothing. Not for a long, long time.

I have, over the many, many turns of my unnatural existence, had to find diversion in otherwise dead—if you'll pardon the pun—boring circumstances. Time spent awaiting trial, for instance, is rarely filled with entertainments beyond the various tortures (most of them quite repetitive after the first few occasions) and tedious interrogations. I have learned, if forced to idleness for an especially long time, to simply cease all sensation and retreat into myself until a certain condition I decide upon is met. I barely mark the passing of time in this state, but I do not do this often, as it requires a great deal of energy to accomplish, leaves me vulnerable to certain *irritations*, and I wake quite ravenous, rendering me a trifle mindless.

So, while I was long accustomed to stretches of boredom, I was not entirely prepared for spending the better part of six days in a lead-lined barrel. Of course, at the time I did not know exactly how many days had passed in my prison, I found out later, when looking at the Three Sisters.

Working backward, I estimate it was sometime on the fifth day that I felt the barrel atop mine being rolled away.

I waited as long as I could, and then some, before pulling the lead sheathing at one end down and working my hands into the shallow holds carved into both heads of the barrel. Here again, Yezzul's planning paid off: the barrel heads had been threaded in place, allowing me to slowly open the barrel without breaking it or making much noise at all.

The cellar was very large and very, very dark. Old when the city beyond was a fishing village, this part of the palace was originally a squat, ugly fortress presided over by an equally ugly little robber. Not that I knew him personally. I may be old but I am not quite *that* old.

I stood and listened for a good long time, making sure no one was likely to walk in on me. Satisfied, I pulled the miniature lantern Yezzul's clever whitesmith had constructed for me and set about lighting it. I could have woven a lens of air to see with, but the concentration such a Working required might make me miss some essential detail. In short, I was still too new to the art of thieving to risk using the art I'd mastered by my seventeenth turn.

Seventeen turns young.

So long ago, even then. Some nights, the past is close enough I might touch it with but a passing thought, dredging forth implications and pains best left in the past. Other times it seems lost in an obscuring mist of present preoccupations—a mountain in fog—never fully visible, yet never fully gone from awareness.

Despite distracting memory, it took but a moment

to light the lantern. From there I spent nearly a full measure locating the door Yezzul had told me of. Part of the Old Palace, meaning the dungeon of the original castle, it was long forgotten by nearly everyone until Yezzul had, through a series of intermediaries, paid a fair amount of stain to obtain certain records from the Guild of Builders.

I examined the door for mundane alarms and, finding none, checked the stone lintel above. Nothing. No charm that might detect my nature or burn any intruder to ash. I smiled and went to work on teasing the lock open. The old, rusty mechanism needed more of brute force than tickling to open, but open it did.

The distant thump and clatter from somewhere else in the cellars made me shield the lantern. Slowly, I saw a ruddy glow resolve into lanterns held aloft by a pair of servants in search of something. I held still and prepared to evade them if I had to. I needn't have worried. After a brief search they collected a cask from another part of the cellar and departed, paying no attention to the disturbed dust at their feet or the monster watching from the darkness.

Once I could no longer hear them, I waited a full count of one hundred before trying the door. It resisted at first, but I pushed it all the way open, leaving a pile of the grayish dust stacked up like a static wave against the prow of a boat sailing some sickly ashen sea.

Pushing it back into position was far easier, though the door did let out a low, bellicose groan as it closed. Trusting that none were alive to hear the noise, I slipped inside the catacombs and began my search.

❖   ❖   ❖

I moved between staring skulls and grasping skeletal fingers, a tiny swaying island of light in an ocean of darkness that only gave up its secrets one dusty step at a time.

I am not sure how long I wandered the narrow confines of the palace catacombs, but I had to refill the lantern's small reservoir twice from the flask I'd brought along. I hoped enough remained for me to finish the job, as what I had to do next would require all my attention.

Unlike the palace catacombs where generations of sworn guardsmen and servants were entombed, the entrance to the ducal family crypt was well protected. An iron gate affixed to the stonework would have to be overcome before the stout, iron-bound door could be unlocked.

According to Yezzul's intelligence, both gate and door had locks designed by different locksmiths and, unlike the catacomb entrance I'd used, the lintel had two charms carved into it, one for detecting Pathless and one for destroying any unauthorized guests, Pathless or not.

The lock on the wrought iron gate proved simple enough to overcome, and the gate itself opened quietly under my hands.

Examining the positioning of the charms, I pulled a piece of the lead sheeting from my belt and started to work it by hand into the required shape. Getting the lead forms to come together required more patient experimentation than I am accustomed to, but eventually I had a stylized L-shape that would hang from the narrow upper lip of the lintel and cover the charm underneath.

Taking an entirely unnecessary deep breath, I cautiously pressed the upper part flush with the stonework above the lintel and then used my other hand to ease the lower part down until the bottom of the L covered the detection charm. I bent close to make sure the shield entirely covered it, then gently removed my left hand from the upper part. It remained in place.

I repeated the process for the other charm, but as I was letting up to see if it would remain in place, the damn thing fell. I was frustrated, not by its falling, but by where it landed: hard against the door and well under the lintel that marked the edge of the charm's ability to detect and therefore explode.

I could Work to move the thing toward me, but marshaling that much air would also disturb the dust around me for a considerable distance. I did not want to leave behind such obvious signs a Select was involved in the theft, at least not here.

I pondered the question a bit longer, examining the engraving that held the charm, considering unmaking and then remaking the thing after I had taken what I was here for. Eventually I dismissed the idea as too time-consuming. While there was time worked into it for delays, I did have a schedule to keep, and there were other obstacles to overcome.

So I settled on a complex Working, planning it out in my head. No mere pull: this time, I would have to form a structure of my Talent, something to channel the air in the directions and manner desired.

I seized the air beyond the door with my Talent and, feeding it through the tortured construct of my intent, anchored it in the windlass of my mind. Before executing my will, I did a final check of my preparations. Finding no imperfections, I allowed myself a moment to enjoy this new application of my Talent before I began the Working.

Responding to the machinations of my Talent, a wind began to build strength just beyond the door. It roiled into a furious knot a handspan above the ground, each knuckle of air building pressure as it bent back on itself.

Notoriously difficult to Work, air has qualities not unlike the energies of spirit I use to prolong my existence beyond that of mere mortals. I sometimes wonder if my early facility with air is the reason I found the Art of Necromancy came naturally to me—

Damn!

I had to stop woolgathering as my Working snagged ever so slightly on the edges of the energy contained in the star charm, dragging it out of form. I corrected the problem, double-checking my work.

Finding all in order, I released the air into the next phase. The lead form leapt away from the door on a gust of air to land at my feet. Dust riding the air rose from the floor to fill the space before me up to my waist. I tugged again with Talent, forcing the air to my will. The dust, far quicker than was natural, settled to the ground like fine-ground flour through a cook's sift.

I picked up the lead form and carefully tweaked it before replacing it on the lintel. It stayed put this time. Relieved, I set to work teasing the door lock open with the tools Yezzul had provided.

A measure I spent. Then a measure more. Had I a need to sweat, I would have been drenched in the stuff. As it was, I am surprised the air did not turn blue with the energy and strength of my curses.

I do not believe I have ever been so frustrated in my life. I, the Dragon of Filbain, the Dread Necromancer, the Death That Came to Carnoz, beaten by a few tiny pieces of iron that would not be arranged according to my will.

I discovered that screaming silently is nowhere near as cathartic as the more natural, audible ones. I resolved to kill every locksmith I came across as blood sacrifices to Hesh. I prayed to Istar for guidance. I even cursed his name.

Then, taking the tatters of my self-control in hand, I tried once more.

I was on the verge of breaking one of my picks when, with a click that sounded like the gates of paradise opening, the last tumbler fell into place and released the latch.

I put my head against the iron-banded wood of the door and wondered which of my preparations for the final bit of effort had done me the most good. I might want to repeat it the next time I was faced with such difficulty.

Deciding I would have no answer from the darkness, I climbed to my feet and entered the royal crypt.

The bones of the noble-born were not stacked one atop the other like their humble-born servants, but in stone sarcophagi carved in the likeness of those interred within. Finding the entrance to the royal crypt had been difficult, as Yezzul's research hadn't been very specific as to the door's location. Thankfully, his work gave me a good idea where the particular sarcophagus I sought lay, allowing me to move more quickly among the dust and bones.

I located the sarcophagus before I had to refill Yezzul's little lantern again. Stopping at her feet, or rather foot, I studied the final resting place of the Duchess of White Boar. The effigy of the woman within was remarkable: the craftsman that carved her likeness had spared her memory not at all. Every wrinkle, every wart, every swollen knuckle, the thinning hair on her head—even the one leg's failure to match the other for length after being lost in the last battle of a storied career—was represented.

There was a reason that even then, two hundred turns after the events known today as the Boar River War, everyone knew who was being referenced when "The Duchess" was mentioned.

She'd been taller when I knew first the noble-born. And in possession of both legs, naturally. Certain of my allies among the merchants of the city had convinced me to join them in petitioning for relief from her latest tax. Levied to fund the war, it had put a crimp that I resented in my lifestyle. The Duchess had been unmoved. We did not know how unmoved until the next night, when she sent her oath-sworn guard to seize us and, more important for her war, our assets.

I harbor no general prejudice against the noble-born, but I have been told I carry grudges a bit too far. And if that night of fire, blood, and looting is not deserving of revenge, by Hesh's sweet song, I don't know what is.

I slipped between her sarcophagus and that of her first husband's and examined her face—or, rather, her head. Atop it, just as Yezzul had said there would be, was a representation of the circlet he had given her on the birth of their first son, and that she'd been interred with as her dying wish.

The circlet I was here to steal.

Content I'd found the right place, I set about clearing the seam between lid and sarcophagus of the dust of two hundred turns. In the course of cleaning it, I found a pair of thin metal sheets of about a handspan in width sealing the lid to the stone of the base.

Yezzul had not warned me the seals would be here, but every necromancer of my experience knows such seals are sometimes imbedded with charms to kill the unwary grave robber when broken. I spun air into an oculus and bent to reexamine the seals. Unable to perceive the telltale glow of a charm on either, I released the oculus and spent some moments cautiously clipping through the soft metal. Once that was done, I contemplated the lift and how to accomplish it with a minimum of noise and effort. The iron pry bar I had would get me under the lid but was far too short to produce the necessary leverage for any natural person of my size to lift the lid.

Thankfully, I am no natural person. I resorted to the Art, channeling necromantic energies into the muscles of my hands, arms, back, hips, buttocks and thighs, causing them to swell and strain against my tunic and pants. I spent a moment ensuring I could control my new-made strength.

Taking hold of the pry bar, I pushed. The lid's slow rise was accompanied by a low grinding noise. Once I had it above the interior lip, I put my shoulder to the lid and pushed sideways with all the unnatural strength in my limbs. Too much strength, as it turned out: the lid slid all the way across, tipped, and fell to the stone floor with an echoing crash I could feel through my feet.

I cursed, froze, and listened for some response. Hearing none, I took the lantern from atop the husband's tomb and looked into the Duchess's sarcophagus.

The bony remains of the Duchess lay in state, cloth of gold robes covering withered, leathery limbs, her wizened head crowned with white hairs held in place with the jeweled circlet of gold I was there for.

It was then I heard the sound of a heavy door opening from somewhere deeper in the catacombs. Guards or Dreamers, my time alone with the Duchess and her jewels was limited.

Hesh did not love her devotees. Istar did not favor me, despite my keeping to Yezzul's rules. And the Duchess did not like guests. I know these things because of what happened next.

When I went to reach for her circlet, the Duchess's leathery eyelids clacked open, revealing white orbs. A malignant, sickly luminescence grew in them, shifting colors without ever steadying to one hue.

I have previously admitted to being a monster. In my time, I've been just as covetous of the better things in life as any other. But even I was impressed by the lengths that old, shriveled bitch had gone to in order to preserve and keep her property.

For a noble-born to invite a necromancer to imbue a carcass's dead flesh with the power to animate when certain conditions were met was almost unheard of. I could have done it for her at the time, had I but been in the region. Even then, I'd had no inkling the Duchess possessed the moral flexibility to engage someone steeped in the Art, let alone to allow someone to do this to her own body.

All these thoughts as well as a few choice complaints

and curses against the gods swept through my mind in the wake of my surprise.

The Duchess wasn't waiting for me to overcome my surprise. One withered arm snapped up, leathery hand closing on my wrist, thickened nails biting into my flesh.

I wish I could say I am immune to fear, but that would be a lie. I am, however, not overly concerned with the things that most people fear. Mine are the more refined fears—denial of my freedom, being burned alive again, the powers of certain god-sworn witch hunters, that sort of thing. That said, startle me sufficiently and those primordial, unrefined fears overcome all experience and intellect. The result is rarely enjoyed by those that startled me.

I yanked my hand back, forgetting the increased strength I had imbued in my limbs just moments before. Again, my flesh tore under the Duchess's long fingernails as I pulled my hand away, but this time I was not the only one to suffer. The outside of her forearm slammed against the lip of the sarcophagus and broke with a crack loud enough to echo through the catacombs.

The Duchess was sitting up, scarce appearing to have moved, reaching for me with her remaining hand. I say "remaining" quite deliberately, as the one she'd grabbed me with now dangled from the torn flesh of my hand, a macabre parody of a lover's handclasp.

Annoyed, as hands require an inordinate amount of focus and energy to repair, I brought the iron pry bar still in my other hand down on the limb now reaching for my throat. Another sickening crack resulted, and the Duchess was reduced to trying to bite me.

I leaned back and spent a moment lining up a strike at the Duchess's head that would not wreck the circlet.

Distantly, I heard guards calling one another as they began a search.

Awkward, the Duchess partially levered herself from her resting place and tried again to sink yellowed teeth into me. Taking the opportunity presented, I drove the pry bar up like a dagger, driving it deep into the dried flesh of her throat beneath the jaw and on into the skull above.

The light flickered in her eyes as the energies that sustained her shied from the iron suddenly interrupting its pathways. Letting nothing go to waste, and suspecting I might soon need the power for myself, I hastily constructed a siphon using the Art.

"Light, over there!" I heard someone cry. Ten paces away, a guard held a lantern aloft as he pounded toward me.

The Duchess's form rapidly took on the gray, lifeless texture of the soul-reaped, and fell into ashes and ruin under the weight of her circlet. My first, frustration-born instinct was to slay the guards, but my promise to Yezzul stayed my hand. I fled into darkness, leaving the Duchess's treasure behind.

Yezzul was not where he'd said he would be. Nor did he ever arrive.

I could bore you with the remaining details of my escape from the palace, but you challenged me on my assertion, so I will only say that I had to improvise my escape, that it took days longer than planned, and that, despite numerous provocations and rather a bit more hunger than I was wont to suffer, I took no one's life in my escape. I kept true to Yezzul's request that I hold to Istar's ways, even though I had failed to retrieve the circlet.

No, the basis of my assertion follows:

Hesh was high in the night sky, a full, deep red eye stalking her silver sisters by the time I returned to Yezzul's hideaway. Something heard as I took position in the casement of his bedroom window gave me pause.

Voices.

A woman.

And Yezzul.

I Worked air and summoned the sounds to me. Such was easier than manipulating the tiny bones and viscous fluid of the inner ear with the Art.

Yezzul's moans proved him near the edge. The woman's, too. I listened to them rut to completion, a small flame of anger lighting the deeps of my lifeless heart.

"But how do you know she didn't escape?" the woman asked, once the natural sounds of their entanglements had ceased.

The quiet chuckle I so liked...then: "The Duchess employed three Select to protect her tomb. One of which, it was later discovered—from the Duchess's own papers—was a necromancer of some power. So, even if Sunderhaven evaded all the obstacles I informed her of, I am confident the Duchess did for her."

"But the guards, they found no corpse."

"No. But they did find the circlet and there was dust and ash in the sarcophagus."

"Surely that only tells us that Sunderhaven fed from the Duchess?"

"Not likely. All my research indicates that necromancers cannot feed from the bodies of those long dead. Something about the spirit having left the body completely."

"Oh? Where did you learn that?"

"The Solamian Venator's library had it."

"They let you see it?"

"The temples have agreed that the witch hunters of all the gods, old and new, should coordinate their efforts. I passed on information to the Sun-God's Own, they reciprocated by allowing me access to their collected wisdom."

"But we of the Crooked Path do not cooperate with those on the straight paths."

"That is a *tradition* of the faith, not a tenet. I broke none of Istar's true tenets. Sunderhaven's own greed is what did her in, nothing more. I did not betray her to the authorities."

"Still, a Shepherd of the Crooked Path should not be so cavalier of our traditions."

"I agree," I said.

I did not recall entering.

I barely recall what the woman looked like as I crossed the carpets of his bedchamber. I remember cutting her screams short, just as I can savor, even now, watching the luster leave Yezzul's shining eyes as I consumed his soul.

Later, I returned to my senses in the midst of ashen carnage. I climbed from the window I had shattered and out into the light of Hesh. I would have cried had summoning tears from dead eyes not required more effort than it was worth.

Turning my face up and glaring at Red Hesh, I asked, not for the first time, nor even the last, "Why?"

The answer came in silence and from the dark corners of my black heart: I had, in my many turns, and no few Ages, come to believe I was immune to betrayal. That Hesh's bloody-handed vengeance served me, not the other way round. I was, once more, being punished for my insolence.

Some nights are made more difficult for an immortal monster.

Still, I persist.

Kuro

Hinkley Correia

A little before midnight on a cold, clear Saturday night in December, Kazue Hikubo should have been spending the night in the arms of a lover, taking in the Tokyo lights and dreaming about the future. Of course, he had neither a lover nor a future, but he had the lights and a half-finished bottle of scotch, so that had to amount to something. He sat in his dim office, with only his tiny desk lamp and the open window for illumination. His old radio in the corner picked up a local jazz station, the music soft and fuzzy with static.

On a night like tonight, he wished he could be like damn near anyone else in this cold city and go to sleep pretending that demons and spirits didn't exist. Unfortunately, he had a paycheck to earn, so here he sat, stuck at his desk, half-finished protection charms piled up on the side like overdue bills, threatening to fall off and scatter across the floor. He almost wished that they would, if only it gave him an excuse to put his job off for just a little while longer.

Kazue had a love-hate relationship with his job. On one hand, he had been practically born into it, so he had to admit that he was pretty good at it. Tokyo generally didn't believe in monsters, but that didn't bother the monsters one bit. Most of the time, he could appease his clients with a simple protection charm that didn't tax his abilities at all. Plus, actual supernatural cases often paid really well, if not by the client then by the Ministry of Supernatural Affairs. On the other hand, being born with the ability to see spirits and other people's memories was torture on his social life. Normal people generally thought of him as either crazy or a fraud.

He briefly wondered what would have happened if he decided to do what his brother did and run off to America. Misogi always had his head on right. Get away from the whole supernatural business, find a decent job that wouldn't land him in an asylum. Maybe find a nice girl to settle down with and forget his past. Of course, Misogi didn't have the family gift, which made it easier for him to escape. That and Kazue never had the talent for English that his brother did, despite all the phrases and mannerisms he had picked up from all the American TV he had watched over the years.

Loud static burst from the little radio, startling the detective out of his tired thoughts about job changes and sensible hours. He stood up and cracked his knuckles before smacking the little machine. The static still continued, albeit a slight bit clearer, before he sighed and turned the volume down.

In the racket, he almost didn't hear the knock at the door. Kazue inwardly cursed. Had he really forgotten to turn off the bright neon OPEN sign in his front window? He decided to ignore it, hoping that whoever it was on the other side of the door would take the hint.

No good, the knocking continued.

"We're closed." He half-yelled, hoping that they would just go away and maybe come back in the morning.

This didn't work either, as the knocking quickly restarted. With a sigh and a grumbled stream of profanity, Kazue went to answer the door.

He could tell from the oversized starlet sunglasses that she was going to be trouble. She had a certain air of sophistication: hair perfectly curled, makeup carefully done. If someone had told him that she had just gotten off the set of her latest movie, he'd be inclined to believe them.

He stepped back to let her in and forgot to speak as he gestured for her to have a seat. Her designer clothes stood out against his second-rate couch. A woman like her belonged on the cover of a tabloid, not the office of some so-called supernatural detective, yet she seemed unphased by the mess of his office.

The mystery woman opted to speak first. "You're Detective Hikubo, correct? The psychic? My name is Tsuyu Kobayashi."

Kazue reclined back into his own seat across from her, barely containing his tired sarcasm. "That's what it says on the front of the building. I can only assume that you're here for something very important if you're calling at this hour."

Tsuyu took a deep breath. "It's my brother." She spoke quietly, with an almost imperceptible stutter as she reached up to pull her sunglasses off. With her other hand, she swiped her gloved hand across the glistening line of tears that ran down her cheek. "He's missing."

Kazue fought not to gasp as an ice pick pierced his chest. Suddenly, it didn't matter that she had arrived in the middle of the night. She looked exactly like *her*. Same face, same lips.

The only difference were the eyes. Tsuyu's were dark, like two pools of ink. Shiori's eyes had been gray, like the storm clouds over a snowy city. If he had been a little less sober, he definitely could have mistaken the two.

Of course, he knew that Shiori was never coming back, but the resemblance shook him to his core.

He wanted to help her, even though helping someone just because they looked like your ex-wife was probably a bad idea.

"I'm sorry to hear that. How long has he been missing?" He spoke carefully, conscious of her feelings. If he was too blunt, it could upset her, making reading her emotions extremely difficult later.

She pulled a dainty cigarette case from her purse and snapped it open before removing a cig and placing it between her lips. Like an old habit, Kazue pulled his lighter from his pocket and lit it for her. Somewhere in the back of his mind, he knew that was a bad idea. His nieces from America were coming to live with him soon and one of them had asthma or something, but he just couldn't bring himself to care in the moment. This woman seemed to steal all attention away from his other thoughts.

Tsuyu took a long drag off her cigarette. "He's been gone for four days. I tried contacting the police, but they just said that he would probably show up within the next few days. I keep trying to call him, but he won't pick up."

"So why did you come to me?" That was the million yen question. Why come to a psychic when there were probably hundreds of detectives willing to take her case?

"My older brother, Touma." She pulled a photograph out of her purse and held it out to him. It trembled in the smoke-streaked air. "He was interested in the occult. I'm worried that he might have stumbled into something that he can't handle by himself."

Kazue took the photo and gave it a good once-over. It looked like an ID picture. It was a bit hard to believe that this man and the woman sitting across from him were siblings. Touma was obviously middle-aged, with a small, squished-in face and a confused and annoyed expression.

Kazue could easily imagine a guy like him pissing off some spirit.

He looked back to Tsuyu, who teetered on the brink of tears again.

This was a bad idea.

She seemed so very sincere.

"Alright, I'll take your case."

They decided to meet at Touma Kobayashi's apartment first thing in the morning. Since Kazue had no idea what he might be facing, he opted to bring Shinrinyoku, glamoured to look like an umbrella, and a pocketful of banishing wards. That was one of the few perks of working with the Ministry of Supernatural Affairs: a weapon specially enchanted to deal with monsters and spirits. Shinrinyoku was a *sasumata*, a large pole with a forked end, used mostly to keep distance between himself and whatever was attacking him.

The apartment building wasn't that good, but it was cheap. Kazue had looked the place up before going to bed. In all honesty, it was probably considered a steal, despite all the wear and tear that it had been through. In his first few scans of the place, he noticed only a few security cameras, and a single sleepy security guard who hadn't been working the night of the disappearance.

The pair of them crossed the worn carpet of the foyer and headed straight for the one working elevator. Kazue punched the call button and glanced around. No cameras. It would have been easy to walk out of here unnoticed.

"Do you come to this side of town often?" Tsuyu asked, her voice high and light, as if she were determined to be cheerful. Her hands still trembled, and Kazue could see her blinking rapidly as if she still fought not to cry.

He shouldn't have brought her... but she had the key.

"Only for work," he said, sounding shorter than he meant to sound. The elevator arrived and the doors slid open. He stepped inside and leaned back against the far wall, glancing around the interior as she stepped in with him.

"My brother liked it here," Tsuyu said, her voice quavering despite her cheery tone. "I was never sure why."

When they got off the elevator, Tsuyu immediately started walking down the maze of hallways, a determined look in her eye.

"This is it," she said, stopping before one of the identical doors that lined the corridor. She put the key into the lock and turned the knob with a satisfying *click*.

"Let me," Kazue said, stepping forward to enter before she could. She followed him in. Then, as he'd made her promise before they entered the building, she promptly sat on the couch to stay out of his way.

Touma's apartment itself gave a weirdly impersonal vibe. It felt more like an unused hotel room than an actual apartment. The kitchen was spotless, and there weren't any dishes in the sink. Kazue could see hardly any personal belongings: only a few pictures of Touma with his parents and an older laptop.

Kazue stood in front of the laptop and concentrated, reaching out with that sense he had. Memories pooled around the keyboard: strings of characters; images of screens; movement patterns of fine, typing skill.

The detective leaned forward and typed in the passwords as they came. Sure enough, Touma's social media sites opened up one by one.

The man wasn't particularly interesting on the internet either. He only rarely posted on social media and the occasional forum. The only place he seemed to regularly interact was an occult website. From what Kazue could read, Touma really was passionate about the supernatural. The detective briefly scanned the actual charms and phenomena just in case this turned out to be an instance of ritual gone wrong. Unfortunately, the worst that would happen if any of these charms had been done wrong was that the user would have bad luck for a couple of weeks.

He glanced around the apartment again. "Hey, Tsuyu, does your brother always keep this place this clean?"

Tsuyu was rooting through her purse before pulling out a lipstick and applying it. She was obviously trying to recall all the times she had been there. "As far as I remember, yeah. He usually works an eight-to-nine, and he works overtime a lot. I think it's just because he's never home."

Kazue concentrated again, pulling memories from the air around him. Touma Kobayashi wasn't the kind of guy who was going to leave his mark on the world. He'd graduated in the middle of his class from a no-name school, working as a midlevel accountant for a big-name manufacturing company. No family outside of his sister, no real friends aside from the occasional drinking buddy from work, and his online presence suggested a definite lack of a girlfriend. It seemed he was yet another faceless salaryman in the sea of millions, destined to live and die and be forgotten within a few generations.

Yes, Touma Kobayashi had never really left an impression anywhere that he had been, which meant that tracking him down was going to be a real pain in the ass. Kazue thrived off of being able to see other people's memories. If no one had any real memories of the guy, he would never be able to figure out where he went.

Kazue continued his search in the cabinets, looking for any kind of clue. Both the pantry and the fridge were almost empty, with the exception of various microwave foods and a jug of milk that was quickly approaching the expiration date. Inspection of the cabinets revealed one of them was completely filled

with bottles of different kinds of alcohol, quite a few
of them unsealed. It looked like Touma liked to drink.

There were two logical possibilities: either Touma
had been kidnapped, or he had willingly dropped
off the face of the earth. Both raised more questions than they answered. If he'd been abducted,
then that meant someone deliberately targeted him,
and that he was in danger. On the other hand, if he
was hiding, then he was probably in a lot of trouble
with someone else. The two groups that immediately
jumped to mind were the government or the yakuza.
Either way, it meant way more trouble than Kazue
was getting paid for.

Well, wherever he was, he probably wasn't dead.
The apartment didn't feel lived in, but the shadow of
death hadn't crept in yet. It always happened when
someone—usually the owner or other occupant of the
home—died, though if another person had been close
enough with the rest of the family or had spent enough
time there, it would affect the place, too. The feeling
was also almost always immediate, forming as soon as
someone found out or, in Kazue's case, as soon as the
person had died. Generally, the feeling would fade
when someone new moved in, but in more extreme
cases, the aura lingered, attracting other yokai.

There was a loud crash from the next apartment,
followed quickly by muffled cursing. The walls must
have been pretty thin, meaning that if there was
any struggle, someone definitely would have noticed.
That ruled out any theory of Touma being forcibly
removed. If he had been kidnapped, it probably didn't
happen here.

Scanning the old energies, he made his way to the

only bedroom in the tiny apartment. From everything he could sense, Touma was just following his daily routine the day he disappeared. There was no sense of urgency, except for worrying if the train would arrive on time. If anything, he seemed quite pleased with himself. Maybe he had done well at his job the night before. Either way, it was not the feeling of someone who knew he was in danger.

The bedroom was tiny, like all the other rooms in the house. A queen-sized bed was squeezed in between a nightstand and the wall. The bed was impeccably made, sheets perfectly straight. Judging by the scent, they had been recently washed and not slept in. Kazue opened the nightstand drawer, praying that he wouldn't find something awkward. Instead, he found a matchbook with the name "The Boiling Note" emblazoned on the front. Looking inside, there were seven matches in it, though it looked like there had been ten originally.

It wasn't much of a clue, but it was the only clue he had.

Despite all the eyelash fluttering, Kazue opted to leave Tsuyu behind rather than take her to a shady bar. Along with regular drunks and other potential creepers, the Boiling Note was located in a hotbed of supernatural activities, being near one of the big rifts in Tokyo where spirits and monsters could easily pass into the human world.

The place itself was actually fairly easy to find. It sat out on one of the main streets, sandwiched in between two much larger and more popular buildings. At least he didn't need to go through any winding back alleyways, where he would inevitably get lost or have a complication with another yokai.

After a few more moments of staring at the old building, Kazue opened the front door.

The soft sound of jazz floated through the smoky air of the bar. Grime stuck to the floor like a shadow, and a thin film clung to the pictures on the wall. The photos were taken in better days, with local celebrities from almost 150 years ago. Dim red lights illuminated the current patrons, both mortal and yokai alike. Glamours were either faded or too easy to see through, and the humans were either too drunk or apathetic to care.

Kazue honestly couldn't blame them. The Boiling Note wasn't the kind of bar you went to looking to have a good time. It was the kind of place you wound up after losing either your job or your wife, to drink until you woke up in Osaka missing your wallet.

He quickly scanned the bar and sat right down in front of the bartender, setting his "umbrella" to the side. He may be here on business, but that didn't mean he couldn't have a little fun. Besides, maybe the only way to get information out of the bartender was to get his trust by ordering drinks. A man could only hope.

"What can I get for you, Detective?"

That gave Kazue a start. He was pretty sure that he had never been in this particular joint before, but he never knew with places like this. When Shiori had left him, he had been in and out of whatever cheap bar would serve him for almost a year. That entire period of his life was spent blacked out, so it was *possible* he could have frequented this place before.

The man across the counter seemed to already know him, so Kazue shrugged. No harm in asking at this point. "I'm sorry, but do I know you?"

The bartender only smiled. "No. Of course not. But I know you. I know everyone."

Kazue took the time to actually look at the man behind the counter. He came across as supremely nondescript. His face looked middle-aged, maybe just a bit on the youthful side, but his eyes had an ancient quality that seemed to pierce straight into his soul. The detective's eyes wandered back to the old photographs on the wall with more attention. The bartender was in almost every single one of them, including the ones from a century ago.

"Your wife is a Yuki-onna, is she not?" The man was casual, as if he hadn't just asked Kazue about a thing very few people knew of. Not to mention he'd just dropped any façade of this being a regular human establishment.

That settled it for the detective. "What are you?"

The man only laughed. "I doubt that you would have ever met something quite like me, and if you have, you probably wouldn't associate them with myself. Now, a good bartender is always willing to lend an ear."

The tiny voice of his common sense spoke up in the back of his mind, wondering why a complete stranger would care so much or why he should spill all of this to him, but the soft music and warm air of the bar drowned it out.

For the first time in a long time, Kazue relaxed. Actually relaxed, not just stayed in bed because he didn't want to face reality. "Shiori and I first met in the Okuchichibu Mountains. I had been asked to find and exorcise a ghost that had been getting hikers lost and attacking them. A snowstorm had come in, and I wound up off the trail and lost. That's when I met her. She was by far the most beautiful woman I had ever seen. She led me back to the trail, made me promise to never tell anybody, and I didn't see her again for another six months. Of course, I recognized her, but I didn't say anything. We started to get to know each other, and pretty soon, we were in love and married before the year was out. But then I had to be an idiot and tell. I broke the promise . . . and made her leave because of it."

Now he just felt exhausted. Part of him wanted to cry, but he reminded himself that he came from a long line of samurai who had been able to remain stoic in the worst of situations. That and he was in a public place, and that would just be embarrassing. Despite this, he had to blink the tears out of his eyes before they fell.

The man across the bar was now wiping out dusty shot glasses. "Of course, what you want, what you truly want, is something only you can repair, but I would be more than happy to assist in your investigation. I am more than willing to answer any question you might have. Kobayashi-san was a regular and I would quite like to see him return. Of course, I believe your ability would be far more useful than most answers I can give."

Kazue could only nod. He supposed that the bartender really did know everyone. He closed his eyes and concentrated on the other world parallel to his own.

The air was so thick with magic it practically buzzed, each unique energy mixing and spinning like some kind of whiskey cocktail. The bartender's magic spread from behind the counter and encompassed all the others in a presence that seemed to comfort and relax. Flickering in and out of all of them were the last traces of Touma's memories from about four days before: the last day anyone had seen him before his disappearance. The magic was wispy and would probably be gone when the sun rose in the morning.

The detective took a deep breath and pulled on the energy like pulling a loose thread from an old shirt. Unraveling from the ambient magic of the bar and the thick presence behind the counter, the memories were flickering in and out of existence. He would have to be careful if he didn't want them to disappear altogether. Images slowly started to filter in and out of focus, fuzzed and blurred with age and alcohol.

The memories were golden and happy, and not just from Touma's inebriated state. Sitting across from him was an extremely pretty woman. Kazue briefly recalled seeing her face on some kind of billboard, releasing some kind of album, but he could not for the life of him remember her name. This mystery woman was smiling and openly flirting with Touma. Warning bells immediately went off in his mind. A pretty, famous singer had come to a little hole-in-the-wall and decided to flirt with Touma Kobayashi, of all people.

Somewhere behind him, the front doors burst open, yanking him out of the memories that weren't his own.

Two men filed in, one human and the other an Oni, both with suits and a nasty look in their eye. The seven-foot-tall Oni ducked his massive shoulders as he stepped through the door frame. His glamour was so flimsy that it definitely couldn't pass the legal test. Not that Kazue was going to go and arrest a guy that was over a foot taller than him without backup. The other was human, probably no older than twenty-five. He had that cocky air that only youths possess, and lots of magic pushed inside the bar with him.

They sat on the two barstools to his right, setting off alarm bells in his head. They weren't looking at him though. Instead, they focused on glaring at the bartender.

Kazue glanced to the fabric bundle at his side. If things got too dicey, he was more than prepared to make a dramatic exit. Not that he thought it would actually come to that. These guys probably weren't supposed to be in here, legally or not. The Oni may have been huge, and the kid may have had magic, but even the strongest stuff he could summon would be nothing but a sparkly parlor trick in comparison to whatever the bartender could do with a snap of his fingers. He could only hope that the two wouldn't start anything because that would only mean more paperwork in the morning and he was already planning to be hungover when he woke up.

The kid leaned forward in his seat. "We're looking for a woman."

The bartender just chuckled and kept wiping the dirty shot glasses. "Aren't we all?"

The kid bared his teeth, even though he held an arm out to hold the Oni back. "Cut the shit, old man. You know who we're talking about. The Hone-onna that set up shop nearby. The one that's been picking off our men."

That piqued Kazue's curiosity. A Hone-onna, also known as a Bone Woman, was somewhere in the neighborhood. Of course his mind jumped to her as a suspect, but from what he remembered off the top of his head, they didn't leave their particular haunts. Unless this one was particularly strong, she should only appear in her lover's home.

A loud bang filled the room as the Oni slammed his hand on the counter so hard he cracked the wood. Now the rest of the patrons were almost completely silent and looking hard in their direction. Kazue let out a sigh. If this continued, people would definitely notice that the unnaturally tall guy wasn't human, which could potentially result in an incident. And since he was technically an agent of the government, he was required to step in if it looked like it would turn into a problem.

He flashed his badge at the two. To most other people, the initials MSA meant absolutely nothing, but almost everyone connected to the supernatural world recognized them on sight.

"I'm going to have to ask you two boys to leave. You're disturbing the peace." Looking specifically at the Oni this time, he lowered his voice and said, "Your glamour doesn't conform to the legal specifications. Go home and fix it now, and I'll let you off with a warning."

The Oni growled, but the young man clicked his tongue before grabbing his friend's arm. "Come on, Motonao, we're going."

Chatter resumed the second the door was fully closed behind them.

Kazue leaned back in his chair. "Mr. Kobayashi left

with a woman the night of his disappearance. Would you happen to know where they went?"

The bartender smiled again. "But of course."

Maybe at one point the neighborhood had been lively, but tonight it just seemed dead. This street wasn't exactly a great part of town, so he at least expected some homeless people, if not a couple of teenage delinquents, but the area seemed to be completely devoid of life. There was nothing around spiritwise, either. On any other night, on any other case, it might have given him the slightest amount of relief, but tonight it just set him on edge. He was not welcome here.

Kazue took a deep breath and focused. Touma's path laid out almost perfectly in front of him, the line glowing and flickering like a dying candle. He could see the effect of alcohol in the way the trail swayed around and sometimes vanished completely before reappearing a few feet later. Every so often, it would turn a corner, winding through the dark neighborhood like a maze.

Eventually the trail stopped at a house. It was plain and undecorated, same style as all the others lining the street. The only thing that set it apart was the sign in the front that was definitely nailed in before the first snow started. Kazue, as quickly as possible, took his hand out of his pocket and brushed off the front side of the sign, just enough to see the "For Sale" and the number for the poor realtor that was charged with selling the joint. He took the number down, just in case it might be important for him in the future.

A single set of footprints led up to the front door.

The yellow line cut off right in front of the door. It didn't fade out or flicker away, it just stopped. Like it hit a wall. Now that he was close he could already tell that the feeling of death had settled in, and it had been there for a while, mixing in with the remnants of old charms and wards.

Kazue reinforced his mental barriers and tightened his hand on his "umbrella." Hopefully, the building was just as dead on the inside as it was on the outside, but he wasn't willing to be reckless. He checked the door, and it opened with no resistance, further fueling his worry.

If he hadn't known any better, he would have thought that he stepped into a meat locker. Somehow, the temperature had dropped a few more degrees from the freezing cold outside, like someone had seen the snowfall and decided to turn on the air conditioning. The only light came from the open door, and the house echoed with stillness. The living room and kitchen were completely devoid of any furniture, and he wasn't expecting much from the rest of the house. Judging by the thin layer of dust, nobody had been here for quite a while.

It would probably be a good idea to stop and come back in the morning, but the idea of closing the case tonight to go to bed without worries was far more tempting. He turned on his flashlight and began to carefully creep through the abandoned house. He placed his feet carefully, so as to not let the floor creak under him, and he was especially cautious not to shine his light directly in the windows.

Even if there was nothing here, the last thing Kazue wanted was to be arrested for trespassing—again. The man in charge of paranormal incidents here was a smug little bastard, and he would never hear the end of it. That, and he really didn't want to spend the night in a jail cell, considering he didn't have anybody to come bail him out. Last time it had happened, he had been a teenager on a case from a pretty girl, and Misogi had to pick him up. His older brother lectured him the entire way home, but at least he hadn't told their father. Good times.

He quietly continued through the house, carefully checking each of the rooms one by one. The aura of death had definitely settled in, seeping into all the corners of the house, but it was getting stronger the closer he was getting to the bedroom. Thick, black miasma seemed to leak from the bottom and the edges of the door. Kazue held Shinrinyoku in front of him, dropping the glamour.

His sasumata was old-school, especially in comparison to the ones regular law enforcement used. The pole extended to just over the length of his arm, though it could telescope out further, ending in a thin fork. Just before the split, several rows of nonlethal spikes jutted out. The tips of the weapon could cut someone if he wasn't careful, but it wasn't supposed to be a deadly weapon. It was designed to keep whatever he was fighting a good distance away from him so he could use wards and perform exorcisms.

With a grimace, he grabbed the doorknob and twisted. The aura clung like sludge, despite not really being there, but the second he got the door open all the way, it seemed to dissipate. Like it had realized it had been beaten and could no longer hide what was inside. And boy, what was inside was a piece of work.

There was a large lump in the center of the room.

Taking the forked end of his weapon and twisting it into the fabric, he yanked the lump over. Recognition hit him like a hammer.

"What the hell?"

It was Touma Kobayashi, lips far too blue and skin far too pale to belong to any living being. His eyes were squeezed shut and his lips were open just a crack in a painful grimace. He was still wearing the suit he went to work in, thin and definitely not protective against the dangerous cold. Of course, it was impossible to get an approximate time of death because of the temperature, but from what he learned at the apartment, Touma probably hadn't been dead for long. Meaning that he had probably been there for several days before death.

Kazue began to dial in the number for the police. This hadn't been accidental, and human murder was very much out of his jurisdiction. As much as he wanted to be there and be the one to help his client, he was far too late. Detective or not, this was now the police's problem. He was about to hit the call button when Touma made a horrible, pained groaning.

He was alive.

Kazue quickly deleted the number he had typed in and instead typed the number for emergency services. The operator was calm, calmer than he was as he explained what had happened and where he was. The operator gave him instructions to sit tight and explained that the ambulance would be there shortly to get them. Kazue thanked them before hanging up.

Once he had done that, he dialed the number for the MSA. Yes, this was attempted murder, and they would probably force him to give the case to them, but the supernatural was still involved and who- or whatever did this was probably still out there. After giving his name and identification number, he was connected to an actual agent. After explaining his case and what he had discovered, he was assured that a squad car would be there in no time to back him up.

Touma groaned again, and Kazue shed his coat to put over the other man like some kind of blanket. He had no idea if this would actually help, but he needed him alive for at least another few minutes, maybe longer, before the actual professionals could take a look at him.

The cold was biting. The almost complete lack of sound made it even worse, as he didn't have anything to focus on. He would love to ask the found man some questions, but Touma was barely conscious. Instead, Kazue focused on the energy around him. Aside from the feeling of death, he could sense the past energy of old protective charms. When he had entered earlier, it hadn't bothered him. Now that he had time to think about it, however, it seemed odd. They were obviously well made considering that they still stuck around for this long. Maybe the owner was really interested in the supernatural.

Kazue pulled out his flip phone for the third time that night. He would have preferred to call her once he knew where Touma was going, but he honestly didn't have anything better to do.

"Ah, Detective. What can I do for you?" Tsuyu's voice was airy and completely relaxed.

"I found him." It was hard to keep the pride out of his voice, but somehow, he managed it.

"What?"

"Your brother. I found him. He's hurt, but an ambulance will be here soon and you'll be able to see him."

"Oh. I see." She sounded surprised. Kazue figured it was because of how fast he found him, considering that they had started looking that morning.

A sharp creak echoed through the small house, then another. It was too loud for it to be the building settling. There were no sirens or lights from the ambulance, and an MSA agent would have announced themselves if they were coming in.

"I'll call you back." He then flipped the phone shut and tightened his grip on Shinrinyoku.

Kazue crept through the house looking for the source of the noise. Peering around a corner, he saw the kid and the Oni from the Boiling Note. They were obviously looking for something, or someone.

He stepped around the corner. "Freeze. Hands where I can see 'em."

They did not freeze. Instead, they looked at each other, the kid giving the Oni a little nod, and they both rushed him. Kazue ducked the Oni's punch, but the kid managed to hit him in the shin, sending him to the ground. He shoved his sasumata at the kid's leg, catching it and sweeping it out from under him.

He scrambled to his feet, avoiding another punch that skimmed his ear, and aimed his own punch to the Oni's neck. It connected, but did not have the desired effect. Instead of spluttering for air, the demon only growled and punched him very hard in the chest.

It knocked the air out of him, but he swung the flat end of Shinrinyoku as hard as he could at the

Oni's face. It didn't knock him down, so he did it again and again. The fourth hit finally sent him to the ground.

Kazue didn't particularly like using his active ability. It required a lot of power that he didn't usually have to use, especially when neither thing was made of metal. Unfortunately, the Oni was just going to get back up again if he didn't use it, so he didn't exactly have a choice. He let the power well up in him, focused on both the yokai and the floor he was on, and magnetized the two together.

In any other circumstances, it would have been comical to watch the massive demon struggle to get off the ground, but he still had other fish to fry. Magic moved and he heard the crackle of electricity behind him. Kazue turned to see the kid, having stood up from his little tumble, with thin bolts of lightning dancing in between his fingers.

Kazue silently cursed. He didn't have enough power to use his active a second time, and the kid was wielding electricity when his weapon was a long metal pole. Kazue had a dispersion charm, but that would only do so much. Suddenly, gravity shifted and forced the kid to his knees, and the power he had been gathering dissipated.

Several men in business suits rushed in, handcuffing both the Oni and the kid, arresting them for the kidnapping and attempted murder of Touma Kobayashi. The Oni stayed mostly silent throughout the ordeal, grunting when the MSA agents tried to ask him any questions. The kid, however, was pissed, and they had to drag him kicking and screaming out to the inconspicuous squad car outside.

The ambulance arrived almost immediately after the others drove off. Paramedics made Kazue wait outside and out of the way; he watched them load Touma's stretcher into the back. One paramedic stopped to ask him if Touma had any family or friends they needed to call.

He only smiled and gave them Tsuyu's number.

"Alright, thank you for your time."

Kazue sighed as he hung up the phone. He called the realtor of the house where Touma was found, but the only thing he had learned was why nobody wanted to buy the house. Basically, it was the first home of a newlywed couple that ended in tragedy. The wife was killed in a drunk driving accident and the husband died soon after of a mysterious illness.

While the easy thing to do would be to blame it on the two troublemakers, something nagged at the detective. It just didn't seem to fit, and if he had learned one thing in all his years of being a private investigator, it was to trust his instincts. So there he was, still working a closed case with nothing but a gut feeling and a bottle of whiskey.

A knock at the door broke him out of his thoughts. This time, he had made sure that the sign was off, so whoever it was knew what they were doing. He got up to answer the door, curious and more than a little annoyed at whoever was calling at this hour. He hadn't planned on going to sleep any time soon, so he wasn't really out anything, but he still wanted to work on the case.

He opened the door to find Tsuyu, dressed in a fur coat and wearing a demure expression.

"You already paid me my fee."

"Yes, but I wanted to thank you *personally*, Hikubo-sama." She entered and headed straight for the bathroom. "Allow me to change into something more comfortable."

He looked at all the old pictures on his desk, memories of a happier time long since passed. Photographs of his family before they had gone their separate ways.

A small ringing of his cellphone broke the silence. Part of him wanted to just put it on silent and throw it somewhere it couldn't bother him, like he had done with a lot of things in his life, but he did check the caller ID first. Probably a good thing he did, considering it was a call from the hospital. With more than a little reluctance, he hit the answer button.

"Detective Kazue Hikubo, Hikubo Psychic Investigations. How can I help you?"

The woman on the other end was clearly tired and obviously didn't want to be there, false politeness lacing her tone. "Hi, I'm from the Tokyo Medical University Hospital, calling about Mister Touma Kobayashi. There's been a problem with the emergency contact you provided, the one for Miss Tsuyu Kobayashi."

That was weird. He was sure that he gave them the right number. Kazue tried to not let the confusion edge into his voice. "What's the problem with it?"

"When we checked the records, it turns out that Mr. Kobayashi doesn't have any sister listed."

This information was decidedly not good. Kazue was quiet, thinking up a lie that wouldn't raise too much suspicion. "Ah, yes, well, I must have made a mistake somewhere. Tell you what, I'll find the number of the girl and call you back."

He then quickly hung up with no intention of calling the hospital back. Hopefully, they wouldn't care enough to follow up, and if they did, he could come up with a different lie that would keep them off his back for good.

Kazue ran through all the information in his head again. Tsuyu Kobayashi had come in with a kidnapping story without involving the police or an actual private detective. The victim, Touma Kobayashi, was a faceless businessman who had an interest in the occult and had been frequenting a bar known to be a stomping ground for the paranormal. Then, while at said bar, a beautiful woman who looked exactly like a famous singer came in and flirted with the unremarkable man. Enough that she presumably got him to meet at a secondary location, presumed to be haunted by a newlywed couple, where she left him for dead. Kazue had gotten there in time to save him, which surprised Tsuyu, who seemed insistent that he was alive. Now he gets a call saying that, according to the paper trail, Tsuyu didn't exist. Tsuyu, who looked almost exactly Shiori, despite her being a yokai. Tsuyu, who looked exactly like his former lover. Tsuyu, who was currently in his office trying to seduce him. And that's when it all clicked.

Exactly one phrase seemed to fit this situation perfectly. "Oh, shit. *Oh, shit.*"

He rushed to the door to get his weapon, only the door slid open before he even had a chance to reach the handle. Faster than he could react, the forked end of Shinrinyoku hit him in the chest, knocking him back into his desk, sending both himself and the stack of half-finished charms onto the floor. The next strike pinned the detective to the floor by his neck. There was just enough space between the metal and skin that he could breathe, but only just barely.

Tsuyu crouched down next to him, a smile that was just a little bit too wide on her face. "You remind me so much of my husband. Always so excited about the paranormal. It's cute, watching guys like you talk about the impossible and then watching your faces when you realize that you're way in over your head."

Kazue stayed silent, eyes scanning the room, looking for anything that could help him. There had to be a way out of this. He just needed to figure out what it was. His eyes rested on the paper charms just within reach. They were minor protective charms, but a little shift in energy would be able to charge one enough to actually hurt her. Now all he had to do was to distract her.

"How many? How many have you killed like this?" If breathing was hard, then talking was even harder.

Tsuyu's grin widened. "Oh, I've lost track. It got hard to keep track after—"

Kazue didn't wait for her to finish. In one fluid motion, he reached for the charm, charged it with as much power as he could muster, and smacked the woman. A horrible screeching filled the room as Tsuyu's glamour faded. Bits of skin began to slough off, leaving a bleached grinning skull: the true visage of a Hone-onna.

He began to pull on the pole that still pinned him to the ground. The spikes dug into his hands but it wouldn't be anything that couldn't heal with time. After a lot of pain and quite a bit of wiggling, he managed to force the sasumata out of the floorboards.

As much as he wanted to just lie there on the ground and catch his breath, he still had a demon serial killer in the room with him. With more than a little struggle, he rose to his feet and tried to maneuver Shinrinyoku into a proper fighting position. By the time he managed that, Tsuyu had mostly gotten over her freakout, and now she looked *pissed.*

She lunged for him, hatred in her eyes, and scratched his arm enough to draw blood. Kazue briefly mourned the loss of one of his good shirts before aiming for the demoness's neck. He believed in karma that way. She dodged, but a quick adjustment allowed him to hit her right shoulder. All he needed to do was to keep her away long enough to send her back to Hell.

The words for the banishment clumsily tumbled out of his mouth, years of misuse finally catching up with him. Tsuyu twisted her body out of his hold, and she began to rush him again, long, bony fingers poised to scratch and cut. Before she got nearly close enough to him, however, a small blue flame caught on her fingertip. It quickly spread across her hand and then her arm, consuming her whole body in the blink of an eye.

Soon, the only evidence of her presence was two large gashes in the floor and the rest of the mess around the office. Banishment was by no means a permanent solution, not like the way a proper exorcism was, but it would keep her from hurting people for a long time.

Kazue Hikubo looked around the complete mess that was his office and sighed. He was going to have to make a few phone calls.

Sweet Seduction

Laurell K. Hamilton

I huddled over my coffee like it was the last sure thing on earth. It wasn't, but since I hadn't been to sleep in almost twenty-four hours, the warm, rich scent seemed more real than the people sitting on the other side of the desk. Or maybe I just liked the coffee better than the two tall, fashionable women sitting across from me. I admit that part of my crankiness was they hit a lot of my issues. They were both nearly six feet tall, vaguely Nordic, and blond: three things I would never be. I was built like my mother, who had been Mexican, as in first generation born in America. The only hint that my father looked more like the two women than me was my skin, which was so pale it really was almost white. I was actually paler than the women. The younger one had a light gold tan, and I couldn't tan at all. I'd inherited my father's Germanic skin, but my curves, my long curly black hair and the deep brown of my eyes were all my mother's. I was also five foot three, a couple of inches taller than my mother, but that wasn't the Mexican heritage, that was just because my mom's family was short. The two women reminded me of my stepmother Judith, who my dad had married after my mom died. Judith had never let me forget that I wasn't like the rest of the family. I was over thirty now and still hated her for it and resented my dad for not protecting me from it.

"Miss Blake, are you listening to me? I told you my grandson is in mortal danger from this money-grubbing hussy."

I hadn't heard the word hussy in maybe a decade and that was from my grandmother, but then Mrs. Chadwick was over seventy, though thanks to fabulous makeup and what I suspected was even more fabulous cosmetic surgery, she certainly didn't look it.

I raised my gaze from my coffee cup to Mrs. Robert Chadwick who sat nearly painfully upright in the client chair. It was a comfortable chair, but she sat in it with some of the most upright posture I'd seen in a long time. Her knees were together, her ankles crossed and to the side. It was a very ladylike posture; my Grandmother Blake would have been proud. In a dress, the knees together made sense, but the ankle crossing had always puzzled me.

Her perfect posture made me fight not to hunch even further over my coffee, but I could only bend so far before the gun and extra ammo that were hidden under my black suit jacket dug into my side, so it wasn't worth it.

"It's Ms. Blake or Marshal Blake, and yes, I heard you the first three times you said something similar. I also told you that you seem to have mistaken my job description. I am not a private detective. I am a U.S. Marshal with the Preternatural Branch, and I raise the dead here at Animators Inc., if you have a good enough reason for me to do it. Since you don't have a rogue vampire or shapeshifter or other preternatural citizen making your life difficult, me being a marshal doesn't help you, and if you don't need a zombie raised, well, I'm not sure how I can help you."

"I paid a great deal of money to your business manager, Mr. Vaughn, to be assured that you would be able to help me, Miss Blake."

"Mr. Vaughn can get overly optimistic about my abilities when it comes to nonrefundable retainers over a certain size."

Part of my growing impatience was that she kept repeating herself and not listening to me, but I knew part of my crankiness was more about my own childhood issues than about the women in front of me, and because I knew that, I tried to be a grownup about it. I tried not to feel short and dark, or not to be bothered that they both looked like they were dressed for a semiformal event from perfect makeup to styled hair and I so wasn't, but they weren't making it easy.

"I don't approve of women calling themselves Ms.; you are a Miss until you marry and then you're a Mrs., all the rest is nonsense."

I sipped my coffee and tried to think of any reply that wouldn't piss her off and then realized I really didn't care. The retainer was nonrefundable, and it had been large enough to get Bert Vaughn so excited he'd called me while I was off doing my duty as a U.S. Marshal. He knew better than to interrupt me when I was Marshal Anita Blake, as opposed to just Anita Blake, animator, so I'd taken his call. The amount of money he mentioned had been a lot of people's salary for a year. It had been enough for my fellow animators to ask me to take the meeting. We worked more like a law firm now, with money being shared out, though the person who brought in the money got a higher percentage, still it was enough that it would help us all out. It was enough to make me go straight to the office instead of going home, cleaning up, and going to bed. The short, curvy, and ethnic I couldn't do anything about, but under normal circumstances I'd have been in a nice business skirt outfit and makeup. I'd stripped off my body armor and most of my weapons, shoved them in the duffel at my feet until I had time to take them home and put them in the gun safe. That had left me in tactical pants, 5.11 boots, and a T-shirt that I'd worn under all of it, so nothing chafed. The T-shirt had a penguin wearing sunglasses on it with the slogan, "Whiskey and Bad Decisions." I didn't like whiskey, but I really liked penguins. I'd thrown the spare suit jacket I kept at the office over the T-shirt to hide the gun and ammo on my belt, but that had been the only concession I'd had time to make, because Mrs. Chadwick had insisted it had to be tonight and before a certain time. Like I said, she'd upped her ante until it was a year's salary for a lot of people. But it hadn't been my year's salary.

"And I don't understand women introducing themselves as Mrs. Anything, as if they have no first name of their own and no identity outside of marriage."

The granddaughter gave a soft laugh that she quickly tried to turn into a cough. Either it fooled

Mrs. Chadwick, or she ignored it. I was betting Mrs. Chadwick was good at ignoring things that didn't meet with her approval. Too bad she couldn't ignore me, or I couldn't ignore her.

"Are you trying to insult me, Miss... Ms. Blake?"

"If you don't pick on me, I won't pick on you."

"This is not recess and we are not children."

"No, we are not," I said, and took another sip of coffee. I had offered them refreshments, but she had refused, and the granddaughter had only wanted water. Them both turning down coffee was reason to dislike them a little. Nothing they had done had really won them the points back.

"You do understand that my grandson, William, is in grave danger."

"I understand that you think he's involved with the wrong woman and that she's after his trust fund. I'm not sure that qualifies as grave danger, but I know a private detective that can follow them around and try to dig up dirt on the woman, but like I keep saying, I am not a private detective."

"We hired private detectives. They could prove nothing substantial."

I blinked at her, inhaled deeply of my coffee again, took another sip and tried not to start yelling. "Then why are you here, Mrs. Chadwick? Why did you pay a year's salary to have this meeting?"

She gave me a look down her perfect nose. "If it was your yearly salary, then your reputation must truly be exaggerated."

"Let me rephrase: you paid what amounts to a year's salary for a lot of people. My reputation as a necromancer and as the nightmare of bad, little supernatural citizens everywhere is not exaggerated, so my pay grade is higher. Since you're wearing a vintage Cartier watch and your granddaughter walked in here in Christian Louboutin stilettos, you might be out of my pay grade, but then again, you might not. But we're not here to play who has the most money, we're here because you told Mr. Vaughn it was a matter of life and death. You keep telling me your grandson is in grave peril, but the only danger seems to be that he's about to marry a woman you don't like? Is she not good enough for him? Too poor, too wild, too ethnic, too what, Mrs. Chadwick?"

"Too fat," she said.

I set my coffee carefully on my desk, so I wouldn't throw it across the room and lose my shit completely. "Get out of my office."

"My grandson was a fitness model for a brief time. He could have had the career I gave up, but he no longer wishes to model..."

I stood up. "Get—out."

"Please, Ms. Blake," the granddaughter spoke at last, "please let me explain."

"Take your grandmother and go and take your weird issues with you."

"Is it wrong to want my grandson to marry someone that matches his beauty?"

"I don't know, maybe not, but it is wrong to hire private detectives to find dirt on her just because you don't like the way the woman looks."

"My grandson comes into control of his trust fund this year. It is quite substantial. All our grandchildren have had fortune hunters after them thanks to how my late father-in-law arranged his will."

"Not my problem, not even sure it is a problem. How did you know they were fortune hunters, just because they came from poorer backgrounds?"

"Not all of them were poor," the granddaughter said, "just not as rich."

"Well, boo-hoo, take your rich kid problems out of my office." I pointed at the door as if that would make them get up and leave.

"You're wearing a gun," Mrs. Chadwick said, and she looked pale, a slender hand touching her thin chest. The hand looked older than the rest of her did, not bad, just closer to her actual age. I guess they can't lift everything.

Raising my arm to point had flashed the gun at my belt. I should have used my left hand instead of my right—my bad—but since I wasn't taking her on as a client, I guess it didn't matter that she didn't like me being armed. I didn't have to impress her, or even be nice. She was crazy, and I didn't have to play along because she had money. Crazy was crazy, and I was done with it for the night.

"Yeah, I have a gun, because I was out of state helping SWAT serve a warrant of execution when I got the message about this meeting. I inherited the warrant after another marshal died trying to serve it. I have been awake for nearly twenty-four hours and I am done with your shit."

The granddaughter asked, "Did you actually execute someone?"

"None of your damn business, and now, for the third time, get out. If you make me say it again, the word fuck will be involved." I pointed even more dramatically at the door, raising my shoulder up so that the

gun was even more visible. It's a Springfield Rangemaster .45, which is a full-frame 1911, which means
it's not a small gun. I couldn't carry it concealed in
civilian clothes, it was just too big, and I was just too
short-waisted. I had female friends with longer torsos
and they could hide bigger guns in places I couldn't.

"Ms. Blake, please, hear us out."

"No," I said, but if they didn't leave soon I was
going to have to lower my arm; some positions you
just can't hold forever.

Mrs. Chadwick glared up at me, so angry that I
could see some of the lines on her face even through
the makeup. She didn't have smile lines: hers were
frown lines, tight and pinched from disapproving of
everyone and everything around her for too long.

"You come in here dressed like a soldier from the
waist down, with that rude T-shirt, and think that
throwing a jacket from some lesser designer over it
will make it acceptable attire for this meeting . . . I
didn't want to come here for so many reasons, but
your attire and your attitude have convinced me that
this has been a mistake. I came here seeking a seductress and all I see is an ill-mannered tomboy that no
man would want on his arm." She stood up, back still
as rigid as when she'd sat down. "Come, Elgin, her
reputation must be exaggerated."

The comment was so weird coming from her that it
stopped me. I dropped my arm and asked one more
question. "Did you say that you came here looking
for a seductress?" I asked.

"I did, but you obviously are not that . . . Well, look
at you." She waved a hand at what I was wearing,
and she was right about me not having dressed for

seduction. I'd dressed so I could move, run, and fight. Priorities, priorities.

Elgin tugged on the older woman's arm. She was trying to go to the door, but Elgin was young enough and strong enough to win the tug of war. "Please, Grandma Chadwick, she's the only hope we have of proving that it's an illegal spell being used on William."

"If it's illegal magic, why not go to the regular police?" I asked.

"We tried," Elgin said, still holding onto Mrs. Chadwick's arm.

Mrs. Chadwick stopped trying to walk out and turned to look at me. "The police said that it's not illegal for a man to change his mind about whom he wants to marry."

"It's not," I said.

Elgin looked at me with tears glistening in her big, blue eyes. "William and I were in love with each other for years, Ms. Blake. We were planning to get married next year."

"Wait, you were going to marry your own cousin? I know that's legal in some states, but isn't that keeping the family money a little too close to home?"

"Elgin is technically my step-granddaughter. Her mother was my son's second wife, but she has been a part of our family from infancy."

"Willie and I grew up together, but we're not related," Elgin said sniffing and trying not to cry.

"We are not some backwoods family to interbreed," Mrs. Chadwick said.

"Royal families did it for centuries," I said.

"Well, we are not royalty, just wealthy," she said.

"I think it was the being raised together that made

me reject Willie for so many years. He was like a brother, I thought. Now I am in love with him and it's too late."

"The venues are already booked," Mrs. Chadwick said. "The designer is too far along on Elgin's dress to stop now."

"Sounds like you're more interested in the money you're going to lose than anything else," I said.

"Why is it wrong to worry about the money I will lose just because I'm wealthy?"

She had a point, I guess. I sipped my coffee, but it was too cold. If I was going to keep dealing with these two, I needed something hot and fresh.

"You're right; weddings aren't cheap, especially big, designer weddings." I'd been looking at price tags for my own recently and I had been shocked. I was more a small-outdoor-ceremony kind of girl, but I was engaged to a great-big-spectacle kind of guy, so that's what we were doing. It wasn't cheap.

"Thank you for conceding that."

The tears began to trail down Elgin's cheeks. "I made Willie happy for four years. He'd had a crush on me since we were children. He said that me loving him back was the most amazing thing that ever happened to him. How does a man go from that to dumping a woman less than a year before the wedding?" Her shoulders started to shake, and Mrs. Chadwick embraced her and let her cry into her designer-clad shoulder.

"I don't know," I said, and had to repeat it louder to be heard above the crying.

"Will you help us?" Mrs. Chadwick asked, patting her granddaughter's perfect blond hair.

"Help you how?" I asked and moved towards the coffee station that had been put to the side of the office. I drank too much coffee to be asking our receptionists for a refill all the time, plus some of my clients got emotional. Pouring my own fresh cup of coffee seemed less heartless than interrupting their grief for someone to bring me another cuppa.

I offered them another chance at coffee as I moved across the office towards the coffeemaker. They refused again.

"How can you think about coffee while my grand-daughter is in such obvious pain?"

I glanced back at them. "You know how you have the right to worry about money, even if you have money?"

"What does that have to do with coffee?"

"I'm sorry Elgin is broken-hearted. I've been there, and it sucks, but I have the right to need more coffee if I haven't slept in twenty-four hours."

Elgin had calmed down enough to turn her face to me. Her expert makeup was smeared across one eye, though the other was holding up better. It made her look more real somehow and made it harder to turn them down.

"I'll ask one more time. Mrs. Chadwick, Elgin, how can I help you?"

"We came here expecting a siren," Mrs. Chadwick said, "but instead we find a rude man of a woman."

"Grandma Chadwick, please," Elgin said, and for the first time I saw a tenderness in the older woman's face. She might be a vain pain in the ass, but she loved her granddaughter.

I inhaled the scent of fresh, hot coffee to give me

courage and tried one more time to get some sense from the two women. "Elgin, tell me what I can do to help you get some closure."

"Closure." She laughed, and it sounded bitter, far too bitter for someone that looked closer to twenty-one than thirty.

"Pick a different word if you want, but what can I do that the police, a private detective, and I'm assuming the family lawyers couldn't do?"

"How did you know we sent our lawyers to pay her off?" Mrs. Chadwick asked.

"If you have enough money, you think people can be bought like things. I've seen it before, and I'll see it again after you leave." I sipped the coffee carefully, savoring it on my tongue and beginning to realize that I might need real food before I slept today. I tried to stay focused on the would-be clients, but I was too tired unless they came up with something that made sense to me soon.

"There is no way that Willie chose that woman over me, unless she used some supernatural power. You have a certain reputation for sexual...conquests."

"Is that a polite way of saying I sleep around?"

"No," she said.

"We were told that you were a siren, or a succubus, and could seduce men in a way that was unnatural just like what has been done to our William," Mrs. Chadwick said.

"So...what, it takes one to know one?" I asked, debating on if I wanted to sit back down at my desk and encourage them to stay longer, or if standing would shorten the interview. I stood.

"Something like that," the older woman said.

I didn't know whether to laugh or yell at them some more. "So, because I have a certain reputation you think I should be able to meet the woman and tell instantly if she's using supernatural wiles on your William?"

"Yes," she said, very sure of herself.

"When you say it that way, it sounds silly," Elgin said, rubbing at the makeup on her good eye so that it began to smear to match the other one.

"Even if I was some kind of supernatural siren, I don't think it would be that easy."

"Can you at least meet her?" Elgin asked, and something about the smeared makeup or the earnestness in her face made her seem younger, vulnerable, someone that you needed to save, or at least help.

"No promises but give me her name and whatever information you have on her, and maybe, just maybe, I'll give her a look."

Elgin's face lit up, suddenly so happy, and she managed to look young, hopeful, and more beautiful than the perfect model that had slunk in on her Louboutin stilettos. Beauty was great to look at, but I always needed something more real, vulnerable, added to that beauty, or it just didn't move me much. Damn it, Elgin had become real to me.

Mrs. Chadwick got a thumb drive out of her purse and held it out towards me. "It has everything we know about Miss Violet Carlin on it."

I took the small piece of technology from her perfectly manicured hand, but I was past worrying that my nails were short and unpainted. I was just glad I didn't have blood under my nails; there were nights when I did.

"If I find out that she's using illegal magic on William, I'll report it to the police first."

"For this much money I would expect you to report directly to me," Mrs. Chadwick said.

"But you can't do anything to her, and if the police can prove she's using magic to seduce people, then it could mean an automatic death sentence."

Elgin looked startled. "Oh, I don't want her dead. I just want Willie back and to marry him."

Mrs. Chadwick gave me the full weight of her pale blue eyes, a small smile touching her lips. "That will be fine, Ms. Blake, whatever you think best."

With that they left my office. I popped the thumb drive into the desktop computer while I finished my coffee. It was good coffee and I didn't want to waste it; besides, I wanted to see what kind of woman could have gotten the Chadwicks up in arms. Just a quick peek and I'd go home to bed.

Violet Carlin was not much taller than me, but she had me beat for curves. In fact, Mrs. Chadwick probably wouldn't be the only one who would call her fat, but she wasn't exactly, she was just built round. It was a step above curvy, but not obese. She looked what once would have been called pleasingly plump. Back when no one thought to starve themselves to be thin, or even that thin was more attractive than curves. She was smiling in almost every photo. I thought her eyes were brown, but when I finally got a closeup they were hazel, or maybe even green with just a little brown in them. Her hair was short, thick, with waves, but not curls, so it looked good just below her ears. In some shots the hair looked darkest brunette, and then in other shots it was a warm chestnut. She was all rich, warm, autumn colors, smiling and plump and happy. She was the antithesis of Elgin and Mrs. Chadwick.

There were pictures with her and William Chadwick together. He was over six feet tall, broad shoulders tapering down to a slender waist, tight hips, muscular legs. The arms, when I finally saw them bare, matched the legs. He wasn't just in shape, he was in fierce shape in the first few pictures. He had that light golden tan that Elgin had had, so even their skin tone matched. Violet Carlin was pale-skinned and looked like she'd burn in the sun. William's face was model perfect with the same high cheekbones that had made his grandmother a supermodel in her day. I dated some beautiful men, but William could have held his own to most of them. But in every picture of him with Violet, he was gazing down at her laughing, smiling, happy, and she looked up at him with the same expressions. I'd seen other people that were dating out of their league lookswise and they didn't look this at ease. Hell, I'd been one of those people. It had taken me a long time to accept that if really beautiful men kept wanting to date me, I must be beautiful, too. Just thinking it made me want to squirm in my chair even now. I was engaged to marry one of those beautiful men, but I still wasn't as comfortable in the beauty politics as Violet Carlin was in these pictures.

It took me a few minutes to realize that William was changing in the photos. I had to go back through them to be sure, but the almost professional level of fitness that he had in the early photos started to soften. He wasn't as lean, so the cut muscles started to be hidden under a little more flesh. He wasn't fat, by any means. He wasn't even overweight, he just wasn't as lean and fiercely fit. She started to lose a little roundness, not much, but a little, about the time I saw a picture of them going into a gym together. Then I saw them go into a shop that read VIOLETS AND HEARTS, CAKES AND MORE on the big front window. Violet Carlin was a baker. She had a multitiered wedding cake in the window of her shop. It was a beautiful cake. There were pictures of them through a telephoto lens from what looked like a car across the street. William and Violet ate cupcakes together. They drank tea with sugar and cream in it. She brought out a pie and sliced it for him, fresh from the oven it looked like. I began to see where William was gaining his weight. Different days, different desserts, but always smiling, holding hands, kissing, just so in love in every picture.

I wondered what had bothered Mrs. Chadwick the most, that William seemed happy with the fat girl, or that he was starting to gain weight himself? Had she taken that as a personal insult that someone in her family wouldn't meet her standard of perfection? Had William losing that nearly harsh cut of muscle been enough to freak her out? Did she envision him getting plump like Violet? She didn't have to worry about that; you carry weight very differently from barely over five feet to over six. As someone short that works out with taller partners, I knew that.

Elgin was broken-hearted, but it must have been insult to injury to see the other woman. The Nordic goddess and the plump baker, it should have been a no-brainer for William to choose, but it hadn't been, or maybe it had, just not the way Elgin thought.

If Elgin was insulted and hurt, what was Grandmother Chadwick? Angry, insulted, and incredulous, she just couldn't believe that her beautiful grandson had chosen this woman. She couldn't believe that Violet Carlin made him happy, it had to be an evil spell. I didn't see anything evil between the two of them, but I understood some of his family's confusion now. Their prince had abandoned his princess at the altar for a peasant, or that's how Mrs. Chadwick seemed to see it.

No wonder the police had sent them packing. I couldn't help Elgin work the issues that this broken heart would give her, but I might be able to reassure Mrs. Chadwick that there was no magical malfeasance involved. I didn't owe them anything else for their money. They'd paid to have a meeting with me and they'd had it, but maybe it was them paying so much for so little that made me want to give them something for it. Or maybe I was curious about how William and Violet had ended up together. Whether it was idle curiosity, or I felt sorry for Elgin and Mrs. Chadwick, I decided I'd visit the Violet and Hearts, Cakes and More after I'd had some sleep and some real food. I didn't think it would be a good idea to go into the bakery on an empty stomach unless I wanted cake for lunch.

By the time I'd eaten, slept for eight hours, and had "hello, honey, I didn't get killed" sex with my sweeties, I was wondering why I'd lost sleep over Mrs. Chadwick and her problem. I chalked it up to the fact that both women had reminded me of my stepmother and I had serious issues attached to her, so I'd bent over backwards to be fair to them, just to make sure I wasn't using them as scapegoats for my own issues. I'd finally realized I did that. It didn't stop me from doing it, but I could let it go later when I figured it out. It was later, I let it go, and got on with my brand new day, which meant I was back at the office looking over potential clients.

Unlike most U.S. Marshals, the Preternatural branch wasn't a full-time job. No government agency wanted to admit they were employing assassins full-time, and no matter how you prettied it up with a badge and court orders of execution, we were government-sanctioned assassins who hunted down and killed supernatural citizens who had gone rogue. We saved lives by killing the predators before they found more prey, but it still meant that most of us had day jobs. Mine was raising the dead for Animators Inc., which made meeting with the two women last night so far outside my area of expertise it was laughable. They'd paid through the nose for that joke, and now I could get back to work.

I had a busy day of client meetings. A historical society wanted me to raise a Civil War soldier so they could question him on a particular battle. The note with it read that I was putting him back in the ground after a two-hour question-and-answer session. I'd stopped letting anyone take any zombie off-site for in-depth interviews. I'd had too many things go wrong that way, so now I kept watch over them and made certain they went back into the grave ASAP. The waiting around and putting them back cut into how many clients I could have in a night, but for safety's sake I thought it was worth it.

A lawyer wanted to double-check a last-minute will

change, there'd be a full court for that one complete with court reporter and judge. Thanks to new laws, a zombie could say which will was the real one, but only with a judge to decide if the zombie was together enough to make the decision. At least the family wasn't allowed at graveside for will disputes anymore. I was all for no family watching their loved one rise from the grave. I didn't do resurrection, I raised zombies. The family did not need their last vision of dear old Dad or Mom to be the shambling dead.

One witness to a homicide had died of natural causes and again the law allowed for post-death testimony with lawyers and court reporter present. You didn't need a judge for that one. Judges were for legal decisions not evidence gathering. There were two requests to bring back the recently dead for a last good-bye. I turned them down. There were other animators at Animators Inc. that could do the jobs and, like I said, I don't believe a family's last view of their loved ones should be as a zombie. Either it's horrific and ruins their memory of the loved one, or the zombie looks too lifelike and the grieving relatives think they've risen from the grave and want to take them home. Sometimes my zombies are so lifelike they don't remember they're dead. It can be truly heartbreaking all around, and I was done with that shit. I had enough emotional anguish attached to my own mother's death when I was eight, I did not need to add anyone else's grief to my own.

I dressed up a little today, probably to make up for going into the office dressed like one of the guys last night. Sometimes just knowing you have the issue doesn't fix it. The trick is to recognize that you have an issue and be kind to yourself while you work through it. So, my therapist tells me, I was trying to honor all that good advice; some days I was better at it than others.

If I hadn't had to worry about carrying my sidearm, I'd have worn a dress, but when outside my house, I had a badge and that meant that legally I was supposed to be ready to do my job at a moment's notice. I'd made a lot of enemies over the years executing people. Just because someone is a murdering psychopath doesn't mean they don't have people who love them and will hunt you down and exact revenge later. You're not paranoid if people really are out to get you.

A royal blue skirt that was a little shorter than I normally wore to see clients, paired with a matching jacket that hit just enough below my waist to hide the gun and badge. I'd had to have the skirt reinforced around the waistband by a tailor so that I could tuck an inner waistband holster complete with gun and badge on my right side, and a holder for one extra magazine on the left side. If I'd been wearing the pants from last night, I'd have had multiple pockets for extra ammo and I wouldn't have had to change from the Springfield Rangemaster to the smaller-framed Springfield EMP, which was a 9mm. But honestly, I was lucky to be able to fit even that much around a suit skirt. I was wearing sheer stockings with high heels that were about two inches taller than I'd usually wear to work. A slightly paler blue silk blouse made the outfit as much of a dress as my paranoia and job could manage.

I even put on eye makeup and lipstick, which was about as girlie as I got. Did I feel shallow that I dressed up because two strangers had made me feel insecure the night before? Yes, yes, I did, but I still did it. The staff at one of my favorite lunch places acted as if they'd never seen me dress like a girl before. It started to make me feel grumpy and then I got a call from our daytime receptionist, Mary, that I had several calls from Mrs. Robert Chadwick. I was about to tell her that wasn't my problem and that I'd met my obligations for the meeting last night, then she mentioned a money amount. It wasn't quite as much as last night, but it was enough that Mary had called me at lunch.

"It's a nice chunk of change, but what does she want me to do for it? I told her last night that wayward grandsons falling in love with the wrong women isn't in my job descriptions."

"The client says she'll pay you just to go talk to the temptress."

"Did she actually call her a temptress?"

"She did," and I could hear the smile in Mary's voice.

"Tell Mrs. Chadwick that I looked over the file she left me last night and her grandson seems happy. I didn't see a temptress in any of those pictures, just an ordinary woman in love."

"I'll tell her, Anita, but she's convinced that if you would just meet the temptress in person, you would know that she's bewitched the grandson."

"I'm just finishing up lunch, and then I have another potential client meeting."

"Bert says he'll find someone else to cover your next meeting if you'll do this for the current client."

"If it was just for Bert, I wouldn't do it," I said.

"I know, but it will help out everyone at the firm, even us lowly desk staff."

"Your grandkids needing new braces or something?"

"The grandkids have parents to pay for their orthodontia. I'm saving up for a romantic trip with my husband."

I laughed. "That's the spirit. Okay, I had salad and soup for lunch. I guess I could get dessert."

"Dessert. Is that your way of refusing to do this, or am I missing something?"

"Didn't the client tell you? The temptress owns a bakery."

"Well, if it's tempting stuff, bring a piece back for me."

"I will." We hung up and I googled the address for Violet and Hearts bakery. I put it into Waze, left a tip, and went to meet Violet Carlin in person.

There was a line at the bakery that stretched nearly to the door. They were in a prime spot for the lunch rush and I wasn't the only one in office clothes. There were also men in work boots, mothers with children in tow, one father with a baby strapped to his chest, a woman dressed to go to her waitress job, teenagers with their phones and earbuds in, and people that I couldn't guess what they did. It was a nice cross section of the city. A little boy in front of me started to squirm, but when his mother told him she'd get out of line and he wouldn't get a cookie, he stopped. Apparently, he'd had the cookies here before and he didn't want to lose a chance to have another.

A woman wearing a black suit skirt asked me, "Which flavor of cupcake are you getting?"

"I've never been here, so I'm not sure."

She beamed at me. "Oh my god, they are the best."

"I heard good things about Violet and Hearts," I said.

The man behind me with his hardhat tucked under his arm said, "We're doing a job just up the road and I come down here on my breaks. If I don't get assigned to a new job site soon, I'm going to have to buy bigger pants." He laughed and the woman laughed with him; apparently, we were supposed to be okay with eating enough sweets to go up a pants size.

"I know that look," the woman said. "Trust me, it's worth the calories." She was thinner than I was, but then she was also about four inches taller and less curvy, but still... "No, really, everything here is amazing. But I don't come down here every lunch hour, more like once a week."

The man laughed again. "I'll be moving to a new job soon, so I'm sampling as many flavors as I can, while I can."

"I work nearby permanently; I have to show more restraint than that," the woman said.

Everyone in line was like that, as if we were all five years old again and eating cake was just a given, not a carbohydrate and calorie guilt fest. It was relaxing just to be around so many adults who all seemed relaxed about eating sweets. It made me begin to wonder if there was some magic in the bakery goods, because Americans didn't enjoy calorie-rich foods like this. Where was the guilt, the excuses, the pledges to do better next week? No one even said the four-letter word—diet. Damn, maybe the crazy grandmother was right and Violet Carlin was a witch. I was going to be disappointed if I had to tell her she was right.

I had to step partially out of line to see through the crowd to the counter. I got glimpses of Violet Carlin. Since we were both short I couldn't see that well, but what I did see was her smiling, chatting up the customers. She knew most of them by name. She remembered who was gluten-free, or had other special needs. She seemed to have something for everyone.

I started trying to look at the baked goods behind the glass rather than at the baker because I'd be having to choose soon. There were tiny cupcakes, full-size cupcakes, cakes that were only a little bigger, and then full-size cakes that they sold by the slice. Cookies came from little larger than a quarter to bigger than my hand. Then there were pies. Again, they came in small, like one-to-two-person servings, or full-size. The icing on the cakes was there, but it wasn't piled on, so that the cakes were stars of the show, not the icing. I liked that a lot. I'd had too many cupcakes over the years where a so-so cake was hidden under too much sweet icing. Or a cake that was decorated as if pretty was more important than how well it tasted. There was none of that here. There was a display wedding cake to one side that showed she could do fancy, but the stuff in the main counter was simpler and all the more appetizing because of it. Maybe one of the reasons I'd stopped being a sweets person wasn't about calories, but about presentation. I didn't want a ton of icing, I wanted a good cake or cupcake. Wasn't that what everyone wanted if they were going to indulge? Maybe cupcakes had become like Mrs. Chadwick, all about outward appearance and not substance.

"Having a hard time deciding?" Violet Carlin asked from behind the counter.

I looked up and couldn't help but meet her smile with my own. Her eyes looked much greener in person, or maybe hazel eyes were like some people with blue-gray eyes and they changed color with her moods. Her hair was a rich chestnut, almost an auburn, tucked up under a dark green cap. I realized that the uniforms were all a rich, pine green, maybe the color brought out the green in her eyes. Whatever the reason, she looked much better in person than any of the pictures had shown. Was it charisma, or was it magic?

"Everything looks so amazing, I don't know what to choose."

She beamed at me, happy with the compliment. It made me want to compliment her more. That wasn't normal for me. Damn it. Was crazy grandma not so crazy?

"Are you getting a snack just for you?"

"I'll definitely get something to try here before I go back to work. I was going to wait and see how good it was before deciding if I should buy some to share at home, but I don't want to brave the line again."

She laughed and just the sound of it made me happier. Fuck, she was using some sort of charm or mind games. The trick was … did she know she was doing it? I'd met one or two people who had some natural abilities and used them without knowing it. It wasn't her mind games that made me want her to be innocent. It was not wanting Mrs. Chadwick to be right, but just because someone is unpleasant, doesn't mean they're wrong.

She helped me pick out a trio of tiny cupcakes so that I didn't have to choose between chocolate-chocolate, cookies and cream, and caramel butterscotch. I told her I'd pick out a cake to match the cupcake I liked best and took them along with a bottle of water to a tiny table that opened up just as I was needing it. Good that something was going right. I hated, hated that Violet Carlin was mind-fucking people, but I was ninety-eight percent certain she was, and that meant that maybe Elgin was right. William wouldn't have dumped her for Violet without the magic whammy. The real problem was that if she was using magic to sway people to buy her cakes, that was illegal. You weren't allowed to use magic to make your merchandise more appealing. It could get you everything from a warning, a fine, to jail time. But if we could prove she'd bewitched William into loving her, proposing to her, that was a potential death penalty. I'd come here to placate a mean-spirited, overprotective grandmother. Now I had to decide how to report Violet Carlin to the regular police. How I worded what I'd seen here would determine if she might end up on trial for her life. Fuck.

I thought it would ruin my appetite, but it didn't. The tiny cupcakes were like two bites apiece. The chocolate wasn't overwhelmingly sweet, but it wasn't too bitterly dark either. Cookies and cream was my least favorite—good, but I'd tasted similar things. The caramel butterscotch on the other hand was like butter pecan ice cream met a caramel sundae and then brushed up against the peanut butter in a Reese's Peanut Butter Cup. I had my cake flavor to take home and then I realized that the cupcakes might all be bespelled to taste better, but if that had been the case, then wouldn't they all three have been equally as good? Shit, this was too complicated for me. I was more an aim-me-at-the-bad-guys-and-pull-the-trigger kind of cop. What I needed was the supernatural fraud division. It was a new subdivision of regular fraud, because people got more upset about us executing humans with psychic or magical gifts than they did about wereanimals or vampires. So, the law had to change to give us another option besides a court order of execution for witches, voodoo priests, Satanists, psychics, etc., that used their powers against others. The one exception to the rule was love or lust spells: that was still seen as rape and that was still under death penalty for the supernaturally gifted.

William Chadwick walked through the door as if just thinking it had conjured him to me. If our happy baker had used her powers to bewitch him into sex, then it was rape, but how do you tell the difference between true love and magic?

He smiled at her and she beamed back at him. She took off her plastic gloves and apron to come around the counter so they could kiss hello. It was a good kiss, the kind of kiss I was still giving my sweeties after years of living together. Like all happy couples, I liked seeing other people happy, but was it real or was it magic?

I had two choices: turn her into the metaphysical fraud division or talk to them together and see if I was psychic enough to figure this out. I might still turn her in to Fraud, but first I needed to know if it was only fraud. Rape, no matter how voluntary it felt to the victim, was considered a violent crime, which was a very different division.

I caught up to them as they were headed back out the door. I flashed my badge at them. They looked surprised, even a little scared. I didn't count that against them; a lot of people react that way when you flash a badge at them out of the blue. They didn't even try and read the badge to see that it listed me as Preternatural Division, or even that it was U.S. Marshal not regular local cops. They also acted as if I had every right to stop and question them. Innocent people who haven't dealt much with the police usually act that way.

We ended up sitting at a larger corner table near the back of the room. It had a sign on the wall over it that read "Baker's Tasting Table." Violet was nervous and that made her talk more than she probably should have. "It's like a chef's table: sometimes for VIPs and sometimes I let people try out new recipes and give feedback."

"I thought chef tables were in the kitchen," I said, smiling and trying to put her at ease. Whatever had been happening while she was waiting on me in line was gone. She was still pretty and pleasant, but I didn't feel happy. That little-kid happy, before the world teaches you about cruelty and loss. It had been that kind of excitement in line for the other customers, too.

"Usually, but I like being out here with the customers. It's about sharing, you know."

"I felt some of that in line," I said.

Her smile brightened then, and there was a hint of . . . what? Was it magic, or just charisma, a type of star power? Except that her star was all about baking and making people happy instead of being in movies or on the stage.

William was silent, watching me as they held hands. He'd gained more weight in his face since the last pictures I'd seen of them together. The perfect cheekbones weren't quite so stark and model-like. He was still handsome, but it wasn't as startling. He was softer around the edges and it wasn't just weight. Even nervous, talking to me, he seemed more at ease than he had in any of the pictures. Or maybe he was like Violet and some things only showed in person.

"Why do you want to talk to Vi and me, Marshal Blake?" Then he frowned and seemed to be thinking harder. "Wait a minute, are you Marshal Anita Blake with the Preternatural Branch?"

I nodded.

He drew Violet closer to him, so that she fit under his arm near his heart, where he could protect her. Her natural blush paled and she looked sort of gray. "I told you, Will, your grandmother wouldn't give up until she got someone to believe her."

"Violet is not a witch," he said, voice low and hissing.

"Being a witch isn't illegal, Mr. Chadwick."

"She has not bewitched me, or whatever my grandmother told you."

"I'm here to get your side of things. I don't want your grandmother to be right. I like both of you better than her, and I just met you." That got a weak smile from Violet. William continued to glare at me.

"Help me understand how your relationship got started, how you fell in love, and maybe I can talk some sense into William's grandmother."

"It won't help," Violet said, sitting up a little straighter. "She hates me."

I debated on what to say and finally went for truth. "That seems accurate. I'm sorry."

"Grandma Chadwick had her heart set on Elgin and I breeding so the great-grandchildren would be up to her standards." He sounded bitter.

"She does seem invested in you and Elgin getting back together," I said.

"Elgin was just a childhood crush. I thought it was love because I'd never felt anything stronger, but once I met Vi, Violet, I knew it hadn't been real." He kissed the top of her head, placing his cheek against her hair. "This is real, Marshal Blake. I'm sorry I hurt Elgin, truly."

"We both are," Violet said and she sat forward in her chair regaining some color as she said, "I've had my heart broken and I would never want to do that to anyone else."

I wanted to believe her. "So how did the two of you meet?"

"I was walking past at lunchtime and saw her waiting on customers. She looked so happy. I don't know if I'd ever seen a woman look so happy doing anything."

"What do you mean?" I asked.

"Women are always unhappy with themselves, or something, or that's how Elgin and all the women I dated were. My grandmother is pleased with herself, but I'm not sure she's happy. She's like all the beautiful women I knew before Violet. They were always saying they needed to lose five more pounds or more, even if they were so thin they'd lost all their curves. I know that some of them had eating disorders—hell, I had one, too—and before you ask, I know that eating disorders are addictions so I'm never really over it. I'm in recovery, except with food, you can't stop without dying. It's the only addiction that you have to keep doing."

"Drinking and drugs you can go cold turkey," I said.

"But not food," he said, and seemed sad.

Violet patted his hand and turned so that he had to look into her green eyes. She touched his face gently. "Food isn't the enemy."

He smiled. "You were the first woman I ever dated that wasn't dieting."

"Even though your family thinks I should," she said.

He hugged her. "They're all crazy about body image. You know Grandmother Chadwick was a famous model?"

"Yeah," I said.

"She wanted me to be a fit model, and Elgin wanted to look that good, so we trained together starting junior year of high school. We even did some modeling. I got lucky and was actually signed to a big agency. I modeled for a while instead of going to college, but I'm a man, I can't marry well like Grandma did. I needed to do something, and I can't act or sing. I move well enough, but if you want to be a professional dancer you need to be devoted to it, and I wasn't. Being beautiful isn't really a career unless you can model or act."

I wasn't sure what this had to do with anything, but I let him talk. Sometimes the best thing you can do when questioning someone is shut up and let them ramble.

Violet gazed up at him adoringly, literally adoring him. I looked at people with love in my eyes, but I wasn't sure I'd ever adored anyone like that. If it was a spell, she had it, too. "The most handsome man I'd ever met walked into my bakery. He was so beautiful that I wasn't shy around him the way I am when I try to talk to men I like. He was so far out of my league that I just talked to him about my cakes and pies."

He smiled down at her and if it wasn't adoring, it was love. "I'd never had a woman talk to me about desserts without complaining about carbs and calories. She just loved what she created. She was so happy in her life, in her work. I'd managed to get a business degree in college, but I didn't enjoy working in an office."

"You just need to find something that you love as much as I love baking," she said, smiling.

He nodded. "I'm trying to figure that out."

"You'll find it," she said, and she sounded utterly convinced that he would.

"Until I do, I have to keep working at the job I have. Did my grandmother tell you that she cut me off financially unless I gave up Vi?"

"No, she didn't mention that."

"She thought I couldn't make it on my actual salary, and maybe I couldn't have paid all my bills. I mean I've never really had to watch my money before."

"That's why I asked you to move in with me. We didn't need to be paying two house payments and double the utilities."

He smiled and squeezed her hand. "I felt like a kept man at first, but what I made helped out."

"Your grandmother didn't mention that you had a job, only that you could have been a model. She didn't say you were living together either."

"She told you Vi was after my trust fund though, didn't she?" He looked tired and sad as he said it.

"She mentioned it," I said.

"Did she tell you that she threw a spell-breaker herb bundle into Violet's face?"

"No."

"She got it from some crackpot that called herself a witch. It was guaranteed to break love spells." He raised Violet's hand up so that he gestured with both their hands. "This is not a spell to be broken. I love Violet and I want to spend the rest of my life with her. I want to grow old with her, and I'm looking forward to aging with a woman that will actually let herself age." That was a definite jab at Grandma Chadwick.

"I love my mom and the fact that I look like she cloned herself. I'm looking forward to looking like her as I get older and having a marriage like her and Dad," Violet said.

I don't know if I'd ever heard a healthier and happier statement from an adult woman about age and romance. I began to see why William had found her a breath of fresh, romantic air.

"Her parents are the happiest couple I've ever met. I want that, too."

"Why can't your family understand that?" Violet asked.

"Because I'm rejecting everything Grandma Chadwick believes in, everything she values."

"What does she value, Will? Beauty? That seems to be all she cares about."

"She thought I was the only grandchild that was as beautiful as she had been, even the girls didn't measure up, not even Elgin, just me. She had her heart set on me having the career she left to marry Grandad."

"A lot of parents want their kids to follow in their footsteps," I said.

"You look in shape. Do you starve yourself to be thin?"

"No, hell no. In fact, I'm the voice of reason with

one of my boyfriends. He has some body dysmorphia from being a dancer."

"Dancing, modeling, acting, all of it will fuck you up with food," he said.

"You don't have to do any of that anymore," Violet said.

He smiled at her and then looked at me, the smile fading. "I don't want to starve myself to keep visible abs anymore. I don't want to weigh my food at every meal. I don't want to treat carbohydrates as if they're evil. I want to eat meat that isn't chicken or turkey."

"Red meat is yummy," I said.

He grinned at me and I could see a younger William, just a glimpse before the sadness fell back over his face. "I love steak. I didn't know how much until I got free of beauty prison."

"Beauty prison?" I asked.

"Between exercise and dieting, looking good consumed my life. It was all Elgin and I did together almost. We'd see an occasional movie or ballet, but mostly we worked out and tried to find ways to eat less, or add protein to build muscles without adding calories, or we worked out harder so we'd burn more calories. If you want that, then great, but Grandma Chadwick made it my life from puberty to a year ago. It was her life, not mine. I didn't know how miserable I was until I met Violet." There was no magic here, the bakery side of things maybe, but not here.

"I'll try to explain that to your grandmother," I said.

"Good luck. I've tried and she just can't accept that I'm happier now with a few more pounds on me than I ever was when I was modeling."

"I'm glad you're both happy and sorry your family can't understand it."

"Thank you, and so am I," he said.

"Now, do you happen to have a caramel butterscotch cake that I can take home with me and a cupcake in the same flavor? I promised someone at the office that I'd bring something back for them if it was good enough, and it was good enough."

Violet smiled and looked a little more relaxed. "Yes, we have both. It's one of our most popular flavors."

The crowd near the door shifted. It was enough to make me look that way. Mrs. Chadwick pushed her way through the happy cupcake crowd and came striding towards us. She looked like an elegant and very expensive ship crashing through a harbor full of rowboats. She was still beautiful and thin and perfect from hair to makeup, to the designer dress with its matching overcoat that seemed a little hot for St. Louis at this time of year, but hey, suffering for fashion was all a part of beauty prison. She looked artificial here. I don't know if it was the more ordinary people all around her, or me understanding her bullshit more. Whatever the cause, she looked like a movie star who was looking for a camera closeup, and that was great if it was your job, but it wasn't her job, and this wasn't a movie set.

"She's bewitched you, too!" She was almost yelling.

Violet stood up, and for the first time, the happy baker was angry. "This is my place of business and you're causing a scene."

"You've put a spell on all these people. It's in the cakes!" She grabbed a cupcake out of a customer's hand and shoved it towards Violet.

"We'll give you a free replacement, sir," Violet said to the customer.

Mrs. Chadwick squeezed the cake in her hand, so that icing and bits of cake squeezed out between her perfect manicure. "I could buy and sell this place."

"You already tried that, Mrs. Chadwick, and I won't sell. I love my bakery." Violet's voice was icy with rage.

"William, come home with me. Can't you see what she's doing to you?"

He was still sitting down. With the two women standing over him, it was like blocking for a play showing him stuck in the middle of it all. "I'm happier than I've ever been in my life; why can't you believe that?"

"She's made you fat. How can you be happy fat?"

William wasn't fat, not even close, he just wasn't as thin as he had been. No wonder he had an eating disorder if that was the message of his childhood. I stood up on my side of the table. "Let's all sit down and be reasonable."

She pointed at me with an icing-covered hand. "How could you eat her cakes and talk to her? I told you what she was!"

"Yelling won't help the situation, Mrs. Chadwick," I said.

"No, you're right, it won't," and she seemed calmer. Great, maybe we were getting somewhere, and then she reached into the pocket of her overcoat and pulled out a gun. It was a small gun, a .380, but as she pointed it at Violet from less than four feet, it would be big enough to kill her. I went for my gun knowing that I'd never get it out in time to stop Mrs. Chadwick from pulling the trigger.

William stood up. He didn't grab the gun, didn't even try, he just stood up so that his body was between Violet and the barrel of his grandmother's gun. I had my gun out and almost aimed when the other gun went off and shot William in the chest.

There was a lot of screaming from the crowd. I was about to shoot her, but the gun fell from her hand and she screamed, "William! No!"

He collapsed into Violet's arms, but he was twice her size, so all she could do was help him fall to the floor. I was screaming at Mrs. Chadwick to put her hands on top of her head, but she didn't seem to hear me. She was just staring at her grandson. I moved around until I could put my foot on her dropped gun, my gun barrel touching her thin chest. I slammed her to the table one-handed. She never protested or tried to fight back. I searched her with one hand while I kept the gun on her. I know I said out loud, "If you move, I will shoot you."

I had to holster my gun to get the handcuffs out of my purse so I could put them on Mrs. Chadwick. The vintage Cartier watch was probably ruined, but I didn't really care. I secured her to a chair and got her gun off the floor, put the safety on and tucked it into the stiff waistband of my skirt.

Someone in a green apron said, "I called an ambulance."

Violet was cradling William in her arms, crying and begging him to be all right. I knelt beside them. He had a pulse, but I could hear that awful wet sound as he breathed. The bullet had hit at least one lung. He was suffocating. Fuck!

"Get me a clean plastic bag and tape," I said to

the aproned employee, who didn't seem to hear me. I grabbed their arm and yelled, "Get me a clean plastic bag and tape, and we might save him for the ambulance. Move, now!" They ran off, but another employee was already there with what I needed.

I put the plastic over the wound and told someone to hold it in place while I taped it down on three sides leaving one side open for air to escape. The plastic should seal off the wound, until an ambulance could get here. I waited to see if it would work, and then his breathing evened out and I saw the plastic be partially sucked in against the bullet wound, and then expand out as he breathed.

"Thank God," I said.

"How did you know how to do that?" the employee asked.

"I've seen this type of wound before." I knelt there with William Chadwick's blood on my hands and prayed that he would be all right—not just that he would live, but that he would heal and be better than ever. I wanted him and Violet to have a life together.

I could hear sirens. The ambulance was coming. I heard police sirens, too. I looked at Mrs. Robert Chadwick handcuffed to a chair. She looked horrified with what she'd done, and even through the makeup and the surgery, somehow she looked older, tireder, as if all the years were catching up with her at once. There was nothing beautiful about her by the time the uniformed police took her away.

The Supernatural Fraud Division cleared Violet. Apparently her only magic was being a fabulous baker who truly enjoyed helping people satisfy their sweet tooth.

Six months later I got a wedding invitation from William and Violet. Mrs. Chadwick pleaded diminished capacity in a bid to get out of jail. Unlucky for her, she shot her grandson in front of a U.S. Marshal. Courts like testimony from federal officers, or at least juries do. She had the best lawyer that money could buy, but money can't buy you everything. I don't think Mrs. Robert Chadwick is going to look good in orange.

A String of Pearls

Alistair Kimble

I stared out the *Sunset Limited*'s window, a one-way ticket on the maglev out of what I called Los Angeles Caidos to New Orleans. Nothing but black out there in the expanse. No horizon. No moon. No moon tonight or any other night in memory.

For three weeks I shocked my liver with bourbon and pummeled my stomach with worry.

Hiding.

Waiting.

Ruminating.

Hid in the black and firmly on the right side of the Veneer. No footprint over on the other side. Nothing. I was clean. In the now and in the real. No virtual.

I waited for a grab that never happened. The law must have been preoccupied or disinterested in a has-been hiding out. I waited in a tenement teeming with the unsavory and the mingled scent of piss and refuse.

No place for a lady, but I left lady behind bottles ago. Lovers ago.

Los Angeles Caidos. Good riddance. I sniffed. The devil summoned his fallen angel and I complied.

The *Sunset Limited* droned a clack-clack-clack in perfect intervals. Sleep hovered, collapse imminent. My eyelids fluttered. A glob of mascara drooped into view as I blinked away melancholy, the lashes clinging as they fought for separation.

The maglev would soon pull into the station. My husband—so old-fashioned of him—Mason would no doubt be there when I arrived, eager for the cargo I carried.

Rattles and clinks. The timbre of ice hitting glass. I ran my tongue over crusty lips. My eyes burned from the trance brought on by the maglev's piped-in clacking, as if some locomotive from a bygone era.

In the window glass, reflections of fire-warped metal and fire-warped screams. The stench of burning hair and scorched skin. Chaos and booze.

I caressed the string of pearls draped around my neck, the precious cargo. I owned no pearls. No one ever sprung for a strand. Special pearls, or so I've been told, as if they'd once touched the princess of Monaco's skin or something. And this bracelet Mason lashed around my left wrist—special. Nothing fancy, but perfect as a restraint and instant inducement device, as if on loan from a dominatrix.

I turned my wrist over, studied the gleaming metal of torture. Oh, how horrid, but goes so well with everything. Does it come ringed in diamonds perhaps? Maybe if I behaved? Mason found humor in precious little, especially me. I'd paid for the remark.

My eyes flitted shut. My head lolled. Filled with mud. Throbbing. Forced my eyes open. Leaden legs. One leg crossed over the other, a flat black gown draped over. A black clutch rested on my lap. Mason's lack of imagination worked overtime when he instructed me on the proper attire for my arrival.

"Lizabeth? Liz?" Haunted. Wounded. Victor. Vic. "How? What?" He choked on the words. A voice out of the past.

The cords in my neck protested, but I forced my head around anyway. A red carnation adorned Vic's white jacket. A bold choice. Bolder by mixing white jacket with black slacks. He fussed with the cufflinks. Nervous. But he wasn't the only one.

My gaze ventured nowhere near his face. Nowhere near his eyes. I could not. Not yet. Beyond Vic, polished wood and brass glared at me, as did a tall uniformed man behind a cherry bar. The crimson furnishings reeked of luxury, as did the few lingering people swathed in evening wear.

"Your hair," Vic said. "I didn't realize—"

Rather than raise my chin, I rolled my eyes up. Hopefully this time the lashes didn't catch. My lips parted.

His breath caught, and those eyes—glassy. Augmented. Replacements from the fire. I fought for control. I once cared for Vic, deeply, and I'd exiled a piece of him deep into a corner of my heart, a heart in no danger of thawing, not while the specter of Mason's designs demanded attention.

"Vic." I cleared my throat. "Victor." His face. Scarred. He'd refused nanotreatment. Wore the scars in defiance. "We'll be pulling in to Union Station soon." I averted my gaze.

He leaned in. My nostrils flared under the assault of bergamot and spice. Damn him. I closed my eyes. Fire-warped metal and fire-warped screams.

Burning hair and scorched skin.

Chaos and booze.

I raked my fingers through straight flaming red hair. "A gift," I said, "from Mason." He wanted my hair restored after the alleged accident. I resisted... until Mason forced, I mean insisted on the augment—though I'd call fixing the swirling mass of scars blanketing my scalp major surgery.

Every once in a while, when I rake my hair, a phantom scar rises up. I should burn it all off.

"Suits you," Vic said. "How about a cocktail?" Though disappointment flashed in those stormy, augmented eyes.

"No."

He blinked.

"Yes, I need one, but no. Another time, okay?" My liver didn't understand, though my liver thanked the fifty-pound brain who discovered nanotherapy. So did I.

"May I contact you," Vic said, "you know, over there?"

"I'm off that other side, strictly a right side of the Veneer woman," I said, "for the time being."

Disappointment.

"What are you doing on the lev, anyway?" I ran a finger along the edge of the empty rocks glass I'd forgotten rested on the arm of the chair. The clacks receded under our sustained conversation. Nice touch.

"Business." No hesitation. I didn't doubt Vic had business in New Orleans.

"If you desire contact," I said, "please try the old-fashioned way."

He ogled me, nonplussed.

Sunset Limited, service from Los Angeles to New Orleans is concluding. The lev will be arriving in New Orleans in five minutes. All passengers should—

The announcement melted away as I stared down Vic. He averted his gaze this time. I could not, *would* not involve myself with him. Not again.

He fought the aversion and brought those steely grays down hard on me.

I kidded no one. I'd broadcast my whereabouts at some point. Vic would find me. The right side of the Veneer wouldn't stop him. Stop me.

Mason would stop everything. That was his plan. Was always his plan.

"The world turns in a funny way, the past always comes back around, doesn't it?" There. The one and only broadcast of where I'd be. Not much. Enough.

"If only I'd discovered your presence on the *Sunset Limited* before now, but I only came aboard in El Paso. See you 'round, Liz." Vic pointed his chin in the direction of the passenger cars and strode off.

I gripped the rocks glass. Not a drop hiding in there. I stared out the window, past the reflection and into the black, swirling night. "Safest way to travel is abstaining." A nanosect swarm, pitch against the gloom congealed and massed, keeping pace with the lev for a few seconds. Curse the fools responsible for unleashing those electromechanical locusts on the world—even if the whole affair was a mistake. My fingers caressed each pearl of the necklace in turn.

The lev hummed into Union Station, the clacks no more. I grabbed my overnight bag, a beat-up old thing, and disembarked into soggy murk. I drank the heavy air into my lungs, the weight settling deep within me.

"Lizabeth." A tall thin man emerged from the gloom. I wished the descent of a black cloud down on my husband's head, the nanosects feeding on that sick mind of Mason's.

"Mace," I said. "Thank you for meeting me."

"You're here for one reason, Lizabeth." His gaze fell to the string of pearls my fingers caressed. "Here, let me take your bag." He wrested the bag from my grip.

"Mace, please."

"What, you want to carry this yourself?"

"No, I—I'm happy to be here is all."

"In this muck? You won't be here long."

"No, come on, be kind. It's been weeks."

Mace's dead eyes livened for a moment, those black-as-a-nanosect-swarm pinpoints of cruelty and hatred, eyeing my wrist.

"Please, Mace, I've done nothing wrong. Did exactly what you told me to do. See?" I pulled the pearls away from my chest. No matter my act, Mace, sadistic Mace, thought first of pain, then pleasure, and often intertwined the two with deftness of mind and of hand.

His gaze followed something behind me. I twisted. Glimpsed Vic stepping off the *Sunset Limited*.

"Eyes on me, Lizabeth," Mace said, "eyes on me."

"What is it?" I braced.

"I think I saw *him*." The inflection of "him" left no doubt. The inflection was only used when speaking of Victor.

"Who, Vic?" I said, "I mean, Victor?"

"No. The mayor of New Orleans, who in the hell do you think I mean? If we weren't in public—"

Mace grabbed my arm with one hand and carried my overnight bag in the other. We strode down the length of the *Limited*. A man and woman stepped off in front of us, Mace tensed.

The man wore dark stubble and his shabby and unkempt appearance paled compared with the rest of the clientele disembarking. He reeked of two things: musk-infused sweaty socks and cop. The woman on the other hand, well, she resided in a neighborhood many miles from his. Black gloves, a crimson handbag dangling from her forearm, and a smart suit. Her shoes, three-inch heels, morphed into elegant but utilitarian boots capable of dealing with the sogginess that was New Orleans.

"What's the score, huh?" Mace asked the man's back.

"Excuse me?" sweaty socks asked. He looked Mace up and down and his eyes widened. Mace had that gravitas. His features denied classification, but the emblazoned graft of the Macau Lotus he wore so brazenly on his hand scared off even the most foolhardy of men and women. "Oh, sorry, didn't mean to—"

"Fine. Get moving," Mace said, "we've a date needs keeping."

The man bowed, but the woman kept her chin high. The pair moved aside, allowing Mace the right of way. At the curbside pickup, his conveyance whirred up, doors opening as the dull metal machine stopped. He tossed my overnight in, gave me as gentle a shove as I've known from him and I slid in. He plopped beside me. "Hotel Monteleone." The conveyance whirred to life, zipping us past the horde of people waiting for transport.

I dared not speak, not until Mace indicated, or I'd—

Pain wormed up my left arm, spreading into my heart, squeezing. Frozen facial nerves prevented any reaction to the pain other than watering eyes, a hot stream bolted down my face.

"I'm happy to see you." Mace stared.

I fought, clenched shut my eyes, closed my lips against the baring of my gritted teeth.

"Let's have a fine night. We'll go to the Carousel Bar at the hotel, start over. I see you've delivered the pearls. Good."

The worming pain retracted. I sucked in breaths, smacked my lips, and got myself under control. They say prolonged use of inducers such as the wrist-worn type causes permanent partial paralysis or, in some people, tics and twitches.

"As beautiful as ever," Mace said, "even under duress. Let's hope these"—his fingers brushed my skin as they caressed the pearls—"weren't damaged in transit."

"Please, Mace," I said, "give me a moment." I breathed slowly. Deliberately.

"Having said that, please fix yourself up before we arrive at the hotel."

"Yes, Mace." I dug into the black clutch, pulled out a mirror and checked my face. Fixed my lipstick. The rivulets of tears tracked through the makeup—

"I really must pay for some skin augmentations," Mace said, "make this fixing up pointless."

Bastard.

"I know, why do I do such things to you, my wife."

I studied the cityscape rather than face my torturer, my husband. "I've seen what you do to those in your organization who aren't your wife."

"Now, now." He touched my knee. "We don't want another performance, do we?" I resisted pulling away, but instead closed my eyes. Waited. Oh, how I wished they'd grabbed me in Los Angeles, in that dank tenement. But I wouldn't have been safe. Not as long as Mace needed the string of pearls draped around my neck, an iridescent albatross.

An indistinguishable mob blocked further passage on Royal Street, a block away from the hotel, whose ancient neon sign blared red through the murk.

"Hotel Monteleone. Override safety." Mace barked the command. The conveyance lurched. People scrambled. People smacked the roof. People kicked the conveyance as the alloyed beast whirred through the crowd.

"What is this?" I asked, keeping my gaze locked on the crowd on the other side of the glass.

"Protest week, I don't know. Not sure why the crowd is over here, unless some impromptu savior hopped up on a soap box." The heat of his words seared my neck. No bergamot. No spice. Mace exuded menace. "At least it isn't Mardi Gras."

The crowd parted.

Mace eased up a bit.

The conveyance whirred and jetted onward for the Hotel Monteleone. In seconds the doors opened and Mace stepped out. He offered his hand, the Lotus graft like a brand for all the world to see. Not just skin on that clawlike hunk of meat some called a hand, but a graft of the same skin containing the same tattoo of Mace's predecessors, thus naming him the Macau Lotus's leader.

I wish Mace would have remained in Macao. Died in Macao. But maybe the devil dying in New Orleans was good enough.

A boy grabbed my overnight bag. I hoped he worked for the Monteleone. Mace led me inside. Not as elegant as it once was, but that was expected given the radical drop in demand for luxury accommodations. Cracks showed in the flooring. A scuff here. A light out there. Mace led me to our room, the top floor. Penthouse. I barely noticed details. So tired.

"Mace—"

"Get ready, in fact, wear what you're already wearing. It's perfect."

"Carousel?"

Mace's left eye phased milky. Snapped back to its lizardlike cold a second later. "The first party's arriving."

I knew nothing of his ultimate plan. I carried the pearls. Told I was to wear the pearls, never take them off, never allow them out of my sight. I followed Mace's instructions. I understood the consequences. And I understood the Carousel Bar was compulsory.

I visited the bathroom. Beautifully decorated, but no joy for me. Not now.

"Don't be long," Mace yelled from the living room. I didn't answer. He wouldn't punish me now, not before the meeting.

Makeup a mess. Hair straight and perfect, even after that display—augments had their place, I suppose. Bags darkened the skin under my eyes. Mirrors didn't lie unless one paid for one that would. Skin augments caused rashes and itchiness, side effects I wanted no part of.

The door banged open. Mace pulled me along, my fingers stretching for the clutch. The pearls bounced on my chest. Our pace steadied into a purposeful walk. No one paid us any mind. I know how I must have appeared to others, but this was New Orleans.

Once on the ground floor, Mace halted our advance

short of the Carousel Bar, eyes searching. I dared take my gaze from him for a moment.

Splendid, though a bit tarnished. A few bulbs out. A haze on the mirrors. But the rotating Carousel Bar remained glorious. Bottles filled the tiered shelving on the carousel's column and patrons filled all the seats but one.

"You'll sit there," Mace said. "That lone seat. Reserved for you."

"Where will you be?"

"Not your concern. Got it?"

"Yes, Mace." I stood still.

"Well?"

I took a step. Mace grabbed my arm, squeezed. The brute didn't need the bracelet on my wrist to inflict pain. "Speak to no one." As if sensing my question: "The bartender knows what to serve you. It's taken care of. No talking."

May I look? May I smell? May I feel? Hear? I guess tasting was on the menu as Mace allowed me a cocktail. What if Mace paid for what some called diminishments—typically only used on criminals as a means of punishment? What if Mace paid for such things—but then his sadistic nature wouldn't be fed. Maybe he'd turn the pain to a new mark.

"Yes, Mace." Straight for the bar. Straight for salvation. I expected the flaws picked out at thirty feet would, up close, smack me in the face, but up close the rococo beauty obfuscated the chips, cracks, and fading paint. A respite, just as the *Sunset Limited* had been, however brief, from the gloom and the black clouds swarming across the expanse and my future.

"Ms. Sheridan."

I blinked. Rubbed my arm. Said nothing. The bartender, a thick man up and down, wore a tuxedo sans vest, and sported a sheening bald head. He slid a cocktail my way. Reeked of virgin something or other.

Screw it. "Splash me a bourbon, neat," I said. "On second thought, make it a double."

"But, Ms. Sheridan, the gentleman."

I sniffed. "The gentleman. Where?"

"The gentleman, he," the bartender said, "he prearranged—"

"Take it easy, sister," the woman sitting beside me said, eyes forward, "you trying to kick a hornet's nest? Doing a good job of it. She'll have what the gentleman ordered."

The bartender sucked in a breath, turned, and attended to guests a few seats down. I turned my head ever so slightly, peripheral vision strained. The well-dressed woman who was with sweaty socks on the maglev platform—

"Yes. Take it easy. You're being watched closely. This appraisal is supposed to happen quietly. No fuss."

"What? You?" I whispered.

"No. Relax."

Who'd this dame think she was?

The bar stool on the other side of me emptied, but was immediately taken by another person. Sweaty socks.

"Those are not the genuine article," sweaty socks said.

My fingers caressed the pearls.

"When did you switch 'em out, huh? That boyfriend of yours?" sweaty socks asked.

"You?" I asked. "You're the one who—"

"Me?" sweaty socks asked. "Bartender, splash me a bourbon"—he winked at me—"neat."

I grabbed the faux cocktail the bartender had shoved under my nose. Sipped. Not a drop of booze. My tongue shot out and I scrunched my face.

Sweaty socks slid a rocks glass into my ready hand. Perfect.

I glanced at my wrist. Please, oh please, not now. I lifted the rocks glass, sniffed. Bourbon. I didn't care, not one whit, what kind. Sipped. The straw liquid washed over my tongue. Heaven. Damn the swarms anyway.

"What do you think?" the woman asked, silky English tinted with Cantonese.

My eyelids fluttered.

"I think these are bogus," sweaty socks said.

"I've worn them the entire time." The words slurred. "And you reek of corrupt cop. And sweaty socks."

The stench of menace, like something rotting deep inside approached me from behind, his nebulous form distorted in the hazy mirrors of the Carousel. Hands grabbed my shoulders. Yanked me backward. Off the stool.

"Mace," I said, "please. Don't."

"I'm sorry," Mace said, "she's had a little—" the rest of the words slurred in my mind. The Carousel spun, faster and faster, as if I'd put my head to pillow after a long day and night of drinking. Sparkling lights swirled before my eyes, like one of those photos people took of the heavens back when they were visible and the stars grew tails, arcing trails across my stupor.

"Mace, I'm—I'm falling." My body smacked a hard surface, but sank deep into—deep into something...

black movement undulating shadows
forced breath choking
fingers in nostrils
fist filling throat
I coughed. Tried coughing. No breath. A dream.
Eyelids glued shut.
Bile pushing upward.
No dream.
Lips glued shut.
Fingers grasping. Pulling. Clawing and tearing.
A muffled chime. The door.
The scream poured down my throat. My eyes burned.
Sinuses stuffed. Quicksand.
I scratched.
Clawed.
The door chimed.
Chimed again. Urgent.
The substance covering my face, my entire head,
undulated.
Fading.
A far-off noise. A crash.
Pulled a hand free of the muck.
Air. Choking.
My fingers scrabbled for the pearls.
Gone.
No. Suffocating.
"Liz." Muffled. "Liz." Hands on me.
My face froze. Electric blue and silver filled my
vision. My body convulsed.
Retreating. The wet sand retreated.
Hissing. Acrid smoke.
I reached for the invading substance. Fingers found
purchase. I ripped. Tore. Gasped.

Rolled on my side. Arcing blue pierced my eyes. I retched. Contents of my insides poured forth and I blinked away the blue and silver and black.

"Liz, please. Wait."

I fell off the bed. Wet. Lukewarm gritlike substance. Used-up bourbon swirling in the mix. I kicked and scrambled with my hands, slipping. Grabbed for the sheets. Hands lifted me. Strong hands. Bergamot and spice.

Fire-warped metal. Fire-warped screams. Burning hair and scorched skin. Chaos and booze. Victor.

I wobbled, but stood. My back arched and rounded as I heaved.

"Liz. I—"

I reached out, put a hand on Vic's chest. Heaved.

Ragged breaths. Burning lungs. I licked crusty lips, got the breathing under control.

"Victor," I gasped. "What—" My eyes adjusted. The gritlike substance congealed. Arcs subsiding.

He raised a wandlike device. "I couldn't risk full power, Liz. Couldn't." Vic's words stuttered as his eyes filled with grief.

I coughed. Grabbed the device. Studied for one second. Aimed. Squeezed the base. Cerulean shot through with silver erupted from the wand, arcing for the mass. My gaze caught the empty bed. No pillow. The mass on the floor was my pillow and where my head had been cradled just minutes before. The charge enveloped the pillow.

The pillow contorted. Stood. Flopped. Constricted. Sizzled. I twisted the end cap, but held the wand steady as the arc thickened. Burnt circuitry and fabric. Acrid smoke.

The pillow came apart, the faux fabric obliterated,

releasing a writhing, charred mass. The mass convulsed. Ceased movement. The arc retracted.

Sizzling. Boiling away. A burnt and jagged hole in the plush carpet. Charred carpet fiber.

Charred brain. Sizzled lungs.

"Vic, I—I'm—" I stumbled for the bathroom. Folded over like a commode-hugging drunk not caring how clean or filthy a toilet was while under the influence.

Bergamot and spice. Victor. Fire-warped—

"Liz. Take your time, but we've a problem."

I fought back the visions of fire and licked my lips. Shivered. Fought the urge. Swallowed. Mistake.

"Vic, please leave," I said, choking, but I reached back, grasped his pant leg. "I mean, just the bathroom, while I"—I gagged—"I get myself together."

The door shut.

After a spell I dragged myself up. Righted myself. Climbed into the clawfoot bathtub. Charming. Pulled the curtain. Showered. Skin-peeling hot. No cleansing nanos. The rational part of my mind understood the difference between helpful and harmful nanos.

Gooseflesh crawled all over me despite the scalding water. I finished showering, toweled off, wondering what everyday item might try to off me next. I tossed the towel on the tile.

Stood at the sink. My hair. I laughed. Coughed. Laughed. Hair straight and perfect, even after the struggle with the pillow. I leaned on the sink. A pillow of all things.

My hair remained perfect. Burn it off. Get back the scars. The bags darkening the skin under my eyes would go so swell with an angry pink scalp covered with scars.

Vic had saved me.

Where was Mace? That bastard. The pearls. I touched the skin where the pearls once rested.

Light raps on the door. "Liz, we need to go."

"I'm almost done. Five minutes."

"We don't have five."

Really? What was going to happen in five?

"Those nanosects—" Right. Tripped an alert somewhere.

My clutch and overnight bag had found their way into the bathroom. Vic, I guessed. I picked fresh undergarments from the bag. I hated having to wear the outfit from the previous day. Mace—

"Vic, any sign of Mace?" I didn't want to mention pearls.

A light rap. The door opened. "No. But he's gone. He left the hotel. Hurriedly. I found these." He thrust clothing on a hanger through the door's opening.

"Vic, I'm not shy."

"I don't want to gawk."

I pushed away the clothes and exited the bathroom wearing only the undergarments. "I've been gawked at before, you know. Never was keen on it. Not from any man. Or anyone for that matter."

Victor averted his gaze.

"You're different, Vic, now hand me the outfit. You don't gawk. You appreciate."

I grabbed the hanger and draped the outfit over an armchair. Not bad. A smart black bolo jacket and sleeveless white shirt, along with a pair of black capris. On the table was a hat: wide downturned brim with a shallow crown covered by a broad white band. A pair of black gloves lay nearby.

"You pick these out, Vic?"

"Afraid not, Liz," His eyes darted about. "Please hurry."

I slipped into the sleeveless number and wiggled into the capris. Vic, always more gentlemanly than I was used to, kept his eyes averted. I ran the white belt around my waist, pulled on the jacket and gloves. "Shoes?"

"Oh. Yes. I think I saw a pair by the closet." Vic retrieved the shoes, a pair of black and white wedge-cut heels. I slipped on the shoes and fixed the hat atop my head at a tilt.

The only downside to this outfit—well, there were two downsides at the moment: Mace's bracelet and the now missing pearls.

"Where are we headed?" I retrieved my clutch. "Hey, was there a handbag to go with this? Never mind, the clutch will do. At least it'll match."

"Out of town."

"How? The *Sunset Limited* won't be back until—"

"I've another way," Vic said. "Trust me."

The air left my lungs. Why did Vic have to utter those words. The last time—

I shuddered. Fire-warped screams. Burning hair. Scorched skin.

"Vic, we have to find Mason."

"What?" His eyes widened, then scrunched shut in pain, pulling on his scarred face, which he dragged a hand down. "Liz. Please. We have a stop to make first."

"Which is? And I don't even want to know how you plan on getting us out of New Orleans, not with those nanosect swarms out there." I glanced at the window but saw only gloom.

Vic opened the door. "We'll discuss on the way,

okay? Please? We don't have time for this." I exited the room, Vic followed and closed the door. "Stairs."

For one second I lamented leaving the luxury of the penthouse atop the Hotel Monteleone. The elevator chimed. Vic opened the doorway to the stairs.

"That'll be the French Quarter Constabulary," Vic said. "At least they have a horrid response time, but there's no way those nanosects and the firing of the arclight wand didn't register on their system."

"I see what you mean about having to leave." I clanked down the metal stairs in the heels, causing a ruckus. Vic followed, his footfalls quieter, but not silent despite the sound-absorbing soles of the type of shoe he always wore.

Once the constabulary arrived on scene, they cared only about containing the nanosects and hauling away the people who'd been in the presence of the nano-sects. There was a good chance some had survived and were now inside me, eating and doing whatever business nanosects conducted. And where Vic obtained the rare and vicious weapon capable of destroying nanosect and human alike, I did not need to know.

I shivered.

I clunked two floors down. Wasn't used to these heels. "Vic, how about an elevator from here?"

He shook his head. "No. They may have people posted at the elevator. These stairs also have a door that leads into an alley along with the usual door to the lobby."

Ugh. I clunked and clunked. Feet already angry on account of the chafing. Too bad they weren't those adjusting shoes like that well-dressed dame from the maglev and Carousel Bar had been wearing.

Vic moved past me, opened the door and peeked left and right before ushering me into the alleyway. The gloom hadn't lifted. The weak daylight in the penthouse had been manufactured. I sighed. A natural sun-filled day wasn't in the cards. Not today. Probably not any day in the future.

A layer of muck covered the alley. No amount of careful steps kept the muck from soiling the new shoes. A pity. My insides roiled. I doubled over before we exited the alley.

"Liz. You need food."

"No, let's keep moving. You said so." Yeah, a little bit of a martyr, but so what. "How far, anyway?"

"We can walk. I don't want to risk an autoconveyance. Unless you absolutely cannot make it."

"Let's just get there. Please. And you still haven't said where we're headed."

Vic grabbed my hand. "To take care of this." His fingers traced the bracelet's edges.

"Oh."

He pulled me down Royal Street, weaving through a meandering crowd. He turned right down an alley, crossed another street and turned down yet another alley. Vic stopped at a beat-up door. He pressed a hand to the surface. A charred fleur-de-lis illuminated.

"What is this?" I asked.

"A refuge."

"A holy refuge?" I laughed. "You sure they take fallen angels in there?"

Vic smiled. Warm, but pained me every time as the scars stretched and contorted. He opened the door. Incense, the heavy sort, poured from a metal censer.

"You found enlightenment or something during our time apart?"

"Liz, don't blaspheme, please. This is serious." He led me inside. Thick incense clouded the room. Men and women in thick drab robes tended a shape on the table in the room immediately to our left upon entering.

Wide plank flooring of deep brown and exposed beams overhead seemed to point the way to an inner sanctum of sorts. The incense cloud dissipated, and we were greeted by a man attired in a curious dark brown jerkin and pants. His eyebrows protruded and tufts of hair poked from his ears in that way of some older men when they ceased careful grooming.

"Victor," the man's voice boomed. "You've arrived. Good. About this device, young lady." I nearly snorted, but held out my left arm. "Ah, yes. A standard device, used to cow and torture."

More torture than cowing, really. Cowing wasn't in my nature no matter how much others believed they'd achieved such a thing with me. I could do without the pain though.

"Brother," Vic said, "she may have ingested nanosects."

The man's face drooped. Shoulders sagged. "Your acts of contrition and penance, Victor, do not falter in them—knowing your deeds have caused such pain in the world should keep you steadfast."

Fire. Screaming. Burning. Scorching. Chaos. I'd been there—been party to the act. Damned. Vic and I were damned.

"Yes, Brother. I seek redemption."

"Now"—the brother turned to me—"come. This

will be uncomfortable, I'm afraid." He led me deeper within the sanctuary. A bubbling pot hung suspended over a small fire, next to which sat urns and jars and mortars, as if I'd entered a medieval laboratory. He fussed with some jars, pouring powders and what looked like seeds into a mortar.

He hid his final preparations from view. I inched closer for a peek at this alchemy, preferring a hint of what I'd soon pour down my gullet.

"A little too curious, I think." He spun on me, a knowing smirk on his face. "We've found the old ways have their uses, even in this deplorable age."

"Liz," Vic said, "let me hold your clutch during this." I passed the clutch to him and dread filled me at what was coming.

"Here"—the man turned, extended calloused hands holding a bowl—"drink this. It will destroy any nanosects coursing through your system."

Lovely. Just how I wanted to think about it. Perhaps this was my penance. I took the bowl. The concoction carried a pleasant odor, of a lily perhaps. I smiled.

"Ah, the scent. Casablanca lily—fragrant, but used in that for the scent only, I'm afraid the taste—"

I tilted the bowl, the first warm drops hit my tongue—tasted like sewage smelled. My nose kinked, but I opened wide and dumped the contents in, wanting those things out of me.

"You'll feel a bit off the next few days," the man said. "Now, for the other matter."

I dragged my hand across my mouth. "How about a bourbon chaser first."

The brother stared into my eyes for a few seconds. Shook his head. Ice water froze my left hand. Ice water wormed up my arm. Squeezed my heart. A thumping ice cube. I gasped. I choked on "please." Mace. Where was Mace? Where had he taken the pearls? My jaw clenched, teeth grinding. "No." With all my might I pulled free. "No. I can't." The fist released my heart. The ice water turned lukewarm.

"But we're trying to help," the man said.

"Liz," Vic said. "You'll be free of Mason."

I laughed. "I'll never be free of Mace, even with the bracelet off; as long as he lives I'll never be free." I rubbed my left arm. The pain receded.

"So what is the alternative?"

"We find Mace." I turned to the man. "Now, is there a way you can assist with that?"

He took a deep breath. "Maybe. We have some equipment here we use on occasion to assist in bringing to justice those who have strayed."

Oh, how I had strayed. The man attached a probe to the bracelet. I pulled free.

"This won't cause discomfort," he said.

"Liz," Vic said, "I still don't think—"

"You're either in or you're out, Vic. Either way, I'm doing this."

The man reattached the probe. Studied a screen. I had no understanding of how this worked, but he explained the bracelet worked via a connection established between the bracelet and the one who implemented the device. He swiped the screen, tapped and poked the screen, and pointed: "Here. This is the spot, but you'll need to access the other side of the Veneer if you're to find Mason of the Lotus."

I'd never heard him called such before, but on the screen I spied the shape of a lotus on a specific spot

on the map. I'd resisted crossing through the Veneer;
doing so would put me on the map—but maybe that's
what I desired. Straddling the Veneer as so many did
twenty-four hours a day was commonplace and I'd
often done so. But I'd grown used to staying on the
right side of the Veneer.

"Liz, I don't think—"

"You keep saying that, Victor, but I have to do this.
Don't you see? To be free of him."

"But you seek something else," the man said, his
eyes glowed beneath the protruding eyebrows.

"I do."

"The pearls," Vic said. "Leave them be, Liz. They
will only cause great stress and great damage. They
should be left to others." He glanced at the man.

Something bothered me about those pearls. The
sweaty sock man and the well-attired woman appraised
them as being fake if I remembered the interaction
at the Carousel Bar at all. And now Vic knew about
them, or maybe had all along. I hadn't said word one
to him regarding the pearls and how I'd been on the
hook for delivering them to Mace and whatever sordid
business he conducted. Vic had said "business" when
he found me on the maglev, said he was in New
Orleans on business. I'd grill him later.

I tapped into the virtual, straddling the Veneer.
Information flooded my brain, too much too soon. I
swept away the detritus, digging for—

"Not within the sanctum," the man said.

I cut it off. Left the sanctum of the fleur-de-
lis. Vic followed. I retraced our path back to Royal
Street. Tapped in once more, straddling the Veneer,
and sipped the information this time. Not far. Mace

remained stationary. The virtual marker given me by
the man at the sanctum guided me: between Royal
and Bourbon streets, a few blocks.

The crowd thickened. The gray muck coated my
shoes, which had been pristine for all of five minutes.
The heavy air stuck to my face and invaded my lungs.
I would not be deterred. Not now. We cut through
the crowd snaking around street performers and ven-
dors. Music cut through the crowd's din. If only music
washed out the stench of trash and tepid water and
grimy people in need of a good scrub.

The overlay projected upon my retinas guided me.
Red dots appeared on the map in the corner of my
vision. "Vic, people are coming for me." Time ran
thin for me. I had to find Mace.

Vic grabbed my arm. "Wait."

"Vic. Let go."

"We should leave. Just leave. Why do this? I never
told you my business in New Orleans."

"No, you didn't."

"Okay. Just stop walking. Please."

I stopped. Muck oozed over the lip of my pumps.
Who knew what lived in the muck on these streets.
"Okay, I'm not walking."

"I was here for you." He stared at the ground.
"And the—"

I shoved Vic. "And the pearls. You were here for
the pearls." The red dots moved for our position on
the map in my eye. "They're coming, Vic, and you
know who they are, don't you?"

"What? No. I don't—don't you see? I was here for
you, and for the pearls, but they're gone. I saved you,
the nanosects at the hotel—"

"Tell me you didn't try to kill me for those pearls. Tell me that." My skin crawled. I stumbled backward, into a wall, the dampness soaked through. "Oh my, I—the pearls. The pearls were gone—those pearls contained the horror—"

"And now there is no more reason for me to be here. For us to be here, don't you see? Those pearls were supposed to be dormant prototypes of cleansing nanosects."

"And someone activated the pearls, which used the pillow as a means, but someone controlled them." Mace practically told me my stay in New Orleans would be short-lived. "Cleansing nanosects? But that was crap, wasn't it, I almost died." I'd been wearing dormant nanosects around my neck. What, posing as pearls? "Even more reason for me to go after Mace."

"Liz, wait. Those pearls, they're our redemption, don't you see? The real strand wields the power for us to atone for the destruction we caused all those years ago."

Yeah. The fire-warped screams. Burnt hair. Scorched skin. Swarms of nanosects. Right. No atonement for my deeds.

I walked away. Maybe Vic followed. Maybe he didn't. The spot where Mace hid came upon me quickly, and the red dots on the map continued their march toward me.

The overlay put me at what was once a club. A jazz club of sorts if memory served with one big room. The end was inside. Either mine or Mace's.

I peeled away from the Veneer slowly, allowing the data to trickle, then drip, then cease. I took a deep breath. Free from the other side once more.

And I liked it. Free of the flow. But now blind to the red dots on the map. They'd likely discover my location, wouldn't be hard, but only Mace mattered. Mace's reckoning.

What would I do inside? The bracelet still adorned my wrist. I'd fight through the pain.

I pushed through the door, harder than I needed, as it swung open and smacked against the wall. Lights streamed from inside, illuminating the gloom in which I stood.

"Lizabeth. I thought I'd never see you again." Mace was bare-chested, tied to a chair. The lights shining on him. Bright. Hot lights.

I stepped inside and took in the room. Every inch illuminated. Wood flooring sagged under my footsteps, soggy and blackened. I could almost make out the mold spores floating before my eyes.

"I bet, Mace. I bet. The pearls. You tried to murder me, and for what?"

Mace struggled against the ropes binding him to the chair. The rope sawed into his sweaty chest. Streaks of red crisscrossed his chest from where he'd struggled, the rope taking on a pink hue.

"You don't understand."

"I'm sure I don't. At least not in any way I care to. Your games. Your position of authority within that little gang of yours in Macau. That graft on your hand." I raked my fingers through my hair, hoping to feel the scars that'd been erased. I spun and glanced at the doorway. No Vic. He hadn't followed me after all. Guess facing Mace wasn't his thing. I closed the door.

Mace's head dipped, chin hitting his chest. "They're coming. They knew you'd come here." Blood-infused drool oozed from his mouth. "You were always a decoy. You never had the real string of pearls." His body went limp.

I slapped him. A nice handprint tattooed his cheek. "Mace, who did this to you? Who is coming?"

He mumbled.

"I'd like to thank them," I said, "after everything you did to me. After—" I saw his hand. Oozing blood and it looked like the skin of someone who'd just gotten a tattoo, that sheen. Not even a faint outline of the lotus from the graft. The graft no longer there. "Mace, what happened?"

"It's over." More blood dribbled from his mouth.

My left hand froze. Arm numbed. Heart seized. "Mace," I gasped. Fell to my knees and collapsed forward on my face. How? The door swung open. A warm draft hit my face.

Two pairs of feet. Dirty shoes and clean pumps.

Sweaty socks. I rolled on my side. Gasped. A vice squeezed my heart. The sweaty sock man and the well-dressed woman stood over me.

"You'll need to come with us," sweaty socks said. "We need to know where your friend Victor is. Take us to him. This one"—sweaty socks nodded at Mace—"has no more use for us now."

The woman smiled, those teeth, so white. Her eyes glinted. Green eyes. Her look softened.

The vise on my heart relaxed. The cold burned as it traced back through my arm. "You assumed Mace's mantle," I said to the man.

"Oh? Did I?" No lotus adorned his hands.

The woman smirked. "Now, get yourself together and come with us. We have use of you. We need to find your friend. Put an end to this business of tracking the pearls."

I groaned. There was no use. They'd ruined the plans I'd had to end Mace. End my pain. Now it'd begin all over again. My hat had settled under Mace's chair, the clutch beside it, peeking open. The arclight wand. Vic must have put the wand in there at the sanctum. It was slender, but barely fit lengthwise. I rolled onto my hands and knees.

The door banged again. Everyone looked. It was Vic. I grabbed the arclight wand while Vic went for sweaty socks. The woman turned, her eyes squinted and a smirk played on her lips. I squeezed the wand. Electricity arced, cerulean laced with silver. Enveloped her face.

She stumbled.

Pain wormed up my left arm. I held steady with my right. The arc widened. Singed hair. Burning hair. Scorched skin.

Bergamot and spice overpowered the sweaty socks.

Fire-warped scream. Her scream. The bracelet on my wrist warped, burned my skin. I held steady.

"Liz, stop. You'll—"

Victor grabbed my right arm. I released my grip on the wand. The woman crumbled. Alive, but gravely injured. The pain in my left arm did not subside.

The bracelet. A wide scar encircled my wrist where the bracelet had—no, the bracelet had become one with my arm. Now a part of me. The pain. Searing. Forever connected to whom?

Victor held me. Mace's breaths ragged behind me. Sweaty socks on the floor moaning. The well-dressed, but ill-mannered woman on her back now. Shallow breaths.

"There's something you can do—if you don't want to be tethered to the person wearing that graft." Vic broke the embrace and put his hands on my shoulders. He glanced at the woman on the floor, the new leader of the Macau Lotus. "But if you do, I can't—"

"I need to know something," I said. "The pearls. Before I do anything else, the pearls. You have the string of pearls, don't you?"

Vic shook his head. "If I find the original strand, they'll be used for good. This time will be different, trust me."

"Why did you say that? The last time ended in pain. Scars for both of us. Inside and out. I've a mind to take back my scars. Use this wand on my head."

"Don't."

"Vic, if you use the pearls you better make sure they don't fall into the wrong hands. Not this time."

I kneeled beside the woman. The graft on her hand fresh. Assimilating. Not yet fully attached. I dug my fingernails under and peeled. The woman screamed. Writhed. Resisted.

My left arm chilled.

I peeled. Ripped the graft from her hand. The lotus hung limp.

Victor nodded. I raised the wand. Aimed.

The chill in my arm subsided.

I dropped the wand and placed the graft atop my left hand.

Victor's shoulders drooped. Crestfallen. Defeated. He walked through the door and out of my life.

Maybe someday. Maybe.

I stared at the bloody lotus grafting to my hand. No more fire-warped screams. No more burnt hair or scorched skin. No more chaos. But there'd still be booze.

The well-dressed woman's chest rose and fell three times. Her clenched fingers opened, releasing a string of pearls. Her chest ceased rising. I snatched them and ran to the door.

"Victor," I yelled, "come back."

Vic turned. Smiled broadly.

"Here, you forgot these." I handed over the string of pearls.

Honey Fall

Sarah A. Hoyt

It was raining. I could hear rain pattering on the roof, singing along gutters. An unaccustomed sound.

There was an odd smell, a sound of gnawing. And I needed to get out and do—

I didn't know what I needed to get out and do.

I was in a small room. There was a window. Dismal gray light shone through, illuminating a series of hooks on the wall, with clothes hanging on them. I sensed more than saw an unmade bed nearby and a large workbench. Smells were chemical with an undertone of bachelor living quarters, all dirty socks and dust. And I had a run in my silk stocking.

I stared at the stocking a long time, knowing that was wrong. I was not the sort of sloppy dame who wandered around with runs in her stocking.

I became aware that I was leaning against the wall, in an uncomfortable position, my legs splayed out gracelessly. The hem of my skirt had gotten torn.

It felt as though someone had flung me in a corner of the room like a broken doll. I blinked. I did not remember being flung. I remembered—

There had been a scene with Ale. I remembered that and made a face at it, but I didn't remember what the scene had been about or what had happened precisely. A quick memory of a shot, and of a bullet... I moved my hand to my left, under my breast, but there was no pain and no wound. A dream.

I got up. It's easier said than done. I had to brace myself against the floor, push with my legs, then pull myself up the wall with my hands. I can't explain it. It's not like something hurt, or like my legs were broken. My body just felt all prickles, like your legs feel if you sit too long.

Standing, I looked around. The room was not familiar. It was a largish bedroom, with a workbench, and the man who lived here must be a natural-born slob. The bed was unmade, and it looked like it was never made. There was stuff scattered on it on top of the tumbled blankets. Getting closer, I saw a wallet. Also a broken magician's wand. A rat was gnawing on it, eliciting sparks for every bite, but not seeming to care.

I'd never been here. I was sure of it.

"Honey," I told myself, "you're getting sloppy in your old age. A woman should not be alone in a man's house without knowing the man rather thoroughly, and if you've descended to slobs like this, you've come a long way since Arty."

And then I realized what I'd said, and clutched the bed clothes as memory returned. I was Honey D'Orio, and Arty was Arthur James Arcana, the love of my life, who had left me, to go chase his dreams—well, chase something, at any rate, in Los Angeles. Not that he didn't have reason to do it, since the Pater did not approve. Or perhaps it was more fair to say that Arty did not approve of the Pater, and refused to work the family business like a good little boy.

I let it go. The words came with a feeling of screamed arguments, in which Ale always took his part against Arty, and where Pater for once listened to him. The whole felt not so much like my memories—though I was sure they were, in fact, mine—but the memories of some other woman, that I'd bought piecemeal at a rummage sale.

The feeling of urgency returned, the one that had caused me to wake. I was supposed to get out of here and go get help.

Help for whom or what?

Five long steps to the door, and I found it unlocked. So I was not a prisoner. Help for whom, then?

I went back to the bed and grabbed the wallet, flipped through it. There were two fifty-dollar bills in it, which made me cast a look around the place again. A lot of money for the owner of this dump.

There was also a much-folded, greasy-looking driver's license listing the owner as Donald Griffin. There was an automobile key. At least it looked like an automobile ignition key and the fob said Chevy. I pocketed that. Something nagged me about that license. I'd swear there was something relating to Donald Griffin. I'd also swear I'd never heard his name.

With no idea where I was going or why it was urgent, I opened the door and stepped out.

And into a steady downpour.

Which caused me to blink in confusion. I was a

Colorado girl, born and bred, and in Colorado you're more likely to get wet with snow than with rain. But every ten years or so, we had a year where it wouldn't stop raining. Spring and summer would come and it kept raining. This had that sort of feel.

I exited the house onto a garden path that descended in a series of very broad steps among a garden more luxurious than Colfax usually was. There was lush grass and old trees and roses blooming in the moisture.

But I knew where I was and looking back at the house confirmed it. I was on East Colfax, the street that ran from Denver to Aurora. Twenty years ago or a bit more, it had been a respectable street, home to mansions with large gardens, but the wars had taken their toll on everything. Now the big Victorian mansions that no one could afford, like the one that rose in front of me in tones of need-to-be-painted grayish blue, had been subdivided into apartments. From the looks of it, Donald Griffin lived in the cottage at the back, which had probably once been a carriage house, or perhaps a gardener's cottage.

I walked down the path, not even bothering to avoid the dripping from above, then climbed down ten steps to the street level. There was a Chevy parked out front. It was a 1926 Chevy Landau that had seen better days. Its rear back panel had been shoved in at least once, maybe more; there was rust on one of the doors, and the whole car was in dire need of a paint job.

But all I needed was a car that would allow me to go somewhere where I could think.

Home, I thought. I wanted to go home. Something in me, some feeling, that same sense of urgency that had awakened me protested, but the urgency could wait. I wanted to go home. And I knew exactly where home was and how to get there.

Acting as if the car belonged to me and I had a right to do it, I opened the door and sat down. There were a gaggle of children playing across the street, and a couple of women, their bags loaded with groceries, walked along the sidewalk talking. None paid any attention to me as I started the car and followed the route I could follow in my sleep.

The Landau didn't purr as I remembered my car purring, my own, beloved Auburn Speedster, painted candy-apple red, that Pater had bought me to celebrate my nineteenth birthday, or perhaps because I'd let Arty go. I still wasn't sure letting Arty go had been a good idea, but at least, dear Lord, I'd got my Speedster out of it.

I blinked unaccountable moisture from my eyes, not sure why it felt like the Speedster was long lost, and took a deep breath, looking up at the gray sky where a couple of broom-flyers sped somewhere, darker against the gray. What a day to be flying. I wouldn't want to try it, not even on the most securely enchanted of brooms. Sure, a lot of veterans flew because they'd done it overseas, but it still seemed like a comfortless form of transportation.

I drove away from Colfax, towards Cherry Creek and the Country Club district. Pater had built the dear old family home less than five years ago. It's an almost embarrassing pile, all golden stone and sweeping European-looking turrets and balconies. I suspected it was his Sicilian grandfather's idea of a palace. The things that get transmitted in the genes!

Because when he'd built the house, he already could see a day when Ale and I would want to move away, and because Pater is unable to bear anyone leaving and going beyond his control, he'd built two apartments into the house, the sort of place where we could live—presumably even after we married—and pretend to be independent.

Mine was around the back, through the terrace at the rear of the house, the same terrace that led to the ballroom where we'd had my coming out ball, and where I'd danced all night with Arty, while Ale glowered.

I hadn't realized how late it was until I pulled into the broad driveway around the house. I could not have known it, of course, not with the overcast sky. But when I got home it must have been well past dinner time. I toyed with going into the dining room and apologizing, but I had a strong feeling I should not. I wasn't sure why, but I reasoned that with my impaired memory, it wasn't a good time to buck my instincts. Not that I had much experience with impaired memory, save a couple of drinking binges, one of them the night Arty left. But even that was enough to show me that sometimes, when you couldn't remember, feeling was all you had.

I got out of the car. A man weeding one of the flower beds straightened up and stared at me, mouth half open. Well, he was probably one of the gardeners and wondering what I was doing driving this pile. Let him go on wondering. I ran across the corner of the terrace, up two stone steps, and took the path to the side that led to my door. Then I stopped. I didn't have my key with me.

Well, it wasn't precisely an unheard-of predicament. Sometimes purses got forgotten. I walked around the edge and felt in the flower bed for the peculiarly shaped stone at the base of the yellow rosebush. The key was there, under the stone, feeling weirdly encrusted with dirt. I couldn't remember when I'd last needed it, but it took me a while to get all the dirt off, so I could put it in the lock and turn it.

The door opened with a creak that nearly pushed me out of my skin.

Inside was . . . my apartment.

See, I chose all of it when I was barely fifteen, which will have to explain why it was decorated in tones of silver and green. My wallpaper was a tracery of delicate green branches, and the furniture was metallic silver, elfin, delicate constructions. Pater had laughed that it was not at all proper furniture, but he liked to indulge me.

My front room was a large sitting room with enough sofas and divans for a party of my closest twenty friends. I walked by the piano and trailed my fingers across the keys before going to my room at the back.

My room was also silver and green, with a soft green coverlet on the silver bed. Next to it was the most expensive bathroom money could buy. I had to make myself decent before going out.

I didn't realize how bad it was. Beyond the torn stocking there were dirt smudges on my cheeks, and the fact that my skirt had collected dust from Griffin's floor. My shoes, too, green patent leather to match my skirt, had become scuffed.

I undressed, washed, and started dressing again before I realized that my entire room was covered in a layer of dust. It made me uncomfortable in a way I couldn't explain, but I shrugged. I might have been away for a few weeks, and Pater been busy with his ventures and not paid any attention. Obviously my maid had taken advantage to take a vacation.

Because it was nighttime and because I had a feeling where I should go, even if not why, I picked a tailored dark green dress, which I wore with my jade beads. At least, whatever I'd been doing with myself, my hair passed muster—which wasn't a given. Left to its own devices, it grew black and in a riot of curls that my father reassured me was exactly the same as his grandmother's when she was young. Fortunately, in the modern era, a girl didn't have to sit under that, and I didn't. Instead, I made it platinum blond and arranged the curls in a stylish fall that blocked my right eye.

The stockings I put on did not have a run, and I picked new heels from the shelf in my closet. Because I had no idea what this was about, I selected my two guns, the ones that Daddy had given me when I turned sixteen, pearl-handled .22 Baby Hammerlesses. One went into my purse, and one into my garter. Because it was raining and the temperature falls fast in the Rocky Mountains once the sun sets, I picked up my fox fur stole and my seldom-used umbrella. Between the two I managed to stay cozy and warm all the way to the car. And yeah, it was the Landau again. My car might still be in the garage at the back, but I was in a hurry.

I backed down the driveway and to the Magic Cat. The Magic Cat is at the edge of the Five Points neighborhood, but it is not colored. Not as such. People of all colors came here. Well, mostly the patrons were white and the personnel, including the excellent jazz bands, were colored. But the thing was no one looked very closely at you there. It was a place I could both be myself and something more than Daddy's little girl.

The parking lot next to it was full, and my car would have passed more unnoticed than the Landau. But I found a spot all the same and walked out, Griffin's two fifty dollar notes burning a hole in my dainty purse.

Coming in from the cool rain, pushing open the polished wood doors of the Magic Cat, with the bas relief of a cat in a fedora playing the trombone, felt like coming home more than my apartment did.

Inside, the club was cool, but dry, and illuminated by golden lampshaded lights that gave an impression of a tropical night.

I didn't recognize the band playing, but the notes wound in a spiral of sound around the usual dancers. Well-dressed, well-coiffed people. Couples who twirled together in every semblance of a passion not acceptable in public. This too felt good. It felt like I'd been away a long long time, and I wanted to warm myself at the fire of human passion and familiarity.

Some people looked oddly at me, but since I didn't know them, I assumed they were new. I pulled my fox stole up over my shoulder, as though to protect myself from stares. It hit me that I'd neither eaten nor drunk in a long time, and I was dying for a drink.

I was skirting the dance floor towards the bar when from the other side, the dark space next to the bar, a hand shot out and grabbed my wrist at the same time a voice said, "Honey."

I turned, ready to freeze with a look whoever had

dared touch me, and stopped. "Arty!" I said, half in a shriek.

He let out a surprised chuckle. "That revolting nickname!" he said, as I reached up to save the fur my startled movement had unsettled.

I didn't know what to say, so I smiled and said, "I didn't know you were in town."

"I wasn't till yesterday," he said. "I arrived by train yesterday morning."

"Oh. From California?"

"From Los Angeles, yes."

"For...you're coming back?"

He shook his head but shrugged a little, as if he wasn't quite sure what to say, so I thought maybe he hadn't made a decision yet. "I'm parched," I said. "You must buy me a drink."

The back of my mind was telling me to let him know everything that had happened since I'd woken up, but I thought I was just going mushy and wanting to unload all my troubles on Arty's very broad shoulders.

He put his arm over my not-so-broad shoulders and led me to the bar. It was Steven serving the drinks. He gave me an odd look, then seemed reassured by Arty's presence, and when Arty ordered a bourbon for himself and a Cosmopolitan for me, he just gave us the drinks. Arty paid, then led me, with his arm still over my shoulder, to one of the booths.

I sipped at my Cosmo, which was precisely how I liked it with the right proportion of lemon and grapefruit, and wondered if I should eat something or if I was going to get sloppy. I couldn't remember when I'd last eaten.

Arty took a sip of his drink and made a face while

looking very attentively at me. He'd gotten older. He was always older than I. When I met him, I was seventeen and he was twenty-five. He'd been in the fourth year of med school when they'd called him for his brief war service as a flyer. Because the moment that John Whiteside Parsons had discovered magic, the army had searched for men who could use it, before the Krauts found it too and used it first. We'd gone into the war on the Allies' side, as magic flyers. And it turned out that Arty was chock full of magic, as well as whatever natural brilliance had propelled him into medical school.

He was still looking at me as if I were a very difficult problem he was trying to solve, even as he reached in his coat for his cigarette case and extended it to me. I was happy to see that it was the one I'd given him, silver, engraved with his initials, as I took a cigarette. I let him light it and blew two puffs before taking another sip of my drink and returning his serious look.

"I came to Denver," he said, "because I got this." He reached into his jacket again and pulled out a postcard. It was one of those they sell at the train station, advertising the newest trains. He turned it over and slid it to me.

The handwriting was crabbed and irregular, and it had been written with thin ink that looked brownish, but it was perfectly legible. "Art, I am in a spot of bother involving the D'Orio family. I don't know what to do, and I can trust no one. It seemed like a good time to call in a favor." It was signed, in a shaky hand, Don Griffin.

"My family?" I said. And to his shrug, "And who is Don Griffin?"

Arty toyed with the corner of the postcard. "Old friend from the war. Same corps. Saved my life. That's the favor he talks about."

"A flyer?" I asked.

Arty shrugged then seemed to think better of it. "I was never a flyer, Honey. Didn't it strike you as peculiar that I would go to California to work in Hollywood? No. My specialty was always illusions."

Illusions. Look, I'm no strategist and, sure, I don't read all those super important accounts of the war and analysis of "how we won." But I do read the pulps. I know what illusions mean. They mean spies and assassins. "And Griffin was in the same corps?"

"Stronger than I. He could create simulacrums."

I raised my eyebrows.

"Simulacrums. Creatures called up by magic, who move and live like the real thing, sometimes for months. Useful when, say, you killed a high-value target but you didn't want the enemy to know it was dead or that it had been compromised. Anyway, too long to tell you and too technical a story, but he saved my bacon once in the war. And then he came here, to Denver, partly because I'd told him about it, to make a living as a magician for hire."

"And you kept in touch?" I said, wondering why I'd never heard of Griffin, not once. At least not that I could remember until I woke up in his pad.

"No. We lived in very different worlds. I met him once or twice when I—when we were keeping company, Honey, and I told him about you."

Well, there was a connection between us, though I was not at all sure what it meant. However, this was Arty, and he obviously knew Don Griffin, and the feeling I should tell him everything and fast was powerful enough that it would be hard to stay quiet. So I smoked my cigarette and drank my Cosmo, while around us jazz wound like a cool wrap, masking our words as I told him everything that had happened to me today. A woman and a man danced by, her head on his shoulder. Arty and I had looked like that once.

Perhaps it was the Cosmo making me tipsy, as I found myself walking to Arty's car—he'd rented one this morning he said, and smiled when he told me he was doing well in L.A. though I didn't understand how well he could do in just six months—and driving back to Griffin's place.

It still wasn't locked and looked exactly as I'd left it, except that the rat had stopped gnawing at the wand.

"What are we looking for?" I asked. I still had the sense of urgency, and it remained unfocused. I'd needed to get to Arty. No. I'd needed to get to someone who could help Griffin, and Arty was one of those people. But other than that, I had nothing except the feeling I should . . . yes, I should be helping Griffin.

"Anything," Arty said. He was going over Griffin's workbench, inch by inch, moving dubious flasks and rearranging various objects I couldn't identify. "Anything that tells us what he was doing or for whom he was making simulacrums."

"Was he making simulacrums?" I asked.

"Sure," he said. "I recognize the materials. Would your family buy simulacrums?"

I shrugged. "Maybe. You know I don't know anything about Pater's business."

"A wise move, since people who do tend to end up dead."

"Arty, Pater just does what he has to do to—"

"Survive and keep the family safe. Yes. Forgive me, Honey. I didn't mean to start the argument again."

He was still giving most of his attention to the workbench and its paraphernalia, so what could I do? I started looking through the bedclothes, to see if there was anything else there. It seemed weird that Griffin had disappeared leaving behind his wallet and his keys, but there was nothing else on the bed, so I started following the path to the door, which is when I saw it.

Look, there were other things on the floor, so I might easily have missed it. It was obvious that Griffin was not one of your natural housekeepers. But there, against the far floorboard, near the rat hole was Ale's pen.

I'd have known it anywhere.

Back when Ale was in school and father still had illusions about being the patriarch of scholars, Father had given him a distinctive silver pen, a thing worked by hand by some craftsman from the old country. It was slick and slim, and it had—I confirmed this as I got closer—Ale's name engraved on it: A. S. D'Orio.

I didn't know what Ale's pen was doing in Griffin's pad, but my first impulse was to hide it and pretend I'd never seen it, because . . .

I paused. Because I'd covered for Ale all his life, at first hiding his bad behavior from Pater so Pater would not be grieved, and eventually just hiding his behavior from everyone because I didn't want to be associated with a man who had turned out to be a common thug. Yeah, I know. You could say the same of Pater and the family business. But it wasn't precisely that way.

The family business had its roots in the old country. It was both vocation and obligation. Sure, Pater lived by crime too, though you might have trouble tracing all his criminal enterprises to him. They were done through flunkies and managers to such an extent that, in the end, even the IRS itself couldn't find the connections needed to bring the business down.

Did Pater's enterprise create misery and loss? I didn't know. Ever since I had realized what Pater did when I was twelve or so—and I can't tell you how, except through adding up the hints and stray words dropped over the years—I'd tried to think of it as little as I could. Pater had certainly broken the law during Prohibition, and I knew there were other things in which he defied the might of the United States of America.

But was it worse than it would have been without him? It would take a better woman than I to know. Arty thought he knew, which was why he'd left me and Denver to go to L.A. and pursue his idea of using his not inconsiderable magic to create movies. He wouldn't sully his hands with Pater's business.

Still, the one thing Pater wasn't was a cheap thug. He didn't knock women about, abuse prostitutes, or plan hare-brained enforcement expeditions to knock out the teeth of some random man he thought had looked at him funny at a bar.

The thought of hiding Ale's pen, and therefore Ale's potential involvement in this, came and went. "Arty," I said, and I walked over and pointed at the pen. I had some idea he might be able to get some sort of emanation or feel from the thing if I didn't touch it. "This is Ale's."

Arty looked over from the workbench, and his eyebrows went up as he stared at the pen on the floor, amid the debris. He flashed a feral grin, "Well, we did know your family was invol—"

"Completely different thing," I said. "If it was Ale. Completely different thing. Ale was a wrong 'un from the beginning, Arty." I looked at his face and explained about Pater breaking the law but being disciplined and an adult. "Ale is just wrong. He beats women and sends thugs to beat men who best him at anything, from a bet to romancing a girl. My father doesn't know. At least I don't think he knows. I've kept it secret from him as much as possible, but Ale couldn't keep it secret from me, not when we went to the same schools and later had the same friends."

Arty took out the cigarette case and offered it to me first. We smoked in silence a long moment.

"I see," he said. "But you're not holding your peace now?"

"I—I don't know why but I have a really strong feeling that it's important we save Don Griffin."

He nodded. "Well, I certainly think so."

He threw his cigarette butt on a clear bit of floor and stomped on it. I put mine out in an overfull ashtray. I noted with interest that some of the cigarettes had exactly the color of my lipstick around the end. I wondered if I'd known Don Griffin. And why didn't I remember?

Arty had picked up Ale's pen with his handkerchief, put it on the workbench, and frowned intensely at it.

I don't know what I expected. Fire or stars, passes or arcane whispers. I'd seen magic on the stage before. I had some idea what it was supposed to look like.

Instead, what came up was a scene. It was foggy or perhaps just distant. Kind of like what it would look like through a window with condensation on it. Behind the workbench, against the wall, a replica of this room formed. Ale, in his brash finery, expensive suit spoiled by a big, yellow-and-white checkered tie held down with a diamond tie pin—that boy never did have any taste—was talking to a thin, dark man with sparse hair combed back from his forehead. I knew without being told that the man was Griffin, which made me wonder what exactly had happened between me and him, and why I recognized him.

He was not what I'd expect, not at all. Not my type. And when one thinks of a spy, one doesn't think of a thin, tired-looking man. Someone like Arty maybe, but not him.

Ale was giving Griffin a picture, "As close as you can, okay? As close as humanly possible."

Griffin mumbled something about time and materials and how expensive it would be. "And then, you know," he said. "She won't be the same. She won't remember the things the original knew. She won't fool anyone who knew her, not once they have a good look. She'll walk different, she'll talk different. She'll be a different person for as long as she lives."

"Doesn't matter," Ale said. "Not for what I need her. Just being seen around town and confirming rumors, that's all."

"Well, that . . . that should be possible."

They were setting a date for delivery. And it was the day after my birthday, on the fourth of July. This confused me for a moment. I thought it was May, maybe April. Suddenly I didn't know what month it was. I'd realized part of my memory was missing, but I didn't know how much of it or what had happened. You know, if I'd used that lost time to take up with the likes of Don Griffin, I needed mental help and would seek it as soon as possible.

"So," I said, "Ale hired Griffin to do a simulacrum, and if I know Ale, he probably welched on payment. Chances are that he took Griffin out to the edge of town and had his thugs beat him, and Griffin is now trying to find his way back, footsore and bruised. What do we do now? How do we find him?"

"We," Arty said, going all of a sudden as solemn and serious as a judge, and one of those judges you couldn't buy for love or money, "aren't going anywhere, Honey. You're going back to your apartment and beddy-bye. And I'm going to get some old friends from the corps and figure this out."

"Arthur Arcana, you rat," I said. "You can't do that. This is my case. This is my story. I'm the one who woke up with the feeling I had to help Griffin. I don't know why, and I don't know how, but I'm sure I'm supposed to do it."

He smiled a little at my calling him a rat, that weird quirk of the lip he used to give when I railed at him or teased him, but his eyes were dead serious and shading to sad. "No, Honey. You have helped him. You told me the whole story. You brought me here. But this will be dangerous, and there is no way I'm going to drag a dame on this kind of errand."

"But, Art, Ale is my brother, and I know his tricks better than you. I know his tricks better than anyone. You need me."

And yet he wouldn't give. He kept looking at me

with those infinitely sad eyes. I thought that once more he had seen me as a D'Orio, someone who wasn't fit to keep company with him. He didn't want anything to do with me.

He started to the door, then surprised me by walking back into the room, kissing my forehead with a butterfly kiss, his lips barely touching. "God bless you, Honey," he said. "You're too good, too fine for this. Stay away."

What is a woman to do with that? Once he'd told me I was good and too fine for my family, and he'd walked away and to California, and if this was July or later, he'd been gone for nine months at least. And I still didn't know what to do with that, except one thing: I couldn't let him go. Not now. Not again. Nor could I let him go off to look for Don Griffin, and maybe die alone. I wouldn't lose Arthur James Arcana again.

I should have told Pater that I was out, and endured his temper tantrum, and told him if he sent anyone after Art, I'd go to the police with a lot of things I'd deduced about the family business. And then I should have left. By now we'd have a little house in the hills in California, and maybe a kid on the way.

"Well, there is no time like the present," I told myself. I took a cigarette from my own case and smoked it down to the nubbins, before stubbing it out on the ashtray with all the other ones with the same lipstick color smeared on them.

By the time I stepped down to the street, there was no sign of Arty's car. I walked in the rain, thinking, to a busier part of the street, where I flagged a cab. I used some of Griffin's money to get back to the Magic Cat and Griffin's car.

Me, I don't use magic. Never have. But everyone knows a magic practitioner or two these days. Basic life necessity, right? Even a girl needs antiwrinkle magic now and then, not to mention getting someone's claws off her best boy's back. If you don't enter in the love philter war in junior high, you're a fool. And if you continue it much after twenty, you're a worse one, I understand. Not that there was magic when I was in junior high of course.

But I knew magic practitioners and had heard of others. The one I decided on, more blind instinct than anything else, was Mother Turner, down by the Cathedral.

There's a welter of little houses down there, a colored neighborhood, and Mother Turner was colored. A middle-aged woman of vast proportions, she was the matriarch of a large and respectable tribe. It was a point of pride to her that one of her sons was a bellman at the Brown Palace, and two more worked for the railroad. But she'd run her foretelling and fortunes business long before Parsons had made magic a scientific reality. I'd consulted her now and then. Nothing much, mind. I knew better than to use magic in love. Except when it came to Arty. I had no brain at all when it came to Arty. Just a blind yearning to be with him, a blind feeling I belonged to Mr. Arcana.

Mother Turner had been straight with me about that too. I remembered the talk after Arty had left, about how I had to choose, how it wouldn't do to run after a man, and she'd refused to bring him back to Denver and particularly into Pater's business. "No, missy," she'd said. "That I won't do because making a man come back against his will is worse than killing him, and making a man participate in crimes against his will is against God's law."

I respected her more for it than if she'd given in. I parked the car in front of her door and walked the little path to her house. Her roses, in her tiny little yard, were full abloom.

The door was opened by a young woman in a severe skirt suit, who gave me a tiny smile before whispering, "Miss D'Orio" and stepping out of the way to let me enter a tiny, oppressively clean living room.

She then walked through an arch to a hallway, murmuring something about "telling Mother."

I didn't know if Mother Turner was her mother or her mother-in-law, and suddenly it occurred to me, more urgently, I didn't know if Mother Turner was even awake. I'd been so taken with my ideas, with the need to let Arty go, I'd forgotten it might be dinnertime or later. Certainly, it was full night outside.

I was relieved when Mother Turner came back with the young woman. She had obviously been awake. She'd also obviously been cooking, judging by the apron she was removing as she walked towards me. "Now, Miss D'Orio, it sure has been a long time," she said, handing the apron to the younger woman, who then vanished back into the back of the house. "Sure has." She extended her hand to me, then frowned a little when I shook it and a little more as she looked at me. She muttered, "Oh, my," under her breath, and sat down on her sofa, while gesturing for me to sit. "I see you're in trouble. Tell me your story, honey. Just tell me."

So I told her. From having decided to let Arty go,

to the things that had happened today since I woke in that closet. Because I'd worked with Mother Turner before, I didn't even hold back that Ale was a bad 'un or that he was involved in this. One had a feeling she had to know already.

After I'd stopped talking—I must have talked a long time, because my throat hurt—she looked at me a long time. She whispered something about not knowing what to do, then she asked, "What would you have me do, Miss D'Orio?"

I shrugged. "Something to find Ale maybe? Or Griffin, wherever he has him? You see I feel I must save him, and I also understand what Ale thinks and how he works, while Arty doesn't. He doesn't. I'm afraid Arty will get hurt."

Mother Turner took a deep breath. "Very well," she said. "I can make you a charm to find your brother. But you must do me a favor in the meantime."

"Find you something of his?" I said. "I was afraid—"

She shook her head. "No. Not that. That won't be a problem. I have a way. No, Miss. I was wondering if you'd eat something before you go, because I can see you haven't eaten in a while."

I would have liked to say no, but I was starving. While Mother Turner disappeared into one of the back rooms, the younger woman brought me rice and beef stew, and then, afterwards, a pastry dusted with powder sugar and a cup of coffee. I felt a new woman when Mother Turner came back.

The charm she'd prepared was a little bit of string, which rose like a charmed snake and pointed in a direction. "That's where he is. Just follow it. You'll find him."

And then before I left, she touched my shoulder. "God bless you, Miss D'Orio. You'll need a lot of courage."

I thought so too, and it would help if my stomach didn't feel like jelly. But damn it, for all of Pater's failings, he'd raised me to be a lady, and a lady doesn't let a man who she's fairly sure loves her, go and kill himself out of being a chivalrous fool.

I set the thread on the dashboard and followed its pointing as much as the roads allowed. I got gas when it became obvious we were headed out of town and north. And then, in the dark, in the narrow mountain roads, I followed the thread.

It took me ever higher, and then down a road that, honestly, was more of a goat track or likely a mule track, used long ago by miners' mules.

Even that ran out, so I grabbed the thread and my purse and continued on foot, cursing myself for seven kinds of fool for not having changed shoes. At least I was going to face death dressed to the nines. It might be some kind of consolation.

The track descended down the rock face, in a narrow, winding path. And below, almost like a ghost, I saw something shine. It appeared and disappeared depending on the rain, and maybe on someone moving it.

Getting closer, I saw it was the entrance to a mine. Colorado is full of abandoned mines. Some played out after the gold rush, when it became too hard to extract what precious metal remained in the rocks. And some . . . well, some were silver mines and still full of the metal, but silver price had fallen too much to be worth working.

They usually had romantic names like the Lucky

Strike Mine, or the Lost Hope Mine. This one could be any one of them. I approached cautiously. So Ale was here. That almost for sure meant Don Griffin, or what remained of him, was here. Good.

At the door, there were two sentinels, I saw. One was fully visible to me as he was holding aloft a lantern, which must be the light I'd seen. Behind him was another man. I knew them both though not their names. They were part of Ale's entourage, his goons to do with as he pleased. They dressed in a cheaper version of Ale's finery: dark suits and screaming ties, and almost for sure fake jewelry.

The guy who wasn't holding the lantern told the other, "Stop swinging it around, fool. As well hang a sign saying we're here, and you won't see anything more than light reflecting on the rain."

"But Ale said—"

The other guy cursed. "I don't know who Ale expects will come in this rain and the dark. If they come, it will be in the morning, and the little wimp magician will be done and gone well before then, and us too."

"There were those headlights!"

"Yeah, but they stopped somewhere up there. Probably some miner's shack there."

So, there was that. The little wimp magician must be Griffin. And it hit me they were probably right at that. He'd be done and gone well before Arty got here.

Which left me.

Well... it was raining just enough and they were far out from the cave enough that I might be able to squeeze behind and into the place. But not with my heels clacking on the rock.

I removed the heels, leaving them without remorse

by the side of the path, and walked on, in my silk stockings, which were going to have far worse than a run in them.

Down the path, stopping every time I loosened some gravel or made something fall, and around the two goons peering blindly into the falling rain.

And then I was in the shaft.

I was blind as the devil's toe, in a winding darkness. I put out my hand, to feel the wall, and walked following it a good hundred feet before I heard a bellow from up ahead. "No, by God, she's not a real person. She's a damned simulacrum and you'll give her to me, you little shite."

Another voice answered, one with whining overtones.

"I paid! I paid good money," Ale bellowed. Hard to miss my brother's dulcet tones. "And you'll give her to me. Or you'll stay in the antimagic cage till you die."

I walked along the wall, towards the voice. As the wall turned—the tunnel turned, I guess—a sort of grayish light filtered in. It let me see a rough-hewn tunnel, turning gently.

I followed it as silently as I could.

From the end of the hallway came Ale's voice, and then another voice murmuring, pleading.

As light became brighter, I knit myself with the wall and slid along it. My dress would be a loss too, and my fur already was.

I couldn't track every word that came from down the hallway, but I could hear the gist and it was this: Ale had paid Griffin to build a simulacrum of some woman, which Griffin had then refused to hand over. Griffin kept insisting his creation had a soul. I wasn't sure what that meant, or how it would be possible.

I also didn't know why Ale wanted a simulacrum of a woman. It had been bothering me since Griffin's place. Except perhaps he wanted to hide the fact he'd knocked one of his women around by having an unmarked duplicate show herself?

I finally reached a point in the hallway from which I could see a round chamber cut into the rock. Down from that there would be more galleries, but this chamber had a lantern hanging from a hook on the timbers bracing the roof, a table and two chairs.

On one of the chairs sat Ale. He sat with the chair reversed, his chin resting on the back. There was an ashtray on the floor next to him. It was full.

On the table, on a cage that looked made of wicker and looked exactly like something you'd keep a canary in, sat a man. I knew it was Griffin. I'd have known it was Griffin even if I hadn't seen the summoning at his place. What surprised me was the sudden rush of need, the desperate need to free him, to let him work, to—

I had my gun out from my garter before I realized it. I was always a half decent shot. And I didn't know how one shattered a magic-dampening cage. I knew such implements existed because they were always a plot device in the pulps. But in the pulps, usually the hero broke them with his bare hands, or unlocked them or something.

Well, breaking it with my bare hands was likely to chip my nail polish. And besides, I had the pistol out. I pointed it above Griffin's head in the cage. And I shot.

The sound was deafening in the mine and Ale got up, his hand going to his gun as he turned to where I stood.

"Honey!" he said. Then stopped. His mouth quirked in an unpleasant smile. "Damn, that's good," he said, turning to look at Griffin.

I looked too.

For just a moment I thought that the cage hadn't broken, that my shot had gone wide. Then I realized that the very top piece had fallen. The next minute there were a dozen of me all around saying, "What do you mean, Ale?"

Ale looked around, he looked back at Griffin, but the cage was empty and the magician was gone.

"You little shit," Ale said. "I'll shoot every one of you."

And then he started firing wildly.

I don't remember shooting him, but I remember his looking very surprised, then falling. I remember the running feet in the hallway, the shouts of "Honey," in two voices I knew all too well.

And then there were Arty's strong arms around me, and I was leaning into him, and I felt cold, really cold.

"Stay with me, Honey," Arty said. "Stay with me."

But I faded into darkness.

I woke with all of them around me. My father, Arty and Griffin.

Pater was saying, "So it's not my daughter?"

And Griffin was saying, in his whining, apologetic way, "Well, it is and it isn't, Mr. D'Orio."

I flowed in and out of a dream hearing bits and pieces: simulacrum, ritual on my birthday. "Sometimes the soul gets captured is what it is. There's no law about it, and that's the truth, Mr. D'Orio, but I didn't feel good giving her to him for who knew what purpose, while it was a living mind and soul in it."

I thought, "Me! They're talking about me."

I shivered, ice cold, and slipped away into a dream where I was just a magical doll of sorts, and no one cared. I woke up again to, "She disappeared a year ago." It was Pater, and his voice was sad, slow. "I thought she'd gone to California, to... I thought she'd gone. But I investigated, and no one could find a trace of her, and I said something to Ale, and I guess he got scared."

"Yeah," Griffin said. "He just wanted her to be seen around. He wanted people to know Honey D'Orio was alive and well. That's all I know. But it... she had the memories and the thoughts. And Jesus, as you see, she bleeds red."

I opened my eyes and there was a lot of red, over my clothes and over Arty's hands, and over the hands of a man I recognized, through foggy vision, as our doctor.

I fell into a dream again. I wasn't real. I wasn't even real. I was a thing. Which is why when Griffin was captured, my mind was the easiest to reach, to send an instruction to save him. He'd made me.

It took a week to be on my feet. They found her meanwhile. They found me, I should say, in one of the deep dark tunnels at the back of the mine. She'd been shot, wearing an evening dress and dancing shoes. Ale shot her in the parking lot of the Magic Cat. And he hid her in the mine, whose name, fading on a board by the entrance, was "Honey Fall."

Pater didn't have the body transferred to the family crypt, though he had a priest come and bless that forgotten tunnel of that lost mine.

He was changed, Pater was. Arty had gotten him

when he'd realized what was going on. He figured
only my father could stop Ale. I'd managed that
well enough, but I couldn't make Pater as he'd been.
He'd lost interest in the business. He'd lost interest
in everything except visiting me every day of my
prolonged convalescence.

It was December before I was back on my feet.
Apparently, a body and a soul is a body and a soul,
even if a body started out as a simulacrum. It takes
the same time to heal. It works the same way, as both
Griffin and the doctor explained.

"That's why Mother Turner wanted you to eat," Griffin had said. "Simulacrums that are just simulacrums—
just dolls made of magic—can't. She sensed you
weren't that. You moved like the original, and you
had thoughts of your own, even under compulsion.
She wanted to make sure."

That had been months ago, and I'd been spending
time in my—in my original's—apartment, in bed and
sitting by the window, while a professional nurse looked
after me. Arty had returned to California. He said he
was building a studio and couldn't leave it for that
long. I'd had two postcards, one showing sunny Los
Angeles, another an orange grove. He'd only written
"Wish you were here" on the back both times.

I'd seen pictures of him in the magazines, with
this platinum blond actress who was the big star of
his new movie.

Then it was a week to Christmas. Snow covered
Denver in sparkling jewels. The house and gardens
had been lit.

"I want you to come with me to the station," Pater
said, coming into my room, where I sat on a chair,

rereading the glossy magazine with a picture of Arty and the blonde.

"Darling," I said. "It is very sweet of you, but I'm no longer five. I've seen the Christmas lights downtown many times before. It doesn't excite me."

"Minx," Pater said but said it approvingly. "I want to take you to the station. There's a young man coming to town to ask you a very important question."

I dropped the magazine. Tears sprang to my eyes unbidden. "Arty? Daddy, I can't."

"Why can't you? Seems to me you should have married him when he first asked, and told me to go to the devil. Well, there is no dynasty here. I'm letting everything go, winding down all my affairs. You two go out, and I'll come and join you when I can. It's time I lived in the sun."

"But, Daddy, you forgot. I'm not the real Honey. I'm a body built who knows how, and a captured soul. What if it all stops working tomorrow and I die?"

Pater patted my hand. "Then, my dear, you're exactly like the rest of the human race. You might as well make the most of it."

So I did.

Three Kates

A STORY OF THE GENIUS WARS

Mike Massa

"Germany calling," the nasal, upper-crust English voice emerged scratchily from the speaker set into the ceiling of the poorly lit pub. "Germany calling."

Erich Hendriksen moodily pulled at his warm pint and leaned back in his chair, listening as the propaganda broadcast began.

Lord Haw-Haw could be counted upon to lie but news cloaked in propaganda was better than nothing, and nothing was all that the Allied censors were offering at the moment. None of the customers sheltering from the intermittent rain objected to the radio selection, each quietly, expectantly awaiting darkness and the possible return of German bombers.

The drinkers ignored his black cassock and white collar, and Hendriksen ignored them in turn. If any thought it strange that the broad-shouldered priest sought out a murky bar for a beer, they kept it to themselves. His damp coat hung from his chairback, the mud blotches along the hem drying in the pub's warmth.

"Tonight the German High Command will again send their irresistible fleet of aircraft to destroy the criminal English war effort. Many civilians are therefore put at risk due to the intransigence of the English Parliament..."

Risk.

Hendriksen knew something about that. His short-fused mission was redolent with the stuff.

And now the familiar risks of failure and capture were newly supplemented by being killed by his own side's bombers.

Haw-Haw's droning voice grated on Hendriksen's nerves. The Abwehr controller in Berlin required him to monitor the nightly broadcasts for the codes inserted into the news program. Each launched successive phases of his mission. That meant that he had to endure Haw-Haw's poorly affected, offensively incorrect upper-class English accent. The sheer absence of professionalism helped the hate come more easily.

That and the instinctive disdain of the field operative on the sharp end, reflecting on the secure, easy life of a rear echelon propagandist.

With an effort, Hendriksen relaxed his white-knuckled grip on his drink before his scarred, powerful hands broke the glass and made a scene.

The pub door banged open, admitting the chill November wind. The latest customer slipped between the blackout curtains which had been in place throughout England since that idiot Goering convinced the general staff that he could bomb the British to the negotiating table. The curtains dragged at a thin, tan coat, revealing a pale flash of thigh.

The newcomer was female, and strikingly so.

She stepped quickly to the bar, her windblown auburn hair obscuring most of her face, permitting only a brief glimpse of carmine lips. The aproned barkeep stepped forward, squinting suspiciously. The new guest leaned across the bar, murmuring quietly to the proprietor as every male customer surreptitiously noted the perfect line of her seamed stockings.

The barkeep nodded towards the shadow where Hendriksen sat.

The agent watched, his trained eyes dark as she turned towards his table, affording him the first look at her youthful face and wide eyes. She was shockingly young and her tentative steps suggested unease, perhaps at being inside a drinking hall. Tapping heels carried her all the way to his table.

So much for not making a scene.

Stepping very close, she leaned inside his personal space. Her low voice, pitched for his ears alone, swept away the illusion of shyness as soon as she spoke.

"Forgive me, Father, for I have sinned," she purred. "It's been *hours* since my last confession. May I join you?"

Hendriksen was a professional. He hid his surprise, beyond a slight firming of the lips. The honeyed tone that the young woman employed suggested that she might be in genuine need of a confession, but her bright eyes lacked any corresponding hint of shame.

Every moment that he kept her standing increased his own visibility, and a collared Anglican priest drinking in a pub was already curious enough.

"Please," he replied, gesturing to the second chair. With an effort he even made the offer seem genial. "Though this is hardly the place for a confession, Miss—?"

"Culpepper," she answered, smiling. "A half would be lovely, Father."

So, clearly not a confession, unless the Anglican church had become even more liberal since his last visit.

Hendriksen signaled the bartender while the young girl with a woman's eyes opened her purse and browsed quietly in that mysterious way that women will.

He watched as she settled herself and opened a compact, peering at the small mirror inside. She carefully patted a few windblown locks into place before closing the case with a satisfied snap. She glanced upwards and her shyness was reborn as the barkeep approached. Despite her suddenly demure manner as she accepted the lager, Hendriksen could tell that this was no waif.

She noted his speculation and smiled.

He studied her openly now. The entire package was pretty spectacular. Her brilliant eyes were an unreal shade of hazel, nearly gold against the perfect unlined skin of her face. A slow, deep pulse of desire bloomed in Hendriksen's gut as she held his gaze. With an effort, he fought the unexpected emotion, preserving his cover and, with it, his life.

Anglican clerics weren't the celibates that Catholics priests were in his native Germany, but even the clergy of the Church of England weren't supposed to ogle schoolgirls.

No matter how perfect their legs may be.

"My child," he said, concealing the effort it required to speak normally, let alone deliver the words in a perfect English accent. "How can I help you?"

"He does prattle on, doesn't he?" the girl said, inclining her head towards the radio speaker as Haw-Haw sonorously described the previous night's bombing on London.

"Perhaps you can tell me your business," Hendriksen insisted quietly. Deliberately, the agent summoned his will and looked away from her eyes.

Still watching him closely, the girl—woman—awarded him a smirk.

And the wave of lust receded as rapidly as it had begun.

MI6, Scotland Yard, even possible "friendly" interference—Hendriksen's premission briefing had mentioned a variety of possible threats, but none of them included incendiary sexuality. He knew himself as well as any man.

The wash of lust had to be . . . unnatural.

"Colour me curious," she replied, sipping her beer as though nothing had occurred. "Don't you wonder why Haw-Haw chose to turn his coat? He's a son of England, after all."

"Miss Culpepper . . ." Hendriksen began as though he was offended by the notion of Haw-Haw as a fellow Briton, and then continued in a measured way. "He's a Yank, and before that, a benighted Irishman. He's no son of . . ."

"Oh, call me Kate." Her perfect cupid's bow smile sharpened a trifle before she lowered her voice and added huskily, "No need for such formality or such sincere protests. I feel quite at home with you . . . Erich."

She breathed his first name as though it was a weapon. Given the way she spoke it, perhaps it was.

Hendriksen deflected another wave of desire and flogged his brain into productivity. He wasn't in Coventry under his own name. There was no reason for this seeming teenager to know that he was anyone but the Right Reverend William Bickel, newly arrived from the south coast where he'd tended a dedicated flock of parishioners.

Another player had entered the game.

But that much was already obvious.

Hendriksen had been trained by the best, so he scanned the room for her partner without moving his head. He took the added precaution of sliding a hand into his jacket pocket before looking back to his tablemate.

Culpepper's smile deepened as Hendriksen touched the grip of the pistol.

"No need for that either, *Father*," she said, keeping her eyes on his. "Neither of us wants to create a scene and I'm here to help you. And you can help me in return."

"Indeed, the time is nigh!" Haw-Haw's voice was suddenly much louder than his previous droning and the key warning phrase arrested Hendriksen's attention. He listened for the next message hidden in the propaganda. It would double as both the mission trigger and the pickup recognition code. "It is time for the English people to decide if they seek the punishment of the Old Testament!"

His eyes never left Culpepper's face, so he saw her smile shift from coy to vulpine, even as Haw-Haw delivered the final words.

She knew.

"Who sent you?" asked Hendriksen, keeping his voice low and his hand in his pocket. "Who're you working for?"

"Someone who wants to make sure that you succeed tonight," Culpepper replied, crossing her legs with a whisper of silk. "Someone who can help you get out. Someone who can ensure that you won't get out unless I help."

"I don't need help," Hendriksen husked, "and I don't respond favorably to threats."

"Oh, don't be so boring," she answered, her lips curving upwards. "I'll show you mine if you show me yours..."

With that, she inclined her head so that an observer might suppose she had become suddenly skeptical. The movement lifted her hair, exposing a closely fitted circlet that adorned her neck. Hendriksen noted the stylized sigil of a raven on the finely wrought silver.

His eyes widened.

Hers just sparkled.

Though the air war against England was only a few months old, the Blitz had already broadened, focusing on military targets, factories and even the English people themselves. However, historical curiosities lacked any relevance to the conflict and neither the Germans nor the Allies had intentionally wasted a bomb on museums and old buildings. Then, quite suddenly, the English had dropped several planeloads of high explosive near the center of old Munich, damaging some of the architecture dating to the eleventh century.

This had generated an even bigger response in the German High Command than the August bombing of Berlin. Personally, Hendriksen believed the RAF Pathfinders has been victims of bad navigation, but for whatever reason, the orders for a new contingency had come straight from the top, or somewhere near it.

At that point, Hendriksen was pulled off his research on the Cairo collection and a new mission was planned. He'd been personally, if hurriedly, briefed by the chief of Germany's military intelligence before being hustled off to the airfield for nighttime flight to the coast of France. Then the agent had infiltrated England in a damp and smelly fishing smack, eventually working his way not to militarily and politically critical London, but instead into central England.

To Coventry, to be precise.

Every night since he had been alerted to the impending mission, Hendriksen had awaited the signal hidden in the nightly broadcast. He'd moved around, trying to avoid a pattern. Two nights ago he'd heard the warning order buried in Haw-Haw's script. It meant that he was to remain within reach of his target, but outside the drop area for the Luftwaffe's bombs.

The German Air Force had previously bombed the factories around the city's perimeter, but so far, the historic quarter in the city center, dating to the Middle Ages, had been spared. In the middle of the quarter lay the largest and oldest of these, the Coventry Cathedral, dedicated to St. Michael.

Admiral Canaris, the German spymaster and Abwehr chief, had lectured the agent without aides or witnesses present.

His superior had outlined the mission with the sketchiest of details while opening a leather satchel, working around the open pair of handcuffs dangling from the handle. A very brief glimpse of the velvet-lined interior was all that Hendriksen had managed. Specially fitted slots held strange devices next to humdrum everyday items. While Canaris carefully withdrew a few items, handling them like spun glass, he explained their relevance to the mission before passing them to the agent.

Hendriksen had memorized what he could before getting on the boat, leaving the notes with his armed escort. The Cathedral was being specifically targeted by the Luftwaffe. And in the center of the Cathedral lay his objective. Not only was he to confirm the destruction of the Cathedral proper and return with proof, but he was also to be alert for certain signs and marks.

Some of the symbols meant danger and some represented allies. A few were to be respected at all costs, even to the point of failing his mission.

Culpepper's silver raven fell unequivocally in the latter category. The sight of the sigil belonging to one of the Unaligned had shaken him. Hendriksen realized that while he had to shed himself of this new complication—and fast—he had to do it *politely*.

So, rather than immediately abandon the woman, he'd stayed seated, nursing his beer.

Despite Culpepper's pout and her pointed look at his wrist, he'd declined to show her the sigil that lay next to his skin, etched into the case of Canaris's wristwatch. Hendriksen might not be perfectly immune to her blandishments, but he'd accumulated his share of scars and not all of them were displayed on his well-used hide.

When the air raid sirens sounded, he quirked an eyebrow at her, but she didn't seem disposed to flee.

As the other patrons relocated to a nearby shelter, he'd slipped a tenner to the owner who shrugged and left them to their table before slipping out the back himself.

Together, the unlikely pair waited out the bombing. Even from kilometers away, the concussions were palpable. Periodically, Hendriksen would study the young woman, but in between occasional glances at her compact, she successfully outblanded him throughout the black night, ignoring even those bombs that fell closer, shaking their building.

Hendriksen kept one eye on his unwanted tablemate, but returned to brooding, something that came naturally. By training, he was an intelligence analyst for the Abwehr's arcane legendarium. If he was caught, they wouldn't shoot him for being an accomplished archaeologist.

Of course, but they sure as hell would shoot him as a spy.

He snorted, earning a sidelong glance from Culpepper.

Hendriksen's family had returned to a Germany that had rediscovered pride. The rise of nationalism had felt good at first. Pride led to a renewed interest in German history. His father had introduced him to the Thule Society, which had developed a genuine antiquities program, albeit one tinged with an uncomfortable amount of mysticism.

A college-age Hendriksen had been skeptical of

the supernatural but had loved the study of historical artifacts.

He'd ignored the politics too, for a time. Hitler seemed almost too good to be true, standing in opposition to the hereditary aristocracy of England and the titans that monopolized American industry—and he had been, for Germany and for Hendriksen's family. First they'd lost their belongings, then he'd lost his parents. His younger sibling had embraced the National Socialist movement and its supremacist ideology.

So he'd lost his brother.

Sitting quietly in the dark, with a beautiful stranger, as his own countrymen dropped bombs around his ears, Hendriksen felt as alone as he'd ever been.

He shook it off, angry at himself for indulging in melancholy, and on a mission at that.

The all clear sounded just before dawn, as the asynchronous thrum of Heinkels faded slowly to the east.

After they donned their coats, Hendriksen escorted Culpepper into the pall of smoke that hung over the city and quickly permeated their clothes. Civilians remained scarce, though overworked firefighters were visible, laboring to knock down dangerous wreckage and quench the fires. The smell of burning wood and oil, and the sharp chemical reek of German incendiaries blanketed everything.

Once clear of the pub, Hendriksen implemented his plan to shake the uninvited woman without directly offering any insult. He accelerated, counting upon his long stride to leave the shorter and slightly built Culpepper behind.

His idea failed. The lithe teen effortlessly matched him, step for step.

Some streets ran with water draining away from the firefighting efforts and soaking the hem of his swirling cassock. The wetness made Hendriksen thankful for the boots hidden under the long garment. If the damp or the smell bothered Culpepper, it wasn't evident.

Mercifully, the heavy stone construction of the old quarter had reduced the amount of fuel for the fires, but broken chunks of that same masonry were strewn everywhere. The streets remained completely blocked to vehicles, but in between the waves of bombers, firefighters had cleared narrow lanes, allowing them to respond to new conflagrations.

The lanes also turned an impossible walk into a merely hazardous, time-consuming scramble. Hendriksen restrained himself from checking his timepiece more than once, even as the sky lightened.

The familiar landmarks he'd relied upon during earlier reconnoiters were changed by the bomb raid, and only the hollowed-out bell tower identified the wreckage of Coventry less than a football pitch away. Relief at finding the target tangled with Hendriksen's impatience. He had to get in and out before full daylight brought the authorities.

Canaris had explained that any bit of the altar or adjoining structure would suffice as proof of Coventry's destruction, so long as it lit the dial of his watch when close by. Hendriksen had no desire to reveal this to Culpepper, so he needed her gone before he started waving his bare forearm about the wreckage.

Ahead lay the smoking ruin.

He spun on his heel to address her. Without witnesses, he could abandon the priestly speech of the last week.

"There it is," he said. "Even a dame like you can see that the place is a wreck. You tell your boss that I respected the forms and leave me to get on with it, right?"

The teenager stepped past him without pausing.

"It was precious how you thought you could simply walk away from me, Erich," said Culpepper, effortlessly threading her way between the piles of shattered masonry. "I thought that..."

She paused.

"Hmm," she said, one foot daintily poised above a detached and dented tailfin of a German fragmentation bomb. "I can't Feel Him."

She waited a moment longer, her head cocked to one side as if listening intently.

"What?" asked Hendriksen, suppressing his irritation. "You can't feel who?"

"We're more than close enough by now that I should Feel Coventry, even if the centrum is shattered," she answered tartly. "And I don't. There's just this...buzzing."

She shot Hendriksen a meaningful look which left him as uninformed as he had been a moment before. He shook his head, but dropped the matter. Instead, he focused on the job and scanned ahead, seeking a way in. Overhead the sky was brightening further, and they had to be gone before someone inquired why they were rooting about in the ruins of a cathedral.

"When the timbers burned, the roof collapsed," he stated, considering the way ahead. "The nave is completely blocked but I...we need to reach the sanctuary."

The entire roof of the cathedral was missing, though

the stout granite walls and the gothic window arches appeared to remain intact. Dull orange flames guttered in the morning breeze, improving visibility enough to show that the cathedral floor was utterly covered by uneven mounds of broken rubble. The firefighter lane led around the rear, where they could see an open door only partially filled with charred wreckage.

Culpepper skipped from one clear patch to the next, and easily navigated the door. Hendriksen followed closely behind her. Inside, thick smoke eddied, and the seemingly young woman darted ahead but then halted so suddenly that the German agent, looking downwards to avoid stumbling on a bits of rubble, actually bumped into her shapely backside.

Before he could apologize, two figures loomed in the smoke, pawing at an object tangled in what remained of the sacristy.

"Jackals," hissed Culpepper, crouching as though she meant to spring.

The dark-suited men turned in unison, and as they straightened, Hendriksen saw that there was something deeply wrong with their faces. Shadowed by the fedoras they wore, their features were smeared and blurred. Unnaturally indistinct, their faces resembled those of cheaply made dolls. The dark smudges of their eyes fixed first on the woman, then himself.

One produced a long-barreled revolver. Hendriksen spared the gun a glance. It appeared to be an antique, chambered in .44 Russian, and the huge bore yawned wider than an open grave. His own pistol was a little light for serious work, but so was any pistol caliber for that matter, unless you had a bullet hose like the Schmeisser. Unfortunately for Hendriksen, even his priestly disguise wouldn't extend to toting along the iconic German submachine gun.

He'd make do with his Walther.

At social distances like this, Hendriksen was confident that he could strike each man twice in the chest within the first second of any exchange. His bullets might be smaller than the monstrous wadcutters in the Russian pistol but Hendriksen was confident in his skill.

It was all about placing the bullets just so.

To one side of the gunman, the second figure clutched at a twisted bit of iron wreckage that it had withdrawn from the heap at their feet. The fire-heated artifact was visibly singeing the man's hands, and his suit smoldered where the iron pressed against his waist. Indifferent to the searing heat, the man moved slightly behind his armed companion.

"Avaunt, demons!" Culpepper said, her voice ringing inside the ruined walls. She stalked forward empty-handed, utterly unimpressed with these possible competitors. "You have no place here. Begone or feel the wrath of the White Keep!"

Hendriksen stepped a little bit to the right, keeping a clear line of sight to the pair. He casually slid his right hand into his overcoat and withdrew his piece, holding it at his side.

The two men, if men they were, didn't reply. One turned its parody of a face towards the second, as if exchanging an idea. The figure holding the hot tangle of metal used one hand to fish about in a trouser pocket before tossing a fist-sized bit of stone towards the newcomers. It crossed the floor, rolling all the way to Hendriksen's feet.

The face of Hendriksen's wristwatch came alive with a lambent glow.

He spared a glance for the fire-scorched chunk of marble as it came to a full stop against his boot. It was the head of a small, white and otherwise unremarkable cherub, which had till that evening been a decoration on the Cathedral's frieze. He looked back up, leaving the marble where it lay.

"All or nothing, beasts!" Culpepper raised both hands, palms out. Her coat flared dramatically outwards with the motion. Something in the set of her shoulders tipped Hendriksen that this was only going to go one way.

"Ah, Miss Kate, just who are these . . . people?" Hendriksen inquired much more mildly than he felt.

"Not people," she replied, her voice taught with anger. "Golems. Tools of the Adversary."

Considering that he was a German intelligence agent inside wartime Britain, he was unmistakably an enemy. If her statement differentiated between what he clearly was and whatever these two were, then the figures were bad news of the worst sort.

The figure with the revolver first looked at her, then towards Hendriksen, as if asking the question.

"Yeah, that's how it's going to be, lads," Hendriksen answered, unbidden. "Like the lady sa—"

Before he could finish, the first golem fired. His old-style revolver spat a cloud of glowing smoke a fraction of a second after a silver curtain of light blew outwards from Culpepper's outstretched hands, staggering the two men and spoiling the gunman's aim. Hendriksen was actually as good as he thought he was, and the little Walther barely jumped in his fist as a pair of slugs hit each "man" right over their respective hearts.

While each twitched slightly at the impact of the bullets, there was no other result, aside from the rippling of the fabric around the fresh bullet holes as the suit jackets appeared to heal themselves.

Which was a bad sign, obvious even to the woefully underinformed Abwher agent.

"Shit!" Hendriksen exclaimed, discarding his useless pistol. He reached for his last weapon as the furthest golem spun away, leaping upward towards a pile of tumbled stone. The shooter crouched and aimed his gun directly at the slip of a girl and fired again, even as Culpepper moved her palms in a complex pattern before thrusting them outwards as fists.

This time her attack and the bullets from the golem's revolver passed each other before striking their targets, with dramatic, if different results.

The golem simply slumped to the ground, the man shape and his weapon collapsing into a mound of what appeared to be wet concrete. Culpepper staggered backwards, her hands clutching her midsection as she tried to keep to her feet.

"You must stop it!" she gasped as Hendriksen caught her, preventing her from falling backwards. "It cannot escape with even a single Splinter!"

Hendriksen heard the unmistakable capitalization in her words. Keeping his left arm around Culpepper, he withdrew a different tool from his cassock vest pocket. The Abwehr chief had cautioned him to employ it only in the most dire circumstance and hadn't offered any instructions on its use, other than the need to aim it approximately but hold onto it most firmly.

The device resembled a cigarette lighter which had been grafted onto a small black pistol grip. The brass artifact was easily concealable and the action was obvious from the trigger, placed just as that of a normal gun.

One-handed, he aimed and "fired" in a single motion, twisting his torso towards the escapee.

The device vibrated fiercely in his hand, the sensation intense and uncomfortable. The snap of discharge was accompanied by a single golden spear of visible light which lanced into the back of the escaping figure, which still clutched the bit of twisted iron against its chest. Struck by the discharge, the golem instantly froze at the top of the very last heap of rubble, poised to leap down into the gray dawn and away from the cathedral.

And then it, too, slumped into a mound of glowing wet sludge that flowed across the jumble of bricks beneath it before congealing into a solid mass.

Hendriksen scanned the immediate area for further threats, keeping his arcane weapon poised. He didn't even know if it could fire again, but his Walther was clearly no use against these things... golems. His surroundings clear, he turned to Culpepper, cradled in his left arm.

"Retrieve the Splinter," she gasped, her face tight with pain. "Get to the train."

This woman knew too much. She was clearly a dangerous figure in her own right. She even had information about his extraction plan, knowledge that threatened Hendriksen personally.

Hendriksen's instinct was to collect the *Splinters*, whatever they were, and strike for his rendezvous. He tucked the little pistol-gripped lighter back into his jacket as Culpepper slumped in his arms, obviously severely injured, though there was no sign of blood.

Hendriksen told himself that he wasn't going to be a sucker for an enemy agent just because she happened to be injured and looked like a pretty fifteen-year-old.

Right.

Her fine, long lashes fluttered as she fought to stay in the moment, before her eyes firmly closed. Her body sank softly into his chest and her face relaxed again into that of a young girl. If that wasn't enough, her head turned as her body went limp, once more exposing that damned raven.

Oh, for fuck's sake.

Hendriksen sat with his head braced against the motion of the swaying train car. The preceding twenty-four hours had been fraught with tension, if not further outright danger. However, he'd exhausted his creativity explaining the condition of his traveling companion and justifying train seats for them towards Leicester, then Lincoln and finally Newcastle-on-Tyne.

After he had collected the twisted iron nails from the mound of slag that his weapon had made of the golem, he'd used his "watch" to look for other bits which caused the dial to glow. The cherub was the heaviest, but there were a few others, including a twisted disc of metal that might have been a paten and a crushed pyx of silver that also showed damage from the intense blaze. All were safely packed in the luggage stowed over his head.

Their itinerary had been shaped as much by his desire to avoid the need to change trains as it had been by their choice of destination.

The northernmost ports were much further from occupied France, but were patrolled less intensely as a result, so he'd accepted tickets that took them directly to Newcastle. Conveniently, his forged papers included an order of ordination from a seminary in nearby Sunderland, so it became a matter of convincing the Coventry stationmaster that he was escorting the young lady, prone to "fits" and suffering from a "poor constitution," to the sanitarium that shared the village with his home seminary.

After their encounter with the golems, Culpepper had roused enough to walk with assistance, but remained logy. He'd pushed her to keep moving, despite her mumbled if heartfelt protests. It had been with relief that he'd finally sat her next to him in a private compartment. Once placed into a sitting position she'd immediately fallen asleep, as though deprived of rest for weeks.

Hendriksen had rapidly examined her for gunshot wounds in the ruins of Coventry, as soon as he'd made sure of their opponents, but although he'd seen her stagger, her clothing and skin were unmarked by bullets. He'd discreetly examined her again in their compartment. Shielded by the ubiquitous blackout curtains, Hendriksen used the electric lamp to discover a peculiar bruising. It spread across her abdomen in an uncanny, fine net pattern. He also found a fine white scar that wrapped completely around her neck, hidden beneath the silver choker. However, apart from her intense fatigue, there were no other symptoms, so he'd kept one arm around her shoulders, holding her upright until the rocking motion of the train took him and sleep closed his eyes.

He woke with a start, one hand instinctively seeking the reassurance of the weapon in his coat pocket. Bright daylight was leaking around the edges of their compartment window.

Hendriksen jerked involuntarily in surprise, his arm grasping around the expected form to his right.

He nearly overbalanced and fell when he encountered only empty air.

Culpepper was gone.

Instead, across from him sat another beautiful woman, her hands folded in her lap. She was perfectly composed in a fashionable gray tweed suit, and swayed ever so slightly as the train continued its journey. Dark, dark blond hair was styled long but pulled back from an expressive, intelligent face. Her beauty was refined, unlike Culpepper's raw sexuality.

She might have been a leading lady from Hollywood, only Hendriksen didn't think that they made actresses quite this beautiful.

Beside her, an expensive camel coat lay draped across the remainder of the bench, dissuading potential joiners from their compartment.

"Good afternoon, sirrah. Thank you for assisting my colleague," the woman said in perfect High German. She raised one gloved hand to pull back one half of the curtain. Bright light filled the compartment, stinging Hendriksen's eyes. Motes of dust became visible, floating through the sunbeam that divided the space between them. "She's been relocated to a safe place to recover and you may trust that she is in capable hands."

Hendriksen only barely kept himself from gaping. At her throat shone the same sigil that Culpepper had worn.

How many of these women were there? Damn the Abwehr and double damn Canaris for sending him into the cold completely ignorant of what he was up against. These two definitely weren't Scotland Yard or MI6.

His new fellow traveler continued speaking.

"We appreciate that you accepted substantial risks in order to ensure she did not remain behind to face other . . . competitors, or the mortal authorities," she said, her hazel eyes twinkling, perhaps as she enjoyed his discomfiture. "If we can agree on the disposition of Coventry, our *employer* may grant you a boon."

Hendriksen shook his head to clear away the last muzziness that inevitably accompanied waking in a strange place. He darted a surreptitious glance upwards.

Above him, the case containing the hard-won fragments still rested in the luggage rack.

"You have me at a disadvantage, madam," he said, once again employing the clipped English of his assumed nationality. Then her use of German fully registered. He barely hesitated before sitting up straighter and smoothing the front of his cassock. "I'm the Reverend Willi . . ."

"We know who you are," interrupted the woman, switching languages and matching his own southern accent with the plummy, round tones usually found in the House of Lords. A calm gaze sought his own but she made no other movement. "Even if you do not. I can call you Reverend or Herr Hauptman or by your birthname if you prefer. I might even share your True Name. In return, you may call me Mrs. Seymour."

Hendriksen paused before answering and found himself relaxing despite the obviously high stakes. The name meant nothing to him, but the tone that she used suggested that she'd imparted useful information.

He spent another moment carefully appraising his new companion and his new situation.

Despite her apparent civility, the woman across from him was obviously as dangerous as anyone he'd ever encountered in the line of duty. She knew what he was and was showing not the least bit concern for bracing a German spy within the borders of wartime England. Either she had ample help nearby or she was absolutely confident that she could manage any force that Hendriksen could bring to bear.

Her perfect calm suggested that she was relying on herself alone against a much larger man. And she liked the odds.

On the other hand, she had information, and she seemed to know much more about him than he knew of her or Culpepper. As long as he had the proof of Coventry's destruction and the train was heading towards his coastal rendezvous, he had nothing to lose from simple conversation. Though he took only moments to consider her words, the delay freighted the air between them with tension.

Without speaking, she abruptly shifted her head to one side, regarding him from a slightly different angle. The motion might have been meant to highlight her perfect, feminine throat but instead reminded Hendriksen of nothing so much as a hunting falcon considering a potentially toothsome morsel.

There was no point in provoking a predator, no matter how elegantly she was dressed. Hell, he might even learn something. Insisting that he was truly a priest seemed pointless.

"Alright, ma'am." His voice relaxed into the flattened vowels of his childhood language, distinct from anything an English vicar might employ. "Seems smart to stick with a name from my cover, all things considered, and English is safer than German," he said, bowing very slightly from the waist. "Maybe you feel like a game of twenty questions, just so's we can pass the time."

"Of course, Reverend," Seymour replied, relaxing backwards a trifle. "That seems equitable. Let us exchange answers as well, until one of us reaches the boundary of permissible truth."

That was a damned odd way to say it, Hendriksen thought. Still, he nodded his acceptance of her terms.

"If I can start?" he asked. She smiled her answer and he went on. "Your friend, Miss Culpepper, looked like she got shot by those whatevers back in Coventry. I looked for a wound but she was fine... mostly. But even without a bullet from that big Russian gun, she still got hit by something—she was weaker than a kitten."

"Katherine Culpepper, as you know her, was struck by a foul device called a soul weapon," Seymour replied decisively. "It was fired by a construct, a golem, manufactured and controlled by our enemy, Stuttgart. The projectile damaged her ability to sustain a Focus, so distant from her own Seat. Her remaining strength was insufficient to handle even one Splinter."

Which told Hendriksen both a very great deal and nearly nothing at all. Before he could fully digest her answer, she immediately continued.

"Would you say that you are a German, a Briton or an American?" Seymour posed the question quite matter-of-factly.

"What the hell do you mean?" Hendriksen said,

allowing some heat to enter his tone. "You know who I work for and you seem to know where I'm going. In case you haven't noticed, Germany is at war with England, and pretty soon with Roosevelt too."

"I didn't ask who you *work* for, Erich," Seymour replied, smiling.

Hendriksen saw that although she was clearly older than Culpepper, she had the same perfect complexion.

She paused, noting his perusal. Purely for his benefit, she took a deep breath and held it, straining her blouse and jacket. He noted that her tailor could have safely added a centimeter or two here and there.

Damn his trained eye anyhow.

"I asked *what* you were," she continued. "A man born in Germany but raised in Pittsburgh, of all places. Then university at Eton, despite the cost. I rather think that a man of so many parts understands exactly what I'm asking. You've walked between masters for a while without choosing a side. Your current arrangement is convenience, not conviction. Whom. Do. You. Serve?"

Her beauty was immediately forgotten as Seymour's question struck Hendriksen like a punch to the gut.

He'd never felt perfectly at home anywhere, preferring out-of-the-way dig sites, foreign museums and travel. The Hendriksen brothers had caught the bug the moment they'd found their first stone arrowhead on a camping trip. The Carnegie Museum's Native American collection had poured accelerant onto their interest, and from then on they'd dragged their parents through every museum and library within reach.

The brothers had drifted apart, but five years in England had only cemented Hendriksen's passion. In the U.S., an antique was something dating to the

American Civil War. In England, regular houses and churches were hundreds of years old. You couldn't swing a dead cat without hitting a Roman hill fort or a medieval castle.

Moving into intelligence had happened almost by accident.

The history degree and his thesis on reliquaries made him a natural for the antiquities collection arm of the Abwehr. It had also kept him out of the meat grinder of regular conscription. Then, just after the Olympics, Canaris had needed an aide for his trip to Spain and Hendriksen's Spanish was as good as his Latin and American English. They'd returned with an ancient Ottoman sword and Franco's promise to help attack Gibraltar when the time came.

The Spanish got the planes and pilots needed to crush the Reds. Hendriksen preferred the sword.

The prewar years had been more than sufficient to scratch his itch. Egypt, Palestine, Sumer, even one trip back to Central America.

Where did he belong? Canaris's service had been a means to an end, not a passion. Was it mere habit at this point, or just stubbornness?

It didn't matter. It wasn't any of this broad's business.

"My parents were German," Hendriksen said, speaking slowly to conceal the anger and apprehension that surged through him. She knew too much. It placed him at an impossible disadvantage. Hendriksen might not have been one of Heydrich's true believers, but he understood loyalty and professionalism, and he owed a debt.

"The Abwehr pays me. That's all you need to know. So let's flip this around. Who're you working for, sister?"

"Working is such an interesting human notion," Seymour answered. "But I suppose that in this, you could say that Bath *borrowed* us."

"*Who?*" Hendriksen's confusion was total. Who the hell was Bath?

"We're both trying to recover fragments of that arrogant snot, Coventry"—the elegant woman glanced upward, before resuming her direct gaze towards Hendriksen—"but your ultimate master would turn those Splinters into weapons that lead to the enslavement of your race. Bath will conserve any viable fragments and will continue her path of benevolent neglect. Believe you me, that's a better path than what Stuttgart and his gathering of fools have planned for all of you."

"But what do you mea—"

"Now, Erich, we must observe the forms...the next question is mine, unless you want to end the exchange right *now*," Seymour said, cutting him off. One cautionary eyebrow angled elegantly upwards.

Hendriksen worked to master his confusion. The incessant clacking of the train wheels against the steel rails reminded him that he was on a timetable. Despite the pressure, he found an unexpected reservoir of calm and exhaled audibly. Then he motioned for Seymour to go on.

She smiled in a self-satisfied way, as though he'd passed a test.

"It should be obvious we've a great deal of insight into your mission. We also have considerable understanding into the relationship between your organization, the Abwehr, and its powerful competitors in the Schutzstaffel," she said, using the full name for the group known to the rest of the world as the SS. "In fact, they're increasingly influencing your operations, even as we speak."

"I don't work for those—" Hendriksen almost said "pigs," but his brother had migrated to the SS from the National Socialist party enforcement squads. Eduard was...well, he was Eduard. However, the friction between the Abwehr and Himmler's personal goons was considerable, occasionally escalating to actual confrontations over their intelligence roles. The SS had no limits, it seemed.

First came the Night of the Long Knives. Then darker rumors of their operations inside Germany had begun to spread.

Meanwhile, the Abwehr had been losing ground and influence. A few agents had even vanished where no English or French could've possibly been involved.

Hendriksen's companion leaned well forward.

"Erich Hendriksen, you're woefully and deliberately uninformed," Seymour replied, poking his lapel before relaxing back into her seat. The motion changed the contours of her calf and one feminine shoe tapped impatiently. "You've been hastily manipulated for a mission that isn't ultimately in your best interest by forces that you can't even see, let alone understand. If you return with the objects in the case, you'll not long survive your victory. So I ask plainly, to whom will you give your full measure of loyalty?"

"I know who I work for," the German agent growled. "Doesn't matter whatever game you and that other dame are playing at. I know about keeping my word. What are you, and what's this really about?"

Hendriksen was rattled. The Steel City accent was in full effect now, and he didn't care.

"Give me a straight answer—or beat it, lady," he said, gritting out the words from a clenched jaw.

He was still absorbing the implications of her information about him, about his hierarchy. Her mention of the SS shook him. His own brother had denounced their father merely to curry favor and gain entrance. The SS had been merciful and merely stripped his father of everything he'd ever earned, even their home. Hendriksen would never transfer his allegiance to them, even if it cost his life. He'd taken the mission for Canaris and the value of his word was worth more than mere survival.

"In plainest language then, little Knight." Seymour sounded as though she was becoming as exasperated as Hendriksen felt.

Good, I'm not the only one, Hendriksen thought, then did a mental double take. *Wait, what?*

"There are naturally useful places where humans have gathered, built, and worshipped for hundreds, sometimes thousands of years. Humans can vest a small piece of themselves in such a place and after a long enough time, that place develops a soul. A consciousness. Sometimes even a conscience."

"You mean like gods?" Hendriksen said skeptically. This woman was sounding more and more crazy. And yet, Hendriksen had seen the golems. Nothing he'd ever studied could explain them.

"The Romans called them Genius Loci, or Spirits of the Place," she answered. "And like the humans that birthed them, they are complicated as well as calculating. They can be dangerous. All these so-called modern countries refer to this dust-up as a World War, as though it is a discrete thing."

She snorted.

"You're all fighting in *their* war. And it has been going on since time immemorial."

Hendriksen didn't know what to believe.

"And what is Coventry to you?" he asked.

"The cathedral that you called Coventry rests on a much older Christian monastery, many hundreds of years old. It rests in turn upon the foundations of a Roman temple. That edifice is sited above a Druidic henge which predates the Christians. And so on, to when men first strode across the land."

"And Bath? Stuttgart?"

"Geniuses as well," Seymour said decisively, one hand rising upwards from her lap, like a sword. "Stuttgart arranged for the murder of Coventry. It remains to be seen if he's succeeded."

"So what does that make you? One of these Geniuses?"

"I?" Seymour laughed, and then covered her mouth and continued. "Heavens, no. Haven't you been paying attention?" Her silver choker flashed. "No, I and my sisters are the Ravens. As ever, alive or dead, we serve the White Keep."

"You're dead?" Hendriksen blinked rapidly, feeling his head spin. He understood the individual words, but he simply couldn't grasp the threads that Seymour wove with them. "That makes no sense."

"Aye," Seymour tapped her heels, impatient. "We're not from this age, but the Geniuses collect useful humans. Both living and deceased."

"But . . ."

"You've to decide what you are, Erich," she added. "You've a great deal of promise, and I'd as lief return with you and the case than the case alone."

A screeching steam whistle drowned out Hendriksen's question, and the train suddenly lurched, braking hard.

Seymour rose, one hand on the rail for balance, and looked outside the car.

"Catterick," she read, as the sign flashed by the slowing train. "This is not a scheduled stop," she added, braced against the deceleration.

"You must Choose!" She looked down at him, her gaze urgent. "Either way, that case over your head must not reach Germany. Your fate is your own to decide."

"The case goes where I go"—Hendriksen withdrew from his pocket not the Walther but Canaris's gadget— "and I'm going home."

"Ahh," Seymour sighed, looking first at the golem-killing gun and then back to Hendriksen. "We'd believed that Culpepper dispatched all the constructs. But it appears that your puppet master anticipated competition. Clever spider."

She didn't seem angry or scared but she also held quite still.

"Enough," Hendriksen said, suddenly standing upright so that he was face to face with Seymour in the tiny floor space. The arcane pistol was pressed into the tweed, just below her chest, but the agent could feel firm muscle beneath the alluring softness of a grown woman. If she was intimidated, it didn't show as she continued to thoroughly examine his face from an intimate distance, close as lovers.

The spy knew that he had spent too long listening. The train was definitely stopping and if MI6 was searching for him, he needed to debark before he was fully in their net.

"I'm legging it, and you're staying here," Hendriksen

ordered. "Don't try to follow me. Stay out of my way and you'll be fine; they'll be looking for me not you. This ain't nothing personal—just business."

"Oh, little Knight," Seymour said, her warm breath palpable on Hendriksen's face. "They don't search just for you. And you're going to discover that it's *quite* personal."

She stayed standing and merely watched as Hendriksen used one arm to pull the leather-strapped case from overhead and banged out of the compartment door.

A few steps later, he glanced over his shoulder to confirm that she wasn't following him.

Through the glass, he could see that the compartment was empty.

On the upside, at least no further unnerving women had appeared to hinder his progress. However, there was always a downside.

Newcastle-on-Tyne was out. The goddamned Luftwaffe had restarted their raids there, forcing him to push towards his *tertiary* pickup point. He had but one night left before the E-boats waiting offshore would assume that he'd been compromised and no longer returned for pickup. The speedy motor craft had been playing hide and seek with the British MTBs, but they couldn't do so forever.

It was tonight or never.

His black cassock had become blotched and smelly from the combination of overland travel needed to stay outside the net of waiting MI6 agents and the dirty bench of the coal wagon whose driver had taken pity on the walking priest. That morning, a sympathetic rector had allowed him a wash and laundered his outfit before he pressed towards his last chance at a rendezvous. It was with a somewhat more presentable appearance and a battered case, that Hendriksen limped into a cafe overlooking the Hartlepool waterfront late on the afternoon of the fourth day.

Using his remaining pocket change, he'd ordered tea and ration biscuits from the short middle-aged proprietress. Wordlessly, she'd inspected his questionable outfit. An abbreviated, if haughty, sniff suggested that his spit bath has been only partially effective.

The heavy mist condensed on his broad-brimmed cleric's hat and dripped onto his cassock as Hendriksen surveyed the waterfront for a suitable pier. He'd need to find a boat small enough to slip outside the still-nascent harbor defenses before he signaled for pickup.

He'd successfully left Seymour behind, but her words had dogged his steps all the way to this dingy cafe. How did he get to this?

His retrieval window was still hours away, but he moved closer, dodging the odd bit of stone or pile of burned timbers before finding a convenient bench along the fishing quay. Finger piers extended into the bay, the details obscured by the profusion of different small craft. The gray winter day sullenly gave way to darkness, as the tall agent caught sight of a wherry for which a single pair of oars would suffice.

Perfect.

A single sentry paced slowly back and forth in front of the pier. The evening mist made the barrel of his slung rifle shine in the dim, yellow light of the pier lamp.

"Pity a poor soldier on a night like this," Hendriksen said aloud. "Could be worse."

He placed the case between his legs and opened a small Bible as camouflage. Meanwhile, Hendriksen began to catalog the major elements of his mission which would be included in his report. How would he describe either woman? Canaris had to have known much more than he let on in order to have equipped his agent with the tools that had saved Hendriksen's life.

But why not tell him more? Was Hendriksen expendable? Of course, if Hendriksen failed, he couldn't have divulged that which he didn't know. Being kept deliberately uninformed rankled. The successful delivery of the case would be an understandable, forgivable point at which to stop working for the Abwehr.

At least directly.

He wasn't certain where he belonged. It probably wasn't there.

"I'm not surprised, young man," a firm, feminine alto caroled into his ear, but with an odd accent.

He started and looked to see the cafe owner sitting next to him. Somehow she'd soundlessly approached the bench at the head of his target pier and sat down.

"Every weapon knows its sheath." She looked over at him. "If you can't even find that, how will you ever find the target?"

Even with them both seated, the woman's head was well beneath his. A round face somehow still gave the impression of firmness, and bright red hair hinted at a temper.

And a hint of silver shone at the open neck of her sturdy coat.

"Oh, god," Hendriksen sighed, burying his face in one hand. "Another one. What's your name, then?"

"That's hardly courteous," replied his latest unwelcome companion haughtily. "My name is Catherine of Lancaster. Of course, I already know who you are."

She pronounced the English words oddly, and Hendriksen recognized that she was no more a son of Albion than he was. Or daughter, rather. Bright blue eyes returned his examination, pausing at the case that he'd tucked between his knees.

"This managed to pass as a priest?" Lancaster said, turning her palms upward above her aproned lap and holding them a handspan apart. The rhythm of her words finally betrayed her Castillian heritage to Hendriksen's trained ear. "The blood of the Church of England always ran thin, courtesy of that whoreson Cromwell, but even he could have organized the hunt for a single false priest traveling on foot. Of course, Wolsey would've had you in a single day."

"Of course," Hendriksen said with some asperity but no greater understanding. What new problems would this bring? He laid his hand on his magical pistol. "Let me save us both some time. My answer is no. The case is mine and you'll leave immediately or I will take measures to protect myself."

"I rather don't think so, young man," replied Lancaster. "You'll require my help before long."

Hendriksen rose angrily to his feet, but before he could refute her, the soldier he'd previously noted stepped into his field of view, the Lee-Enfield rifle still slung.

"Wot's this, then?" the guard asked. "Are a body seeking th' punishment of th' Old Testimint, then?"

It wasn't the slung rifle that totally arrested Hendriksen's attention, nor was it the terrible parody of a Cockney accent pronouncing the recognition code.

The German agent looked, really looked at the guardsman.

It was the shockingly familiar features on the guardsman's face. Hendriksen should know. He saw their facsimile in the mirror often enough.

"Eduard, what the hell?" Hendriksen said, looking around the pier as three more men appeared from shadowed doors or climbed up from boats. "What's this, what's going on?"

"Hello, brother," the "soldier" replied. A tight smile from Eduard Hendriksen was the extent of his filial greeting. "You certainly don't sound like an English priest, so I guess that it really is you. But who's this?"

Hendriksen's brother turned to look at Lancaster, his head swiveling like a cannon slewing onto a new target. Lancaster sat quietly, a small smile playing across her mouth as she watched the family reunion.

"She's nobody, a cafe owner who was chatting with me," answered the confused agent. "Where's my pickup? The Abwehr was supposed to meet me beyond the breakwate—"

"Change of plans, big brother." Eduard didn't sneer, but his oily, satisfied smile spoke volumes and something dark reflected in his gray eyes. "The SS is taking responsibility for that case you're holding. You're to come with me immediately. Your friend can come with us as well. If she behaves, we may even let her stay on the boat after we make the Channel."

Instinctively, Hendriksen turned his body to shield the case that bore the treasure.

"I'm working for Canaris," he said. "This case goes only to him."

Hendriksen's mind churned. The relationship between the Abwehr and the SS hadn't devolved into open violence. Or at least it hadn't until there was something important enough at stake. His brother would've been sent to guarantee positive identification of Hendriksen himself. As a fervent believer, he could be relied upon to see the matter through.

Regardless of cost.

Hendriksen's left hand slowly lowered the briefcase to sit on the ground.

"Well, plans change," Eduard said, raising a pistol in one hand. Hendriksen noted it was the new Steyr with a bulbous cylinder screwed onto the muzzle. Standard SS issue.

"In addition to the boy who guarded this pier until a short time ago, your Abwehr friend on the E-boat also resisted, so now we have an additional space for a new passenger," his brother went on, smiling thinly down at Lancaster.

"Lucky you," he added with a jerk of his weapon. "Now get up!"

Lancaster didn't budge. Her bright eyes flicked about the scene, calculating.

"Oh, I don't think so, Herr Master Race," she answered. Her strange accent visibly registered on Hendriksen's brother, who looked briefly puzzled. "I rather think I'll stay right here. I'm waiting, you see."

To Hendriksen's left, an additional guard moved to flank him. This one held a Schmeisser in the shadow of a long overcoat. Hendriksen glanced at the man's face. His features were unfinished, like unfired clay.

Once again, two dark smears of eyes regarded Hendriksen steadily.

"Have it your way." Eduard sneered and began to raise the pistol.

Hendriksen couldn't have explained the compulsion. He didn't know why he dove at his brother, leaving the case to fall over next to the bench. At least his brother was a man, unlike the golem that was raising the submachine gun. There wasn't time enough to think, only react.

All he could be sure of was the overwhelming impulse to keep Eduard from shooting Lancaster. At this distance, a miss was impossible.

The seated woman raised one hand quite quickly, as though shooing a fly.

The Steyr coughed once, twice, before Hendriksen's shoulder drove through his brother's midriff.

The whine of two ricochets accompanied Eduard's wheezing exhalation as his diaphragm made violent contact with his spine, courtesy of Hendriksen's tackle. The little Steyr flew several feet across the slick cobblestones with a metallic clatter. It would be a few moments before the SS man could breathe, let alone fight.

But the golem's line of fire to both Lancaster and Hendriksen was now clear, and the Schmeisser chattered as the construct began to empty the thirty-two-round magazine in a long burst. Mercifully, its accuracy was atrocious, but three rounds stitched through Hendriksen's cassock, driving spikes of frozen fire through his back and legs.

Lancaster abandoned the bench and stepped forward, crouching. Her other hand joined the first in a complicated gesture. Half of a hemisphere of silver light glittered as the remaining bullets splashed ineffectively into an invisible shield which she extended to cover not only herself, but also Hendriksen.

He grunted as he tried to roll over. His own body had protected his brother, who began crawling away.

Figures.

Fighting the growing pain, Hendriksen lay on his side and made a fumbling draw with his lighter pistol. A brilliant snap of light reduced the golem to a pile of glowing sludge.

"There it is," Lancaster said brightly as she finally rose to a standing position, eyeing his little brass gun. "I'd wondered where that had gotten to." She surveyed the rapid action that surrounded them, adding, "The modifications made by your artificers are inferior."

Another SS golem snapped off some shots at Lancaster, but her shield intercepted the bullets with a single wave of her right hand. The enemy agent dove for a garbage tip as his own rounds rebounded.

Eduard was several meters away now, nearly all the way to the quay's edge. He put his hand in a pocket, making Hendriksen tense, but his brother remained prone and, with a grunt of effort, scattered a handful of pea-sized bits of ivory across the pier.

"Oriuntur!" he shouted. *"Fidelius militum, oriuntur!"*

Hendriksen stiffened. He knew his Latin.

Apparently, so did Eduard.

More than a dozen new shapes grew upwards into a standing position. As they straightened, arms separated from their claylike trunks. These didn't even attempt a pretense at clothing or faces. Short lashes of golden light dripped from each black hand as the bottom half of the trunks split to become legs.

Hendriksen attempted to fire at the nearest, but his arcane firearm emitted only an angry yellow spark.

The dozen or more golems began to step towards the diminutive woman and the wounded agent as Eduard scrambled sideways to avoid their advance.

"Dragon's teeth!" Catherine of Lancaster said, more seriously this time. "I underestimated Stuttgart's interest. And his resources."

She raised her voice.

"About now, if you please, ladies!"

Hendriksen had been watching his death approach, so he had an excellent view as both Culpepper and Seymour appeared quite suddenly, as though they had been behind an insubstantial but otherwise perfect drapery.

Instead of skirts and heels, this time they were clad in what looked like sleek plate armor. They interposed themselves between the mob of golems and the bench. The first swung his glowing whip of light, but Culpepper bent backwards from the waist as gracefully as a gymnast, and the weapon swung past her face, missing by a hairsbreadth. Her return stroke with a silver axe did not, and the golem slumped into the now-familiar pile of mush. She thrust a palm outwards and a silver wave of force knocked a pair of nearby golems from their feet. Seymour adopted a classic fencing position, and with very rapid steps, she advanced, the little silver foil in her fist dipping first to deflect a whip, and then to run a golem through.

In four seconds, she dispatched four more constructs, her movements so fast that Hendriksen's blurring vision couldn't quite follow.

Together, the two ladies performed a whirling dance of death, and with each stroke, another golem dropped.

The sound of a hissing crack jerked Hendriksen's attention. The bench exploded into splinters as a light whip crashed through it, swung by a golem who, luckier or faster than its fellows, had made it to the place where the case lay.

Hendriksen could feel himself beginning to fade and tried to scrabble away, but his legs were not responding properly. By dint of a desperate roll, he only just missed another forehand blow, and watched his death approach as the golem cocked its hand for a backhand swing.

A silver knife blade grew quite suddenly from its chest, and it too collapsed. Nearly within touching distance, Hendriksen could hear a slight hissing sound as whatever the being was made from flowed across the planks. As it shrank, Lancaster's slight form appeared behind the felled creature.

The sound of a motor launch roared from the far side of the quay. A quick glance revealed that the younger Hendriksen was missing. The sound of alarm whistles punctuated the night and, from the far quay, a searchlight stabbed out, illuminating a white curving wake.

"Corporal of the Guard, Post Number Three!"

Laying on his back, Hendriksen could make out the distant sound of shouted orders.

"Well, my sisters," Seymour said, stepping into his field of vision. "You saw him intervene. It seems that he has Chosen."

"Should we save him?" Culpepper asked brightly, also stepping forward. Her little axe was nowhere to be seen and instead she folded her arms, all angles and attitude. She leaned forward, staring into Hendriksen's eyes, even as he tasted the blood rising in his mouth.

"The Keep has ever considered adding as many of

the Blood to our strength as we could find," replied Seymour. She still held the little foil but made a moue of distaste as she regarded the golem sludge spattered on her vambraces.

With a considering glance back at Hendriksen, she offered, "Another properly owned Knight could be decisive."

Screw that. No one owns me.

Hendriksen made an effort to rise to his elbows so he could tell them what to do with their idea but failed as his strength fled his limbs.

"I don't know that this Knight-in-being is salvageable, Madam Seymour," the shortest Catherine said. Her blue eyes were cold, devoid of emotion. "Untrained. Uncouth. Proud of it, just like our unlamented Henry. Can you not see the Stain upon this man?"

She held the case in one hand. "We have what we came for."

Seymour stepped closer. Her regard was so intense, it was as though she was looking through Hendriksen.

"He could be useful. He lacks only focus and a reason to belong," she said.

The one-time German agent tried to roll to one side, but couldn't even manage that much, let alone reach the little arcane pistol that lay only a foot or two away on a glowing mound of sludge. Culpepper negligently toed it a little further away.

"He's tenacious," she said.

Stooping closer, the youngest Raven moved Hendriksen's wide-brimmed hat away from the spreading blood puddle and brushed a forelock out of his eyes.

Lancaster wasn't so solicitous.

"Have you considered your Choice?" she asked.

"Whom do you belong to? Scavengers like your brother, twisted by distant masters? Your admiral, a doomed Knight already irredeemably Stained? Or something else?"

His field of view began to narrow as blood loss affected his vision. He knew that Culpepper's eyes were golden. Lancaster stepped closer still, and her eyes should have been blue.

Instead the world was rendering in shades of gray.

He tried to speak, but a bloody cough was as good as he could manage.

I belong to no one, not the SS, not Canaris, and especially not these three dames.

Lancaster squinted suspiciously, as though she could hear him.

"Good enough," Culpepper said, smiling. "We can work with that, for now."

She turned to her partners. "Well?"

The pier light had been growing dim and now it was nearly out. He sagged backwards, lying in his own blood. Through rapidly fluttering eyelids, he could see all three Kates looking down at him now, side by side. They didn't seem to be in a hurry to make up their damned minds.

Going.

Going.

Fade to black.

Worth the Scars of Dying

Patrick M. Tracy

The most beautiful woman in the city leaned against the wall of my shop, sobbing into a scrap of green silk. A glimmer of light flashed inside a tear as it traced down her knuckles. Her indrawn breath carried to my ears, a soft shiver. My mouth opened, hoping for the scent of her against my palette. I didn't know the door would blow in a moment later. I didn't know the dead would pile high on the floor, or that I'd be turning down the darkest streets in town on her behalf. I just knew that a gorgeous redhead crying was a damned shame.

I grew up in Remnar, the biggest city in the world. Not the pretty surface city, but the seedy subterranean part. I don't daze easy. Seeing her, though? She hit me across the eyes like a warhammer. Everything slowed down. The smooth lines of her body beneath that green dress told me stories about worlds I'd never known. Her red hair swayed, powered by the action of her tears.

I'm not the kind to help. Never been a hero or cared to be. I try to be kind, but this place will break you ten ways if you can't build a wall around your heart. Tragedy rolls down every street like trash blown by the wind. Seeing her there, just this side of the stairs up to Lex's, I found myself wanting to be different than I am. I wished for something I'd always shied away from. Goodness, I guess. In retrospect, probably a mistake. In the sordid underground of a city built by demons, reaching for goodness will get you killed.

I only had a moment to gawk at her and be a bad host to my customers before the door smashed inward, falling in four parts, sliding across the floor at jagged angles. A human in heavy armor burst in, shield lowered and heavy sword glinting in the orange light of the witchlamps.

A cup of darkbrew shattered on the floor, spraying hot liquid on my shoes. The lady dwarf who I'd been handing the beverage swore, jumping back from the mess. I turned, meeting the human attacker's eyes. His pupils hardened down to pinpoints. Rank sweat cooked from out of his mail, a tail of greasy black hair across his shoulders.

He headed straight for the woman. Her. The High Queen of all redheads.

Crying, she hardly jumped at the sudden crash and motion. Even if she had, her dress couldn't stop a breeze, let alone a blade. I'd seen what a sword did to bare flesh. My mind flashed forward, hearing the wet tearing sound as the sword cut deep and freed her living blood. I saw her on the boards, eyes gone blank, the miracle of the living dissipated.

Oh, hell no. Not in my shop.

I didn't know I'd summoned the Emperor's Rush until my hand whipped out, the forked sign of death forming, power like congealed shadow and fire burning down my bones. I didn't think about it until the magic lashed out, smashing through the human's shield, his armor, his flesh. He flew back out the broken door, a hole in his body where life used to be. His soul ripped free of his corpse, lingering there, confused and pale. When they die in strife, their spirit isn't ready for the journey. Most people can't see them, but they can feel the chill of their ghosts haunting an empty room.

Another warrior rushed in. I shouted in the barking tongue of the underworld. His face disappeared into black fire, his scalp drifting down to the floorboards far more slowly than his nerveless body fell. The sound of the body landing touched the air like a fallen grain sack.

The redhead's face turned to me, locking on mine as my brow burned with the shadow crown of evil magic. She didn't flinch. Even as my horns manifested and I could feel my teeth grow bestial in my jaw, her eyes stayed steady, looking at me as a savior. No one had ever looked at me that way. I didn't think anyone ever would. That's what makes you lose your head. When a beautiful dream walks in the door and treats you like a better person than you know you are.

I ran to her side, shielding her from the other two as they trampled over the fallen bodies of their comrades. I closed my right fist, and the power of the Emperor's Rush glided across my clavicles, seething in my shoulder joint and down my left arm. Beyond gods and devils, beyond the passing of eons, the everlasting power of death flared in me. You don't tell it what you want, you simply call it forth and reap its dark reward.

A giant shadow fell across them. A single monstrous arm pushed through the fabric between worlds. Made of burning shadow, it shed hot darkness and a slow crawl of smoke. The third attacker, a massive orc female, ducked under the fist of darkness and swung a flanged mace at me. I juked to the side, and the mace smashed a fist-sized divot in the stairwell next to me. I pushed the redhead up the stairs with my right hand, then swung the shadow fist. The scrawny fourth warrior's breastplate buckled. He flew through the window, dead before the sound of shattering glass reached his ears. The very expensive window that I'd just had replaced. Lex, my upstairs tenant, had gone through it in a brawl a few weeks prior. The glazier had only mounted the new pane that morning. At great expense, in case I didn't mention that.

I kicked out at the female orc. A clumsy attack, but right on the point of her knee, slowing her down just enough. The mace missed me by an inch. Her swing destroyed a stair riser right beneath me. I fell. The redhead caught me before my head bounced against a stair, and we went down in a heap. The orc loomed above us, mace rising for her next swing. I clenched my left fist. The claw of burning shadow engulfed the orc female, shaking her like a rat in the jaws of a hound. Her bones broke, her tissue tearing from its tendon locks. Being an orc, she bore three times the punishment that would kill anything else. That just prolonged things for another few moments.

She died. Bad. Screaming. The spell dissipated,

and what fell from its grasp looked like stew meat inside torn splint mail.

The quiet after a killing comes down hard and fast. It presses on your ears like diving into the deep ocean. My heart hammering, I scrambled to my feet, passing my palms over my forehead. I replaced the glamour that hides the shadow of my horns. The jagged teeth of a monster folded away, leaving my jaw and gums soaked in blood. My unholy patron, Skolle, released his grip on my skeleton, and the loss of the power ached to my core. It felt like the hunger of a starving man, the envy of the cuckold, the shiver of the dry drunk.

Just like every time.

The echoes of the dark fire chattered down the empty hallways of my long bones, and I wavered on my feet.

"Whore's bastards and motherless dogs," I whispered.

I stepped back down into the shop. It would take hours to get the blood out of the floors. I almost wished I was a wizard, with all those handy spells. The six customers sat at their tables, their faces filled with shock and horror. Well, mostly. Sebastian, my most loyal customer, sipped at his darkbrew, a look of vague interest playing at the corners of his mouth.

"Folks, I'm going to have to close the shop for a while. Please finish up and go out the back. You all have a comped darkbrew on your next visit, and I apologize for the inconvenience."

I didn't need to ask them twice. They filed out, old Meurin still holding a half-eaten pastry, stepping over the unrecognizable gore where the orc had fallen. This incident would probably lose me a customer or two. Then again, the action might bring a few others. I took a big breath and let it loose.

Turning, I saw the redhead had caught hold of herself and wiped away the tears. She looked at me steadily, maybe to avoid looking at what lay below us on the boards. Maybe because, when the glamour is up and the helltouched features are smoothed over, I'm pretty dashing.

"You all right?" My voice felt tight and hoarse. You don't spend the morning serving darkbrew and baking pastries, thinking you're going to be standing over dead bodies. You don't expect to taste the bitter stress of almost dying in your throat. The stink of the fallen rose into the air. The redhead's emerald eyes had never flinched away from me, but that smell caught her. Some of the color fell away from her cheeks. Her fingers reached out, steadying herself against the wall.

"Why?" she asked.

Oh, her voice reached in and shook me inside. It took me a minute to find my words again. "They were coming for you, sweetness."

Her brow crinkled. When she thought of it, flashes of a thousand jade shards splashed across the narrow stairwell, signaling emotions I could only guess at. "I didn't expect them to look like that."

"But you expected them—someone."

She shot me a pained look, evading the question. "You saved my life."

I shrugged. "I killed some guys."

"Not for me, then?"

"I didn't say that."

"You're a careful one, aren't you?" She brushed past me, trailing her fingers across my chest. Every touch

burned a trail across my skin. She walked behind the
bar and poured herself a darkbrew, bolting it down
scalding hot. She stood there, putting me to the weight
and measure with her eyes. I stepped between her
and the worst of the scene while she did so. I'm no
Iron District prizefighter, but I don't get fat on my
own baked goods.

"I have to clean up." It seemed like the dumbest
thing I could say. The redhead waved at me and carried on helping herself to the darkbrew. Her hand
hovered over a honey scone, but she thought better
of it and stayed with her drink.

I dragged the bodies into a pile. She sat at a nearby
table. Even though she hid it, her hand shook as she
held her cup. Giving me a smile that shocked the
dimness of the room, she tried to indicate that she
was all right. A noble effort, and not necessary. I felt
off balance, about to say something stupid. I made
myself turn away.

In the back, I found my box of ravening and brought
it with me. "You may not want to watch this part."

"It's fine, Professor Orman," she said, but she did
look down at her hands as they held her now-empty
cup. "I trust you."

"You know my name."

"It's on the door. Well, it was, when I came in."

Right. Professor Orman's Sweet Darkness. My shop.
Where food is. And a pile of dead people. If the
food server's guild caught wind of this, I'd be paying
a nasty fine. I knelt and whispered into the box of
ravening, awakening those within.

"Upon the flesh and bone, upon the sinew and
blood. Feast and slake the eternal hunger." You didn't

really need to give them any enticement, but I'm not one to stint on my necromancy. Lazy spells go astray. Sloppy necro work pulls strange shit into the world, and that's never good.

I set the box on the floor, no bigger than a man's palm in each direction. The scuttling horde emerged. A thousand shining, black beetles, clicking across the worn wooden boards, hurling themselves at the congealing blood and cooling flesh. For any normal person, the sound of meat being devoured from the bone by a writhing carpet of magical insects is pretty horrid. You get used to it. Your soul stops screaming against it. It's that or go mad, so you adapt.

I helped the redhead to the back room, where the big baking prep table lay empty and shining. I eased the door closed, hoping that no local rogues would sneak in and rob the till. Doubtful. The Iron Hand guards would be coming to check things out. Even in Remnar's Underhalls, four dead is enough to have the constabulary show up eventually. You didn't want to be caught thieving by the Iron Hand, who were selected for muscularity and sadism.

"I hope this doesn't splash back on you, Professor. I don't want to get you into trouble."

"Just Orman is fine. The Irons know me. I'm a licensed necro, all my papers in order." My voice sounded assured, but you just never knew. I'd find out by how many guards they sent over. More than three, and I'd have good reason to worry.

"A few minutes ago, I didn't have much hope left." She smiled. It hinted at a lot of things, but it came and went so quickly that it felt like an illusion, something you doubted you'd really seen.

"Remnar isn't known for kindness. People get burnt down to ashes every day. No one's ever figured a way to make it stop."

She reached out, covering my hand with her own. Her touch felt so warm. "Maybe it's not all bad, Just Orman."

I knew trouble when I saw it. I couldn't seem to do anything but get closer. "Since we'll be questioned, maybe I should know your name. We should have our stories straight when they arrive, or this'll look like something worse than it was."

"Call me Kariel. Or Kara, since we have a certain bond now."

A certain bond. All the dark powers preserve me. I'd never seen trouble like her.

Varduk, the Iron Hand captain, listened to the end of my story about the attack. I'd mostly given him the truth, where it suited me. Telling the whole truth is for suckers.

"You don't know why they attacked?" He hooked his thumb at the pile of bones, shoes, and armor where the bodies had been. I caught him shivering when he thought about how I'd stripped the bones.

I shrugged. "It happened in a moment. They didn't say a word. Just kicked down the door and attacked."

"Any enemies? Jilted lovers? Rivals in the necro business?"

"I'm not the guy who makes enemies. My tenant who lives upstairs is always in some kind of trouble though. You might know him. Lex Custos?"

Varduk made a face. "That guy. He has enemies everywhere. I should talk to him."

"He's out of town."

The hobgoblin shook his head. "Figures. Looks like you might have caught some of the backlash for all his ... antics."

I hunched, putting my hands in my pockets. "Yeah, could be." Lex was a Bonded Agent of the city and could do all kinds of strongarm work and investigation on retainer. Mostly, though, he drank himself half stupid and lamented losing his job as a detective in the Falcon's Eye, the most respected constables in Remnar's richest district.

I put on the "I'm just a meek shopkeeper" expression, though it was a tough sell with four dead on my ledger for that morning. "Is there anything else you need from me? I need to start getting the shop cleaned up and arrange for someone to fix the window and the door."

Varduk gave me a come-along gesture with his chin and I walked out onto the street. I met eyes with Kara, who sat at the back table and answered questions from another cop. She flashed a smile and all the fight went out of him. She'd be fine.

We hooked into an alley. My eyes pierced the gloom. No one else lingered back here. They weren't going to try and grab me up. Good for me. Good for them, because I wouldn't have gone quietly.

"That girl," Varduk started. A tall hobgoblin, he touched the pointed black beard at his chin before continuing. "You should watch out around her."

I stiffened. "Why? What do you know about Kara?"

He shook his head. "I know enough, just seeing her once."

I stepped closer, not even sure why a flare of anger kindled in my chest. "What do you mean by that?"

Varduk smiled ruefully, not giving any ground. "Even guys like you aren't immune to...well, you saw her. That's not what I'm saying though. She ain't afraid of you, and that's the biggest giveaway."

"Afraid of me? I'm a baker," I said, gesturing at my apron.

"Not what you look like, Orman Orphesias. What you are. What you do after the shop is shut. Tell me she shivered and looked away when you put the black across their eyes, and I'll tell you you're safe."

I remembered that look. The look women only give the good guys and the suckers. The look that told me I was her favorite person in town, that the shadow crown and the horns of hell didn't frighten her.

"Yeah. Beautiful woman who stares straight into your eyes when you kill? Those are some deep waters, my friend. That's all I'll say."

He turned, walking back in the direction of the nearest district station. I shook my head, doing my best to dismiss all he'd implied. By the time I came back to the shop, it was down to Kara and me.

"They rough you up?" I asked. Clearly, they hadn't, as her dress still hung perfect and pristine across her shoulders. No shadow of a bruise, no hair out of place. Like none of this had ever happened. I really took her in for a few heartbeats. Not just the improbable perfection. Everything. She wasn't human. She probably carried Fey blood, but asking about that seemed like a rude thing to do.

Kara suddenly loomed close to me, her hand on my cheek. "I'm fine. They didn't...threaten you, did they? I couldn't stand it if whatever I brought to your doorstep put you in danger." She shook her head. "Again, I guess." So close, her delicate scent revealed itself. Crushed flowers. Jasmine and a hint of sweet orange. Below that, something earthy, like the remnants of an old hardwood fire.

I hadn't gotten beyond her nearness, the warmth of her palm against my cheek. I do okay with the ladies, but they always want either one side or the other. The pleasant guy behind the counter or the warlock who can summon up the powers of the black force domain. When they see both, it seems to always chase them away. Kara? I could see her taking in the paradox without a single hitch. What could I say in the face of that kind of acceptance?

"I'm going to go. I don't want to see you hurt, Orman. What you did today, though, I'll never forget." She surprised me. With more strength than I expected, she brought my face down to hers, kissing me gently. "Thank you. Remnar has at least one hero on its hands."

She turned and walked out of my shop, lost in the press of the darkened street of a subterranean city built on the bones of an ancient demon civilization. Kara disappeared into the night that never lifted, and I stood there, mute as a stone pillar.

You can't just stand there being lovesick. Not as a small business owner. Not as a licensed necro for the city of Remnar. I shook it off and started scrubbing at the stains in the floor, the sad faces of the spirits in the room watching me. They weren't going to leave on their own power. It would be up to me to show them the way. A warlock's work goes on and on.

I went and got the black chalk and the dust of rusted coffin nails. In a moment of inspiration, I grabbed an empty quill and poked it into my arm, filling it with blood. Small ritual wounds? Part of the gig. You get inured to it.

The female orc's spirit hung there, blood red in the air. The agony of her death filled her, shaking her ghost like wind against sailcloth. She recoiled from me when I came near. Usually, spirits and haunts come toward me like an old friend.

But when you kill them, it's different. It has to be, I guess.

"I can't hurt you now," I told her. Which was a lie, but she didn't know that. "Let me take that pain away. One less thing to carry into the void. I don't have anything against any of you. You did what you did, and I did what I did. It's the law of the city. Whatever gets you through, whatever it takes."

That seemed to settle her down. All of them stopped retreating from me. I produced the quill and said the abyssal spell that draws pain into the blood and binds it. The orc's spirit went from crimson to the same washed-out gray of the other three, who'd died cleaner.

"There. That's a little better, isn't it?"

Not that she'd answer. If I didn't kill them, they'd sometimes have a lot to say, but these ghosts stood there, mute as I'd been when the woman of my dreams walked away. I took a breath and knelt again.

There's a mystical name for the portal into the spirit realms that I made with the black chalk and rusted iron. Some dark wizards and eldritch tinkerers love to throw that lingo around, but I just call it the door in the floor.

Like a corpse draws flies, the door draws all the ghosts and lingering spirits in the nearby vicinity. It's a service I can perform. For a fee, of course. The elves and Fey, especially, seem to like it better when there aren't a lot of unquiet dead hanging around.

One by one, the four attackers from that morning gave themselves to the door, dragged down to the Grand Necropolis, where Skolle would sort them and send them to their final reward. I had some thoughts about where these four would end up. Paid killers didn't tend to fare well at the far end of the road.

Only bones and broken armor remained. I'd sell the armor and use the bones. I'd go on. I'd try to forget the day ever happened.

"She'll come back," Sebastian said. An elf, he stood taller than I, all fine bones and boringly flawless skin. A stalwart regular, he always floated in after the rush, stayed an hour, and had interesting, enigmatic things to say. I suspected he was a deposed king or a former spy.

"I don't know," I told Sebastian. "Why would she?"

A slow smile bloomed on his features, putting the lie to all that nobility one would normally ascribe to an urbane elf gentleman.

"You killed for her. You threw yourself between her and death. That sort of thing makes an impression. Just remember though—that's how it started. When she comes back, your window is the least of what might get broken."

I sighed. "I guess I'm a sucker, because I want to say that I'd take that risk. For her...yeah. Maybe I'd stick my neck out."

He took his second cup of darkbrew and gave me a little toast. "And she knows that."

"Maybe I'm losing my edge. This thing, being down in the mouth about a woman, isn't normal for me." I pretended to clean, just rubbing a cloth back and forth on the counter to have something to do.

"No matter how tough you are, you always fall for someone. Or something, I guess. If you don't, maybe that's the real tragedy in life."

"The tragedy? I could have said something, anything, and she might have stayed. No, I just stood there. Like a sap."

Sebastian handed me his empty cup. "Like I said. She'll come back. Blood always buys another trip around the ring."

The shop door opened. A group of dwarves came in, calling for their midmorning ale. "Blood usually just buys more blood," I said, mostly to myself.

The CLOSED sign had been up for an hour, the chairs upended on the tabletops and the floor dusted clean. The street outside whispered through the shaded window and shuttered door, no more than the simple noises of the Underhalls that we never notice.

But the back door eased open. Was that the slightest hint of a footstep on the hard floor of the kitchen? That caught me, strange as daylight underground. I reached beneath the counter, wrapping my fingers around the orc's flanged mace. Somehow, I'd grown used to it, attached. The one that didn't quite kill me.

I expanded my glamour to make my steps silent, edging closer to the back door. Right shoulder against the wall, I gripped the weapon and waited. I heard the intruder's breath.

Helltouched, I can see in the dark, and only a

single lamp burned in the back. Shadows danced in over the half door between the public area and the kitchen, strange and misshapen.

The half door opened, and my muscles tensed. "Orman?" a female voice asked. Her voice. Kara.

I nearly dropped the mace. My body relaxed, the weapon held by my leg now, breath finally returning to my lungs. "You could have knocked on the window. The closed sign doesn't apply to you."

I didn't think about how that would sound, coming out of the dark and from behind her shoulder. She spun, her eyes snapped wide, just picking up the light of the distant lamp as she searched for me.

Her hand went to her chest. She stood very still, the prettiest of the shadows in the dark. No scolding, no shrieking, just a moment of forced calm. That kind of control? You can't buy that, can't earn it reading a book. That strength is paid for with tough years with no one but yourself to trust. Something in my heart clenched just watching her.

She scanned me, and I could tell her vision pierced the dark, at least a little. "You just about fed me a mouthful of that mace, didn't you?"

I reached out, setting it on the countertop with a thud. "I came closer than I wanted to. I didn't think you'd ever come back, especially not creeping in like a thief."

"If they saw... if they knew I'd doubled back, even once, it'd be all over for me."

Her whole body shook, the resolve that clenched her jaw and hardened her eyes weakening. I stepped closer.

"I'm all alone, Orman. I didn't know where else to turn."

She grabbed my hand, squeezing so hard, her eyes bright as candles up close. The way my arms went around her shoulders felt like that's where they'd always belonged. She nestled against me without the slightest resistance. "You're here. I've got you. Everything's fine."

The words sounded like I believed them. Maybe I did.

So warm. Anyone I'd ever held this way, their bodies felt cool against my own. Helltouched isn't just the horns and obsidian eyes. It goes down to the bones and sinew, into the hot cauldron of your blood. I can reach into fire unharmed. Disease and poison burn away in my veins like ice hitting a hot stove. Certain churches, I can't get past the front door.

But Kara's heat hadn't been illusion before. Her cheek against my shoulder, her hands at the small of my back—they baked through my shirt. What did that? Sanguivore Fey? I didn't smell blood on her. I couldn't keep my mind on it. The silent trust of her body against me in the dark spun all thoughts away. Her heart and breath quieted. Was that me? Was that the safety of having me close?

"What are you into?" I asked, voice just loud enough to reach her ear.

"You probably shouldn't know. It's my weight to carry. I've been trying, but things went so bad. I had nowhere else to turn. Everything I'd built up over these years, and they burned it down in a night. These clothes are all I have left."

"Who's trying to hurt you, Kara?" I moved my palm against her back. No silk dress this time, just a rough-spun tunic over wool trousers and soldier's boots. Not even her clothes, I didn't believe. Maybe a part of a disguise, or simply stolen. It didn't matter. Her kind of beauty didn't need any adornment.

"I...got away from a place where these villains were holding me like a prisoner. My whole life, they held me captive, but I got away. It took them a long time to find me, but they know I'm here. At first, maybe they were trying to bring me back, but I've found out too much now. They need to kill me before I get my chance."

My head spun. It took me a minute to even decide what question to ask. "How long have we got before they track you here?"

"I think I lost them, but they were close. All around." She squeezed me harder, the strength of her arms locked against me almost painful.

"All right. We're getting out of here."

"If we go out there, they'll find us. They're on the street, searching. I don't know how many hunters they sent, but too many to fight."

"Fighting's not my first choice, sweetness. Much as I don't want to ask, I need you to let go for a minute."

Her hands slipped free. I ignored the sudden rush of want burning at her absence. I centered myself and spoke out the guttural words of a spell, concentrating on my left hand. My fingernails grew and thickened into claws, then talons. Maybe clever wizards knew how to do this stuff a more graceful way. A way that didn't send agony crashing through their system as the magic ripped them and remade them. Not me.

Kara's teeth clicked together. She touched her own fingertips but didn't say anything.

I reached out, clawing at the surface of the air.

Bleeding through the wounds in the fabric of the world, I gathered the insubstantial stuff of darkness itself. I painted it across us, until we were merely shapes. Speaking the words to heal the rift, my own voice sounded like wind whistling down a long tunnel.

My left hand returned to normal, a process equally as painful as the transformation. Blood dripped to the boards. I forced the hand into a fist, sweat breaking on my face. Not that anyone could see beneath the shroud of gloom.

"Come on." I took her hand, and we stole upstairs, through a hidden door at the back of Lex's broom closet, and out onto the roof. We floated from roof to roof until we were out of the nearby vicinity, then dropped down to street level, taking narrow, winding alleys back to my apartment.

"We should be safe here," I whispered.

Inside the courtyard, I dismissed the darkness.

That's when they attacked.

Six robed figures rushed out of my neighbor's door, the yellow witchlight from the courtyard lamps glistening on their swords. I smelled dwarf blood: Berek, my neighbor's. I pushed Kara behind me and stepped closer to them.

"My flesh the doorway, my blood the road, my bones the bridge of death," I spoke, casting a spell I'd never imagined I'd need. I made no effort to evade them, standing with my arms held out, like they were old friends. The hooded figures struck as one. The agony of six swords cleaving into me made anything else I'd ever felt pale in comparison.

The pain of dying is like that.

❖   ❖   ❖

I couldn't get off my knees. Their cloaks lay empty on the ground, their weapons still skewered through my flesh at odd angles. Kara's eyes met mine.

"How are you alive?"

I shook my head. "Just help me get the swords... out."

She did. Slow, dark blood oozed out of the wounds before they knit back together. By the end, I lay on my back, looking up at the far-off roof of the Underhalls, at the witchlamps flickering against the gloom. Yellow lamps. The Guildsman's District. Most times, that's what I called myself. A guildsman. A baker, by trade. Not tonight.

"Are you going to survive this?" she asked, kneeling at my side.

Fair question. Every strike had been a killing blow. Six deaths. The pain faded, but not the touch of the dark realm, where I'd been just for a flickering moment. I turned my mind aside from what I'd seen over there, the fact that time is meaningless, and the sounds of screams go on forever.

"Looks like. Help me up. We have to get out of here."

"What happened to them?" Her hair hung down around my face. Even in the shaky aftermath of death, the view of her seemed pretty perfect.

"That's a complicated question. They're suffering in the jaws of hell. Ain't that enough?"

She took my hand and pulled me to standing. I slewed into her, pointing at my own door. Kara half-carried me into my place. With clumsy hands, I fumbled through my cupboards until I found a bottle. Breaking the seal, I upended and drank it all down.

Maybe it was lion blood, rum, and powdered Tahash flower. Whatever it was, it got me moving again. We had minutes, at best. I drew a ward upon the door with the blood from my own wounds.

"They weren't alone. More will be along soon, if they had a lookout. They can still smash down the door with enough effort."

"Then we're trapped." A moment of defeat crossed her features, then her strength chased it away. "Why is there a human arm bone?"

I ignored the question. "Grab that. We might need it. Come on."

Walking fast, I couldn't do. I could walk, and I didn't have far to go. I didn't keep a big place. Just two rooms, the second being my bedchamber. I led her there.

Kara raised an eyebrow.

"No time. Help me move the bed."

Her strength proved useful. Recovering from death, even with a draught to keep me going, left me weak and uncoordinated. The floor beneath the bed held a permanent portal. I took her hand and brought her into it, beginning the incantation I'd crafted in secret. Even if they had a mage of some kind, the best they could do was try and predict where it would take us. No one else could come through.

I looked around at my place, wondering if any of it would be left when this was over. Sebastian said it. More than a window. A hell of a lot more.

Utter darkness and dead silence. Kara pushed closer to me, so I could feel the bone of her hip and the way her ribs rose with her sharp, indrawn breath. I led her to a torch stand and removed the hood from a witchlamp.

"Where are we?" She looked around at all the vague outlines of furniture covered with drop cloths against the dust.

"My secret lair, I guess you'd call it. We're a long way below the city. No one's ever been here but me." I slumped down on a couch, glad for the drop cloth. My blood covered me to below the waist. I'd have to clean up, but I didn't have the energy yet.

Kara watched me for a long moment, pain in her eyes, then folded her legs and sat on the ground in front of me. She leaned her back against my knees and gathered her arms around herself.

I ran the back of my knuckles through her hair, letting my eyes close for a moment. Just the feel of her there, the way she smelled, seemed like enough.

"I destroy everything I touch," she said. "Everyone who tries to help me loses everything. I'm a walking curse, and I can't seem to stop hurting people. Maybe I should just stop running. Let them kill me. I'm just so tired."

What could I say to that? I put it aside. "Those guys were cultists. Tell me they weren't."

"No, you're right," she replied after a pause.

"So this cult of lunatics...that's the people you got away from? Tell me something, so I can figure out what we can do from here."

"You're...going to keep helping me?"

"I've already killed ten of their goons. They murdered my neighbor. I'm in it now."

She stood up, turning to face me. Kara pulled her tunic over her head. For a moment, I struggled to take in everything I saw. Perfection made flesh. An answer to prayers someone like me has no business uttering. But what she really meant to show me only arrived a distant second in the race.

A rune so complex that it deflected the eye had been drawn upon her belly. It covered much of her torso, stretching from the cleft of her ribcage to just above her belly button. I reached out and touched her hips, drawing her onto my lap. She didn't resist, but I saw a flash of something cross her features.

So close, her hips against me and legs straddling my waist, her scent overwhelmed the blood, intoxicating. That hint of old fire, of hot metal beneath the jasmine. I never wanted to stop drawing that into my lungs. I put my palm against the rune, and it hummed with power. Invisible waves of energy washed out of the rune with every heartbeat. I didn't know what they were, or what they meant.

"They caught me when I was a baby. My parents were dead, and so there was no one to look, no one to save me. They put this on me to contain my power, to harvest it for their own. The cult didn't hurt me. I didn't know to fear them for a long, long time. One day I learned, though. When I reached my full strength, they were going to use me in a ritual. Something about bringing the glory of the fire god out of the earth. They were going to kill me. I started to plan my escape that day."

I swallowed. "That's how they always find you. The rune. I'm not the right guy to understand all it does, but I bet the power coming off of it is unmistakable."

"That means we're not safe, even here."

"Not forever, no. A day or two, that's it. I have to . . . do something. I have to get moving again."

Kara pulled my face against her chest. "You have to rest. They hurt you so much." I realized that my glamour had slipped, that my hellish features had been there for her to see since the attack. Her hand curled around one of my horns, holding me against her, pushing the warmth of her life back into my half-dead frame.

"Are those scars going to fade?"

She stood behind me, the chilling spray of the waterfall swirling across us. I stuck a cloth out into the falling flow and watched the darkness of my blood wash away. I'd let Kara go first to get cleaned up, and she had one of my cloaks wrapped around her. Outside of necro work, I don't have that many spells, but I can summon up a fire, just like any helltouched. The one throwing heat and light across us had taken the last little dregs of my powers, but I counted it worthwhile.

I touched the raised seams on my flesh. "No. They're forever." I continued to scrub down as she looked on. I'd done the same, so fair play. She never made me feel self-conscious about what I was. Remarkable. Another helltouched couldn't have made me feel more at ease.

"I'm so sorry, Orman."

I turned around, letting the spray go against my back. A natural cold, not like the clinging tendrils of the grave. "You don't have to be."

Clean, we went along a narrow ledge to my lair, sealing a door shut behind us. I had some supplies dried and sealed. Not enough for anything special, but I managed a stew of rice, beans, and dried meat. Kara ate like she'd been starving. Seeing her in this one moment of calm, being able to do one normal thing, meant as much as any number of dead cultists and hired killers.

"You still need to rest," she told me. Her own eyes looked heavy after the meal.

"Soon. Tell me this, though: If you get away, what's the plan?"

She pressed her lips together, finally coming to a decision. "I have to evade them, build a power base for myself, and grow stronger. When I do, I come back and kill them all. First thing, though, I must find a way to break this rune. I'll never have a chance if they can steal my power and find me no matter how far I run."

"About that," I started, but she stopped the words with a kiss. Kara pushed me over onto my back, opening the cloak to let it fall over us like a blanket. Everything I wanted to know burned away like parchment before a blaze.

Gwethieri and Qess looked us over. The two witches had been friends of mine for years, and if anyone could find out about Kara's rune, they could. They were also librarians, so they had access to all kinds of scrolls and tomes. All the stuff warlocks don't really need.

"You look bedraggled." Gwethieri looked amused. I usually try to be dashing. "When you asked us to summon you, I figured you'd finally gotten yourself in over your head."

"We wondered what you were into. Your shop is closed and your apartment building burned down last night. Hashem said you killed some guys. Doesn't sound like the careful necro we all know and love." Qess took Gwethieri's hand and squeezed.

"No one gets out intact, not even warlocks."

"You've been hanging around that Lex guy too much," Qess said. "He's a reckless madman."

Kara peered around at the shelves of books, ill at ease. She flicked a questioning glance to me, but I tried to seem sure of myself. I introduced her to the witches. They looked between us, trying to figure out how I'd thought up whatever con game I was running. They whisked further into the library, chatting and hugging and laughing. I trailed along behind, now at their mercy.

"Of course we'll do Orman a favor! We've been waiting years to get him into our debt, the scoundrel," Gwethieri said.

Yeah. In debt to witches. That would hurt, but not as bad as replacing all the stuff I'd lost when the bastard cultists burned down my house.

Underneath the cloak, Kara wore one of my shirts. This fact didn't get lost on the witches, who looked back and grinned at me, Qess even giving me a sign that meant something crude in Fey silent language. They removed Kara's shirt and had a look at the rune for themselves. They studied the weave of magic, and other parts of the nearby terrain, for several minutes.

"So. There's a lot going on. Whoever did this wasn't kidding around," Qess told us. "We'll need a circle to learn more."

"Can you disjoin it?" I asked.

"I wouldn't even try," Gwethieri said, no hint in her tone that we could change her mind. "But when we feel the flow of energy around it, maybe we can help you get to someone who could."

The witches joined hands with each other, bringing Kara into the group. Between them, a tiger eye stone as big as an apple sat on the table. As they closed their eyes and chanted, it burned with golden light. The room pulsed and throbbed with earth energy. I walked to the front of the library. Not my kind of magic, and it made my teeth ache to be nearby.

I glanced outside.

Cultists.

Their hooded robes clashed with the normal foot traffic of the city. The lunatic bastards had found us again. Drawing away from the windows, I said a lot of unkind things under my breath. The other librarian came to chastise me about drawing a sigil on the floor. Something in my look caused her to think twice about it.

We just had to have a few more minutes of luck. Yeah. Like that would happen. A whole squad of hooded madmen rushed the entryway.

They kicked the door in. The sigil went off, pulling all light and life and hope out of the room. The cultists sagged on their feet, some of them going to their knees.

"Lady, run to the back and don't turn around!" I shouted at the librarian. "Tell 'em it's about to get loud."

She bolted. I began casting another spell, feeling all the meager energy I'd built up ebb away.

"By the long shadows of the endless twilight valley, let down your rope. By the chill, fast waters of the river where the black swans float, let down your rope. By your leave, I bring forth the mournful clamor of the doom bells, all ye Kings of Night!"

Next to me, out of the sudden gloom above, an old and roughened rope appeared. I leaped up, just as the whole squad of cultists gathered themselves and prepared to charge. I seized the rope and pulled with every ounce of my weight, every measure of my strength.

The tolling of the doom bell crashed across the library entrance, catching all the cultists and tossing them backward. Books flew from the shelves. The nearest cultists collapsed, every bone shattered. They were fortunate. The rear rank, their eyes and ears burst from the blast wave, would not go so quickly to their demise. No, they were doomed to atonal yells of agony, clawing at their own faces. They couldn't stop the maddening reverberation of the otherworldly clang and rumble. Only death could.

The rope faded, and I ran to Kara. Everyone in the district would have heard that. Gawkers and guards would be along in a moment.

The witches looked shaken but unhurt. Kara shrugged into her oversized shirt ready to run. She lifted her hand toward me, but no time for anything but essentials remained.

"What did you do?" Qess shouted. I imagined everyone's ears were ringing, even from this distance.

I shrugged. "Doom bell. Sorry about that. Did you learn anything?"

"We know who could help, but you're not going to like it." Gwithieri handed me a scrap of parchment with a name on it.

"Her? With them? These are scary people. Even for a guy like me."

"She's the only one who can help. Now get your asses moving. You owe us really big, Orman," Gwithieri reminded.

Yeah. If there was anything left of me to pay.

❖   ❖   ❖

The deepest, darkest settled street in the Underhalls. Demons lived here long eons ago. The horror of their magic still echoed in the stone. It's how people like me come to exist. Helltouched, the darkness of those ancient spells changing us before we're ever born.

Most people didn't think the place existed. To the world outside Remnar, the Humans of Leng were just a bad dream, a scary story for children. I knew better. Brutal, calculating outsiders from another world, they played by their own rules, and no one could trust them.

Four warriors stood before the gate, hands on the hilts of their swords. I'd seen those swords once before. They flashed and disappeared so fast your eye couldn't track it. Something damn close to magic.

"These aren't the humans you've always known, Kara. These guys are cruel and nasty," I whispered.

"Many of the cultists were human, Orman. I have little faith in anyone, save those who prove themselves friends." She squeezed my hand. I approached and made my plea.

"We have come to see the Blood Mother," I said, feigning confidence I didn't have.

The lead warrior scowled. "No. She sees no one. Leave, or be slain."

"I can make it worth her while. Please, at least pass along a gift I've brought her." Slowly, so they wouldn't murder me, I drew out the arm bone from my place. On every surface, crimson runes spiraled across it, written as small as I'd been able to form them. It was all the blood I'd infused with the orc's spirit-taint. I offered it to the lead guard, whose expression hardened even more.

"What nonsense is this?"

"It's a powerful magic item. It holds the very agony of death in battle."

The lead warrior sniffed, then motioned one of his subordinates to take it. The man left in haste, the gate closing behind him. I stepped back, not wanting to make the stone-faced warrior any more likely to kill us.

It took all my effort not to glance around like a fugitive. After what felt like forever, they ushered us through. Every door we passed was closed and had no marking. Not a single decoration appeared on any wall of the hallway. We went down a long stairway, then another featureless hall, then through a green door.

The austerity of the hall gave way to such intricate decoration that it hurt my mind. I stood before a tall dais, looking up at a woman whose age I couldn't guess. She looked neither young nor old. Her olive complexion had no flaws, and her black hair shimmered in the light of the lamps. True, burning lamps, a rarity down here.

She looked at us with a shrewd eye for a moment before speaking. "I am intrigued by this. Did you invent such magic?"

"I . . . yes, Mother."

"Tell me how it is done. Every detail." The way she spoke, I knew that argument would be fruitless. This was our way in, and our way out. The grandest practitioner of blood magic in the world got what she desired. Every time.

"Of course." I told her everything I'd done and learned. A secret worth a kingdom, maybe, and I had to give it away.

The Blood Mother snapped her fingers and two

scribes entered, each taking down every word I said. As much as I didn't want to stand there discussing theoretical necromancy, explaining it to someone who understood did feel invigorating. Before I knew it, I'd spilled the whole thing.

A slow smile appeared on the Blood Mother's face. She reached over, hitting a small gong next to her on the throne. They brought in a heavily built guy who struggled every step of the way. His eyes were blackened and he had healing wounds across his bare torso. A prisoner, and one I wouldn't want to switch places with.

The Blood Mother walked down to the center of the room, nodding for her warriors to let the prisoner free. She gave him a false smile, then motioned to him. "If you can kill me, they will let you free."

He needed no further enticement. He rushed at her, teeth bared. She touched him on the shoulder with the arm bone, sliding aside like a fencer. A scream broke from his lips, and he fell, curled into a ball of agony.

The Blood Mother nodded. The guards dragged his body away. She put the bone in her belt and retook the throne.

"You wish a boon, then."

"If we may." I made my voice humble.

"For the . . . lady, I would suppose." I didn't care for the way the Blood Mother looked at Kara. Her distant reserve had given way to unwholesome interest.

"She . . ." I didn't get to finish.

"Oh, I know what Kariel came for, Orman Orphesias. I could feel it when she first arrived in Remnar."

She reached into a hidden pocket beside her throne

chair, bringing out the tooth of some primordial creature. As long as a dagger, it came to a wicked point. She threw it to me, and I managed to catch it without being skewered.

"I have gotten the best side of this deal. Then again, I always do. Remember, breaking the spell will bring as much sadness as leaving it intact."

"How is the spell broken?" I asked.

Her hard eyes bored into me. "By an act of will."

Guards grabbed us and hauled us out a different way than we came in. By the time the door slammed behind us, I had no idea where we were or what direction we faced.

The cult had guessed, however. Outside on the street, a mob of twenty robed figures lurked, waiting to cut us to ribbons.

I gathered Kara in my arms. Like every time, her embrace felt like the home I'd never known to look for.

"Hey, it's not over. We'll think of something," she told me. I could hear the last dregs of hope fading as she spoke.

"I'm not giving up, Kara. Hold on tight."

She did what I asked, burying her face in my shoulder. How could anyone want more than this? She was worth the pain, worth the scars of dying.

"Beyond the Gloomreach Mountains, in the valley where all night goes when the burning chariot circles, I call to the living stuff of shadows. I have need of you, wings of Doldimmengard."

The incantation's power thrummed across us, encompassing our bodies with demi-real substance, like the breast of a giant raven. Wings three times as wide as

my own height unfolded. Leaping, I took to the air,
the wash of my passage forcing many of the cultists
to the ground. We surmounted the walls of the Blood
Mother's sanctum and soared above the Screaming
Hollows, where nightmares lingered.

"It's wonderful," she shouted against the wind.

"It's temporary."

The wings shed shadow, weakening with every
beat. I circled above the edge of the great crevasse,
looking for anywhere we could put down and have
a defensible position. We couldn't get away. No real
escape remained. Only a place to defend, and maybe
figure out how to free Kara from the rune.

I saw it. An ancient ossuary where a hundred
generations of goblins moldered. It stood, the last
vestige of an age when that race held sway over the
city and the whole of the known world. We landed at
the broken gates just as my wings dissipated.

"It's not far enough. If we had managed to cross the
chasm..." Kara's face began to crumple as hope left.

I touched her chin. "Hey. You said it. It's not over."

Pulling free the tooth we'd been given, I pushed
back my sleeves and cut my forearms. The artifact's
magic buzzed against my palms, the pain roaring in
my veins. The tooth glimmered purple as it tasted
my blood.

"Why?" she breathed.

"I'm a necro. This is what we do."

I clenched my fists and the blood poured down my
arms. I ran from one open crypt to the next, making
handprints on the skulls of the ancient dead. To each,
I only said a few words. The moment I released my
hold, the skeletons clattered out of their funerary

nooks and struggled to comply with my command. "Get up and kill."

In the end, Kara had to throw me over her shoulder and carry me to a wide empty place beyond the crypts. How many did I raise? No one will ever know. More than anyone should. More than I thought myself capable of, even under the best conditions.

I lay there, a hollow husk. Breathing hurt. Everything hurt. The sound of battle echoed from out in the crypts. Time ran short. I struggled to my knees, then to my feet. I swayed like a drunkard. Kara held the tooth in one clenched fist, her shirt discarded. Her jaw clenched, I saw the determination gleam in her eyes again. The glory of her presence caused me to stand straight, though every fiber of my being ached to simply stop, to quit the business of being conscious and even living.

"An act of will," she said. Kara looked right in my eyes and drew the point of the tooth across the rune, cutting so deep I could see muscle in the opening wound.

She didn't cry out. I tried to, but my protest drowned in the sound of a battle cry and the footfalls of our enemies rushing closer.

I turned away. I couldn't watch her bleed to death. I couldn't let the cultists touch her while I still lived. Bereft of magic, with nothing but bare hands, I staggered toward them. I could throw my body against their steel. I'd already died six times. What was once more? What did a guy like me have to fear from death, anyway?

The charging lunatics never reached me. Something titanic settled upon the ground behind me, wind blasting against my shoulders. The shadow of utter terror fell across the nearest faces, and then everything went away, burned to red, then to white in a torrent of flames that knocked me to my knees.

My clothes burned away, even my belt and boots turned to sudden ash. Heat beyond anything I had ever imagined bathed me. I made myself small within the maelstrom, eyes clamped shut, unable to breathe or think.

As suddenly as it came, the fire winked out. Blinking the blindness out of my eyes, I stood. Naked, scoured, and steaming, I saw that nothing but cracked bones remained of our enemies. Even the steel of their weapons twisted, the temper of the metal broken.

I turned. She filled my vision. "This is you. I should have known you'd be beautiful, no matter what the rune kept secret." My voice sounded dry and raspy, like it came from inside a grave.

Kariel shook her long neck. Her talons gripped the rock, cutting half a foot into the pure granite. I'd never seen a dragon close up. Every scale began as dark as wrought iron, but glittered with a crescent moon like platinum at the edge. Her eyes still gleamed emerald, the ruff of fur behind her horns crimson like her hair had been. More than weakness drove me to my knees. The realization of what I'd done, what I had touched, settled on my shoulders.

"Oh, Orman," she sighed. The magnitude of her voice shook the bones inside my skin. A mighty claw reached out. She gently stroked my scarred back with the smooth edge of one talon. How could her touch, even like this, make my heart clench and burn?

"Did you always know what you were?"

"Not for a long time. Even when I finally guessed, I didn't know it would feel like this. So bittersweet. For two hundred years, I was the woman you knew. It's all I've ever known."

Her claw encompassed me, lifting me up to her eye level. "They stole so many years from me, Orman. You gave me back my destiny."

"And you have to live it."

"I do." That close, the intensity of her attention almost hurt. "And I don't know where that will lead me."

"Show them revenge like they've never imagined," I told her. I couldn't think of anything else that wouldn't break me up inside.

"You know I will. Thoughts of you, though, will always be on my mind. A regular hero could never have done what you did. It had to be you." She touched her snout to me, as near as she could get to a kiss goodbye.

"I would go with you. I'd leave everything behind."

"I know . . . and I'd get you killed. I can't face that." She pushed her face against me one last time before she left.

Sitting on the edge of the crevasse, I watched until her shape disappeared into the distance, the thunder of her wingbeats fading away.

I found the back door to my shop unlocked. Lex and Sebastian had been behind the counter and helped themselves to the old pastries and the darkbrew press.

"You look like a wreck," Lex said. "What the hell happened to you? And what are you wearing?"

I slumped down on the third chair at the table.

Sebastian gave me a knowing and bemused look. "I caught one of your cases."

Lex pushed the brim of his battered hat upward and sat forward. "How did that go?"

"About like you'd expect. I killed a lot of guys, did some magic, made love to a dragon."

Lex's eyes went wide. "You should tell me more about that part."

"No. He shouldn't," Sebastian said. The look on the elf's face showed that he knew. At least some of it.

I struggled to my feet. "I should go and get some rest. This place doesn't open itself."

Slipping out, I managed to keep it together, to act like things were fine. I walked, not knowing which way to go, not having any place to lay my head. Time went by. I found myself slumped in an alley, the stolen clothes too tight across my shoulders. Something went wrong with my eyes, because every witchlamp smeared like chalk in rain.

"She'll be back. Blood always buys another turn around the ring." I told myself that. The elf had been right the first time.

Somewhere down deep, I knew you never got that lucky twice.

The Frost Queen

Robert Buettner

To this day, of all days, my mother blames herself for what is now described in the Moon as "The Frost Queen Tragedy." But Mom is one of the original '59ers. So, she's used to sucking it up, and taking onto herself responsibility for bad things that happen.

Me, no. I'm Jason Cho, Looney-born, Looney-raised, for all twelve of the years I had lived at that time. So, like all Looneys, Lithium Luna Limited coddled me from cradle to crematorium. Personal responsibility was optional. All I needed to know about the Big Blue Ball, that I saw up there in the sky when I went Topside, was: As long as the twelve billion people who lived on the Ball needed batteries, all of us who dug lithium out of the Moon would have jobs.

Of course, because Triple-L controlled all the jobs, even the franchise concessions, you couldn't job-hop. Other hopping was easy, because on the Moon we weighed one-sixth of Earth weight.

Carrying around five more of me throughout every wake cycle, and battling twelve billion competitors for a stupid McDonalds entry-level job were just two reasons I wanted no truck with the Big Ball on which Mom grew up.

That's why Mom insisted on force-feeding me Earth culture since I was old enough to swipe. She said that Earth had been producing great art, great literature, and great music since cavemen first painted their walls. By comparison, Triple-L hadn't introduced a permanent, nonrobotic community into the mining tunnels and galleries beneath the Moon's surface until 2059.

So, Mom said, the Moon's total creative output, since the year I was born, would fit in a flea's navel.

I had to look up "flea."

Me looking it up was what Mom was going for. Me looking stuff up for myself was what Mom was *always* going for. Other Looney slackers might punt personal responsibility. But in Cho-ville, personal responsibility was Job One. And Mom meant to keep it that way.

I had to consult Earth-generated sources to learn about fleas. That proved her point about Moon culture. Or lack thereof.

Fleas are insects. I didn't know about insects because the Moon had none. And Triple-L meant to keep it that way.

Therefore Earth people flew down to the Moon for jobs, not vacations. That was because visitors' first Moon experiences after disembarking the shuttle were normal gravity, which they found abnormal; Delousing, which they found degrading and disgusting; then Quarantine, in a windowless bus.

But I digress from my point, which involves fleas.

They're smaller than Nanoborers. Because insects hatch from eggs, fleas lack navels. Navels are the leftover attachment points of the cords that connect placental mammal mothers to their children during gestation.

Just like fleas don't need navels, human children don't need to be jerked around by those invisible cords after their twelfth birthdays. I realized that sooner than Mom did.

Which is what started the trouble.

Mom said, "This month a Broadway show touring company's coming down. I had to push my wake cycle an hour to queue. But I scored us front-row seats, with backstage passes, for a classic revival."

The last Earth classic revival for which Mom had scored us front-row seats was *The Comedy of Errors* ... which I thought was more error than comedy.

I said, "Do I have to go?"

She said, "If you've previously committed to, and taken responsibility for, something else, then no."

"How long do I have to think up something else?"

Therefore, twelve wake cycles later, Mom and I sat in the center of Armstrong Auditorium's first row. Mom sat alongside me, across the center aisle, as I watched actual human beings in the orchestra pit tune actual, wooden violas for opening night.

Mom fanned herself with her paper program as she leaned across the aisle and whispered, "Isn't this exciting? Shakespeare, Stan Lee, Disney. The giants of the classics never grow older."

She said it wrong on purpose. To test whether I had looked it up. I had, but I didn't take her bait that time.

The classics might never grow older, but the giants

were as dead as the guy whose name was on the auditorium.

Lee's work was the most revered, and his death the best documented. Shakespeare plagiarized. So, who knew *exactly* when whoever wrote his plays died. But *The Comedy of Errors* was first performed in 1594. As for Disney, some sources insisted there had been a real person, but the body of work was produced over so long an interval that I doubted it. Plus, "Walt" sounded like a made-up name.

The overture started, so I watched the musicians try to saw their violas in half for three minutes before the curtain even rose.

The story concerned a princess who shot ice from her fingertips. The actress who played her was spectacular and was the only reason I stayed awake.

The reason that a Broadway show came down to us in the Moon was so that it could be performed in reduced gravity, holoed, then marketed in that more acrobatic version.

Based on opening night, I doubted it would sell enough clicks to fill a flea's navel. The cast members could sing, but they flailed when they danced. Earth newbies always flailed in normal gravity, which they found abnormal.

But when *she* danced, she flew higher than any Looney—ever. With an angel's grace. She sang like an angel, too. I cried when she cried. I laughed when she laughed.

After the final curtain, Mom stretched and yawned. "I don't suppose you want to wait around for autographs."

"Autographs?"

❖   ❖   ❖

Backstage passes, like the ones Mom and I wore on lanyards around our necks, must have been easy scores after all, because half the audience seemed to be wedged into the space between the dressing area's door and the Airtight that exited into Centerline Passage.

Mom had stepped back from the crowd, into the lobby.

She's claustrophobic. Claustrophobia and living in caves didn't mix. Since the 2059 Breaches, Triple-L pre-screened for, and rejected, claustrophobics' applications.

But, like I said, Mom was a '59er, and they were a tough bunch. To belabor the obvious, she was among the half that survived the first year. That's part of why I never wanted to visit Earth. If the early years *here* were that bad, how much worse must conditions on Earth be, that people like Mom resorted to Triple-L?

While half the audience and I waited, with our programs opened to the cast member pages, two people also waited, apart from us because they wore zootier neck tags.

The first cast member who came out I didn't recognize, but a girl squealed, and some grown-ups applauded.

The cast member held up both hands and waggled them, then grinned and shouted, "Hellooo, Moon!"

The crowd roared, and from the gesture and his voice, I realized that he had played the snowman. Playing a snowman seemed like a stupid job.

He stepped up to the crowd and people pressed forward. They held out stuff for him to sign, ranging from programs to Topside helmets.

One of the zoot-pass people, a woman Mom's age but way more flash, walked over to him and clung to his arm while he signed with his free hand.

If she was his girlfriend, maybe playing a snowman wasn't stupid.

More actors emerged, the crowd split into clusters surrounding each of them, and the room grew quiet.

The door opened again, and a girl stepped out. She wore a tiger-striped skinsuit, just like any girl in my class might have worn after school.

The program said that the title role of the princess who became the Frost Queen was played by Isis Lavender and that she was fourteen. That was credible because her skinsuit had bumps in places where the girls in my class hardly had skin.

The other zoot-pass person, a man with a mustache, stepped over to her. Alongside himself he wheeled a scooter, tiger-striped, with a little stuffed tiger tied to the handlebar. Scooters were very big with girls then.

He said to her, "Honey, do you want to skip signing tonight? You have homework, and a matinee tomorrow."

She looked around, saw me standing alone there, holding up my program like a dooz. She pushed the scooter aside, then produced a jeweled pen. That seemed magical because skinsuits lacked pockets.

She said, "Dad, I'm signing."

She made it two steps toward me before the first person, other than me, recognized her.

A heartbeat later the stampede was on, like the story where the sea parted, except in reverse.

Then suddenly she stood in front of me. She brushed aside the hands and the things that the hands thrust toward her.

When she took my program, it was as though we were the only two people in the Moon.

With her pen poised over my program, she looked up. Without her makeup and costume, she looked *more* beautiful.

Since what Mom called my "growth spurt," I was so tall—for a Looney—that I had outgrown my clothes. But when her eyes, bigger and lovelier blue than the Ball itself, stared into mine, she was almost as tall.

She said, "What's your name, One K?"

"One K?"

"Your seat. I saw you. How do you want me to sign?"

"Jason."

She smiled. "I'm Isis, Jason. But my friends call me 'Ice.'" She swayed and wiggled her shoulders to music that wasn't there. "You know. 'Chill like ice cubes, sweet like ice cream.'"

We get pop music six months behind Earth, so I didn't know the song, but admitting that would make me out a stupid hick.

So I filled the void with facts. "There's no water on the Moon. So, there's no ice."

Her smile faded, and her big blue eyes turned down toward the floor.

She whispered, "I'm sorry. I was trying to say something you would think was interesting. Not make myself look like a stupid hick."

Then the human sea rolled over her and swept me away.

Ten minutes later Mom and I rode the Centerline Passage slidewalk, northbound to our Kube.

She said, "So, what did you think of the play?"

"It was okay."

Mom said, "The girl was extraordinary. *Variety's*

reviewer wrote she was a precocious talent. That understated it, I think."

"She was okay."

"What was your takeaway from the show?"

I had read the online synopsis. "That true love takes many forms, and triumphs if the will is strong."

"You read the synopsis."

"Yeah."

"Well, *I* sat next to you. And *I* thought your take-away was that the blue-eyed girl was flash."

Mom tracked my wake cycles, and the next wake cycle was my forty-five-hundred fifth. And my worst.

After I thought it through, I realized that the most exquisite female in the universe had *hit* on me. And I had not only doozed it up, I had hurt her feelings. It creeped me that Mom used a word like "flash." And creeped me worse that she knew exactly what I was thinking.

As I rode the slidewalk home after school, I set down my backpack and took out the playbill that I had tucked into the front pocket. Even though seeing her face would remind me I was a dooz.

In purple ink across her picture was written:

"I get one hour a day free, to scoot in the park across from the Ritz. If you're interested, 16:00. —Ice"

After her name, she had drawn a heart.

I looked up at the chronometer, where Centerline intersected Aldrin. The big red one above the McDonalds advert. As I watched, the time ticked over to 15:46.

A slidewalk slides fifteen kilometers per hour.

On Earth, the fastest human-over-ground foot speed ever recorded peaked at forty-nine kilometers per hour, at the 2040 Reykjavik Olympics. Tested human-over-ground foot speeds in the Moon averaged twenty-four-percent improvement.

Therefore, the fastest combined speed possible for a human running on a slidewalk in the Moon was seventy-nine kilometers per hour. Or, as Mom would say it, forty-nine *miles* per hour "in old money."

Even at that speed, I would arrive at the park entrance across from the Ritz at 16:02.

At 15:59, I was fifty meters from the Ritz's Portico, half-dead, when I saw her. She walked her scooter past the hotel's doorman, crossing the slidewalk to the park via the overhead footbridge. He smiled, then tipped his top hat to her as she passed him.

She paused at the park's entrance, looked right, then left, saw me and waved.

She said, "I didn't think you'd come."

With my hands on my knees, I wheezed, "Just along the way home."

She said, "Do you work out on your way home every day?"

Gasps punctuated my answer. "Moon. No days. Wake cycles."

"If you're going to make obtuse corrections to everything I say, maybe you should just keep running."

I recovered enough to straighten, then shook my head. "No. Please."

She said, "Maybe we should just *walk* together instead."

I couldn't speak, just nodded and gave her a thumbs up.

She laughed. "I'm just as flogged as you are. Matinees suck it."

My jaw dropped.

I'd never heard a girl drop the S-bomb before. But when she said it, it didn't sound dirty. It sounded funny.

I said, "If you had a matinee, how are you here?"

"You're smart. After the show, I skipped signing and my shower because I was afraid I would miss my scooting time."

"Oh."

"Do I stink too bad?"

She smelled like lemon and strawberry extract. Maybe she lied about skipping her shower. But only an idiot probes a witness's truth and veracity by cross-examining on collateral matters.

I just said, "No."

The next day, Ice didn't have a matinee. She met me at the park entrance, without her scooter, and looking flash.

As we walked, she hopped and touched the sky with her fingertips.

The Moon's living spaces are covered in animated Threedee foil, two centimeters deep, laid over hewn rock. Triple-L says they're visually indistinguishable from reality.

Ice said, "I nearly bashed my brains out on this wallpaper the first day we got out of Quarantine. I don't understand Quarantine."

I shrugged. "And I didn't understand fleas. I didn't understand them *because* of Quarantine."

"What?"

"It's my obtuse way of saying that you and I come from different worlds."

"'Thank you, Captain Obvious.'"

"What?"

She said, "When I was eight, I played a precocious brat, in a sitcom, set in the two-thousand-teens. A grown-up character would say something self-evident. I would wait two beats, then say the line. The show only lasted two seasons, but I said the line so often in rehearsals and on talk shows that I think I still say it in my sleep. And it's become my signature line."

I shook my head slowly. "I can't imagine having my own signature line."

"It's not that great. When I'm not rehearsing, or performing, or touring, or suffering through gymnastics and free weights, my parents homeschool me. So, I have no friends my age. I've broken each ankle three times. I haven't eaten a french fry or a cupcake since I grew bumps, to keep my weight down. And all the money goes into a trust."

I said, "That sucks it."

Her jaw dropped. "I never heard a *boy* say 'sucks it' before. But when you say it, it doesn't sound dirty. It sounds funny."

Maybe we were more alike than I thought.

She said, "My agent swears at me like a gangsta. My gymnastics and lifting coaches, too. And *all* the dressers and caterers swear."

Maybe we weren't so alike.

"Why do your parents make you do it?"

"They don't. Going all-in on acting was my idea. After every injury or bad review that makes me cry, they tell me it's fine if I want to quit."

"But you don't?"

"Because when your song stops the show, or your acting quiets the audience so that you hear people cry, the emotion rolls forward from way back in the cheap seats. Then it crashes over you, like a wave. And you know you've touched people. So I made my choice."

"Your parents expect you to take personal responsibility for your choices. And you do."

She stared at me. "Exactly. You really are smart. What do *your* parents tell *you*?"

"Parent. My mother tells me the same... and to do the right thing."

I really didn't want to dive deep on the parent subject. I said, "Do you like Earth?"

"Compared to *here*? Uh, *yes*! This is like *living* in the subway. Not just commuting to rehearsals in it."

"Earth is even more crowded than here."

"Manhattan and Beijing and London are. But on the Serengeti, the only crowds are wildebeest. My parents bought a compound on the Serengeti. We live there when I'm between projects."

"Are there fleas in your compound?"

She laughed. "Only if you count fleas on the elephants that walk through."

"You have *elephants*?"

"We don't *have* elephants. We see elephants when they decide to walk by there. I like that."

"I'd like to see an elephant walk by here."

She pointed up and laughed again. "An elephant walking by here would bump its head on the sky."

"Oh."

"Jason, the *real* sky is so big that *nothing* can bump it. Sometimes, even in daytime, this Moon, that we're standing in right now, floats in the sky. Like a white ghost. And there's water everywhere. So much water cascades over the Victoria Falls that their real name means 'smoke that thunders.' And when you're close to the Falls, the Earth shakes."

When Ice described Earth, it didn't sound awful. It sounded like a place I ached to see. And, more than anything, ached to see with her.

When I got home to the Kube following my fifth after-school walk with Ice, Mom was already home.

As she punched in dinner, she said, over her shoulder, "You're late. What's the big attraction at the park across from the Ritz?"

Kids in the Moon knew that, with personal device location systems, their parents *could* spy on them. I just assumed my life was so boring, and so much my personal responsibility, that my parent didn't. But, apparently, the invisible cord was still attached.

I said, "It's a nice park for walking."

"Was it your idea—or hers?"

Parental spying in the Moon was not limited to a tracking dot that identified a child's phone. In the Moon, the public could access public surveillance cam records, so long as the cam surveilled a place where the surveilled subject had no reasonable expectation of privacy—like a public park.

I said, "Mom, she's nothing like my father."

Mom's head snapped around from whatever she was doing at the kitchen counter.

I knew all of Mom's faces. This was the first time I saw the surprised face looking toward *me*. And also her sad face, at the same time.

She punched dinner to warm and hold, then pointed to the kitchen table. "Sit."

She sat across from me, then leaned forward on her elbows. "I've never told you about your father."

"You never tell me about anything. I figured that meant I should look it up."

I began at the beginning.

In the Moon, birth records carried no more reasonable expectation of privacy than walking in a park. And there weren't many births to look up.

Amanda Lin Cho was the name my Mom was born with in Vancouver, British Columbia, Canada. My father's name, entered on my birth certificate in her handwriting, was Ricky Ringo Wallace, of Malibu, California.

Finding "Ricky Ringo Wallace" was easy. Percussionist for Apocalypse, the American rock band, he was best known for his drum solo on the album *Suck it!*

I clicked up a couple tracks. When Apocalypse said it, it definitely sounded dirty.

Apocalypse's 2058 tour stopped at Vancouver for one night only, in December.

Ricky had obviously noticed an intriguing face in his audience, the way Ice had noticed mine in hers. I hoped that Ricky would do the right thing by an eighteen-year-old girl, who he had left behind to take personal responsibility for a questionable personal choice—a choice that was to become me. My hope vanished when I learned how he died.

Two months before I was born, Ricky self-drove his gasoline-powered antique Maserati convertible off the Pacific Coast Highway. Top down, at two hundred seventy kilometers per hour. Buck naked, drunk, and lit up on blow. In the company of three similarly clad females...which challenged the imagination, because his Maserati only seated the driver plus one.

I overlaid an online photo of Ricky with a selfie of me, using facial recognition software, which nailed it. Ricky was voted one of "Rock's Ten Hottest, Rudest Dudes" in 2055, so I did have that going for me.

That was bleak enough. Then I inferred the rest, from the 2050s world situation.

Earth's population had exploded past all predictions, and past twelve billion, in 2054. So, birth taxes trended, even in low-population-density democracies like Canada. Democracies don't forbid questionable personal choices. They just tax the hell out of them.

A young, single mother-to-be who had made one questionable personal choice had therefore confronted three more: a tax she couldn't pay, an abortion she couldn't bear, or a long-term indenture with Triple-L. Triple-L offered cradle-to-crematorium job security. Plus, a bonus for women who agreed to give birth in the Moon.

The Moon needed expectant mothers. Not just because the Moon got two inhabitants for one price. Triple-L also got baseline data about subsurface Lunar births. That was why Mom texted my height, weight, and vital signs to Central Records each wake cycle.

At that time, the only certainty about permanent residents *on* the Moon was that cosmic radiation exposure would kill them. *In* the Moon, that hazard vanished. Beyond that, Triple-L didn't even know what it didn't know.

Mom sat silent for a long time after I shut up.

Then she said, "Isis is attractive, talented. So was your father. So are you. So, her interest in you is as unsurprising as yours in her.

"But, Jason, you have to understand, her world

and your world are even further apart than Earth and the Moon."

"But that's the point."

Mom smiled. *"Vive la différence?* Sure. She's exotic to you. And you are far more exotic to her. But she *will* leave you behind. That's the real distance between you."

Mom tapped the table, it lit, and she swiped until she stopped on a story, in an Earth entertainment 'zine called *Variety*, about a sixteen-year-old male actor. His photo showed him shirtless. He had muscles where I didn't, in the way that Ice had bumps where my female classmates didn't.

Mom pointed at the story's text. "The Moon is her tour's last stop. Her next project is a feature film, acting opposite this young man."

I said, "That doesn't mean she's going to hypothetically fall in love with his pecs. That's why they call it 'acting.'"

"No. But her broken heart will have healing opportunities that yours won't. That's not a hypothetical. That's the voice of experience."

"Mom, Ricky left you with more than a broken heart. Ice and I are placental mammals. And I'm the male. You don't need to worry that I'll be left behind, penniless and pregnant."

Mom smiled. "Thank you, Captain Obvious."

I wrinkled my forehead.

Ice's signature line, about truths so obvious that they were self-evident, appeared to be better known than I thought.

"Jason, what Ricky left behind was *you*. You are the most precious gift anyone could ever have given me. I don't want to see you hurt by a fourteen-year-old *femme fatale*."

"Mom, Ice is barely even a *femme*. She's a fourteen-year-old girl who's precocious."

"And you're a twelve-year-old boy who's precocious. Girls grow up much faster than boys. The maturity delta between you and Isis is even greater than the chronological one."

"Meaning what?"

"Meaning she knows what she wants from you—and how to get it. But what makes a regular *femme* into a *fatale* is less what she *wants* than how much *you* are willing to sacrifice to give it to her."

"You're saying I shouldn't die for her."

"I'm saying you should do the right thing."

I sat with Ice in her dressing room, backstage at the Armstrong, before the show's last performance, which was a matinee.

Costume trunks stood open in the room's corners, along with makeup kits the size of suitcases, all where the people who had dressed Ice and made her up, had left them when they left the room.

It was, I realized, the first time we had been alone together. We had never even touched, not so much as fingertips.

But by next wake cycle every stitch, bottle, bangle, and false fingernail would be packed aboard the Upshuttle, Earthbound with its lithium. And with Ice.

It would be as though none of the last month had happened.

The Frost Queen sat, staring into the mirror above her dressing table like a frozen statue, protecting her makeup and costume. And, I supposed, to get her performance game face on.

I said, "Ice—"

She raised her palm. "Stop! This is hard enough."

Close like this, I could see the skin-toned tubes glued to her forearms' undersides. They connected her false fingernails to the pumps and projectors, concealed in her costume, that produced the illusion that she could shoot ice from her fingertips. Yet she had to perform spins and flips like a gymnast, while dancing and singing, and projecting emotion, as though the machinery wasn't even there.

I said, "Game face. Got it."

She said, "No. I've played the Frost Queen so often that I can be her in my sleep. But saying good-bye? Don't say one word. I'll cry, and my makeup will run. And my last performance will be my worst performance."

A guy wearing an earpiece and carrying a chipboard stuck his head in after rapping on the door jamb. "Ten minutes, Ms. Lavender."

That broke her tension.

She stood, then turned in front of the full-length mirror opposite her dressing table. "What do you think?"

With her hair upswept and her eyelids painted with purple glitter that would be visible from the cheap seats, she looked electric. Her costume accentuated her bumps, and it dripped jewels that bedazzled me.

"What I think is that you look like a *femme fatale*."

"I'll take that as a compliment. I'll have extra scoot time after this last show...if you can handle it."

"What do you want to do?"

"I want you to take me Topside."

I cocked my head. "Topside? Why?"

"I've been on the Moon a month. But I've haven't been *on* the Moon. I haven't seen the Earth. Or the black sky with the stars that don't twinkle. Or the shadows so dark that you can't see into them. And tomorrow—that is, next wake cycle—I leave. And I still won't see them. The bus that Quarantined us, and that takes us back to the shuttle, doesn't even have windows."

"You should have done it earlier."

"Instead of spending every minute of my free time, of which I have so little that it fits into a flea's navel, with you?"

"Okay. Got it. But I can't just 'take you Topside.' You don't even have a Topside suit."

"I'm sure the Ritz concierge can rent me one."

"He can. After you hand him your certification card. The course takes at least two wake cycles."

"Why? You just put on a puffy suit, then walk around. Kevin does that in the snowman costume nine shows a week."

"Walking around Topside isn't difficult . . . just dangerous. The only thing between you and vacuum is Flextex fabric. Flextex is long on impermeability and reflectivity, and short on durability. The suit's lined with a conductive heating and cooling grid. But without the suit's battery and oxygen tank, you're dead anyway."

"Oh."

"Direct-sun temperatures can be one hundred degrees C. That's plus two hundred twelve degrees in old-money Fahrenheit. But as soon as you step into a black shadow, the temperature drops instantly. That's the range a Topside suit protects. Short-exposure daytime."

"Daytime? Somebody dissed me once for saying the Moon had daytime."

"On the *surface*, the Moon has days. And nights. Night temperature is minus one hundred seventy-three degrees C. That's minus two hundred seventy-nine degrees in old-money Fahrenheit. Night-rated suits are strictly for the Emergency Rescue pros."

"I thought the law was everybody had to have a Topside suit."

"Permanent residents, yes. The law passed after the 2059 Breaches. Half of the first human mining crews froze, or decompressed, because they couldn't cross a few hundred meters of surface to move from a breached tunnel to an intact tunnel.

"The resident suit isn't a real Topside suit. It's a Pressurized Lunar Escape Suit. The PLES battery and oxygen last maybe thirty minutes. The old airlocks were supplemented with redesigned ones when the complex expanded west. PLES suits are junk, built to satisfy an obsolete law."

"Is there *anything* you don't know everything about?"

The guy with the headset and chipboard returned. "Four minutes, Ms. Lavender."

Ice spun while she watched herself in the mirror, shimmied some of her dance moves, then smoothed her costume back into place over her bumps.

She said, "You're the smartest person I've ever met, but you can't figure out a way to take me Topside after the show?"

"It's not a matter of figuring something out. It's dangerous. Going Topside uncertified, or aiding and abetting another to do it, is still against the law. It's really a matter of principle."

She wriggled her bottom while she watched it in the mirror, then tugged at her skirt to straighten its back seam. "Final offer. Take me Topside after the show, and when we get back, I'll let you touch my bumps. All of them."

Even a principled man has his price.

I met Ice outside the Armstrong's stage door, after the Frost Queen made her final curtsies.

As we rode the slidewalk side by side, she hummed along with music in her head, danced, and spun back flips.

People sliding toward us in the opposite lane smiled. Maybe they recognized her. More likely she just projected exuberance.

I said, "I take it you were good today?"

"I was *invincible* today. I always finish a project strong . . . because I'm sick of it and jacked to move on to the next one. Plus, the hiatus between projects is like a furlough from my prison."

If she would be free again, however briefly, among her beloved elephants, I loved her more for it. Even though it would break my heart.

If I was a project that she was already sick of and she was already jacked up about the next guy's pecs, my heart would be shattered beyond repair.

With her bumps on the line, I shut up.

But if I had asked her which it was and shared what was in my heart, perhaps things would have ended differently.

The abandoned pre-2059 passages were sealed from the new areas by Airtights, marked "Hazard."

The passages and airlocks remained, just in case. But even entering the passages broke the law. Every parent in the Moon forbade every kid in the Moon from entering them.

Therefore, every kid in the Moon who wasn't an utter dooz had dodged the sensors, snuck through the Airtights, and explored the passages. Some of us more than others.

Guided by my utility light's beam and by my fingers on the passage's cold, bare, rock wall, we had arrived at the old Topside Egress lock nearest the new areas.

Behind me, Ice's whisper echoed in the dark, "This place is colder, creepier, and stinkier than I expected."

A principled man would have said, "You're right. Let's go back." However, her deal was Topside first, bumps after. Failure was not an option.

I said, "But we're here."

I shrugged out of my backpack, then unloaded it.

While Ice had played the Frost Queen one last time, I had retrieved my PLES Topside suit and helmet from home. And also the never-worn PLES Topside suit and helmet that I had grown out of the prior month, which Mom hadn't gotten around to turning in for credit.

I gathered the smaller suit and helmet, stood, then shone my light on the control console that cycled open the lock's inner, then outer, doors.

I said, "Go behind that, strip naked. Everything. And do it fast."

In the dark I didn't see the slap coming. It spun my head, and I dropped my light.

She said, "If you thought *that* was my deal, you don't know me at all. And I don't know you."

I retrieved my light as I rubbed my cheek.

I wasn't even precisely sure how placental mammals like us did "that," so her inference seemed monstrously unfair.

I said, "Topside suits heat and cool by conduction against bare skin. We have to be naked inside them. Topside sundown's in forty-three minutes. That's our literal *dead*line to be back inside."

"Oh."

Never underestimate a stage actress's quick-change ability.

When she emerged from behind the console, she was Topside-ready, except for her phone in one mittened hand.

I said, "Our phones can't go past here. Most of the fail-safes in these passages are dead, but they left in place the sensors that shut down the lock in case somebody tries to open it from inside. Phones trip the sensors. I discovered that the hard way."

She pouted at me through her faceplate. "Just one selfie? With the Earth behind me? Because 'no picture, nothing happened.'"

I shone my light on a yellow stripe on the passage floor. "You cross that line, with that phone, and 'nothing' is *exactly* what will happen."

She sighed. "Well, that sucks it!"

But she left her phone alongside mine, on top of our clothes.

The inner lock had cycled closed behind us, as we stood side by side in the lock's darkness, watching our helmet displays count down from thirty minutes.

I said, "You're hearing me through the intersuit walkie-talkie. If it fails—which it won't, don't worry— we can still talk by touching helmets. 'Talkie range is maybe forty meters. So stay right behind me. Shuffle. No running. No jumping. We look at the Big Blue Ball. We say 'Wow.' We return. Period."

"Don't worry, Safety Boy. The Frost Queen's invincible."

"Ice, stop. This environment is more unforgivingly hostile than anything you've ever experienced."

Her snort echoed inside my helmet. "You sure don't read *Variety*."

The lock evacuated, its outer doors opened, and I led the way out onto the Moon.

The sun reflected so bright off the landscape that I squinted, even as my faceplate darkened itself.

The old lock cycled shut behind us. Ahead stretched a boulder field. The boulders had been ejected by a four-billion-year-old impact, then hadn't budged or weathered one millimeter since.

Armstrong had barely missed one boulder like these when he landed in 1969. His footprints, and Aldrin's, remained in the dust at the Memorial out east. And would remain there for another four billion years.

Beyond the boulders, the Big Blue Ball floated in the black sky.

I said, "Worth the trip?"

Silence.

The view left newbies mute.

I let her drink it in.

I said, "Ice?"

No answer.

I turned.

She was gone.

Stupid! Stupid, stupid, stupid.

Why hadn't I made the Invincible One go first, so I could keep an eye on her?

I finally spotted her. In a vast, dead landscape, she was the sole moving object. Already distant, she popped up from behind one boulder, then hopped to another, like a flea.

I skipped toward her, fifteen meters per low stride, kicking dust that didn't float, while screaming in silent vacuum. She had escaped walkie-talkie range.

When I finally caught up, she posed, hands-on-hips, staring down on me like a victorious pirate, atop a boulder that resembled the Rock of Gibraltar.

Inside my helmet, I heard her pant.

I said, "Show's over! Come down. Carefully."

"God! This is the best. I may never leave the Moon."

"Get down here or you won't."

"Fine. But watch this."

She hopped once, bounded skyward, somersaulted above my head, then landed feet together, knees bent, on the point of a tilted rock cube three meters behind me.

She straightened, raised her arms so her body formed a "Y," then crowed, "And she *stuck* the landing!"

The cube had balanced just as it landed for four billion years, until her miniscule mass unbalanced it.

The cube tipped beneath her, and she toppled backward into the dust. Relieved of her weight, the cube plopped back, without a sound.

Ice shrieked through the walkie-talkie.

I reached her in one skip, knelt beside her.

She squeezed her helmet's sides with both hands

as she thrashed her head. Behind her faceplate, she hissed through clenched teeth. "It's broken."

"Your suit's not broken. You'd be dead."

"Not my suit. My sucking *ankle!*"

"You're sure?" I turned to look at her legs.

"Of *course* I'm sure! I've broken six of 'em. Just get this father-sucking rock off it."

She lay on her butt in the Moondust. The cube pinned her right leg. Below the knee it was...

My head snapped back and I sucked air so hard that my throat whistled. I nearly barfed inside my helmet.

She said, "How does it look?"

"Not too bad."

"At acting, you suck."

I reached out and pushed the cube. It didn't budge. I stepped close and pushed again using my shoulder. Nothing.

She said, "Put more weight behind it."

"Ice, this is the Moon. I don't *have* more weight. With a lever long enough, I could move the world. But I don't have a lever either."

"Then grab my leg and yank. Say 'On the count of three.' Then count two and yank. So I don't tense up. That's what they do when I dislocate something during a show. I suck it up and the show goes on. Suffering is a child actor's life."

Inside my helmet I shook my head. "No. Hundred percent probability your suit will tear. We couldn't even cut off your foot, if we had a knife, because cutting your suit would kill you."

"Stop cheering me up. Jason, it's no big deal. Just leave me here. Run and get help. I'll just suck it up 'til you get back."

"You don't understand. In vacuum, when the sun disappears, the temperature drops like somebody flicked off an old-money light switch. And by the time I phone, and ER gets here..."

She didn't speak as it sunk in.

Then she said, "Even more reason that you have to go. There's no sense both of us..."

She turned her face away inside her helmet, so I couldn't see her eyes...but I heard her sob.

I glanced at the chrono display projected on the inside of my faceplate.

Four minutes to sundown.

I stood and scraped pumice against her suit with my boot's instep.

She said, "What are you doing?"

"Insulating us."

"Us?"

"I'm piling it up around you. Moondust has about as much insulating value as it sounds like it does. But it's all we have. Then I'll lay on top of you."

"That's a cheese excuse to touch my bumps."

"Why are you joking?"

"To distract me from panicking." She paused. "Jason, will any of that really help? Or are *you* just distracting me?"

"Shut up."

I packed the pumice around her. It was a pathetic imitation of insulation. Then I laid on top of her. With two puffy suits between us, it was a pathetic imitation of touching her bumps.

I thumbed off her walkie-talkie function, and her internal helmet display, by pressing the Buddy Button on her helmet's side, then shut my walkie-talkie off, too.

Seconds later, she realized that she could no longer hear me breathing. Her eyes widened, her lips moved, and I felt her squirm beneath me.

I lowered my head until our faceplates touched, then said, "Don't panic. Can you hear me now?"

"Yes. Not as well."

"I cut both our walkie-talkies. We need heat more than anything else, and the 'talkies eat battery."

"How much time will all this you're doing buy us?"

The answer was maybe an extra minute or two.

I said, "Maybe enough."

"This is the worst feeling-up I've ever had."

I said, "Well, they were working in better conditions."

"There is no 'they.' You were going to be the first... and the last...for as long as I lived. Now only half of those lines will be true. Jason, leave me...while you can."

I said, "Save your breath. I mean really. It wastes oxygen."

We both saved our breath and lay as still as a Popsicle sandwich.

I had chosen to get her into this. My choice had been a bad choice, but I was taking responsibility for it.

The outside temperature, visible on my helmet display, started dropping. So did my suit's inside temperature. Telling her would just make her breathe faster.

She whispered, "Jason, I can't feel the toes on my good foot. And I can't feel the broken one at all now."

I hadn't thought it through, but just drifting off painlessly was a better way to die than explosive decompression—or driving off a cliff.

She whispered again. "In a few minutes I really will be the Frost Queen. I told my father this morning that if I played her one more time after today's show, I would die. Bad joke."

She cried, so softly that I could barely hear.

The battery and oxygen warning lights on her helmet crest, which were there to inform first responders, began flashing red. My red lights had been flashing in my interior display for a while.

When they all went solid red, we were done. But after sundown we would be done anyway. If I had any last words, and expected her to hear them, it was time.

I said, "I loved you from the first moment I saw you. I will love you forever. And I know that whatever happens next, somewhere, sometime, we will be together again. And you'll love me, too."

She was so near the end that it took me awhile to figure out what she mumbled back.

What she had said was, "Thank you, Captain Obvious."

The worst was that, as the dark became absolute, her lips were four inches from mine.

But I couldn't kiss her goodbye.

I sat there on the Armstrong Auditorium's stage, dressed in black, head bowed as I stared down at my hands.

The huge room was silent, packed SRO with her fans. Their emotion rolled forward, from way back in the cheap seats, and I felt it wash over me on the stage. She had told me about that feeling once. And finally, I understood it.

But the emotion wasn't for me, it was for her. Isis Lavender was more beloved than I had ever realized. Her performances had touched so many during a career cut short.

Ice's mother sat in the front row, just beyond the orchestra pit, in seat 1K—the seat I had occupied the first time I saw her. Her mother dabbed her right eye with a hanky, then tilted her head, dabbed the left. She then stretched out her arm and handed the hanky back to my mother, who was sitting across the center aisle.

Mom blinked, then dabbed at her own eyes.

It was going to be easier for them. *I* was the one who would have to suck it up, and stand up, and speak.

I thought I would be able to hold it together. Her father had told me he thought he couldn't. I couldn't tell whether he had predicted accurately, because he wasn't seated with his wife. I couldn't even see him.

The guy seated alongside me whispered, "Will you say anything to console her grieving fans?"

I leaned toward him and said, "I might say that her grieving fans can suck it."

He recoiled. "What?"

"Look, I just told you most of the story. The rest is that, when I was late, my mother, because the invisible cord was still attached, checked my phone's location. She found it stationary, in an off-limits passage. She called me. I didn't answer. She did the right thing and called Emergency Rescue, even though the problem could have been nothing. Our clothes and phones, alongside the airlock console, told ER everything. They pulled us in from the Lunar night, one minute short of dead. They say my improvisations had bought the time that saved her life. And, less consequentially, mine. That was nine years ago."

I said to the *Variety* reporter, "Having you here today is her agent's and the studio's idea, not ours. If he, and they, and her grieving fans, think her retiring at twenty-three is a 'tragedy,' they can suck it."

The orchestra in the pit began Pachelbel's Canon in D. Bang on cue, Isis Lavender appeared at the distant end of the auditorium's center aisle. For the last time. After today, she had chosen to disappear, and my wife would be known by her birth name, Mary Elizabeth Baker.

Everyone in the place stood, then stared at my bride.

Even from where *I* stood, I saw that Mr. Baker, whose arm she held, had been right. He wasn't holding it together.

Ice and her teary-eyed father glided down the aisle toward me as I stood there in my tux.

From way back in the cheap seats, she smiled at me. And we were, once again, the only two people in the Moon.

Then I couldn't hold it together either.

Bombshell

Larry Correia

New York City, New York
1955

The body had been mutilated and then left out with the trash. It was so mangled that he couldn't even tell if it had been a man or a woman. It was just...parts.

"What're you gawking at, Rookie?"

Henry looked up to get a flashlight beam right in the eyes. He squinted. "I was just assessing the crime scene." He couldn't see the speaker, but he'd spoken with authority, so Henry added "sir" onto the end just to be on the safe side.

"That's my job. You should be over there with the rest of the flatfeet shooing off the lookie-loos."

It was after midnight. There weren't that many bystanders to chase off. The light moved from him to point toward the pile of garbage bags, which was when he saw that the homicide detective who'd caught the case was Jeff Richards, one of the hard cases out of the 69th Precinct. Richards had a problem with Actives, so it was a good thing he'd tacked on the "sir."

"You'd better not have messed with—" Richards froze when he saw the mess. As his eyes widened, he whispered, "Dear lord. Not another one."

That got Henry's attention. For four months he'd walked this beat and never heard a peep about anything this grisly. The city had plenty of murders, but you'd think someone getting rendered into chum would at least make the morning briefing.

But before he could ask, the detective composed himself and got back to business. "Give me the lowdown."

Henry rattled off the pertinent details, as matter-of-fact as he could. "I was on foot patrol nearby. When they found the body, I heard the commotion clear down the block. One of the cooks at the diner had been taking out the garbage. He entered the alley, stepped in a puddle, realized what it was, and started hollering. I used the booth on the corner to call it in and then secured the area."

"Witnesses?"

"Just the cook who found it. The poor guy's back in the kitchen now, hyperventilating into a paper bag. I told him to stick around until detectives could take his statement."

"That it?"

"Yes, sir." He'd been staring at this horror in the dim, flickering light for the last half an hour, while listening to the buzzing of flies and the scurrying of rats in the dark waiting for him to leave so they could have a nibble. All that considered, his report had been remarkably composed and succinct. His goal was to make detective in record time, so he couldn't ever let anyone see him rattled.

But even Richards, who was in his fifties—and you didn't make it that long as an NYPD homicide detective without seeing some awful shit—looked like he was trying not to be sick.

"If you don't mind me asking, Detective, what did you mean 'another?' You've seen this before?"

"Afraid so, kid. Fifth one this month, spread across the city. Bodies like they got turned inside out, but you didn't hear that from me. The brass is keeping it hush-hush but they're forming a task force. They don't want to cause a panic over a magical psycho killer on the rampage."

"You think this is the work of an Active?"

"Our vic is splattered all over the walls. What do you think?" Then the detective scowled as he realized who he was talking to. "You're Officer Garrett, right?"

The shift in his voice warned Henry which direction this was heading. "Yes, sir."

"You're one of *them.*"

He didn't like the accusatory tone, but he was used to it. "If you mean an Active, no, sir. I've got no magical abilities to speak of."

"Not a magical yourself, but friendly with a bunch of magical vigilantes. You're that famous Mouth's kid. The Mouth and the Healer's rich boy. I heard about you."

Half the NYPD had heard about him, and not in a good way. Suspicions ran deep here, and even nowadays, when Actives were relatively common—hell, they'd elected one president—not everybody was comfortable around magic, especially the old-timers. Henry caught extra flak because his mom and dad had been all over the papers for years, lightning rods for controversy.

"I guess I'll go man the perimeter."

"You do that."

Out on the sidewalk he could no longer hear the flies buzzing. The air was fresh. Well, fresher. This was Brooklyn after all. Two other uniforms were holding back the crowd, but since the crowd was only a couple of curious bums, they had it well in hand. He caught a whiff of death stink, and then realized it must have soaked into his uniform. Somehow he'd gotten some blood on his Sam Browne. *Damn it.* So he wiped it off best as he could, lit a cigarette to drown out the smell, and waited for the coroner to arrive.

Cops came and went for the next hour. More detectives arrived. More brass arrived, and when they showed up, then the press realized something big was up, so they began arriving too. With less than a year on the force, Henry was still a probationary officer, which meant he was low man on the totem pole. If anybody in his chain of command saw him here, they'd probably order him back on foot patrol, so he did his best not to be noticed and joined in holding the rapidly growing crowd back, repeating the policeman's mantra of *there's nothing to see here, move along*, while getting repeatedly eyeball-stabbed by camera flashes.

The whole time he kept thinking that he'd been first on scene of a murder, more than likely committed by an Active. He knew more about magic than probably any other cop in this city. This was his shot. Not that he minded wearing the uniform, and maybe it was naïve, but he wanted to be a detective. Always had, long as he could remember.

So he watched and waited until Richards came out of the alley. He might not have inherited his father's magical gifts, but he'd learned from the master, so he was pretty good at persuading people even without Power. Dan Garrett's words could reach right into someone's brain and subtly twist their way of thinking. Henry had to get by on good old-fashioned charm.

Richards was heading for his car. This was his chance, so Henry broke off the line and chased him down. "Hey, Detective!"

Richards turned around and scowled. "What now, Garrett?"

"Look, I've got no Power myself, but I do know a lot about it. If this killer is an Active, I can help with the investigation."

"Why? So you can squeal to your wizard pals about any suspects I've got, so they can take the law into their own hands and be judge, jury, and executioner? I've got no use for divided loyalties."

"That was a long time ago." Henry tried not to sound defensive, but truth was, it wasn't really that long ago, since Grimnoir knights were still doing it today. However, usually only in places that weren't quite as civilized, or where the local authorities were corrupt, incompetent, or tyrannical when it came to dealing with people who had magical abilities.

"So I'm supposed to believe you're just some college boy bucking for rank, eh?"

"I dropped out of college. It wasn't a good fit. Come on. I've got connections."

"Meaning Grimnoir-type connections."

"Well, yeah..." It wasn't much fun being a member of a secret society which wasn't much of a secret anymore, especially when everybody figured you were probably a member of it.

"Actives protect their own."

"Not murderers they don't." That was just downright insulting. If it weren't for the Grimnoir—including one of the men he was named after—this city would've been vaporized by a Tesla super weapon back in '08. And if it hadn't been for other knights—including the one he'd gotten his first name from—the whole world would've been torn apart by an outer space monster in 1934. The only reason Richards could stand there, grumpy, smug, and—most importantly—alive was because of the Grimnoir. But he was sworn to secrecy about that sort of thing, so he just tried his best to look earnest.

"I can help you catch this killer. Just ask my captain to send me to your task force. I'll pull my weight. If I don't, just kick me back to patrol."

Richards mulled it over for all of ten seconds before he turned back to his car.

"Beat it, weirdo. I got work to do."

There were two reasons Heinrich Pershing Garrett had always wanted to be a detective. First, he'd always looked up to Jake Sullivan, literally and figuratively. It was hard not to since the man was a mountain, six foot five with fists of stone and a voice like an avalanche. In a way it was ironic that Heavy Jake Sullivan would inspire someone to become a cop, since he'd rarely been on the side of the law himself. In fact, he was an ex-con. But he had been a private detective, a manhunter for the BI, and from all the stories Henry had heard as a kid, damned good at it.

Growing up, Henry had spent a lot of summers at the Sullivan family's Montana ranch, constantly bugging Jake for stories about the old days. It was a challenge to get the notably taciturn Heavy to speak more than a few sentences at a time, but Henry had always been remarkably dogged and had worn him down. Sure, there had been stories about world-saving, battling magical samurai, and even tales of fighting beings from other worlds, but Henry had gotten plenty of that from his folks. It was the stories about tracking down dangerous criminals that had floated his boat.

The whole time, Jake had tried to warn Henry that detective work wasn't like the pulps or the movies. He was a smart kid. He would be better off listening to his folks, going to school, and using his family connections to get involved in great things. There was nothing fancy about solving crimes. Hell, Sullivan's most common PI work had been unglamorous strike-breaking, and he'd spent most of those years barely scraping by... But of course, despite all those warnings, when Henry had traded Harvard for the police academy, his parents had still blamed Jake Sullivan for it.

Which wasn't fair, because the second reason had really been the big one.

Born without a connection to the Power, Henry had been the oddball of the bunch. When you grow up Grimnoir, it was always talk about protecting the innocent, standing up for what was right, liberty and justice and all that jazz... but it took big magic to be a knight.

It didn't take any magic to stop a crook.

❖   ❖   ❖

The killings continued.

The whole department was told to be on the lookout, and though the task force had sworn everyone to secrecy, word had immediately started to spread. Cops talk, especially when they were ordered not to. The NYPD leaked like a sieve and the press was a big old sponge.

Even though he'd dropped three bodies in Manhattan and one on Staten Island, the papers had started calling the mystery killer the Bensonhurst Bomber. Reporters loved their alliteration. One headline had declared him the most powerful Boomer since Zangara, a name which still got all the rabid antimagic protesters foaming at the mouth.

The new mayor had given a big speech urging everyone to remain calm. It hadn't worked, but at least a riot hadn't broken out, which was something. Henry figured that by now, New Yorkers would be blasé about murders, since they had so damned many of them. They were in year two of a crime wave that the chief had publically declared they weren't going to allow to turn into a trilogy, but these murders were special. Good old-fashioned shootings and stabbings weren't exciting enough to grab press anymore. Randomly explode a bunch of people and even the most jaded New Yorker was bound to get jumpy.

Henry spent the next few nights questioning everybody on his beat, but nobody had seen anything suspicious. He then spent the days doing research and quietly chasing down leads. He didn't get much sleep, but he made up the difference with coffee.

More bodies were found, and as far as he could tell, Richards's task force was wasting its time questioning known Actives. Like they all knew each other and had a mailing list or something. Homicide was harassing anybody they heard about possessing energy-based magic, most of whom were regular law-abiding citizens who'd never exploded a fly.

You didn't need magic to catch a crook, but it sure could speed up the process.

Detective Richards might be old-school, but word was he'd already tried using a Finder. The department even kept one on retainer. Problem was, without anything connected to the killer, the demon he summoned wouldn't know who to track. They needed blood, hair, clothing, an item he'd had in his possession—something. Otherwise the demon would just float around aimless and invisible, looking for their Boomer, and since most demons were fairly stupid, and there were almost eight million people in this city, good luck with that. Sadly, their killer hadn't left much evidence behind.

The NYPD didn't have a Justice on retainer. Actives who could literally see the truth of things were so rare they made Healers seem common. Despite that, Henry knew two personally. The better of them had just been appointed director of the Bureau of Investigation and was probably too busy dealing with Imperium spies and Soviet agents to worry about a single homicidal maniac.

However, the second one might be available. Jack Moody worked for United Blimp and Freight out of Detroit, though Henry didn't know if Moody actually worked for UBF, or if they just kept him on the payroll while his real job was secret assignments from the Society. And therein lay the problem. If he called Moody in, then the Grimnoir would find out. And as much as he tried to assure Richards that the Grimnoir would stay out of local police business, he knew they probably wouldn't. Once they found the guy, it would be a .45 to the skull, some cinder blocks tied to the ankles, and a quick trip to the Hudson.

Nothing wrong with that per se. The bastard certainly deserved it, but Henry really wanted to catch him the right way. The Wild West days of Grimnoir knights dispensing indiscriminate justice were supposed to be over. Hell, Dad had even told that to Edward R. Murrow on TV the other night.

It was a tough call, but their Boomer was dropping a body every few days. The longer they dithered, the more innocents would die. The two of them didn't really get along—Henry thought Moody was a lout—but surely a Justice would jump at the shot to help take down a maniac.

Only when Henry used the phone number he had to make a long distance call to Moody's home, nobody picked up. He then tried the UBF offices. He didn't know which department they'd stuck Moody in, he assumed janitorial, but the secretary told him that "*Mister* Moody" was actually in something called "aerospace engineering." He had laughed at the idea of that thug helping design rocket ships, but apparently she was serious. Only he was on vacation, gone hunting, and hadn't left a number where he could be reached.

"Are you insane? Running an off-the-books investigation could get you in a lot of trouble."

"You came to me and asked what I was up to. Now you know. Come on, Rebecca. It'll be fun."

"The killer *explodes* people, Henry. We've got a drastically different definition of fun."

The two of them were sitting on a bench in the park, being menaced by a gang of pigeons. That was Rebecca's fault because she'd dropped some of her pretzel and the birds had taken it as an invitation to join them for supper. To a casual passerby, the two of them might have been mistaken for an attractive young couple having a date on a mild September evening. He had to admit Rebecca looked a lot better in a floral print dress than in her uniform.

They'd met in the police academy. It had only been the last three classes which had allowed women to train with men, and only two since they'd allowed known Actives to be hired at all. Lady cops were a tiny minority in the department, Actives even fewer. Rebecca Langford, or Crash as most of them had taken to calling her, was both. As his dad liked to say, "the times are a-changing."

"Look at this." He opened up his briefcase and pulled out the file. He showed her the latest crime scene photographs and the typewritten notes from the coroner's office. "I think Jeff Richards is right. The killer is using magic."

"That's awful!" She blanched when she saw the photos. They were far grislier than the ones that somebody had leaked to the papers. "Hang on. How'd you get this?"

"I stole it from the task force's ready room."

"What? You're going to get fired."

"Only if I get caught."

"Like getting caught is unlikely sneaking into a room filled with homicide dicks?" She gave him a very incredulous frown. "From that superior look on your face, they weren't there, were they?"

"It's lonely on the night shift."

"Oh my gosh. You *broke* into the task force room?"

Henry shrugged. He came from a family where children learned useful skills like how to hotwire cars, tail a mark, or fight back in case Imperium ninjas all of a sudden materialized out of thin air and tried to assassinate you. Grimnoir tradecraft was way better than being an Eagle Scout. "You'd think a police department would spring for better locks."

She just shook her head in disbelief. "You're a nut."

"Like I was saying, Richards is onto something. The coroner said that each victim died from a series of small detonations which appeared to have come from inside their body. But there were no traces of explosives or chemicals or anything like that. Which can only mean one thing."

Crash stared at him blankly. "A wizard did it?"

He had to remember that most people—even the ones capable of touching the Power in some way themselves—had very little exposure to the various types of magic. Most Actives could fudge one little part of the laws of physics, while the rest remained a mystery to them. Then their knowledge was limited to the garbage they read in the papers or the nonsense versions they saw at the movies like everybody else. Just because Crash was good at one thing didn't make her an expert on anything else.

"Well, yeah, but specifically it sounds like we're dealing with a Boomer. They're rare."

She nodded. "Like that lunatic who tried to assassinate FDR."

Everybody had heard of that mook. "Giuseppe Zangara. Sort of like that, but he had a spell carved on him to augment his Power." There was another case he knew a lot about, but he couldn't say much to someone who'd not taken the oath. Not the protect and serve oath, but the other one... the Grimnoir one... which he supposed was also a protecting and serving kind of thing. "Never mind him. He was an anomaly. Most Boomers, they can create a little explosion out of thin air. It has something to do with gathering up energy and then releasing it all of a sudden. Usually we're talking firecrackers, tops. Zangara was like cannon shells. From the pictures, I'm betting what our murderer can conjure up is more like half a stick of dynamite at a time."

"Oh, that doesn't sound bad at all—unless he puts it inside your *head*."

"Actually, the task force says that the fatal blows originated inside the abdomen or chest, or at least that's what they think from the way everything got sprayed around the crime scene. I think it's because that's one of the types of Power you have to charge up and aim, and the body is a bigger target." Then he realized he shouldn't have corrected her, because that really wasn't helping, and this was a hard enough sell as is.

Crash was an attractive girl. Short, strawberry blond, perky and athletic, she looked more like she should be wielding a cheerleader's pom-poms than a .38 Special and a nightstick. *Wait...* Did they issue nightsticks to the lady cops? He didn't actually know.

"It isn't like you don't know bigwigs. Why don't you just have *mommy* call in some favors? Everybody loves a Healer. I'm sure she's cured the mayor's ingrown toenail at some point. Just have him order Richards to officially put you on the unit."

That was just her being petty, but to be fair, Crash's family was stevedores union without two nickels to rub together, while Henry's played golf with the president.

"You know damned good and well I can't ask my family for help like that."

"You mean won't."

"Same difference. I'll make my bones on my own, or not at all." She didn't come from that world. She couldn't understand. "You asked what I was up to and you offered to help. Well, this is it, and I could use some help. I know you're frustrated where you're at, Crash. You're a walking tank they've got fetching coffee and running a typewriter. This maniac will be running around New York blowing people up until we stop him. The task force has got squat. Help me crack this case and we'll be heroes. It's your ticket out of the office and onto the streets."

She snorted. Like they were ever going to let her bust skulls? She might break a nail. But from the way she gave him the sly eye, he knew he'd hooked her. "What do you want from me, Henry?"

Crash probably thought it was because of her Power—which, frankly, was nothing to sneeze at—or maybe because she was clever. But in reality, it was because he needed backup and another set of eyes, and none of the other cops he was friends with would be desperate enough to risk career suicide. She always talked like she was motivated to climb the ladder.

"I need a partner."

"Sure. But I've got a condition."

Of course she did. It was that union upbringing. "Name it."

"If we get caught poking our nose into someone

else's case, you take the blame and say I was just some poor innocent girl you suckered into helping you."

"That hardly seems equitable."

"You get fired and you can just ask your pals at the country club to loan you a wad. I'll end up waiting tables to pay the rent. Which, come to think of it, wouldn't be that bad. Waitresses probably make more than we do once you factor in tips."

"Deal."

"Deal." They shook on it. Despite her petite hands she had a grip that felt like he'd gotten his fingers stuck in an industrial press. She was burning a bit of Power to let him know that she wasn't messing around.

"I'd save the magic if I were you. You might need it where we're going."

An hour later they arrived at their destination in Manhattan. Judging by the line of cabs picking up and dropping off, the club was a popular nightspot.

"When you said you needed a partner, you didn't say it was for dancing."

"The victims seem random, the ones we can identify at least, but I heard that two of them were regulars here. I wanted to look around, but it's a couples place and I didn't want to stick out being by myself."

"Why, Henry Garrett, if you wanted to take me out on a date you could've just asked nice."

"It's a slim lead, but I want to start checking out all the places the victims were last seen." Then he realized what she'd just said and gave her a lopsided grin. *So much for keeping it professional.* "Well, maybe after we catch this guy we can go celebrate."

"I'd like that."

He pulled his Chrysler around to the lot in back. Most of the cars were fairly normal, but there were a few hot rods. There would probably be boys racing for pink slips later tonight.

He had his .38 Police Colt beneath his suit jacket but didn't know if Crash was packing. "I've got a spare heater in the glove box if you need it."

"I've got one in my purse." She giggled. "Heater? You've been reading too many Chandler novels."

He didn't reply to that, but all his copies were autographed.

Inside, the dance floor was so full they had to be bribing the fire marshal. Henry's musical knowledge was limited to being forced to take a few piano lessons when he was ten, but he immediately liked the catchy tune. The band was playing that weird mix of electrical powered guitars, drums, and saxophones, that sounded like a bunch of excitable hillbillies were trying to speed up rhythm and blues. But whatever it was, the affluent white kids loved dancing around to it enough to come to this part of town to slum it with the poor ones.

From the smell in here, some of them also loved smoking reefer. Luckily, neither he nor Crash particularly looked like police so nobody made a run for it. With the suit and fedora, Henry was a little overdressed for this crowd, but if Crash was going to get mistaken for a cheerleader, then they'd figure him for the quarterback.

"How do you want to play this?" she asked him. "You want to dance? You know...to sell our cover."

That wasn't dancing. It was twirling and gyrating. Actually that sounded kind of fun with Crash as his partner, but if he was going to try something that silly looking, he'd definitely need some beers in him first. Jake Sullivan had said when you're looking for information always start with the bartender. They're the one person who saw everybody. Plus, they were usually easy to bribe. "Let me buy you a drink."

Crash looked a little disappointed.

The bar was too crowded for stools. It was shove your way up, shout your order, and then hope someone heard you over the amplified music. He got bumped into by some guys in leather jackets. Henry tried to be polite about the shoving. Besides the greasers, bikers, street racers, and general hooliganry, from the short and awful haircuts there were a lot of soldiers and sailors in here on leave too, and every one of those groups was easily inclined to give somebody a knuckle sandwich to show their lady how tough they were.

Unfortunately, politeness went right out the window when he saw who was already talking to the bartender. "You poaching ass!"

And as soon as he shouted that, Lance Browning Garrett looked up from his conversation with the bartender. Henry had taken after their mother—tall, effortlessly fit, and classically good-looking—while his twin brother had taken after their father—short, stocky, and perpetually disheveled. Lance seemed really surprised. It looked like he said, "What're you doing here?" but it was hard to tell over the blaring noise.

This was no coincidence. There was only one reason Lance would be here. He'd taken after Dad in more than just looks. Unlike Henry, who was a magical dud, the Power had picked Lance to be a Mouth, and a really potent one at that. Lance was local and a secret knight of the Grimnoir Society. They were hunting the Bomber too.

But before Henry could articulate any of that, the nearest greaser shoved him hard. "Who you calling an ass, germ?"

"That short dumpy guy at the bar," he tried to explain, but of course as he looked back over, Lance had already disappeared. "I wasn't talking to you."

"What, you think you're too good to talk to me now?" With a response that dumb, this guy was obviously spoiling for a fight. If it hadn't been with Henry, it would've been someone else.

"Pretty boy's cruisin' for a bruisin'," said another one of the kids, egging on his buddy.

Henry slowly moved one hand to the leather sap he kept in his back pocket as he flashed his most disarming smile. "Sorry about the misunderstanding. Let me buy you a beer."

The mope telegraphed the punch. He must've been used to fighting drunks. Henry easily dodged to the side, and then cracked him over the melon with the sap. It made a very satisfying noise on impact. If there was one thing a beat cop learned fast, it was how to sap a fool. The kid must've had a thick skull though, because he wobbled and blinked, but didn't drop. So Henry gut-punched him. That put him down, wide-eyed and gasping like a fish.

Apparently, fighting in this club was a team sport, because all the greaser's friends suddenly decided they got a turn too. Henry easily ducked the next fist, and he responded with an uppercut that dropped the guy and left his fist stinging. That's why you should always stick with the sap.

The beer bottle that got flung at his face probably would've hit, if Crash hadn't suddenly stepped in the way. It shattered against her forehead.

"Oh shit! Sorry, baby!" shouted the kid who'd thrown the bottle. Sure, it was one thing to break a bottle over a guy's head, but you didn't go around giving concussions to girls. That kind of thing was downright impolite.

Except Crash was unharmed. She just reached up and wiped the beer out of her eyes. "You got glass in my hair," she snarled. And with a surge of magical energy, she crossed the distance, grabbed him by the leather jacket and, despite the fact he was double her size, hurled him violently over the bar. He hit the cash register and bounced off with a *clang*.

You never ever wanted to get into a physical altercation with a Brute.

Everything might have been fine, and everyone could have gone about their business, but it was always the little sawed-off runts who escalated stuff. Henry didn't even see the switchblade until it was too late. The tiniest greaser he'd ever seen slashed at him. Henry thought he'd gotten out of the way, except all of a sudden there was a rip in his sleeve. He didn't even realize he'd been cut until blood started coming out. Then it hurt.

The greaser lunged at him again, knife pointed at his stomach.

"*Stop!*"

The word hit with such magical impact that everybody immediately did as they were told. Not just the combatants, but the dancers, and even the band. Everybody in the room froze. It was suddenly, painfully silent.

Even Henry found that the shock of the word had momentarily stunned him. And he'd had his whole life to learn how to resist that kind of Power. He still managed to move away from the knife. Not that it mattered, since the greaser was pretty much stuck there, quivering and confused.

Every eye in the joint was on them. *Way to go, Lance.*

Now that his brother wasn't in immediate danger of being disemboweled, Lance moved to a conversational tone and used his Power of suggestion in a calm and soothing fashion, now directed only at the punk. "The fight is over. There are no hard feelings. Put the knife back in your pocket."

"Sure thing," the greaser said. And Henry knew that to him, Lance's words sounded like the most reasonable thing he'd ever heard, and it was coming from his bestest best friend in the whole wide world. So he immediately shoved the knife back in the pocket of his jeans . . . Only the kid was dumb, and Lance hadn't specified that he should close the switchblade first. "Ahhhhhhh!" He screamed as he stabbed himself in the leg.

Which was the moment when everybody in the club realized that there was a wizard fight, and nobody wanted to be in the middle of a wizard fight.

"Time to go," Henry said as he grabbed Crash by the arm and tugged. Since she was all fired up, her arm was as hard as an iron bar, and he might as well have been trying to pull a locomotive. "Unless you want to stick around and explain what we were doing here."

"Nope." Her arm returned to normal.

He caught a glimpse of his brother innocuously walking toward another exit. They shared a knowing glance. They had some business to discuss. He and

Crash headed for the door, mixed in with the crowd, and got the hell out.

There was a twenty-four-hour drive-in both he and Lance liked, only four blocks from the club. When he pulled in there, Crash seemed a little surprised. "What're you doing?"

"I'm craving a milkshake. Want one?"

"You just got knifed."

"It's only a scratch." Actually, his sleeve was damp with blood and he was probably going to need a few stitches. He parked the Chrysler next to one of the speakers. Then he struggled out of his jacket and took a look at the cut. It wasn't that bad. "There's a flask in the glove box."

Crash got it out and unscrewed the cap. "Ladies first." She took a swig.

"Hey. I need that." He snatched the flask from her, took a deep breath, and then poured the rest on his arm. It stung enough to make his eyes water. Muttering obscenities, he wrapped his sleeve around the cut like a makeshift bandage. Most of the obscenities were related to the ruined clothing. The arm would heal. He'd liked the suit.

Sure enough, a big black sedan pulled into the space next to them a moment later. The passenger side window rolled down revealing that Lance was in the passenger seat. Henry shouldn't have been surprised to see he had a partner driving. Grimnoir only worked alone when they had no choice. But he was surprised to see who it was.

"If it isn't Justice Jack Moody. Hey, I called your office the other day."

Moody was a big, heavyset man, with a thick black beard. "I'm on vacation."

"I can see that."

Moody just gave him a noncommittal grunt.

Lance leaned out the window a bit and clucked disapprovingly when he saw the bloody jacket around his arm. "You're hurt. You should go see Mom and let her Mend that."

"I'm fine."

"Whatever, tough guy. She was just complaining you never come to dinner anymore." Then Lance whistled. "Say, who's the lovely lady?"

Instead of answering him, Crash asked, "You know these clowns, Henry?"

"Unfortunately. This is my brother, Lance, and his associate, Jack. Considering where we ran into them, they're looking for the killer too."

"Maybe I just really like rock and roll music."

Crash leaned forward so she could address Lance directly. "You two are Grimnoir knights like Henry?"

Lance and Moody shared a look. "Hang on a minute. Henry's no knight."

"I never claimed I was."

"Yeah, but you love letting regular folks assume it! My brother here is in the Society. Anybody can be. It's all about protecting magicals from the world, and protecting the world from magic. But he's not one of the knights. Oh, he's tried. But you don't ask to be one, they ask you. Knights are special. We're like the commando problem solvers who step in when necessary, for example when the cops can't do their jobs, to take care of problems. And to be one nowadays, you need to have magic. Strong magic."

"You talk too much, kid," Moody muttered. He was the senior and far more experienced of the two.

"If blondie here is chasing a lunatic with my brother, she needs to know what she's getting into."

Henry chuckled to hide his embarrassment. Yeah, it ticked him off that they wouldn't let him be a knight, but so what? "Lance here is just bitter that I got all the height, smarts, and good looks, so he likes to rub it in that he got all the magic."

"You need to stay in your lane. The Bomber isn't an average killer. He's got skills. You're getting in over your heads. Let us deal with him before you get hurt."

"The Society is supposed to let the law take care of it. This is NYPD's turf."

"Well, they need to handle their business faster," Moody said.

"Why haven't you caught him, then? With your Power you should be able to track this guy down no problem."

"Can't. He's warded."

"What?" That was unexpected. Lots of people had magic that was just naturally attached to them, but very few knew how to craft different kinds of spells. Creating a ward that could keep you from being magically spied on took skill, and you couldn't learn a spell like that just anywhere. "So he's a pro? We talking Imperium? Soviet?"

Moody shrugged. "Wherever he learned it, his warding's solid."

"Wait . . . That's why you've stepped in. You're worried he might've learned it from the Grimnoir."

"Now which one of us talks too much?" Lance asked Moody.

The intercom buzzed next to his window. *"May I take your order please?"*

He was trying to emulate the great Jake Sullivan, who in this situation would probably have gone to a smoky bar to down shots of whiskey in a most hard-boiled manner, but he really did want that shake. "Large vanilla shake, please."

"Two double cheeseburgers, two orders of fries, and a Coca-Cola," Crash said. Henry looked over at the dainty girl, impressed. "What? Using my Power makes me hungry. Besides, you're paying."

"Hey, lover boy," his brother snapped. "Pay attention. This one is dangerous. I'm talking maybe even Iron Guard dangerous. If the cops find him, he's going to pop a bunch of them like balloons before they take him down."

His brother had the ability to put ideas into your mind and twist thoughts, nothing near as strong as Dad, but if he used his Power and ordered Henry to back off, it would suddenly sound like the best suggestion he'd ever heard. Only Mouths had to tread carefully when dealing with their loved ones, and despite the name calling and rivalry, the two of them had way too much mutual respect for that kind of thing.

"I'm begging you, Henry, stay out of this."

"And if I don't?"

Lance's eyes narrowed dangerously. "I'll tell Mom."

"Oh, that's low even for you."

Their intercom started squawking, but Moody put their car in reverse and backed out. Lance rolled up the window as they drove away.

"Your brother seems nice." The sparkle in Crash's

eye matched the tiny bits of broken glass still stuck
in her hair.

"He's a good sort in his own unique and annoy-
ing way."

It was sad that after all these years, Lance was still
under the mistaken impression that anyone could get
Henry to back off once he'd set his mind to something.

On the bright side, now Henry knew they were
doing the right thing. Normally, Jack Moody could
track anyone. A Justice could come to a fork in the
road and simply ask the Power which way his target
had gone and it would tell him. With the Bomber
warded, Jack was as blind as anyone else, and yet the
experienced knight had still wound up looking in the
same place that they had.

The victims were the key. The killer was picking
them somehow. If they figured out how he was choosing them, then they could get ahead of him.

For the next few days, he and Crash hit up every
spot the victims had last been seen. They went to restaurants, bars, even a movie together. Ronald Reagan
played a cowboy. They'd shared a bucket of popcorn
and, afterwards, watched the people coming and going,
but saw nothing suspicious. All of the subsequent fishing expeditions went better than their initial brawl.
He was really enjoying the company. Except for the
hunting-a-maniac part, these were some of the more
enjoyable dates he'd had.

They interviewed people at each spot, trying to
play it gentle, never identifying themselves as cops.
All these folks had already been grilled by Richards or
his men and left with business cards, so the last thing

he wanted was for one of them to call the detective and ask why they were getting hassled again.

Once they'd exhausted the leads listed in the first file, he'd tried to break back into the task force room to swipe a more up-to-date file. Only Richards must've realized they'd been burgled, because the locks were new and improved, and they'd left another uniform there for the night. Stymied, Henry had just gone on with his shift.

On his night off, Crash had come over to his apartment after she'd gotten off work. They were supposed to go out sleuthing, but he was out of ideas. A corkboard was taking up one wall of his tiny kitchen. He'd put up a map of the city with a tack stuck in it representing each body. A red string ran from each tack to a photo of the vic while they were still alive. The board was getting mighty crowded.

"That's creepy," Crash said as she hopped up and sat on his kitchen counter in a very unladylike sort of way. She was still in her uniform. Main difference between his and hers was that she had to wear a wool skirt and he at least got to wear pants.

"I'm trying to be thorough." He had his notebook open and was going through the things he'd written down after each interview. "We're up to fourteen victims. Eleven men, three women. Ages between eighteen and fifty. He's not picky. So why these?"

"Targets of opportunity?"

"Maybe that's part of it. But my gut tells me it isn't all of it. They've got different kinds of jobs, from assembly lines in Hoboken to banks on Wall Street. Different political parties: Democrats, Republicans, and one Communist." He snorted. *No great loss on that one.* "One openly magical, one possible who was keeping it to herself, and the rest were normal, so it wasn't magically motivated. Half didn't go to church and the other half were all different religions. Different educations, from nothing at all to one guy with a master's. Backgrounds from lower middle to upper class. Nobody real poor. Don't know why that is..."

"Luck of the draw maybe? My folks are safe. Yours aren't."

If the Bomber made a move on the Garretts, that would be the end of the Bomber. They'd fought Iron Guard and won. "He's not robbing them. He's left wallets, purses, and nice watches behind. There's no rhyme nor reason to where they're killed compared to where they're last seen. Nobody ever sees the killer with them. He's highly mobile and leaves no trace. He moves around the city with impunity, and even with everybody so nervous, not so much as a single eyewitness."

"Can Boomers turn invisible?" Crash asked. When he looked over at her to see if she'd lost her mind, she was grinning at him. "I'm being silly. Henry, come on. You've basically been working round the clock. You're frazzled and it shows. Why don't we take tonight off and just stay home?"

It was sorely tempting. And he liked the way she said *we.* Crash was adorable and virtually indestructible; it was a nice combo. Only he couldn't let go of the feeling he was close to the truth. Every minute the killer went free was another minute his city was in danger.

"While you ponder on it, I'll make dinner." She slid off the counter, turned around, and opened his cupboard. "You've got...one can of green beans and, wow, that's a lot of Spam... How are you still alive?"

"He knows the streets really well," Henry muttered to himself. He was chewing on his pencil, which he tended to do when he wasn't smoking. "He knows all these spots where there won't be witnesses, and he knows when it's quiet. You're onto something. He's not invisible, but he's damn close."

"You're fixated again." Crash sighed. "If you want to just stare at your murder board all night, I'm leaving. This girl's got standards. I deserve better than green beans and Spam. You could at least be a gentleman and offer to drive me home. I had to take the subway to get here."

Henry owned a car because he'd been given this one for his eighteenth birthday. Crash didn't have her own car, but that wasn't too odd in a city that had lousy traffic, no places to park, and plenty of other ways to get around. "Yeah. Sorry, let me get my keys."

And then he stopped, and glanced back at his board, scowling.

"What now? You get this funny look on your face when gears start turning."

"New York State requires licenses to drive. When they were trying to identify the victims, the ones they got quick were because they had license cards in their wallets with their names and addresses printed on them, but that was only a few of them. Most took longer to identify because they had to be compared to missing persons reports because they didn't have a license."

"So?"

Henry started flipping through his notepad. "When I talked to one vic's doorman, he said our guy's car was in the shop. So the doorman hailed a taxi to take him to a restaurant that evening."

"Which one? Because I liked that Italian place we tried on Wednesday. We should go again."

"He ate, left, and was never seen again. He would've taken a cab home." He started flipping through the pages faster and faster. "Most of these, they weren't seen after leaving the establishment. We don't know how they planned on getting home. I don't remember in the inventory anybody having subway or bus tokens on them."

Cabs weren't invisible, but they were so common that nobody noticed they were around unless you were trying to hail one.

"You can put a warding spell on your own skin, but that's really challenging. Only the most talented spellbinders I know can pull that off. Carving one on a vehicle is comparatively easy. You'd just scratch it someplace nobody would see. The second anyone got inside, they'd be camouflaged to demons, Finders, Justices, the works."

It was starting to dawn on her. "Cabbies know the streets better than anyone, every back alley and short cut."

"Why'd you take the subway to get here tonight?"

"Because you were too distracted to pick me up at the precinct."

"And?"

"And because the subway's *cheaper* than cab fare... He's not sparing the poor, they just don't ride in cabs as often!" Crash came over and stood next to him, staring at the board. "Oh my gosh. It all makes sense."

"The Bomber is a taxi driver."

They both stared at the map for a long time as the enormity of the challenge sunk in. Finally, Crash asked, "Now what?"

There were thousands of taxis in New York City. He could've emptied out his savings account to pay for cab fare, and caught rides from dawn to dusk every day for the rest of his life, and still not had good odds of getting picked up by the Bomber.

"I don't rightly know."

"This is too big for us. We need to take this to the task force."

Henry shook his head. "From what I've seen of Richards's ham-fisted methods so far, *if* he believes us, he'll probably just send dicks to every taxi company in the city to browbeat them into identifying any driver they've got who might be able to do magic. The Bomber's not stupid. He'll find out we're onto him and go to ground. We'll never catch the guy."

"Elephant in the room. What about telling your brother?"

Lance was sharp. There wouldn't be any fumbling around. He'd pull some strings, call in some favors, do the legwork, and then some random cabby would just disappear into thin air. The killings would stop. Nobody would ever know why. Problem solved.

"I don't know. Maybe."

"I know you want to be the one to do this, but don't let your pride get in the way. You want to prove something, but there're lives at stake. Call Lance."

The Grimnoir had the most effective way, but it wasn't always the right way.

The killings had evened out. They were having one every three days. Henry figured that was because that was how long it took for the killer's Power to charge back up after completely obliterating someone. There had been a killing last night. That meant they had roughly forty-eight hours before the next body dropped.

He tried to deliver the next line with more confidence than he felt. "I've got a plan."

"Taxi!"

Henry waved one hand and stepped aggressively into the darkened street. He really wanted to catch this particular cab.

It was raining hard. A cold, sopping downpour that leeched the warmth right out of his flesh. *Yeah . . . the rain. That's the reason.*

The yellow cab pulled to the curb. He confirmed the number painted on the side was the one he was looking for. This was it. Henry took a deep breath, opened the back door, and climbed inside.

The interior was uncomfortably warm. The heater was going full blast. The windows immediately began to fog. The wipers were beating a fast rhythm.

"Where to?" asked the Bensonhurst Bomber.

Or at least he hoped it was the Bomber and this wasn't a wild goose chase. But that was why they were going to take a nice long ride together to find out. He rattled off an address across the river.

He could see the cabby had tilted his head to look at him in the rearview mirror. It was dark enough that the only thing he could make out were the eyes. He wanted to describe them as piercing or cunning, but really, they seemed completely normal. Heavy-lidded. Maybe a little tired. It seemed they were just two regular guys stuck on the night shift.

The cab pulled out. At this hour there wasn't much in the way of traffic. The headlights behind them belonged to his Chrysler, with Crash at the wheel. They'd been following this particular cab for a while as he picked up and dropped off fares, knowing that he didn't like to strike until it was late enough to avoid witnesses. The hour was getting late. When the cabby had stopped for a coffee, they'd had the opportunity to get ahead of him. Crash had hated the idea, she'd begged him not to do it, but Henry had told her he'd be fine and gone for it.

He had to know if this was the one.

Some cabbies liked the quiet. Others liked to make conversation. Henry needed him to talk. "Hell of a night, isn't it?"

"Sure is." Luckily, it appeared this cabby might be a chatty one. "Where you from?"

"All over. Here mostly," Henry answered truthfully. "How about you?"

"Nowheresville." The cabby had a normal voice, not too deep, not too high, no lisp, no rasp. He'd kind of been expecting a psycho killer to at least sound different.

They drove the next few blocks without a word, except for the thump of the wipers and the sound of rubber on wet road. They stopped at a red light. Now he could see that the cabby was younger than expected. They were probably about the same age.

When all else failed, talk about the weather. "It's pouring cats and dogs out there."

"Yeah." The cabby sounded a little wistful. "I kind of like it though. The only time this place smells clean is when it rains."

"That never lasts long." Henry kept one hand in the pocket of his trench coat, wrapped around the grip of his snub .38. "It smells like garbage before, and then it smells like wet garbage right after."

There were pedestrians walking by beneath umbrellas. Henry studied the back of the suspect's head. He was wearing a tweed cap, and the hair beneath was brown and bristly.

The light turned green. The cabby looked at him in the mirror again before proceeding. He was doing the math. Tonight was a killing night. This fare would take a while. It was either pop this one, or take his chances finding somebody after. At least that's what Henry assumed was going through that crazy mind. Who could tell?

He must have made his decision because he put his eyes back on the road.

"Things don't have to be dirty, you know. If there was somebody strong enough, they could clean this place up. Make everything work right. It just takes will."

"Uh-huh." Henry tried to keep it noncommittal to keep him talking. "So you don't like the new mayor?"

"That's not what I mean. If somebody had the will and the power, they could really turn things around, fix the country, fix the whole world even."

That sounded like old-fashioned Imperium propaganda, from back when Okubo Tokugawa's eugenic madness conquered a third of the world. Unfortunately, the Imperium didn't have a monopoly on that kind of authoritarian crazy. "The world sure does have a lot of problems."

"Those problems are too big for regular folks to fix. It would take God to fix things. Only if he's real, then he sure don't care about us anymore. When somebody don't care about doing his job no more, he needs to be replaced." Those eyes flicked back to the mirror again. This was probably the part where his fares started feeling uncomfortable and saying they'd just get out here, but Henry kept his mouth shut.

The cabby started up again. He seemed enthusiastic about the topic. "You know, somebody had the chance once to become a god, but she chickened out. You ever heard of the Spellbound?"

Not only had he heard, they were on a first-name basis. "Nope."

"The story goes that there was once this Active who was extra special. The Power loved her more than any of its other children. So whenever somebody died near her, she took their magic for herself. She got stronger and stronger. All the magic in the world was hers to take if she wanted it. And you know what she did when she needed to do something extra hard?"

He already knew. "She killed her enemies and stole their magic."

"I thought you said you hadn't heard of her?"

"Just a guess."

"Well, that she did. She took what she needed to do what needed doing, but then after... nothing... she walked away. Gave up her magic entirely. Can you imagine? Being able to change the world however you wanted, but then just leaving it alone? Ruthlessly alone."

"It's hard to imagine."

He waved one hand at the passing city. "But how could you leave it like this? This filth. This squalor."

The longer he talked, the more erratic he sounded.

Was he compelled to explain himself to all his victims? Did he try to justify it as he was driving them to someplace other than their destination? Was he still talking as they walked away and he was drawing his Power together to blow them to pieces? The cab was approaching the Brooklyn Bridge. On the other side, they'd either go to his destination or divert to a killing ground. Henry needed to push him. He needed to be sure this was the one.

"It's a big job, being a god," Henry said.

"Yeah, but somebody's got to do it."

"I feel bad for all the poor bastards who'd have to die just so their magic could get stolen."

"Sacrifices get made for the greater good. You know, a few months ago, I picked up this old man. And while we were driving, he had a stroke. Can you believe it? He had a stroke right where you're sitting now. Died on the spot...I tried to help him, swear I did, but there was nothing could be done."

"Tragic." At least the cab company would've disinfected the seat.

"But right afterwards, I felt *something*. He'd had magic. Only after he died, it lingered, like it didn't know where else to go. I couldn't let it go to waste. So I took it. Made it mine."

That was impossible. It had taken one of the greatest minds in the history of magic to come up with a spell that could do that. It sure as hell didn't happen by accident. This guy was delusional.

"Problem is that spell's long gone," Henry stated, flat and calm. "It was one of a kind. It was undone. Gone. Kaput."

"No it's not."

"Oh, it's done. It was a special one-time offer from the Power, trying to protect itself. Mission accomplished."

"You don't know what you're talking about!" Now he was getting really upset. "You lied. You said you didn't know about it."

Better a liar than a murderer. "You'd have to be crazy to think you could kill somebody and take their connection to the Power. You'd have to be insane to believe that."

"It's real." There was an audible creak because he was squeezing the leather-wrapped steering wheel so hard. "It talked to me."

Enough of this. "The voices in your head are imaginary. Most of the people you killed didn't even have any magic, you sick son of a bitch."

"No! I felt it! I felt it as they died! I'm stronger now! I'm doing what has to be done."

"You killed them for nothing." The air started to hum with energy. As the killer's crazed emotions grew hotter, so did the magic inside the car. Henry shoved his .38 against the back of the driver's head. "Try anything and your brains end up in your lap."

The cab swerved wildly, first into the oncoming headlights, and then back for the tires to strike the curb and bounce off. But thankfully, the gathered magic dissipated.

"Keep driving." You didn't need to cock the hammer to fire a double action, but Henry did so anyway, just to hear the *click* that let him know he meant business. "No matter how fast you think you are with your Power, bullets are faster. You're under arrest."

They got back in their lane. "How'd you find me?"

"Once we figured out your cab was warded, I paid a bunch of Finders to look for something that wasn't there." It had taken every dime he had to hire every Finder and Summoner in the city for the last two days. He'd put them on major intersections or sent them past every cab company until one had found a parking space filled with a cab his demon couldn't see.

Shaking, the driver asked, "So where are we really going?"

"My station house. You're going to jail."

"They can't lock up a man who can kill a guard just by looking at him."

"Not my problem." There were prisons with special lead-lined isolation cells specifically for guys like this. Maybe they had a padded one for the crazies. Yet now that Henry knew the why, he wanted to know the how. Very few people in the world knew about the Spellbound, and being able to make wards was a very specialized skill. "I've got to know, were you Grimnoir?

"Briefly. They learned what I could do. Some of them took me in when I was a kid, tried to teach me. I was good at it, but I didn't like being bossed around, so I left. I threw my Grimnoir ring in the Hudson and changed my name so they'd never find me."

No wonder the elders had sent Moody. The Society knew they'd lost track of a dangerous Boomer. They were trying to do the right thing by stopping him, but they were also trying to save face by stopping him quietly. They tried to do good but caught a lot of hate. Having it come out in court that they'd trained this murderer would make it even worse for them.

They'd reached the bridge, but there was a whole lot of brake lights ahead. Red and blue flashing lights reflected off the puddles. Henry looked ahead and saw that a pair of patrol cars were blocking traffic. It was a roadblock.

Damn it. He'd installed a police radio in his personal car. Crash must have been so worried about him that she'd called for help.

The cabby stared at the flashing lights ahead of them as they came to a gentle stop. The wipers were still beating. The rain made a thrumming sound against their metal roof. The red and blues cast odd shadows inside the cab.

When he spoke again, the killer sounded resigned. "It's working. I know it. I can still do it. I can't let you ruin my plans. I'm not the one who wasted all those lives. I was going to use them to build something better. You're the one trying to throw away their sacrifices."

Energy was gathering again.

"Don't do it."

Henry didn't have magic himself, but he was no stranger to its use. Even he could feel the spike. This was every bit of magic the killer had, all at once. The hair on his arms stood up. The Bomber was going to blast himself, his passenger, the cab, and probably a big chunk of the Brooklyn Bridge to kingdom come.

Henry's finger was on the trigger. Now it was his turn to have a shaking hand. "Don't make me kill you."

The killer just looked at the mirror and gave him an eerie smile. "You can't kill a god, cop."

And then the back window shattered.

Henry flinched as his face was splattered with blood.

The cabby's head had been thrown forward by the impact. The inside of the windshield was dripping red.

The wipers still beat on the other side. He looked at the .38 in his hand, just to make sure he hadn't just burst the cabby's skull by accident, but the Smith hadn't been fired. He turned around to catch a face full of cold rain and got partially blinded by the headlights of the car behind—probably his own car—but that wasn't where the shot had come from.

There was a big black sedan stopped a little further back. As he watched, a broad-shouldered shape that was most likely Jack Moody lowered a scoped rifle, got back into the car, flipped a U-turn, and drove away.

It was another week before he talked to Crash again. After giving their statements, she'd been transferred, while he had been *retroactively* assigned to the now unnecessary Bomber task force. He had been ordered to smile for the cameras; when the media asked, all he was supposed to say was that he'd been following Detective Richards's orders when he'd gotten into the killer's cab, and that he'd been forced to shoot him in the head to keep him from blowing up the Brooklyn Bridge.

The carrot was that if he managed to keep his stupid rookie mouth shut, they'd give him a commendation for valor and fast-track a promotion. The stick, if he didn't, was getting put on something like harbor patrol for the rest of his life.

Detective Garrett. He liked the sound of that.

He'd called and stopped by her apartment but she never answered the phone or the door. Crash had been avoiding him since that night, and he had a pretty good idea why. He found out where she'd been transferred to—headquarters, ironically enough—and then waited outside until she got off shift.

Crash came down the stairs, looking lovely in plain-clothes, and didn't seem the least bit surprised to see him. Sad, but not surprised. "Henry."

"Rebecca." He nodded, then tossed his cigarette butt down and crushed it beneath his heel. "You lied to me. You want to have it out here in front of all your coworkers, or talk someplace private?"

The answer was obvious, and they strolled away from the front doors so nobody would overhear them. It was a much grayer and colder afternoon than when they'd launched their partnership. Steam came up through the grates.

"I heard you're getting a commendation."

"It's my reward for keeping secrets. Luckily, I'm good at that from all the practice. I tried to give you equal credit for finding the Bomber. Imagine my surprise when it turned out your version of events made it sound like it was all my doing."

Crash shrugged. "I'm just humble, I guess."

"So how long have you secretly been a Grimnoir knight?"

She sighed. "I suppose I could protest and act offended, but you're too smart and I've got too much dignity. How'd you figure it out?"

"Moody knew how to find us in time to erase their embarrassing mistake. So I got suspicious and looked in your purse. You left it on the seat of my car while you were getting questioned on the bridge. You had a communication spell etched on your little makeup mirror. From the runes, Grimnoir. A powerful Brute like you, with lots of brains and all sweet and innocent-looking, you're an ideal recruit. Now they've got somebody who will overhear lots while not being noticed, working inside the biggest police department in the country. So how long?"

"Years and years before we met. It was tempting back in the academy to tell you that I already knew your parents. It's kind of funny actually."

What wasn't funny was all the grief he took from his fellow cops because they thought he was the one with divided loyalties, even though he was no rat. Nobody would ever suspect the pretty girl with the bubbly personality of leaking information to a magical secret society.

"Did my folks order you to help me?"

She laughed. It wasn't mean, but it was honest. "Don't kid yourself. You're not that important in the grand scheme of things. I wanted to help because I believed in you."

"Well, too bad I can't ever believe you now."

"That's on you. The elders suspected the killer might be their missing Boomer who'd gone rogue. He was always a little off. That's why they sent Moody. He's a thug, but he's reliable. When he came up with nothing, that's when Moody recruited your brother. Nobody can squeeze information out of people like a Mouth. You should be proud; you cracked the case when they couldn't."

"I was bringing him in, Crash. The right way."

"Him babbling would've hurt a lot of innocent people. I told you not to get in that cab. If Moody hadn't shot him, you would've had to. Or maybe the real reason you're so angry at me is deep down you're afraid you would've hesitated a second too long and he would've killed himself, and you, and me, and everybody on that bridge. Flash-fried so a maniac could go out in a blaze of glory. And now you'll never know."

"I would've done whatever I had to do."

"I'm sure Moody would say the same thing. So are you going to blow my cover now, or are you going to let me keep doing what I need to do?"

Police headquarters was a massive edifice rising behind her. The first night he'd stumbled into this case, Detective Richards had told him that Actives protect their own. In the case of the Grimnoir, that was the God's honest truth. Sometimes that meant taking out their trash. They weren't perfect, but they did a lot more good in the world than harm.

"I take all my oaths seriously. Your secret's safe... Just tell me though, Lance at least honestly didn't know who you were, right? I can only handle being lied to by one person I like at a time."

"Not that night at the rock and roll club." She shook her head in the negative, but then a mischievous smile formed on her lips. "But we've gotten to know each other better since."

He groaned. "You've got to be kidding me."

A cherry-red hot rod pulled up to the curb next to them. The driver had to shout to be heard over the noisy engine. "Hey, babe, ready to go? I got us reservations at that little Italian place you talked about." Then Lance Garrett glanced over and saw his brother. "Henry! Didn't expect to see you here. I heard how it shook out with the Bomber. Way to clean up the streets, Johnny Law."

Henry looked at Crash. "You can do better."

"He's sweet." She gave Henry a kiss on the cheek and then went to the passenger door. "Take care. I'll see you around."

As the hot rod drove off into the sunset, Henry Garrett went back to work.

About the Authors

A native Texan by birth (if not geography), **Christopher L. Smith** moved "home" as soon as he could. While there, he also met a wonderful lady who somehow found him to be funny, charming, and worth marrying. (She has since changed her mind on the funny and charming but figures he's still a keeper.) Chris began writing fiction in 2012. His short stories can be found in the following anthologies: "Bad Blood and Old Silver" (*Luna's Children: Stranger Worlds*, Dark Oak Press); "Isaac Crane and the Ancient Hunger" (*Dark Corners*, Fantom Enterprises); "200 miles to Huntsville" (*Black Tide Rising*, Baen Books); "What Manner of Fool" (*Sha'Daa: Inked*, Copper Dog Publishing); "Case Hardened" (*Forged in Blood*, Baen Books); and "Velut Luna" (*The Good, the Bad, and the Merc*, Seventh Seal Press). He has cowritten two novels, *Kraken Mare* (Severed Press) with Jason Cordova, and *Gunpowder and Embers: Last Judgement's Fire Book 1* (Baen Books, Spring 2020) with John Ringo and Kacey Ezell. A solo urban fantasy novel is currently under construction. His cats allow his family and three dogs to reside with them outside of San Antonio.

Michael J. Ferguson is a Master Brewer, a nationally syndicated TV host and now Director of Business Development at Aalberts Dispense Technologies. After eleven years of field engineering, R&D, and tech writing at IBM, Michael set off to find the next step to his personal growth. Michael always enjoyed motorcycles, reading, and writing as hobbies, but in 1989 Michael found himself at the ground floor of a craft brewing start-up named Gordon Biersch Brewing. This began the journey from apprentice brewer to Master Brewer. After helping to install and open six breweries, a move to Director of Brewery Operations at Station Casinos allowed Michael the independence to garner several industry awards including five medals from the GABF (Great American Beer Festival). Michael also accepted an Associate Professorship at the University of Nevada Las Vegas College of Hospitality before moving on to BJ's Restaurants Inc. in 2004 as Director of Brewery Operations and Beer Training. Michael helped open over 120 restaurants for the company and trained countless team members about the ins and outs of craft beer. It was at BJ's Restaurants that Michael's high profile within the craft brewing industry caught the eye of talent scouts at Discovery Channel, which led to the inception and production of *Beer Geeks* television show, the only nationally syndicated TV show about craft beer, the people who make, follow and love craft beer, and the industries it encompasses. *Beer Geeks* received a national Emmy nomination for

Best Culinary Show in 2015. Michael's love of writing and science fiction is now the newest phase of a long career. Michael Ferguson lives in Houston, Texas.

David Weber was born in Cleveland in 1952 but grew up in rural South Carolina. He was a bookworm from childhood, with an interest in history which perplexed his parents, who nonetheless encouraged and supported him in it. He was also blessed with a father from the south side of Chicago who collected autographed copies of every E. E. Smith hardcover and introduced him to Jack Williamson at the age of ten, and with a mother who taught high school and college English, ran her own advertising agency, and encouraged him to write. (And who went back to graduate school in her sixties to earn her PhD in Literature.) An avid tabletop gamer (who, alas, no longer has room in his schedule for his hobby), he's wargamed every era from ancient Rome to World War II armored conflict, and began RPG playing with Gary Gygax's *Chainmail* rules in 1972. His younger sister went on to become a hand weaver and his younger brother was a production potter for thirty years, so it's probably not too surprising that from that start he would find his way into the world of science fiction and fantasy rather than pursue honest work. He sold his first novel to Jim Baen at Baen Books in 1989. Since then he has published sixty-eight solo and collaborative novels, and another has been delivered but not yet scheduled. He has also edited six anthologies and appeared in several more. He is best known for his Honorverse, with twenty-seven solo and collaborative novels in print (the twenty-seventh, *Uncompromising Honor,* was an October 2018 release from Baen Books) centered around his character Honor Harrington and her universe, and the Safehold series, with ten novels in print (the tenth, *Through Fiery Trials*, was released in January 2019). He still lives in South Carolina with a wife, Sharon, who fortunately loves him enough to put up with him, their three children, two dogs, and six cats. And, as Sharon is fond of saying, don't get him started talking if you expect him to ever shut up again.

Kacey Ezell is an active duty USAF instructor pilot with 2500+ hours in the UH-1N Huey and Mi-171 helicopters. When not teaching young pilots to beat the air into submission, she writes sci-fi/fantasy/horror/noir/alternate history fiction. Her first novel, *Minds of Men*, was a Dragon Award Finalist for Best Alternate History. She's contributed to multiple Baen anthologies and has twice been selected for inclusion in the Year's Best Military and Adventure Science Fiction compilations. In 2018, her story "Family Over Blood" won the Year's Best Military and Adventure Science Fiction Readers' Choice Award. Her collaboration with John Ringo and Christopher L. Smith, *Gunpowder and Embers*, was released in January 2020. In addition to writing for Baen, she has published several novels and short stories with independent publisher Chris Kennedy Publishing. She is married with two daughters. You can find out more and join her mailing list at www.kaceyezell.net.

Steve Diamond is the author of the YA supernatural thriller, *Residue*. He writes for Baen Books, WordFire Press, Gallant Knight Games, Privateer Press, and numerous other publications. He founded the

Hugo-nominated review site, Elitist Book Reviews, and is the editor of the horror anthology, *Shared Nightmares*.

Steve lives in Utah with his wife and two children. He works as a finance manager for a Department of Defense contractor, and does all his writing in the evenings. He's an avid baseball (Oakland A's) and football (New Orleans Saints) fan. You can follow him at thestevendiamond.wordpress.com.

A veteran police officer in a major metropolitan police department out west, **Griffin Barber** is also a lifelong speculative fiction fan and gamer. He's had shorts published in the *Grantvile Gazette* and penned a well-received novella for Roberts Space Industries' website called *A Separate Law*. His novel *1636: Mission to the Mughals*, with Eric Flint, is available from Baen Books. He and Kacey Ezell coauthored a little noir-ish SF novel called *Second Chance Angel*. Madame Sunderhaven features in a novel he swears will be completed soon, tentatively titled *A Petty Necromancy*.

Hinkley Correia is currently a college student aiming to get a degree in digital forensics. She has written one other short story, "Blood on the Water," appearing in the *Target Rich Environment* anthology, and currently has in the works a full-length novel set in the world of "Kuro." In the small amount of free time that she has, she enjoys playing video games, making music, and basic photography.

Laurell K. Hamilton is an American multigenre writer. She is best known as the author of two series of stories, Anita Blake: Vampire Hunter and Merry Gentry.

Her *New York Times* best-selling Anita Blake: Vampire Hunter series centers on Anita Blake, a professional zombie raiser, vampire executioner and supernatural consultant for the police. The series includes novels, short story collections, and comic books. Six million copies of Anita Blake novels are in print. Her *New York Times* best-selling Merry Gentry series centers on Meredith Gentry, Princess of the Unseelie court of Faerie, a private detective facing repeated assassination attempts.

Both fantasy series follow their protagonists as they gain in power and deal with the dangerous "realities" of worlds in which creatures of legend live.

Laurell was born in rural Arkansas but grew up in northern Indiana with her grandmother. Her education includes degrees in English and biology from Marion College (now called Indiana Wesleyan University).

Hamilton is involved with a number of animal charities, particularly supporting dog rescue efforts and wildlife preservation.

Hamilton currently lives with her family in St. Louis, Missouri.

Alistair Kimble is a Special Agent with the Federal Bureau of Investigation working with Violent Crimes Against Children and is a team leader for the FBI's Evidence Response Team, responding to and processing crime scenes. He's worked a variety of matters throughout his career, including foreign counterintelligence and counterespionage. He served in the U.S. Navy, where he dangled from helicopters while performing search and rescue operations as well as mission support for NASA projects such as the Mars Pathfinder, space shuttle recoveries at Edwards AFB, and X projects such as the X-36 tailless fighter. *Iron Angels*, an urban fantasy detective novel, co-written with Eric Flint, was chosen by *Publishers Weekly* as one of its top ten science fiction, fantasy & horror picks for the fall of 2017.

Sarah A. Hoyt has published over thirty books (she hasn't counted lately) and over a hundred short stories. Her first novel was a finalist for the Mythopoeic Award, her novel *Darkship Thieves* won the Prometheus Award and *Uncharted* (with Kevin J. Anderson) won the Dragon Award.

Sarah lives in Denver, Colorado, with her husband and a variable number of cats. When not writing furiously, she's usually engaged in some inadvisable construction, earthy moving or furniture refinishing work. Successful attempts to divert her from such enterprises include trips to museums and diners.

Mike Massa has lived an adventurous life, including stints as a Navy SEAL officer, an investment banker and a technologist. He's lived outside the U.S. for several years, plus the usual military deployments. Mike writes novels and shorts in MilSF, SF, fantasy, horror and nonfiction. Currently he's working on two novels: a second collaboration with *NYT* best seller John Ringo as well as the first novel in his Genius War universe. Mike is married with three sons, who check daily to see if today is the day they can pull down the old lion. Not yet . . .

Patrick M. Tracy: You can find him in darkness. Often underground. Word on the street says he can bring computers back to life. Salt Lake City pays him to do it. He writes about horrible things, fantastical things, even stuff from the future. He's been known to pen a song or make up a game. He helped create *The Crimson Pact*. You can find him in *Kaiju Rising: Age of Monsters*, and *Mech: Age of Steel*. For fun, he practices archery and plays bass guitar. He used to rip phone books in half, but they're hard to find now. It's possible that he drove them to the brink of extinction. More clues can be found at pmtracy.com.

National best-selling author **Robert Buettner**'s novel, *Orphanage*, 2004 Quill Award nominee for Best SF/ fantasy/horror novel, has been called "one of the great works of modern military science fiction." Baen Books released his tenth novel, *My Enemy's Enemy*, in June 2019. His short fiction appears regularly in print and online venues, and he has served as the author judge for the National Space Society Jim Baen Memorial short story writing contest. A former intelligence officer, National Science Foundation Fellow in Paleontology, and attorney, he lives in Georgia with his family and more bicycles than a grownup needs.

Larry Correia is the *New York Times* best-selling author of the Monster Hunter International series, the Grimnoir Chronicles, the Saga of the Forgotten Warrior, the Dead Six thrillers with Mike Kupari, novels set in the Warmachine universe, and *The Adventures of Tom Stranger Interdimensional Insurance Agent* on Audible, and a whole lot of short fiction. Before becoming an author, Larry was an accountant, a gun dealer, and a firearms instructor. He lives in Yard Moose Mountain, Utah, with his very patient wife and children.

Monster Hunter Memoirs: Sinners
9781481482875 • $7.99 US/$10.99 Can.

Monster Hunter Memoirs: Saints
9781481483070 • $7.99 US/$10.99 Can.

THE FORGOTTEN WARRIOR SAGA
Son of the Black Sword
9781476781570 • $9.99 US/$12.99 Can.

House of Assassins
9781982124458 • $8.99 US/$11.99 Can.

THE GRIMNOIR CHRONICLES
Hard Magic
9781439134344 • $15.00 US/$17.00 Can.

Spellbound
9781451638592 • $7.99 US/$9.99 Can.

Warbound
9781476736525 • $7.99 US/$9.99 Can.

MILITARY ADVENTURE
with Mike Kupari
Dead Six
9781451637588 • $7.99 US/$9.99 Can.

Alliance of Shadows
9781481482912 • $7.99 US/$10.99 Can.

Invisible Wars
9781481484336 • $18.00 US/$25.00 Can.